MOONLIGHT OVER STUDLAND BAY

DELLA GALTON

Boldwood

First published in Great Britain in 2020 by Boldwood Books Ltd.

This paperback edition first published in 2021.

1

Cover Design by Debbie Clement Design

Cover Photography: Shutterstock

A CIP catalogue record for this book is available from the British Library.

Paperback ISBN: 978-1-80280-366-2

Ebook ISBN: 978-1-83889-176-3

Kindle ISBN: 978-1-83889-175-6

Audio CD ISBN: 978-1-83889-245-6

Digital audio download ISBN: 978-1-83889-173-2

Large Print ISBN: 978-1-83889-816-8

Boldwood Books Ltd.

23 Bowerdean Street, London, SW6 3TN

www.boldwoodbooks.com

FSC www.fsc.org MIX Paper from responsible sources FSC® C171272

To my very dear friend and fellow writer, Nancy Henshaw.

1

Sam Jones was beginning to feel a great deal more stressed than she had when she had left Beach Cottage, her home overlooking Studland Bay in one of the most beautiful spots in Dorset, fifteen minutes earlier. Her hands felt slippery on the steering wheel. It was hot for June, plus annoyingly a section of her long dark hair had escaped from its butterfly clip and was flicking round her face as she drove. This was because all of the car windows were down. Abby, who was half sitting, half lying on the back seat, had said she needed the air.

'Can't you drive any bloody faster, Sam? I'm in agony here.'

She glanced in the rear view mirror and saw that her best friend and housemate – they'd met in year seven and had been inseparable ever since – was thrashing about. Her head was thrown back, her white blonde hair fanned out against the headrest and her flushed face was screwed up in a very good impression of someone in agony. But, as Abby was prone to exaggeration, if not a full-on drama queen, Sam was nowhere near as worried as she might otherwise have been.

Sometimes she thought the only thing she and Abby now had

in common was the fact they were both thirty-six. They had been born exactly a month apart – Sam on 10 May and Abby on 10 June. A month had a lot to answer for in astrology terms. Not that Sam put as much faith in astrology as Abby did. This morning, Abby's Three-Word Fun Horoscope, which she read every day on her app, had said, '*Don't go yet*'. Abby, as ever, had put her faith in that until she couldn't hold off any longer, which is why they were racing along in the car now.

'Honey, half an hour ago you didn't want to come,' Sam pointed out gently. 'You were dead set on having a home birth. And I can't drive any faster, it won't do us any good if I crash.' Also, she was worried about the two mousetraps, both of which contained live mice, which she'd just remembered were on the back seat of the car in a brown paper bag. The traps were shut, but if they tipped off the seat they might open and release their cargo and Abby was terrified of mice. If there was one thing worse than having a pain-ridden Abby in labour in her car, it was having a pain-ridden and panic-stricken Abby in labour in her car.

Sam knew she should have moved the humane mousetraps before they'd set out, but in all the panic of racing around the house gathering up all the stuff that Abby hadn't bothered packing because 'no way am I having an unnatural hospital birth,' it had slipped her mind that they were there. Fortunately they hadn't been in situ very long; she had planned to release the occupants in the woods on her way back to get Abby, before she'd realised quite how urgent things had become.

'Anyway,' Sam added, hoping she sounded more confident than she felt, 'first babies always take their time, you've got hours yet.' Not that she was any kind of expert, most of her knowledge having been gleaned from One Born Every Minute.

'I bloody well better not have,' Abby snapped, pausing from writhing to glare at her. 'Anyway, you don't know anything about it.

You haven't had one and don't start telling me that dogs don't make all this fuss because I'm not a dog. I'm a woman. And it's different for women. When we get there, I want an epidural and a caesarean and I want one of them injections that numbs you from the neck down and I want some gas and air too, a bucketload, and – for God's sake, that was an amber light, why are we stopping?'

'It was red.' Sam took the chance to refasten her hair back out of her face. She was well used to Abby's outbursts. 'How long is it between contractions?'

'I don't know. I haven't got a stopwatch. I'm going to have it on the back seat if you don't hurry up.' She groaned dramatically. 'It bloody hurts, I know that. Yeooww, fuck, can you please just bloody well hurrreeeeee up.' Her voice disappeared into a long wail as she thrashed about and Sam thought she heard the thud of something falling off the back seat. Hopefully it was Abby's bag and not the one with the mousetraps in.

'Count,' Sam suggested, tapping her fingers on the steering wheel and wishing the red light would change. 'Start counting now and see how long it is between contractions, that's the first thing they'll ask us.' At least that's what she remembered from the antenatal classes Abby had dragged her along to.

'You could be a bit more sympathetic.'

Sam put the handbrake on and turned in her seat to study her friend's red sweaty face. 'I am. I'm very sympathetic, honestly, but there's absolutely no point in us both getting in a state.'

'I am NOT in a state. The lights have changed. Try and pay attention. Do you think I should take my knickers off to save time?'

'No,' Sam said, putting her foot down and resisting the urge to say there probably wasn't much point as Abby was also wearing pink super-stretch maternity leggings – unless she intended to streak across the hospital car park naked from the waist down. 'Are you still counting?'

Perhaps she ought to be counting too, she thought anxiously, but it was difficult to navigate through the seaside traffic, drive safely, be sympathetic and stay calm, as well as to count, when she had a deranged woman flailing about in the back of her car. Abby was hard enough to deal with when she had a headache.

Sam's mobile blared from somewhere behind her seat. She glanced in her rear view mirror, relieved to see Abby's face was no longer contorted in pain. 'Any chance you could get that?' Perhaps it might help to distract her from what was happening.

This hope was rudely dashed two seconds later when Abby snatched up the phone and yelled, 'Eff off!' at the top of her voice.

Sam sighed. 'Who was it?'

'Your boss, I think.'

'Please tell me you're joking.'

'It sounded like him. You'll have to tell him it was extenuating circumstances. Anyway, he shouldn't be phoning you on your afternoon off.'

Realising she was in the wrong lane, Sam nipped in front of a black 4x4, ignoring the driver's furious horn blowing.

'It's not my afternoon off. I said I had raging toothache and I'd got an emergency appointment with my dentist.' She hadn't told Rex Fielding that she was responding to a panic-stricken call from Abby, because when she'd got the call just before lunch she hadn't been 100 percent sure Abby was actually in labour. There had been several false alarms so far and she'd wanted to save the official mercy dash day off for a time when she really needed it.

Hopefully it hadn't been Rex.

'Are we nearly there? I don't think I can hold on much longer.'

'We're very nearly there,' Sam soothed, indicating to turn into the road that led to the hospital.

'And you are going to stay with me, aren't you? You're not dashing back to work?' Abby sounded vulnerable for the first time.

'Of course I'm going to stay with you.'

'Even if it takes twenty-six hours.'

'I thought you said it was going to be born any minute,' Sam said, pulling up in a drop-off bay outside the hospital and wondering if she was still supposed to buy a ticket.

'Yes, well I might have got that wrong. I've never had a baby before. Arghhhh-eeeeeee.'

Shocked, because the scream was ear-splitting, even by Abby's standards, Sam leaned into the back. 'Stay there, I'll go and get a wheelchair and a doctor.'

But Abby wasn't listening. She'd snatched her legs up onto the back seat and was pointing at something in the rear footwell. 'There's a bloody mouse in your car. I just saw its tail.' She grabbed Sam's hand, her eyes wide with horror. 'I'm not staying in here with a mouse. You wait. I'll get the wheelchair.' As she spoke, she shuffled across the seat, the pain of labour obviously totally eclipsed by her terror of mice, and flung open the door.

Sam leapt out of the driver's seat into the hot tarmac-scented air just in time to see a cute brown field mouse, no bigger than a matchbox, hop down onto the wheel arch and twitch its nose curiously.

Abby screamed again and the mouse, presumably deciding enough was enough, having already endured the forty-minute drive with Abby's pain-filled monologue, skipped onto the tarmac and then scurried up onto the ramp that led up to the main entrance, causing two paramedics to sidestep rapidly.

'Ugh, I just saw a rat,' exclaimed a young mother with a blue-coated toddler. 'There must be vermin all over the hospital.' She scooped up her child and started muttering about the falling standards of the NHS.

Sam kept her head down, relieved that at least the woman

hadn't seen it emerging from her car, and prayed to all the gods in heaven that the other mouse was still safely in its trap.

'Why didn't you tell me there was a mouse in your car?' Abby accused. 'What's it doing in there anyway?'

'We've had a bit of a mouse problem at work,' Sam said, relieved that Abby hadn't asked if there were any more. 'I've been catching them in live mouse traps and you have to release them two miles away or they come back, so I've been dropping them off in the woods on my way home.'

'Why can't you use poison like normal people? Sometimes I think you rate all creatures higher than humans... What do you mean, *THEM*?'

'Because it's cruel,' Sam said, avoiding answering the second question. 'Are you getting out or shall I find a wheelchair?' She crouched by the open door, her eyes fixed on Abby's face. Her friend's damp blonde hair was stuck in tendrils to her forehead as she screwed up her eyes once more and braced against the pain.

'I'm scared,' Abby panted when it had passed. 'I don't think I want to go to hospital any more. I hate hospitals. What if something goes wrong?'

'Nothing's going to go wrong and even if it did, you're in the right place. The very best place.' Sam was aware that her voice had taken on a maternal, soothing tone in response to the childlike fear in Abby's.

'You promise you won't leave me. You really, really promise.'

'I really, really promise,' She caught hold of Abby's hand again and squeezed her hot fingers. 'I'm going to be right beside you for every push and every pain. We're going to have this baby together, OK?'

Abby smiled for the first time since Sam had arrived home an hour and a half earlier and Sam smiled back reassuringly. She had a feeling it was going to be a very long day.

* * *

Nineteen hours and thirty-six minutes later, at 11.15 a.m. on 24 June, which also happened to be Midsummer's day, literally the longest day of the year, Abby finally pushed her son into the world and Sam, who couldn't remember the last time she'd cried, found that her neck was wet with tears of joy and wonder. She felt weak with exhaustion and lack of food. She'd kept her promise and hadn't left the delivery room, except to go to the loo and to free the second mouse from her car at a reasonable distance from the hospital – she didn't want to be responsible for a vermin problem. She'd also tried to phone Rex, but her battery had been flat by the time she'd remembered she should call work. Never mind, she was sure he'd understand when she explained. Her throat was hoarse from shouting encouragement and her forearm was covered with finger-mark bruises. But – wow, was it worth it.

Even in her most idealistic, rose-tinted-glasses moments, which she had to admit she was prone to, Sam had never imagined that seeing a baby come into the world could be so amazing. She'd expected it to be bloody and messy and involve a lot of yelling and it had. Abby wasn't one to do anything quietly and no amount of pain relief was going to stop her letting an opportunity to do a lot of legitimate screaming slip through her fingers. But Sam had watched in awe as the slithering, pink baby had been gently placed in his mother's arms. Her throat had closed with tears as she'd seen something switch on in Abby's eyes.

Love, she had realised in wonderment. Abby had looked down into her son's red, screwed-up face and in that flick of a moment, everything had changed. Peace had ironed out all the lines of pain on Abby's brow and there had been a huge sense of joy in the room. Such intense joy that it was almost holy. Sam wouldn't have been at all surprised to see an angel with a halo standing at the foot of the bed playing a harp – and she didn't even believe in angels.

Life. New life just beginning. Wondrous. Magical. Rapturous. Amazing new life with all the hope and optimism and years of possibilities that it brought with it. The midwife was smiling. Abby was smiling. The delivery room itself was smiling. How many new lives had these walls welcomed? Sam wondered. How much pain too, all that intense emotion swirling about. Heaven and hell meeting. She shook her head and swiped tears from her eyes. Why on earth was she thinking about heaven and hell? She must be more exhausted than she thought.

'What?' Abby demanded.

'I was just thinking that you were right,' Sam said, blinking. 'It's nothing like dogs.'

The midwife shot them a curious glance but didn't comment on this. She probably already thought they were crazy. During Abby's early labour, which seemed like a lifetime ago now, rather than a mere eighteen or so hours, she had insisted they sing 'Ten Green Bottles' between contractions, followed by 'Always Look on the Bright Side of Life'. Towards the end, she'd spent the time in between screaming that she no longer wanted a baby and swearing – whole chains of swear words strung together so that most of them were indistinguishable. Fortunately. Not that Sam had anything against swearing. Women in labour were entitled to swear, although Abby's profanities were, perhaps, a little too colourful for a hospital.

But maybe midwives were used to the eccentricities of women in labour. None of them had batted an eyelid. Sam wondered if they ever got bored of this moment: the pinnacle of all that effort when one life miraculously became two separate ones. She couldn't imagine ever getting bored of it. Perhaps she should change career and become a midwife instead of an audio typist for a group of structural engineers. Not that she planned to stay an audio typist for very much longer. That was just her day job.

Her dreams lay elsewhere. She'd always loved animals, especially dogs, and just over two years ago she had begun a business, Purbeck Pooches, which she hoped would one day become her full-time career. She walked dogs in every spare minute she had, early mornings, summer lunchtimes and after work. She also did weekend boarding. Purbeck Pooches was her passion and she ran it from her home at Studland, on the Isle of Purbeck, where there was a footpath that ran down onto the beach. Her cottage came with a one-acre field and she rented both for a pittance because Ben Campbell, her landlord and also a good friend, needed a tenant who wouldn't complain about the place's numerous faults.

She was building up a small but regular clientele, although things had slowed down a bit since Abby had moved in with her on a cold December night six and a half months ago.

Prior to that Abby had shared a flat with her on/off boyfriend, Paul Kent, who was also the father of Abby's newborn son and conspicuous by his absence today. It wasn't the first time Abby had turned up on Sam's doorstep in tears after they'd rowed, vowing never to go back to that 'waste of space wanker' again, but this time had lasted longer than the rest.

Sam had expected Paul, who was notoriously flaky and a (mostly) out-of-work musician, to come back into Abby's life as the birth approached, but he hadn't. This was a new level of flakiness, even for Paul, and although Abby made light of it, Sam suspected she was heartbroken beneath her bravado. Abby and Paul had been childhood sweethearts. They always got back together eventually.

Much as she loved Abby, it had been harder to concentrate on Purbeck Pooches with her living at Beach Cottage. She'd been side-tracked by accompanying her to antenatal classes, having officially been recruited as Abby's birthing partner, and long girly chats into the night weren't conducive to getting up at the crack of dawn to walk dogs. Despite this, Sam had started to get recommendations from happy clients. When she had a few more regular bookings, she planned to tell her boss to get lost herself.

No she wouldn't. Rex Fielding, owner of Fielding & Son Structural Engineers, was a bit pompous, but he wasn't a bad boss most of the time. She couldn't really blame him. He'd been expecting her back yesterday and she should have started at 9 a.m. today – it was now nearly midday. For all Rex knew, she could be lying in a ditch somewhere. And after the rude response he'd got on the phone yesterday afternoon, he had every right to be a bit snotty.

'Sam...?' Abby's voice was as honey-soft sweetness now as it had been raucous, grating agony a little while earlier. 'You know I said I was going to call him Jack after my grandad? Well, I think I'm going to make his middle name Sam after you. Samuel, not Samantha obviously. What do you think? Jack Samuel Martin.'

'That sounds like a very fine name.' Sam surreptitiously wiped another tear from her face.

'And there's something else,' Abby added.

'What kind of something?'

'Do you fancy being his godmother?'

Sam looked down into the baby's squashed little face. He had a lot of dark hair – he must get that from his father – and he was so little, from his tiny curling fingers to his tiny pink toes. A mewling, vulnerable scrap of helplessness. She had never been a fan of babies, but now something twisted in the region of her heart.

'I'd really, really love that.'

2

Sam was dreading going into work on Thursday morning. She had spoken briefly to Rex late the previous afternoon once she'd got back from the hospital and recharged her phone. She had begun with an apology. Experience had taught her that if you just put your hands up straight away and said, 'I'm really sorry, I mucked up, I am totally at fault,' it usually worked in your favour.

But it probably hadn't helped that she had caught him just dashing out of the office to an appointment.

He had cut through her apologies, 'Save it, Sam. I don't have time to do this now. We can talk tomorrow. I take it there are extenuating circumstances and you didn't just decide to head for the beach to top up your tan.'

'There are. Of course there are. I—'

'As I said, save it for tomorrow. My office, nine o'clock.'

'I would never just—'

'Tomorrow.'

'Sure.' She knew when she was beaten. 'Tomorrow...'

She'd been talking to empty air. He'd already gone.

And now it was tomorrow. There hadn't been time to wash her

hair, which was prone to be flyaway, so she'd tugged it back into a stern and efficient-looking ponytail, rather than her normal colourful clips. She was wearing her most sensible, toned-down, stiff-upper-lip office outfit, a white blouse with silver buttons, long black skirt and herringbone jacket. It was a bit warm for the jacket, but she was wearing it anyway. Rex was a fan of the traditional, and although they didn't meet the public that often in their office, so they could wear what they wanted, she suspected he wasn't altogether approving of the ultra-casual outfits she occasionally wore in summer.

She could do contrite when the occasion demanded it. She'd even ditched the rainbow earrings Abby had bought for her last birthday in favour of smallish silver hoops. The moment of reckoning had come. She walked nervously across the car park.

Fielding & Son had second-floor offices on an out-of-town industrial estate just outside Swanage. They shared the building with a private dentist on the ground floor – you could occasionally hear the sound of drilling from below – and K. R. Lacey's Accountancy Services which was on the same floor as them.

The main entrance of the building led immediately to a flight of stairs and then a second door led into their office space, which, apart from Rex's office, was open plan. Rex's office was tucked at the back, alongside the kitchen, and shielded from the main area by a glass wall.

Sam had to pass the desks of the other three structural engineers on the way to her own workstation. None of them were in. They must all have gone straight out to jobs. Rex's PA, Elannah Lewis, who was dark and petite with huge geek-girl glasses and was super mature for her twenty-seven years, had the desk just across the way from Sam's and she glanced up as Sam arrived.

Sam went over to talk to her. 'What sort of mood is he in?'

Elannah widened her eyes so they looked even bigger behind

the glasses, sucked in her cheeks and whistled softly. 'Not great... But you know what he's like. He'll bang on for a bit about you letting him down and the good name of the company, blah blah blah, and then he'll offer you a Murray Mint and forgive you. He never loses his rag. But you did drop him in it.' She leaned forwards. 'Where were you anyway?'

'I was with Abby. She had the baby yesterday.'

'Oh wow, really – what did she have?' Elannah was a sucker for babies and all things cute. There was a picture of a fluffy cat in a stripy hat pinned on the noticeboard over her desk.

'Boy. Seven pounds.'

'Are they OK?'

'Yes, they're doing great. Fingers crossed, they're coming home today. I'm picking them up after work. They let them out early these days.' She'd got the impression when she'd gone back to visit last night that the nurses would be glad to see the back of Abby. Maybe that was unfair, but she was a handful at the best of times and Sam suspected she'd be treating her hospital stay like a visit to a hotel, and expecting on tap room service thrown in.

She yawned and covered her mouth. 'Sorry... I haven't had much sleep the last couple of days.' She was going to have even less from now on, much as she was looking forward to having Abby and baby Jack at Beach Cottage for the foreseeable future.

'I bet.'

'Shall I go in?' It was five to nine.

'I'll tell him you're here.' Elannah picked up the phone on her desk.

There was no need for her to do this, due to the fact there was only a glass partition between Rex's office and the main area where Elannah's desk was – if he looked up he would see her – but Rex was a man of protocol. He liked things to be done properly. He was only forty-two, but he acted like a man a decade older. He'd inherited Fielding's from his father when he was in his early thirties and he'd taken the responsibility very seriously.

'Our reputation is so concrete you can build on it.' Rex was fond of trotting out this line at regular intervals and it was also part of the company's branding, as was the line, 'Our word is our bond.'

'You can go in,' Elannah said, hanging up after the briefest of conversations with Rex and crossing her fingers surreptitiously. 'Good luck.'

Sam stepped into the little office, which smelled of old books and coffee and still had battleship-grey metal filing cabinets that looked as though they had been made at the end of the war. On the wall hung a portrait of an unsmiling man, Mr Fielding senior, who had started the company.

Rex glanced up. Like his father, he had brown slightly receding hair and sideburns and he always wore a suit and tie – today's tie was maroon. His blue grey eyes were serious, but other than that it was difficult to read his expression.

'Samantha, take a seat.' Oops, he only used her full name when he was cross.

He came out from behind his ornate cherry wood desk, which had clawed feet and fancy twirly bits on the corners, and pulled up one of the two wooden chairs that were on her side. Elannah had once told her that the last book he'd read on management, which had belonged to his father and been published in 1998, had been called, *How to Deal With Staff Without Drama*. His favourite chapter, apparently, had been the one that suggested barriers and boundaries were outmoded and should be avoided at all costs when talking to staff. He'd been greatly impressed with this and was still using these tactics, especially if he had to say anything unpleasant.

Blimey, he wasn't going to give her a disciplinary, was he? She probably deserved one.

He hadn't even offered her a Murray Mint. He kept a bowl of

them on his desk; he drank very strong coffee but hated the aftertaste apparently. Today it was clear that the Murray Mints were not forthcoming.

Feeling more nervous than ever, Sam sat and smoothed down her black wool-mix skirt – work was the only place she ever wore a skirt, she was a jeggings and trainers girl – and decided that much as she wanted to blurt out another apology it would probably be best to let him start the conversation.

He cleared his throat. 'I'd like to know where you've been for the last day and a half.'

Sam knew that she needed to tell him the truth, so she told him and he listened thoughtfully without interrupting while she laid it on as thick as she dared about the unexpectedness of Abby's labour and the high drama of being in the delivery room – she decided it would be best not to give any details about that – and how she'd completely lost track of time and then her battery had gone dead or she would, of course, have phoned him.

When she'd finished, he said that he hoped mother and baby were doing well.

'They are.'

'But, Samantha, what I don't understand is why you felt the need to lie to me about the dentist appointment. Could you not have been truthful?'

She felt a rush of shame. Lying was one of his pet hates. She wasn't a huge fan of it either.

'I wasn't sure that Abby was actually in labour, there had been a couple of false alarms. I thought it might be easier if…' she tailed off. The thinking that had seemed so rational the day before yesterday now seemed sly and underhand. 'I'm sorry,' she said, aware of his eyes on her. 'I should have been honest.'

'Yes, you should. Our word is our bond. Trust is at the basis of all good working relationships.'

'I know.' She felt about two inches high. 'I'll make up the time, obviously.'

'Heather had to cover for you and she wasn't feeling at all well.'

No change there then. Hypochondriac Heather, as they all secretly called her, was the other audio typist. She was always complaining about aches and pains and mysterious untraceable symptoms that never came to anything.

She was good at her job though. Between them, Heather and Sam typed up and made sense of the convoluted and often lengthy structural surveys – filled with tricky terminology that, luckily, they were both au fait with – that the engineers gave them on a daily basis. They were usually voice files, so it wasn't just typing, but translation. Most of the engineers were aware of the difficulties and spoke clearly, but there was one, Mike, who mumbled, despite the subtle and not-so-subtle hints they'd made to him over the years. Sam hoped Heather hadn't been stuck with Mumbling Mike's surveys.

She realised suddenly that Heather hadn't been at her desk either this morning. No doubt she had stayed at home then today with some imaginary illness: payback for Sam having an unauthorised day and a half off work.

'Is she all right now?' Sam asked.

'No. She had stomach pains, so I had to send her home.' Rex's already grave voice went a shade graver. 'In fact, I just had a phone call from her partner saying that she was rushed to hospital last night with suspected appendicitis.'

'Oh my goodness.' Sam felt guiltier than ever. 'Is she going to be OK?'

'I'm sure she'll be fine. As soon as I get some more news, I will let you and everyone else know.'

There was another little silence. Sam would have preferred him to shout at her and pace about, but he wasn't the shouty, pace-about type.

Finally he broke it. 'There is a fair bit of work in your inbox, I should think. I would appreciate it if you could do the urgent ones at least today.'

'Of course. I'm on it,' Sam said, realising the meeting was over and getting to her feet with relief. 'And I'm really sorry again, about not being honest.'

'Your apology has been noted and accepted,' Rex said, rubbing at a spot on one of his angular cheekbones as he met her gaze.

She guessed he had found this whole discussion as excruciating as she had. She had never had much to do with Rex. In the three years that she'd worked at Fielding & Son, he had mostly been in his office when she arrived and still there when she left, unless he was out surveying. Even her annual reviews were dealt with in a matter of minutes. She'd only seen him out socially on a handful of occasions. The Christmas meals, a team bonding day out at Salisbury races once and a summer meal that Elannah had organized last year to celebrate the forty years of Fielding & Son being in business. At all of them, he'd looked stiff and uncomfortable in the same kind of suit and tie he wore for work and he'd made his excuses and left as soon as possible.

She'd always had the impression he was far more at ease around buildings – the older, the better – than people and Elannah was good at shielding him.

It was only when she was on the other side of the door once more and heading towards her desk that she realised that he hadn't even mentioned being told to 'eff off' by a pain-ridden Abby. That was something. With a bit of luck, Abby had been wrong and it hadn't been him on the other end of the phone after all. The call had been from a withheld number so she hadn't been able to confirm one way or another.

* * *

For the first time in ages Sam didn't switch off her Mac on the dot of five. She was still typing furiously at five to six when Rex went by with his laptop bag in his hand. He gave her a nod of acknowledgement. 'If you're later than Elannah, get her to show you how to set the alarm.'

'I will,' she said, realising that she had never, in her entire time at Fielding & Son, been the last one to leave the building. She wasn't a slacker but she religiously observed her working hours so she could get back to her real love – Purbeck Pooches.

She carried on listening and typing, both of which she could do on autopilot, but she couldn't get Rex's comment out of her head. Flaming heck, was she that much of a lightweight? What kind of nickname did they have for her? Everyone had a nickname in the office. Elannah's was Geek Girl. Rex's was Suit Man, or RoboBoss if people were feeling mean. Andy Jakes, the senior surveyor who was in his fifties, was known as Lightning because he fitted more surveys into his day than anyone else and also had a habit of talking really fast. The younger surveyor, James Carr, was known as Magpie because he had glossy, jet-black hair and was always stealing pens and 'borrowing' bits of kit from the other surveyors. And, of course, there was Mumbling Mike.

For the first time, she wondered what her nickname was and why she didn't know already. Slope off Sam, Workshy Sam maybe. God no – that way lies madness. Besides, she wasn't workshy – she just had a job she loved at home. Not that Purbeck Pooches earned her much money. This job was her mainstay. Rex was a fair employer and he paid well. She couldn't afford to lose her job.

A cough from Elannah interrupted her thoughts and she realised that she was standing on the other side of the desk and had possibly been trying to attract her attention for a while.

Sam took her headset off. 'Sorry, did you want to show me the alarm?'

'Please. If you're OK with that? I'd have thought you'd be rushing of to see the new arrival.' Elannah tilted her head to one side in a question. 'Or are you avoiding going home? I've just remembered you prefer puppies to babies, don't you?'

'I'm not avoiding going home. I've got some serious grovelling to do to make up for the last couple of days, remember? I'm on the last survey with today's date on. But, yes, you're right. I do prefer puppies. Although Jack is quite cute, as babies go. He's got the tiniest little hands and fingernails. Like a doll's. And he has quite a bit of dark hair. I wasn't expecting that. I don't know why and he's so small and…' She'd been about to add 'cute' again, but she stopped herself just in time. She did not want to turn into one of those women who went on and on about babies, boring the pants off everyone around them, and this wasn't even her baby, for goodness' sake.

Elannah was looking at her curiously. 'You're actually quite smitten, aren't you? What was it like being a birth partner?'

Sam let her mind flick back over the past forty-eight hours. 'It was kind of what you'd expect. There was a lot of waiting about and a lot of shouting. From Abby, not me, obviously. Although it was quite painful for me too.' She pulled up the sleeve of her blouse and showed Elannah the bruising on her left forearm.

'Ouch.'

'Yes, that's what I said.' She paused. 'It was also totally not what I expected. The end bit was amazing. I wasn't prepared for that.'

Elannah screwed up her face.

'The emotions, I mean. It was overwhelming. I felt really privileged to be there. I mean, usually a maternity unit's the last place I'd choose to be. Although I was glad that Abby had changed her mind about the home birth bit, which was what she had planned. I was never so keen on that as she was. It's much better to know there are plenty of experts on hand.'

Elannah was nodding. 'I bet.'

'I'm never having kids though. From what everyone says, the birth is the easy bit. It's all downhill after that.' Motherhood wasn't something that had ever featured largely in her life plans. Also, she'd need a man, and she was single and had every intention of staying that way.

'Robbie and I are planning to have two once we've got our own place. Although it's taking forever to save the deposit. There's nothing round here that's affordable. Even the tiniest flat's a premium price.'

'People buy them as holiday homes, don't they,' Sam commiserated. 'The downside of living in one of the most beautiful parts of Dorset, I guess.' She knew she was really lucky. If Beach Cottage had been in a pristine state of repair, Ben Campbell, her landlord, could have got double the rent. Luckily, he was too lazy to do more than the basic essentials and he didn't need the money anyway. He did something that made megabucks in the City and already owned more than one property. Beach Cottage would one day be his pension, he had told her. But in the meantime he was more than happy for Sam to live in it. In fact, she'd be doing him a favour because he trusted her to take good care of it.

'Changing the subject completely,' Elannah said suddenly, 'I've just remembered we caught another mouse in the back utility room this morning. Did you get rid of the others?'

'Yep.' Sam remembered the field mouse heading up the hospital ramp and frowned. 'Although possibly not in the best place. The traps are still in my car. Shall I bring them in?'

'No, it's OK. Later's fine. I'm not putting any more out. That's the first one we've caught for a couple of days. I think we may be on top of things. Rex has stopped muttering about getting the council in.'

'Good.'

'I'll go and get it while you finish your typing.'

Elannah might be a geek girl, but she was eminently practical too. She disappeared and Sam went back to her survey and realised that Mumbling Mike was wrapping up and almost onto the disclaimer section of the survey, which was part of their standard letter. She was done by the time Elannah came back with the mousetrap.

'Sam, if you like, I can drop this one off in Wareham Forest on my way home. Then you can get on with picking up Abby and Jack. Do you have to go home first?'

'Thanks, yes, I need to get the car seat and stuff. She only just texted to tell me she's ready. She's been on the phone to everyone apparently, announcing the new arrival. Her parents live in Spain, but her brother's local.'

Elannah clapped her hands. 'How exciting. Having a little one in the house. I bet you're really looking forward to seeing them both.'

'Yes,' Sam said, realising with surprise that she very much was.

3

One of the other good things about her job was that it was close to home so she could get back for lunchtime dog walking, Sam thought, as she walked out to her Chevrolet in Fielding's almost empty car park. She and Abby often joked that she had a 57 Chevy because the first part of the number plate was HG57, but her car was actually an old black hatchback with four doors and a big enough space in the back to get a medium-size golden retriever in, standing up.

If the back seats were folded flat, you could get an Irish wolfhound *and* a golden retriever in the back. The wolfhound had to hunker down a bit as he jumped in, but it was doable. Sam knew this because she'd tried it. Seamus, a shaggy grey gentle giant of a dog and Goldie, his bossy female companion, were two of her regular canine customers. She walked them two lunchtimes a week when their owner, Barbara Oldfield, who reminded Sam of a young Fiona Bruce, was working. She also house-sat for them sometimes.

'I know they could go to kennels,' Barbara said. 'But they trust you. And so do I.'

The house-sitting at Barbara's had evolved into Sam having the two dogs at Beach Cottage on the occasional weekend. She had use of the field abutting the big garden, so there was plenty of space and the dogs were just as happy there.

She also boarded other animals that didn't need her to be around 24/7. Barbara had a friend with horses – they'd stayed once at livery because their owners had wanted to bring their horses on holiday with them to Studland. The riding was amazing. Beach rides and forest rides were both accessible directly from Sam's field.

The Isle of Purbeck, which wasn't an island, but a peninsular with water on three sides, the English Channel to the south and the east and Poole harbour and the marshlands of the River Frome to the north, was a tourist paradise. It was chock-a-block with pubs, restaurants, cafes and hotels and attractions like Monkey World Ape Rescue Centre – Sam had tried to get a job there once, but there was a huge waiting list – and The Tank Museum at Bovington. Sam had never visited Bovington, let alone tried to get a job there, but each to their own.

The tourists came for the stunning coastal beauty spots like Durdle Door – an impressive archway through limestone rock at Lulworth Cove. Not to mention the man-made attractions like Swanage Railway, where you could have a slap-up meal on a steam train while travelling past an unforgettable view of Corfe Castle, built by William the Conqueror and still hugely impressive, even in ruins.

Another reason Sam would have hated to lose her job at Fielding's was because it was one of the few places she could work that didn't involve being around members of the public 24/7. She'd had a brilliant childhood, but she felt as though she'd grown up in a business, not a family home. Her parents ran Belinda's B&B (named after her mother), which was close to Swanage seafront. They loved it. Her dad was a born front-of-house man. He was brilliant at putting people at their ease by being totally interested in them and making silly jokes, mostly at his own expense.

Her mum was an ace cook and a gifted artisan, who could turn her hand to all kinds of creative projects, from upcycling a piece of furniture to making a patchwork quilt. She was also a great person to have around in a crisis because she was level-headed and calm.

Sam had inherited her mother's level-headedness but not her creative flair. She often wished it had been the other way round. Cooking and crafting would be a far more useful skill to have than the ability to keep calm in a crisis. Although she supposed it had come in pretty handy when Abby had been in labour.

But the flip side of being a peacemaker was people-pleasing. Over the years, Sam had watched her parents turn themselves inside out to please other people. She didn't want to spend her life doing the same thing. People were fine in small doses, but her real passion was for animals. Anything that was four-legged and furry, anything that woofed, meowed, neighed or squeaked. She'd had a small menagerie when she was younger: guinea pigs, a rabbit, a Jack Russell terrier called Spot and a ginger cat called Felix.

Hers wasn't the kind of family that could afford a pony, although she had blagged rides at the local riding school in return for helping out. She'd had dreams of being a vet, but she'd known full well that her parents couldn't afford to put her through vet school and so she hadn't ever mooted the idea. Instead, when she'd finished her A Levels, she'd done a small animal husbandry course, alongside a basic IT skills course. Then, for a couple of years, she'd worked on the admin side of a magazine called *Dogs R Us*, which had been started by a husband and wife team of entrepreneur publishers based in Poole, but which had unfortunately been axed because of low circulation.

It was at *Dogs R Us* she'd met Ben Campbell. He'd been part of the sales team. They'd dated for a while before drifting apart but had stayed friends. When the magazine had closed, Ben had moved from Poole, where he'd grown up, to London to become a commodities broker, a job he'd excelled at, and he'd soared into the stratosphere as far as income had gone.

He'd bought Beach Cottage with one of his annual bonuses. Sam's jaw had literally dropped when he'd taken her there for the first time. The three-bedroom property was one of the oldest in Studland village. A Grade II listed period cottage, the colour of vanilla ice cream with a thatched roof, it looked like a child's painting of a cottage with smiley-faced frontage and a messy thatched fringe. Inside, it needed a new kitchen and a new bathroom. The plumbing was temperamental and the back cloakroom at the lowest part of the house flooded when the water table was high. But, luckily, the ground floor was mostly flagstones so it didn't matter too much.

All of these inconveniences could be forgiven totally as far as Sam was concerned because of its amazing location. It was on a quiet road within walking distance of the beach and looked out across pasture meadows towards Old Harry Rocks – three great chalk formations that jutted out of the sea, marking the most eastern part of the Jurassic coast. Legend had it that Old Harry was a devil that had once slept on the rocks and the smaller white chalk stack alongside him was his wife. Sam didn't care much for legends, but it was certainly an impressive set of rocks and a great story for the tourists, her mother always said.

There was a footpath a stone's throw from the cottage which led through woodland to an idyllic white sandy beach and was very handy for walking dogs. If you walked far enough to the left at low tide, towards the chain ferry that linked the Isle of Purbeck to Bournemouth, you reached the golden sands of Studland – there was a naturist beach en route. If you went right, you would end up at Old Harry rocks.

Beach Cottage was everything Sam had ever wanted in a house. She'd lived there for five years and every time she drew up outside it, she felt the same thrill of pleasure as she glanced up at the lime-washed vanilla walls, the pretty hanging baskets on either side of the duck egg blue front door and the wooden house sign with the picture of a fat seagull on one corner.

Never live in a house that doesn't make your heart sing, her mum had told her once. Sam had to pinch herself sometimes to believe she truly lived here and wasn't dreaming.

She had that feeling tonight as she stepped out of her car and into the honeysuckle-scented air and was instantly surrounded by the sounds of birdsong and the more distant haunting cries of the gulls.

She let herself in, ran along the flagstone hall and into the wood-beamed lounge, found the car seat propped against the inglenook fireplace and was out again in the midsummer air. She was really looking forward to fetching Abby and Jack home.

On the way to Poole, she phoned her mum hands-free from the car.

'Give them both my best, darling. It's so exciting having a new baby in the house and what a privilege to be there to hold her hand. I hope he doesn't keep you both awake all night.'

Sam put the phone down smiling.

* * *

A couple of hours later, Sam was feeling slightly less peaceful. Abby had been buoyant when she'd picked them up, but since they'd got back, her mood had dipped lower and lower.

Sam had just gone into the lounge to find her in tears.

'Darling, what is it? Is Jack all right?'

'Jack's fine, he's asleep.' She gestured with her hand towards the carrycot and Sam saw that he was breathing peacefully, long dark eyelashes curled against his cheeks, his face serene.

She sat down on the sofa beside her best friend. 'So what's wrong?'

'Everything's wrong. I'm a hopeless mother. I can't hold him properly, I can't relax around him. I made a right pig's ear of changing his nappy. I can't get him to stop crying. I can't comfort him.' Her voice was growing more anguished by the second. 'I don't know what to do.'

'But he's not crying now, he's asleep. He looks ever so peaceful. Look at him.'

'That's because he's so exhausted, I expect.'

Abby was the one who looked exhausted, but Sam didn't think pointing this out would help. She held her hand instead. 'It's all so new – it's a big adjustment. It's bound to be emotional and it must be difficult with your mum and dad in Spain. When are they coming over?'

'Not for a couple of weeks. I told Mum I needed to get into a routine first, which I do. I'm used to them not being here. Anyway, I've got to get used to doing things alone.' She sniffed. 'My horoscope said, "*Go it alone.*"'

Those bloody horoscopes had a lot to answer for.

'This is just the baby blues, darling. They said it would be like this at the classes. Remember?'

Abby blew her nose with a crumpled-up tissue she was clutching.

'No. But maybe I didn't listen properly. I don't know. I'm not like you.'

One of the reasons Sam and Abby got on so well was because they were so different. Sam was a planner. If she was embarking on something new, from buying a new car to moving house to setting up in business, she would gather information. She would consult her friends, read every book, blog and feature going, watch vlogs, go in chat rooms, make lists and then decide on the best way forward.

Abby liked to do things on the spur of the moment. She found plans and structure and lists tedious and said they stifled her creativity – she designed websites and website interfaces for a living. She was innovative and brilliantly original and very good at her job and she hated being tied down with rules and regulations.

'Shouldn't you be seeing to animals and stuff?' Abby asked, turning tear-washed eyes towards her.

'There are only the rabbits. They won't take me long.' The lop-eared rabbits, which belonged to a family in the village, were in the run in the garden. Fortunately, they were not time intensive guests.

'Go and sort them out, honey. I'm fine, honestly.' She gave Sam a little shove and Sam went, reluctantly.

* * *

After Sam had checked the rabbits were secure and made sure their water and food were topped up – they were doing a great job on her grass – she went back into the farmhouse kitchen and cooked frozen pizzas for her and Abby's tea – the range oven was wasted on her.

Then they spent the rest of the evening focused on Jack, who slept soundly throughout, and watching YouTube videos on baby's first days – it was amazing what you could find on YouTube. Abby practised nappy changing, while Sam read posts from new mum sites and shared helpful tips.

When he woke, Jack was amazingly obliging. He was a happy little thing and while he was quite vocal, giving little squaws and snuffles, he didn't cry or screech. He just gazed at Abby adoringly while she breastfed him and Sam felt a twinge of what she had felt back in the hospital – awe, joy and that intense feeling of peace and wonder that was almost holy.

'Do you think he's too laid-back for a Cancerian?' Abby brought her back to earth with a bang. 'Cancerian babies are supposed to be moody and clingy. Do you think maybe that means there's something wrong?' She sounded slightly panicky again.

'No. He's probably a bit young to be showing his star sign traits. I think you're worrying too much.'

'Do you think so?'

'Yes. He's just laid-back.'

'He certainly doesn't get that from me.' Her voice was wistful.

Sam said, as casually as she could because it was a contentious subject, 'Have you heard from Paul? Have you told him Jack's arrived?' She'd wanted to raise it before, but they'd almost fallen out last time she'd tried.

'Nope.' Abby compressed her lips into a tight line. 'And I'm not planning to speak to him any time soon.'

'He'll want to see him though, won't he? And what about registering the birth – don't you need to do that together?'

'I'll cross that bridge when I come to it. Paul made it perfectly clear last time we spoke that he's not interested in babies.' Abby busied herself with a nipple pad and then changed the subject pointedly. 'Did you get into any trouble for missing work?'

'Not too much.'

'That's a relief. Did I tell you Matt's coming over on Sunday morning to see his new nephew?'

'No, but that'll be nice. I like your brother.'

'He likes you too. I always thought you two might get together one day. You've got loads in common.'

Fortunately that was the moment Sam's phone beeped with a text and so she was saved from answering.

It was true she did like Matt, but she had never seen Abby's older brother as prospective boyfriend material. Matt was the opposite of Abby, at least in personality. He was the archetypal surf dude, totally in tune with nature and pretty laid-back. He was the soothing balm to her drama queen. He even spoke slowly. He had a habit of saying things like, 'It is what it is.' Or 'The future brings what the future brings.' He had no sense of urgency about anything, something that secretly irritated the hell out of Sam, although she would never have told Abby this.

Matt's heart was in the right place and she imagined his relaxed attitude went down very well in his job – he worked as a scrub nurse in the theatre at Dorchester Hospital. She bet he had a very calming effect on patients. When they weren't asleep, that was!

Maybe she didn't see him as boyfriend material because she had known him all her life. He was more like the big brother she'd never had. Or maybe it was just because she didn't do rangy, fair-haired men with freckly arms. She wasn't sure what she did do – she'd avoided men lately – but freckly arms were a no-no.

'I'm going to put sir here, to bed,' Abby's voice interrupted her thoughts at exactly the same moment as another text pinged on Sam's phone.

She glanced up.

Abby was standing up now by the lounge door with a sleeping Jack in her arms. 'Someone's anxious to get hold of you.'

'The first one was from Elannah. Hypochondriac Heather's off work for a week and they're asking if I'll do a few extra hours.' She knew she couldn't exactly say no, as she was still trying to get back into Rex's good books.

'The cheek. Is she actually ill?'

'She had suspected appendicitis apparently, so yes I think this one is real.' She glanced back at her phone. 'The other text is from some guy asking if Purbeck Pooches has accreditation or expertise or any qualifications for looking after Kunekune pigs.'

Abby snorted with laughter so that Jack shook slightly in her arms. 'That has to be a wind-up, right?'

'I'm not sure. He included a link. There's quite a lot of information.' She scrolled through the website she was now on. 'There's a big section on the history of Kunekunes. Apparently they come from an Asian domestic breed introduced to New Zealand in the early nineteenth century. Have you heard of them?'

'Are they like teacup pigs? I think that might have been a celeb thing a few years back. Didn't Victoria Beckham have one?'

'You'd need a pretty big teacup for one of these. Apparently they can grow up to about four feet long.' They do look quite cute though. I've just found some pictures.

'Oh. Are you sure that text isn't a wind-up? Who's it actually from?'

'Someone called Mr B. No first name, no proper surname. Just a capital B. He wants me to give him a ring at my earliest convenience.'

'It's definitely a wind-up. You'll ring him and it'll be one of your mad friends or one of the blokes from work or something laughing their heads off on the other end.'

'You're the only mad friend I've got,' Sam said, but Abby had stopped listening. Jack had just stretched up an arm towards her face and she dipped her head down to meet him.

'OK, little man. Let's get you bathed and in bed. Wave goodnight to your godmummy.'

'Never mind waving goodnight. I need a kiss.' Sam leapt to her feet. 'Can I help with his bath?'

'I'd love that. Do you mind?'

'Of course I don't mind. I told you I'd help. Then I think we should all have an early-ish night.' She glanced at her watch. 'We deserve one.'

To her relief, Abby was looking a lot happier than she had earlier. Everything was going to be fine.

As she followed Abby up the steep cottage stairs to the big bathroom that was next door to Abby's bedroom she decided that Mr B and his pigs, real or imaginary, would have to wait until the morning.

4

Those first few days of having a new baby in the cottage were a mixture of panic and peace. Most of the panic came from Abby. No surprises there, Sam thought. Abby thrived on drama and motherhood was all very new.

Sam had suspected there would be a lot of crying – she hadn't expected quite so much of it to come from Abby, but she was glad she could be there for her. She was also very glad that Beach Cottage had thick stone walls. She was also very, very glad they had no neighbours, as once she had caught Abby screaming, 'I can't effing do this...!' at the top of her voice out of the first-floor landing window, which overlooked the garden and field. Abby had said she hadn't wanted to disturb Jack, who'd been asleep at the time.

The first-floor landing was big enough to be a bedroom, but the only bits of furniture on it were an antique dark wood French dresser that Ben had apparently bought with the cottage because it was too big and heavy to remove and an old wooden rocking chair that squeaked when you rocked back and forth. Sam had put the rocking chair there. It was a lovely place to sit and she thought Abby might like a change of scenery when she was feeding Jack.

Jack was oblivious to his mother's dramas. He seemed to spend most of his time either asleep or gurgling peacefully and had to be woken up for feeds. Were all babies like that? Sam knew they couldn't be. In the limited experience she'd had second-hand from friends, babies were sleep stealers who cried 24/7. She'd heard horror stories of babies who didn't sleep through the night until they were three years old, babies who had to be driven around the block to get them to go off, babies whose parents became walking zombies.

Jack did have his moments. He yelled when he needed his nappy changed, but even that was more squawk than decibel screech. Sam was beginning to wonder whether she was seeing him through rose-tinted glasses because he was a part of Abby and she loved Abby so dearly – and if so, when the rose-tinted lenses might shatter.

It was gorgeous weather, which helped make everything seem brighter anyway. Beach Cottage was beautiful every day of the year but summer made it spectacular. You could see the sea from all of the front-facing first floor windows. It was wonderful waking up and throwing back the windows to look out across the meadows, their long yellowing grass sprinkled with daisies and pink thistles and the occasional scarlet red splash of a poppy. Beyond the meadows, the sea sparkled blue as it lapped around Old Harry beneath an arch of turquoise sky. There was nothing better than the salt smell of the sea carried on the coastal breeze across the fields. It was the smell of summer and Sam loved the summer.

Sam had moved out of the biggest bedroom into the middle-sized one when she'd known Abby and her baby were going to be stopping for a while. Abby was untidy at the best of times and the bigger bedroom was also beside the bathroom. If Sam had owned the place, she would have made en suites for both bedrooms by pinching a bit of the spacious landing. She couldn't imagine ever owning a place like Beach Cottage, but she was incredibly grateful that she had the chance to live here.

She had volunteered to help with the night feeds, but so far Abby had resisted.

'You haven't got the equipment, girlfriend,' she had pointed out, eyeing Sam's front and arching a blonde eyebrow. 'Well, you have, obviously, but it's out of commission.'

'Sad but true,' Sam said, glancing downwards and screwing up her face. 'These boobs have been out of commission for far too long.'

'I meant for babies.' Abby looked flustered.

'I know what you meant.' Sam smiled to show she was joking.

'Be grateful. My girls are never going to be the same again.' She rubbed at two damp patches on her t-shirt with the palms of her hands. 'I'm sure I have enough milk for a dozen babies. I never stop leaking.'

'You could always express some. Then I could help out with the night feeds and you could catch up on some sleep.'

'I might do that,' Abby said. But so far she hadn't. Sam was half relieved and half disappointed. But she was mostly relieved that her closest friend was beginning to settle into motherhood.

* * *

On Sunday afternoon, Matt turned up as planned. Sam and Abby were sitting in the garden on sun loungers beneath the shade of a huge old beech tree alongside a dilapidated green-painted wooden summerhouse that could be lovely with some TLC. Sam planned to do something with it when she had the time. Presently it was empty, apart from dust and a family of huge spiders that she'd disturbed the one time she had ventured in. She'd made a very hasty retreat.

She felt the same about huge spiders as Abby did about mice. She hadn't risked going in again.

'Hey ho,' Matt called as he walked around the side of the house, carrying a bunch of blue and pink helium balloons and an enormous teddy that was wearing a pink tank top. 'I tried ringing the bell but no one answered.'

'It doesn't work,' Abby told him. 'Like most things round here.' She jumped to her feet, beaming. 'It's brilliant to see you. Why have you bought Jack a teddy in a pink top.'

'It's gender neutral. It's blue on the back. Same thing with the balloons. I'm on trend, Sis.' He clicked his fingers. 'Down with the kids.'

'Are kids gender neutral, these days?' Sam asked from her position on the sun lounger in the leaf-dappled shade. She was holding Jack, who was wearing a tiny sunhat and also sunblock for babies.

'Wow, and there he is.' Matt's face crinkled up with affection. 'The little man himself. Should he be out here in the middle of the day?'

'It's not the middle of the day,' Abby pointed out. 'It's four o'clock. You're late, as usual. Anyway, a little bit of sunlight is good for him. I've got an app on my phone which tells you what the UV levels are…' Her voice was rising defensively.

Matt put his hands up. 'OK, calm down. It's all good. I'm not having a go at you. And I'm not late. I said afternoon and 4 p.m. is afternoon.' He kissed his sister, winked at Sam and, having divested himself of the teddy and balloons, he hunkered down beside her on the grass to get a closer look at Jack. 'Wow,' he said again. 'He's so tiny. He's got some hair, hasn't he?' He held out a finger close to Jack's hand and the baby gripped it. 'And he's got a grip on him too. The little bruiser.'

Sam watched the look of wonder spread over his face and she knew exactly what he was feeling. Only it must be stronger than it was for her because he was actually related to Jack. This baby had some of his genes. For the first time in her life, she wondered what it would be like to actually hold the warm solid weight of her own baby in her arms and she felt her throat close tightly with emotion. A sense of longing spread through her. Bloody hell, where had that come from?

Abby's voice broke the moment. 'You can hold him if you can prise him away from Sam. She's totally smitten.'

'I am,' Sam said, shaking her head slightly. 'Here you are then, Uncle Matt. While you're saying hello to your nephew, I'll go and fix us some drinks.'

She half expected him to refuse. Newborn babies were a scary prospect if you'd never had any of your own, which Matt hadn't. He'd always said he wasn't going to settle down until he was at least forty-five – he'd been forty-one on his last birthday and he was still playing the field. He didn't refuse though. He took Jack from Sam's arms with infinite care and looked at him with that same sense of awestruck wonder.

When Sam looked back at them from the oak stable-style back door of the house, she saw a little trio framed by sunlight and love and her heart gave another hard kick.

Good grief, she surely wasn't getting broody, was she? Up until now, settling down and having a family had been the very last thing on her wish list. In fact, never mind the last thing, it hadn't actually featured at all. This was not all that surprising, given her relationship history.

Sam's last relationship had not ended well. Gary Collins had been one of her first clients when she'd started Purbeck Pooches. She'd looked after his dog, a soft-eyed, soft-furred grey lurcher called Mitzi, and once, when he was away for a week, the two bay horses that he used to pull the Cinderella coach he hired out via his wedding carriage business. Gary himself had been married and divorced twice before he'd hit thirty-five. Both marriages had been fleeting and neither of his first wives still spoke to him. This should have been warning enough, Sam had thought with hindsight, but at the time she'd been too besotted to be rational.

Gary Collins was a mix of bad boy and brilliant entrepreneur. Dark-haired and silver-tongued and hotter than a sizzling summer's day, he had swept her off her feet. In the nine months, they were together, they'd had a couple of fantastic holidays, one in Greece, where they had spent all day in bed, and one in the Highlands, where, Sam mused, they had also spent a great deal of time in bed. If you took the bed part out of their relationship, there wouldn't have been much left. But that was another thing she had only realised with hindsight.

At the time, she had thought herself in love. She had thought Gary was the one and he had professed himself to be head over heels with her too. Then, one Thursday evening, just as she was settling down to watch her favourite drama – they didn't see each other on Thursdays – the whole thing had come crashing down. It had begun when her phone had beeped with a mysterious text from a withheld number. It had said simply,

He's cheating on you. Just like he cheated on me. Where do you think he is right now?

Sam had thought he was in The Anchor because that's where he'd told her he was going. To have a pint with his mate, Jez. They both agreed it was important to have their own lives. To not be so completely wrapped up in each other that they had nothing fresh to bring to the relationship.

'It's a matter of trust, babe,' Gary had said, looking deep into her eyes. 'I trust you utterly. And you can trust me too. Why would I be tempted out for a burger when I've got steak at home.'

It was typical of Gary to use a food metaphor. He loved food. He was one of the few men she'd met who could knock up a gourmet meal in his bachelor pad. His kitchen was full of spices like fenugreek and asafoetida and sumac, which she had never even heard of before she'd met him, let alone used. Even her mother had been impressed when she'd told her.

'I trust you too,' Sam had replied and she did. But the text had niggled her. It had been sent at 8 p.m. and had put her in a quandary. Random strangers who sent unsigned texts from withheld numbers could not be considered reliable sources. It was probably from an ex who had an axe to grind or maybe it was from someone he'd never even been out with who had an axe to grind. Gary was the kind of man who turned heads wherever they went. (Abby had once nicknamed him TaDah, which stood for Tall and Dark and Handsome.) He never seemed to notice the female attention, but Sam noticed. It had occasionally given her a twinge of uneasiness and she'd wondered if she was punching above her weight, but she'd been secure enough for this to be only a fleeting thought and one that was swiftly dismissed.

She could just treat the text with the contempt it deserved and delete it from her phone and forget all about it. Well, she could do the first two things anyway. Forgetting all about it would be tricky. On the other hand, maybe she shouldn't delete it. She should probably show it to Gary the following night when they were meeting for dinner.

Sam had glanced at her phone. The other thought that had been competing for space in her head was that it would be very easy to check. The Anchor was their local pub and it was less than a twenty-minute drive. She could casually wander over and see if his car was there. His silver Audi TT had red stripes – he'd had a custom paint job – so it wouldn't be hard to spot. She could maybe even peek in the window. Would that be a controlling jealous girlfriend kind of thing to do? She had struggled with herself and eventually decided that, in the circumstances, it wouldn't.

Gary's car had not been in the car park of The Anchor. Neither had Jez's pickup truck. There was no other way they could have got to the pub; it was too far from their homes in Swanage to have walked. They could, of course, have simply decided to go somewhere else. There were dozens of watering holes in Swanage; they could be anywhere. Sam had decided that as she was out she had nothing to lose by swinging past Jez's house, which was closest. His truck was parked outside, so they must have gone in Gary's. Feeling reluctant but committed to finding out what was going on, she had driven over to Gary's.

It was harder to casually drive past Gary's as he lived in a cul-de-sac in a nice estate on the outskirts of Swanage. She could feel her heart pounding as she got closer. When she was at the end of the road, she had been tempted to abandon the idea and go home. She felt insanely guilty. Surely she wasn't really going to drive past his house. What if he saw her? That was unlikely, she had reminded herself, as he wasn't supposed to be in.

But if he was in, she didn't want to be spotted, and it might be nearly nine, but it was still light. Making a split-second decision, she had pulled over and parked and then walked down. She could see before she got anywhere near his house that Gary's Audi was in the drive. It wasn't alone. There was a brand-new fuchsia pink Citroen C1 tucked up behind it. It was a car that screamed female, from its garish colour to its shiny alloy wheels, to the pretty pink and jade scarf that was draped over the back seat.

Sam's guilt for spying on him had morphed into outraged anger. She had tried to damp it down. There could be a perfectly rational explanation.

'*Like what?*' Abby's voice had suddenly popped up in her head.

'*Like he has a sister.*' Sam knew he didn't have a sister. '*A cousin then.*'

She was pretty sure he didn't have any cousins either. It was one of the things they had in common. They were only children of parents who had also been only children.

If she'd been Abby, she would have already marched up to the door and hammered on it and demanded to know what was going on. Sam had still been trying to decide whether this was the right thing to do – it wasn't in her nature to cause a scene – when she'd seen movement behind the front room bay window. Gary had slatted wooden blinds, but he rarely closed them fully and now he and a stunning tawny-haired beauty had just come into view.

The body language had said everything. They were standing very close together and, as Sam had watched, Gary cupped the girl's face in his hands and bent his head to kiss her. It looked like the closing scene in a romantic movie. Well, maybe not quite the closing scene, but Sam had seen enough.

They say that in moments of shock you remember every detail and the details that froze in her mind that night were the almond smell of the forsythia that grew against the side wall, the sickly pink colour of the car and the sick feeling in her stomach. She had hated the smell of almonds and the colour fuchsia ever since.

In the end, she never had confronted him that night. She had driven home, her hands clenched tight on the steering wheel, and she had let him lie to her for another twenty-four hours on the phone before finally telling him what she had seen and ending their relationship. Abby had been brilliant. She had ranted with her, hugged her, supplied endless prosecco and suggested several revenge strategies, most of which were illegal or immoral and all of which Sam had declined to carry out, being of the opinion that the best revenge was to pretend he had had never existed.

Then, while Sam's heart had slowly healed, Abby had phoned or WhatsApped every single day to make sure she was OK. Abby had been the ultimate best friend. Sam sometimes thought that they couldn't have been closer if they were sisters.

She thought this now as she took a tray on which were three glasses and a jug of ice-cold lemonade with lime slices – Abby's favourite drink since she'd been breastfeeding – out into the garden of Beach Cottage.

Jack was back on Abby's lap and she and Matt were halfway through a conversation about their parents.

'Mum's already seen him on Skype,' Abby was saying proudly. 'Dad had a bit more trouble. His eyesight's bad at the best of times. But they're coming back in August to meet him properly.' She shielded her eyes to look up at Sam. 'Matt's just agreed to be a godparent too. So if anything ever happens to me, you two will have to take care of my beautiful boy.'

Sam didn't want to think about anything ever happening to Abby, but she knew with absolute certainty that she would do whatever was needed for Abby's son. Abby continued, 'I was telling Matt just now about the odd text you got about the Kunekunes. Did you ever hear any more from that guy?'

'Funnily enough, I had an email from him this morning, asking if I'd received his message.' She frowned at the memory. 'I was going to answer it, but he went on to say that he thought his phone may have been intercepted by the Chinese government. He's clearly bonkers. I'm still thinking about what to say.'

'Lots of your clients are bonkers,' Abby replied. 'I mean who takes their horses on holiday with them?'

'I can see why they'd bring them to Studland,' Matt said. 'It's a great place to go horseback riding. Trotting through the sea with the wind in your hair, that's living the dream, isn't it? What's not to like?'

Sam put the tray on the grass and Matt jumped up and went to get the metal patio table from the hardstanding alongside the summerhouse.

'This will be easier,' he said, repositioning it beside them.

Abby wrinkled up her nose. 'Kunekune pigs though! I mean, why would you want something that snouts around in the mud!'

'Because they're cute,' Sam said. 'Apparently pigs are as trainable as dogs.' She'd read that on the website.

'They're not cute, they're gross.'

Matt glanced at Sam. 'I've often wondered how you and my sister ever became friends.'

'Because opposites attract,' Sam said. At exactly the same moment as Abby did.

5

Sam went to work before the post was delivered, but halfway through the following week, Abby WhatsApped her a picture of a handwritten envelope with a message that said,

This had to be signed for, do you want me to open it?

Sam read the message in her break. Abby must be bored and she was quite curious herself. She had no idea who would be sending her letters requiring a signature. She messaged back:

Yes please.

A few moments later she got another WhatsApp.

You are NOT going to believe this. The word OMG was followed by several whole rows of exclamation marks.

God, Abby was infuriating sometimes.

Just tell me who it's from

Sam messaged, glancing up to check if anyone was looking in her direction. Using mobiles at work was frowned upon unless they weren't busy – which they were because Hypochondriac Heather wasn't in – and Sam had rather foolishly, she'd realised with hindsight, told Elannah not to bother getting a temp in. She could cover for a week or two, she'd said.

She was still trying to make up for lying to Rex about the dentist appointment. Not that he'd mentioned it again. He wasn't in today, as it happened. All of the engineers were out doing surveys, apart from Lightning who'd just dashed in – he'd probably done two already; it was nearly eleven thirty. Rex was probably out on a survey too. He did the top-end ones. Elannah hadn't said where he was. She'd been on the phone when Sam had got to work and, apart from a brief nod, she'd had her head down all morning. She was obviously busy. She wasn't currently at her desk either.

Sam's phone, which was on silent, but had the vibrate mode on, buzzed again and she snatched it up.

This time, Abby had photographed the letter, which was typed but long. Sam tapped on it to make it big enough to read and looked at the sender's address, which she didn't recognise, and then the first line.

> Further to my recent correspondence via text and email, which I fear you may not have received, I am writing in connection with a possible booking. I have a pair of Kunekune pigs. You may have heard of them…

As Sam was scanning the rest of the letter with a growing sense of disbelief, her phone vibrated with another message from Abby.

He says he's coming over to discuss the booking with you today as he's in the area. You have to stop him. I don't want to be dealing with a mad person. Not with Jack here.

Sam sighed. This was all she needed.

I'll phone him

She WhatsApped:

Don't worry

Please can you do it now

I'm on it

As luck would have it, Lightning chose that moment to hotfoot it over to her desk and drop a USB stick onto it.

'Couple of surveys from the weekend. Any chance you could prioritise the first one on it. They're in a hurry.' So was he by the look of it. He was hopping from one foot to the other.

Sam liked the senior surveyor. He was like the archetypal avuncular uncle, kind to everybody in the office and always appreciative, and he occasionally brought in big pink boxes of cream cakes that smelled sweetly of cinnamon and vanilla from the bakery in Swanage to show his appreciation. He always knew what everyone's favourites were and this earned him a lot of brownie points.

'Will do,' she said.

'Thanks, you're a star, Sam. Better go.' He turned and headed for the door. 'Just going to that bungalow in Wareham,' he called back over his shoulder. 'Laters.'

Elannah hadn't returned to her desk. There would never be a

better time to do it. Sam made a split-second decision. She would phone the bonkers pig man now. He had signed his letter with some incomprehensible signature, the only letter of which she could read was B, so she still didn't know what his name was, but at least she could put him off visiting Beach Cottage.

She picked up the cordless landline on her desk. To her relief, he answered almost immediately.

'I'm phoning from Purbeck Pooches,' she said. 'I had a letter from you.'

'Ms Jones, I presume. Thank you so much for getting back to me.' He sounded quite normal. That was a relief. 'Did you also receive a text from me?' he enquired. 'It would have come from a Mr B. I think I had the correct mobile number. I do hope that got through.'

'I saw an email,' she hedged deciding it might be best not to mention she'd had both his messages and had decided that the B stood for bonkers or barking mad or barmy – nothing good anyway. 'I'm so sorry I didn't get back to you sooner. I've been rather busy. Summer holidays, you know.' She didn't want to get into explanations about new babies being time stealers.

'Don't worry. I understand completely. I'm Head Chef at the Bluebell Cliff. This time of year is manic.'

Sam sat up a little straighter. She knew of the Bluebell Cliff. Not many locals didn't know of it. It was a gorgeous boutique hotel set up on the cliffs at Ballard Down and had undergone a total update and refurbishment about four years ago by its new owner, who was an eccentric multi-millionaire apparently. It had a really good reputation, both for service and for food. In fact, it was one of the few places in the area that had a Michelin star. It was out of her price range but firmly on her To Do list for when she was richer.

Sam had once met Clara King, the manager, at a lunch at the Chamber of Commerce when she'd been networking to promote

Purbeck Pooches. Clara had been lovely. She'd had the most gorgeous Radley bag, which had led to a discussion about dogs and she'd subsequently directed more than one person looking for a pet-sitting service in the direction of Purbeck Pooches.

'Clara King, my manager, gave me your details,' Mr B said, right on cue. 'She said she had heard very good things about you.'

'That was nice of her.' Sam was now completely disarmed. If Mr B worked for Clara, he couldn't be all bad and weren't brilliant chefs supposed to be a bit on the eccentric side? She relaxed into the conversation, spinning around on her office chair, as she was prone to when she was thinking. 'I've never actually looked after any Kunekune pigs, but I don't think it would be a problem. What dates are we talking about?'

'There's plenty of time. I'm not going away until the middle of September, but I need to make sure I'm leaving Portia and Percy in safe hands.'

'I'll need to check the diary,' Sam began, 'but in principle it should be fine.'

'Marvellous,' Mr B said. 'Excellent news. I have to say that Kunekunes are a joy to keep as pets. If you haven't met any, you're in for a treat. Is today convenient to swing by and discuss it? Or should I make another appointment?'

'Today's not brilliant. I haven't got my diary in front of me, but could I possibly call you back?' Sam thought she had just heard the bang of the front door downstairs. Someone must be on their way up. She should probably get off the phone.

She glanced over her shoulder. Yes, she should definitely get off the phone. It was Rex. He had just come through the internal door and was crossing the office, his laptop case in his hand.

Mr B was still waxing lyrical about the joy of keeping Kunekune pigs. She didn't want to cut him off mid-flow. But Rex was heading her way. Not that Rex would know who she was talking to, she realised suddenly. She could easily have picked up Elannah's phone. She could even get extra brownie points if she kept her cool.

'As I say, sir, I don't have the appointments diary in front of me right at this moment, but I will have someone call you back very shortly.'

Rex had stopped by her desk and was now looking at her curiously.

She gave him her best professional smile. Mr B was still squawking away on the other end of the phone. The man could talk, that was for sure.

'I can take the call if you like,' Rex offered, holding out his hand for the cordless phone.

'Um, thanks, great. I'll put it through to your extension.'

'No need. Just give me the phone.'

Sam pretended not to hear and turned her head slightly to shield the phone so she could press the disconnect button without him seeing.

That wasn't going to go down very well with her eccentric caller, but she could always sneak out and phone Mr B back in a minute from her mobile. Tell him she had lost the signal or something. She should probably have phoned him from her mobile in the first place. In the ladies. Just in case. She hadn't expected Rex to sneak up on her unannounced.

'I, um, seem to have cut him off,' she said, feeling her face flame scarlet and willing Mr B not to phone back. 'I'll call him back in a minute. Shall I come and get the diary first?'

As she spoke, the work phone began to ring again. It was bound to be him. He must have dialled 1471 and hit redial. She already knew he was persistent. Shit, shit, shit!

'Are you going to answer that?' Rex said, straightening his navy tie and looking agitated.

'Yes. I am. I am most definitely going to answer it... yes, I am...'

She nodded slowly and made no move to answer the phone, which was still in her hand. Rex was looking at it too. Fortunately, other than physically grab it out of her hand, there wasn't much he could do about it.

It carried on ringing. The familiar electronic trill sounded ultra loud in the silent office. Trill, trill. Trill, trill. Trill, trill. It was excruciating.

'Samantha,' Rex said. She didn't dare look at him, but she could hear the incredulous disbelief in his voice.

So she did the only thing she could think of doing, she leaped up and still holding the phone she ran as fast as she could across the office, past the empty desks of the other engineers, out of the internal door onto the first-floor landing and then down the staircase until she reached the front door of the building, where she leaned back against a wall, her heart pounding madly as the adrenaline flooded through her. The flaming phone still hadn't stopped ringing.

She pressed the connect button, just as it did finally stop. Rex hadn't followed her. He must think she was totally mad. Better that than him knowing that she was lying to his face again. Maybe she could say that she'd had a medical emergency. But then why would she have taken the phone with her? Oh God.

The front door opened and someone who she recognised as working in K. R. Lacey's Accountants came in, glanced at her curiously and went on up the stairs. He'd only just gone in through Lacey's door, which was in line of sight from Sam's vantage point, when Elannah appeared at the top of the stairs.

'Sam...?' she called and then when she spotted her standing there, 'Sam, are you OK?'

There was no avoiding Elannah. She was coming down, her pretty face anxious. She paused on the bottom stair, adjusted her Geek Girl glasses and leaned forward.

'Only Rex said you'd left in a massive hurry. Are you ill?'

'No. No. I'm OK now.' Sam felt numb. She would have preferred to have made some excuse and fled home, but she couldn't. Things were hectic enough without Hypochondriac Heather. She was going to have to face Rex and explain.

'Is it a man thing? You don't have to tell me.' Elannah touched her arm in a little gesture of sisterly solidarity that made Sam feel even worse. 'Look. Whatever it is, I'm sure it will be OK.'

'Thanks. I'm sure it will too.' The upside was that Rex was unlikely to sack her for moonlighting, she thought as she followed Elannah back up to the office. They were far too busy.

* * *

A few minutes later, she was in Rex's office, surrounded by the familiar smell of old books and coffee. She had a feeling of déjà vu as he came out from behind his desk and sat in the visitor's chair next to her.

He wasn't smiling, but he didn't look angry either. She had no idea what he was thinking.

'Is everything OK, Samantha?' he began.

'Sam,' she said automatically. 'Yes, I'm sorry. I owe you an apology. That call. It wasn't a work call.'

'I gathered that.'

He was clearly waiting for her to say something else and she was struggling to work out how much she should tell him. No one at work knew about Purbeck Pooches. Although it didn't affect her ability to work for Fielding's, it probably counted as moonlighting and she was loath to give him a reason to sack her.

After a pause that seemed to go on forever but could only have been a few seconds, he said, 'I thought it couldn't be when I heard you mention pigs.'

'You heard me mention – um – pigs,' she repeated, slightly thrown. How had he heard that from outside the door? She could have sworn he had only overheard the final part of her conversation.

'I came into the office a little before you realised,' he said at around the same moment she had worked this out for herself.

'Right.' Bloody hell, he must have been wearing super quiet shoes. She glanced at his feet. Brown brogues like the ones her father wore. You couldn't ever hear him coming either.

'I thought you'd heard me come in and then I realised you hadn't.'

So he had gone out again and had banged the downstairs door extra hard. He had given her the opportunity to get off the phone. Somewhere in the conflicting mix of emotions rushing through her head was the thought, *That was nice of him*.

It made her want to tell him the truth. She told him about Purbeck Pooches, about how she was lucky enough to be renting a cottage with a field where she could board horses and the occasional more unusual guest. 'I was hoping I could use the field more, but there are so many rules and regulations. There are forms galore just for boarding dogs. If you have bigger animals, it takes things on to a whole new level. Although I do actually have a pet goat coming in a couple of weeks. Just for the weekend. She's called Snowy.'

He didn't react to that snippet, so she rushed on. She told him how Purbeck Pooches had been both a sideline and a passion for the last two years of her life and then, in for a penny in for a pound, she told him about her hopes that it would one day become a full-time business.

He didn't interrupt at all and she still couldn't read his face.

'So being an audio typist for a firm of structural engineers is not your dream job,' he said when she had finished.

'No.' Sam felt a trickle of sweat running down the back of her neck. She was suddenly very conscious of the fact that telling your boss you were planning to leave just as soon as you could make enough money from your part-time extra job may not have been one of her best ideas.

But Rex didn't react as she'd feared he might. In fact he was a hair's breadth from a smile. 'I'm not surprised really, Sam. You're bright. So who was the man with the pigs?'

Had he really just said she was bright or had she imagined that bit? Relaxing slightly, she told him about Mr B and the Kunekunes and how that had all evolved into what had happened today.

At the end of that, instead of reprimanding her or laughing at her plans, he offered her a mint from the bowl on his desk.

'I do love... like,' she amended, '...working for Fielding's.'

'And you fit in very well,' he replied on the back of this very clear olive branch. 'So you had better get back to it.'

'You're not going to sack me?' she blurted before she'd had the chance to edit the thought. It probably wasn't a particularly good plan to put that idea in his head either.

'We're too busy,' he said and she could hear the slightly amused irony in his voice. 'If you need to phone that Mr B chap back, then go and do it. But, Sam... Please don't lie to me again.' His face was serious.

'I won't.' She fled before he had the chance to say anything else.

* * *

That night when Sam got in an hour later than she'd intended, because once again she had felt honour-bound to catch up on her work, Abby listened to her rendition of the day's events with a horrified fascination.

'Oh my God, I'm sorry. If I hadn't opened that letter none of that would have happened, would it?'

They were in the kitchen. Abby was sitting at the table breastfeeding an unusually uncooperative Jack, who was grumbling, and Sam was making them some tea. Cheese on toast that she was just cutting into squares and sprinkling with Worcester sauce because it was late and she couldn't be bothered to do anything that involved proper cooking or even putting ready meals in the oven.

'It's not your fault, Abby. It's mine. The bottom line is that I shouldn't be trying to do two things at once. I've always thought that me running Purbeck Pooches doesn't have any impact on my job at Fielding's. But I guess it does. Even if it's only to the extent that it takes away my energy and attention.' She sighed as she brought the plate of cheese squares to the table. 'I haven't even got any boarders and it's buggered up things today.'

Abby nodded as she moved Jack patiently back to her breast. 'I don't think this little one's hungry, bless him. So what happened with the Kunekune man?'

'He's coming over to see me in a couple of weeks. I offered to go there, but he wants to come here. I think he wants to vet me. He's clearly on the paranoid side – understatement! I'll be looking after his Kunekunes at his place, I think. Not here.'

'How come? Wouldn't they be OK in your field?'

'Probably, but pigs are classed as farm animals. You need paperwork from DEFRA to move them around. You probably need a licence to look after them too. I'm not sure. Anyway, I won't be needed to babysit Portia and Percy – that's their names – until the middle of September apparently, so there's no great rush.'

'Mmmm.'

Sam could tell Abby was no longer listening. She was focused on Jack. So she didn't say anything else. But she was still feeling rattled. Rex had been incredibly nice and understanding today when, to be honest, he'd have been perfectly entitled to blow his top. It was the second time in just over a week that he had caught her out and he hadn't even given her a formal warning.

This didn't stop her feeling as guilty as hell. The truth was she wasn't sure how much longer she could run Purbeck Pooches and work at Fielding's without one or both of them being severely compromised.

6

To Sam's intense relief, the next fortnight went without a hitch. She had a proper catch-up with her mother on the phone, promising to go and see them when they weren't so rushed off their feet with guests and in between her day job and her Purbeck Pooches bookings.

Fortunately, Hypochondriac Heather was back at work too, having recovered from being ill. She hadn't had appendicitis in the end. Apparently the doctors never had got to the bottom of her tummy pains and Heather had come in for a fair bit of good-natured ribbing in the office ever since.

'It was all in the mind,' Magpie had said when she'd first got back. 'As usual.'

'I was not skiving, if that's what you're trying to imply.' Heather had glared at him and tossed back her two blonde plaits – a nod to her Dutch lineage. Her father was from Holland and her mother was from the Isle of Wight. They had met when they were skiing in Switzerland.

'I didn't say you didn't *think* you were ill,' Magpie said, picking up a pen absentmindedly from her desk. 'Just that it was a psychopathetic illness.'

'I think you mean psychosomatic,' Lightning said smugly. 'That means that your physical symptoms were real, but they were caused by your mind.'

'That's what I just said,' Magpie pointed out. 'Exactly that.'

Heather retrieved her pen from his hand. 'Nothing was in my head. The pain was here.' She gestured irritably towards her stomach, but they both ignored her.

'You were having a psycho-sabbatical, weren't you, love.' Lightning laughed loudly at his own joke.

'I should leave her alone if you want any typing done today.' Rex's quiet authoritative voice had cut through their hilarity and Sam had glanced at him. Where had he sprung from? He must have been wearing his super quiet shoes again.

'Quite right,' Heather puffed out her chest and pursed her lips. 'The next person who mentions psycho anything will be struck off my typing list for the rest of the week. And don't go thinking you can butter up Sam. She can't do two people's work.'

Sam was tempted to point out that actually she could if she put her mind to it. She had done it while Heather was absent without too much trouble, but that would have felt unkind and the girls stuck together in this office. 'Correct,' she said. 'Be nice to typists. I don't think we've had any cakes lately, have we, Lightning?'

She had also liked the way that Rex had stuck up for Heather. He might be a pain in the butt as a boss sometimes when it came to rules and regulations, but he had a gentlemanly integrity that you didn't see very often. And he was good at inspiring them as a team.

Things had gone smoothly at Purbeck Pooches too. Sam had built up some flexi time covering for Heather, which meant she'd been able to look after Seamus and Goldie for Barbara Oldfield for three full days.

They were her favourite customers and so far it had been a fabulous July for her fledgling business. Sam had been in her element walking the Irish wolfhound and his partner in crime, the sweet-natured, but bossy golden retriever, taking them for a play on her local beach and a race in and out of the waves a couple of times a day.

Once, when Jack had woken at 2.00 am and wouldn't go back to sleep, she and Abby had gone on a night walk to the beach. The dogs had been delighted to go out at such an unorthodox hour and Jack, who'd been grizzling relentlessly indoors, had calmed down once he was outside in the still air beneath the stars.

'He was probably too hot, bless him,' Sam had said, as they negotiated the pitch-black footpath (tarmac fortunately) through the woods with a torch and went across the powder-soft sand to the harder shore at the water's edge. The tide was out, so it had been easier to push the buggy there and a cool breath of air blew in off the sea to touch their faces and bare arms. Neither of them had bothered with jackets. It was a muggy night.

'It's so peaceful here,' Abby had said as they strolled, soothed by the endless shushing of the surf, with the two dogs loping like ghostly shadows alongside them. A huge disc of a silvery moon had sailed high over Studland Bay, turning the sand to palest gold and the sea to indigo and casting a glittering moon path across the water. As each wave broke against the shore, phosphorescence had twinkled beneath it like silver sparkles. It was an enchantingly beautiful night.

Jack had been asleep by the time they got home again and both girls had the luxury of lie-ins the next day. Fortunately so had Jack. And so had Seamus and Goldie.

Now it was Friday evening. Seamus and Goldie had gone home and Mrs Alsop, or Mrs A as she was known affectionately, the owner of Snowy the goat, had just dropped her off for the weekend while she went off to a meditation retreat in Weymouth.

'It's brilliant to find somewhere that will have her,' Mrs A had gushed, perhaps a little too keenly, Sam had thought. 'My kennels used to take her, but they didn't have the space this time. She's no trouble. She just ambles around.' She had giggled and made vague 'ambling around' motions with her hands.

Snowy had arrived in a horsebox towed by Mrs A and had certainly seemed benign enough when she emerged into the evening sunshine. They had released her in the field and Sam and Mrs A had watched her for a while, but all had seemed well.

How much trouble could one small nanny goat cause? Sam had wondered when Mrs A had finally left and she'd gone in to touch base with Abby and Jack. What with her dog-sitting duties and Abby's visits from friends and a couple of people she worked with, all of whom were keen to see Jack, they'd been like ships in the night lately.

'I'm going to have an early night,' Abby said, yawning, 'But how about we have a girly evening tomorrow? Wine, the works. We haven't done that for ages. And...' she paused and looked at her phone, 'my weekend horoscope says, "*Schedule an escape.*"'

'For once I'm in agreement with your astrologer,' Sam said, arching an eyebrow.

* * *

Sam was woken at an unearthly hour the next morning by a piercing shriek. It sounded like Abby.

Terrified there was a problem with Jack and with her heart thudding madly, Sam leaped out of bed and raced out onto the landing and found Abby leaning out of the open window.

'There's a goat on your car,' she said, darting her blonde head back inside and turning towards Sam with a stricken look. 'It's got blood around its mouth. Do goats kill things?'

'No, they're herbivores. Are you sure? Let me see.'

Abby moved aside and Sam took her place. Snowy was indeed on the roof of her car, which was parked inside the five-bar gate in their garden. How had she got up there? More to the point, how had she got out of the field? At least she hadn't escaped into the road... yet.

Snowy was facing towards the road, but there was something red smeared around her muzzle. She must have hurt herself during the escape. Sam felt sick. One of her worst fears was that a boarder would be hurt while in her care. She was so careful to make sure this didn't happen. Today it had obviously gone wrong.

She flew downstairs. She closed the back door as quietly as she could so as not to scare Snowy, who, it had to be said, didn't look as though much would scare her. She was staring over the walled garden at a car that was just going by. Sam saw the driver's startled face. From his position, it must look as though there was a white goat suspended in mid-air.

Snowy was chewing peacefully. Despite her unusual vantage point, she didn't look stressed, but Sam could see a splodge of blood on her creamy white chest.

Oh God.

She walked slowly forward. As she got closer, she realised that what she'd taken for blood was actually the petal of a red rose.

Snowy was chewing a rose. Oh thank God. There were more petals, along with several bits of stalk and leaves scattered around her hooves on the black car roof.

She clearly wasn't hurt, thank goodness, although getting her down was going to be an issue. Especially as she was in no hurry at all to come down from the nice viewing platform she'd found. In the end, Sam had to resort to bribery – a bucket and some carrots. It was amazing how many animals responded to a bucket, she thought, as Snowy was finally enticed back on to terra firma.

'How are you going to stop her doing it again?' Abby asked with interest when Sam got back inside and was washing her hands at the Belfast sink in the utility room that led off the kitchen. 'I take it you don't want her to be jumping up onto your car whenever the mood takes her. Did she do any damage by the way?' She was holding Jack, who blinked sleepily and yawned. The drama had clearly passed him by.

'No damage as far as I can see,' Sam said, following them back into the kitchen. 'At least, I don't think so. I've checked her mouth. She must be impervious to thorns! I just need to google whether goats can eat roses safely.'

'I meant to your car,' Abby said tutting. 'Not to the flaming goat.'

'Oh. There were a few scratch marks, that's all. It's had worse.' Sam hadn't thought too much about her car, she'd been too concerned about Snowy.

'That would be an interesting one for the insurance company,' Abby said, smirking. 'Can you tell us exactly how the damage was incurred to your car please Modom? Yes, certainly, Mr Insurance Company man – a goat leapt up onto it and did a little dance on the roof. It wasn't the goat's fault. I shouldn't have parked the car outside my own house in my own garden. I should have put it somewhere less accessible to goats.'

Abby was a very good mimic. She had Sam's slightly defensive It's-Not-The-Animal's-Fault tone spot on.

'To answer your other question,' Sam said, 'I've left her in the garden for now and I've parked my car outside on the road. I'm pretty sure she can't get out. I might have to tether her, though, to be on the safe side. Thank goodness it's only until tomorrow.'

Abby's eyes widened in horror. 'Is it safe to go out there with Jack? What if she charges at the buggy?'

'Goats don't charge. That's bulls.'

'Yes, but they headbutt, don't they? I don't fancy being head-butted by a goat.' Who will look after Jack if I end up in hospital impaled on a goat horn?

'I will. Anyway, she hasn't got horns. And she's as daft as anything. She likes having her chin scratched.'

'Even so.' Abby shook her head. 'I'd feel safer if she was tethered, I think.'

'Can I sort it out once I've seen Mr B? He's coming at nine thirty.'

'Is that Bonkers Pig Man? Did he tell you why he sent you a letter by the way? Isn't that a pretty strange thing to do?'

'I guess because I didn't answer his messages quick enough. Maybe he was anxious I hadn't received them. He sounded like he could be the anxious type. Did I tell you he's the Head Chef at the Bluebell Cliff Hotel?'

'No.' Abby sniffed the air. 'I think this one needs changing. You can tell me about the mad chef later.'

* * *

Sam's first impression of Mr B, who arrived in a very unassuming car, an old Sierra, on the dot of nine thirty, was that he was very tall. He was also very thin – wasn't there a saying, 'never trust a thin chef'? He reminded her of a young Rowan Atkinson. Her dad was a huge fan of the old Mr Bean shows.

Mr B got out of his car, which he had parked on the road behind hers, and stood for a few seconds with his hands in his pockets scanning the house intently. It would have been unnerving if she hadn't known who he was.

She went out to meet him.

'Good morning. I'm Sam Jones. Are you Mr B? Does that stand

for anything?' She held out her hand and he shook it with a grip much heartier than his appearance suggested.

'I prefer to be known as Mr B.' There was no question mark in his voice, but Sam nodded anyway. She was used to the eccentricities of people. Her parents had once had a couple stay at the B&B who had insisted they be addressed as Princess Laura and Prince Albert. They had been happy to comply.

'As long as they pay cash up front for the room, they can call themselves the Queen of flaming Sheba, for all I care,' her dad had said at the time.

'And as long as they don't expect me to curtsey when I take in their bacon and eggs,' her mother had said, 'I agree with you, love.'

Sam didn't think she'd need to get cash up front from Mr B. He was clearly who he said he was. She had looked him up on the Bluebell Cliff Hotel website. He was referred to on there as 'Mr B, our brilliant chef'.

Sam didn't have an office, she had never needed one, so she'd said she'd talk to Mr B in the kitchen and Abby had agreed to make herself scarce. As Sam led him through the garden around to the back door of the kitchen, Abby was ostensibly hanging out her smalls on the rotary washing line. She had timed that well, Sam thought as Abby gave them a cheery wave and stared with undisguised curiosity at Mr B.

He stared unsmilingly back.

'This way,' Sam said, leading him towards the back door, where Snowy was now grazing peacefully on a patch of grass. According to Google, goats loved roses and it was perfectly safe for them to eat them. Sam planned to give her a couple more later if she behaved during Mr B's visit.

'Nice goat,' Mr B said approvingly. 'I like goats.'

'She's supposed to be in the field, but she escaped.'

'Your fence isn't high enough,' he remarked, glancing across at the four-foot-high panelled fencing. 'You need an electric fence. They can get out of anywhere. My parents used to keep goats. They took them to nightclubs.'

'The goats?' Sam asked, assuming she'd got the wrong end of the stick.

'Yes.' He looked at her as if this was the most natural statement in the world. 'You could tell the calibre of a nightclub by whether they would let your goat in. The good ones would give you a dustpan and brush and tell you to clear up after them. Mind you, that was back in the mid eighties. Before government departments jumped in with a million and one regulations. In those days, you could keep whatever animals you wanted in your garden – pigs, donkeys, goats, chickens – you didn't have to fill in ten forms in triplicate to shift an animal from one place to another. Big Brother wasn't breathing down your neck, spying on you through your phone or your own security camera.' He put his hand over his face, fingers splayed, before glancing up at the security camera that was fitted on the wall above the back door behind them. 'Did you know that security cameras are continuously sending images back to China?'

'No,' Sam said, expecting him to break into laughter at any moment.

He didn't. 'Well, they are. Have you never checked your data transmission on your laptop?'

She shook her head, not entirely sure what he was talking about, but not wanting to show herself up as being too much of a technophobe.

'If you do, you will find that your camera is in constant communication with China. They're spying on us. Have been for years. It started with security cameras and digital televisions, then phones and laptops. In fact, anything at all that's connected up to the internet. They gather information and compile it.'

'But for what purpose?' The words slipped out of her mouth before she had time to consider that she probably didn't want to know the answer.

'Infiltration. Some people say I'm paranoid.' He glanced at her suspiciously. 'But I am not paranoid. A few years ago, I singlehandedly uncovered a conspiracy to bring down the Bluebell Cliff Hotel.'

'I see.' Sam was momentarily lost for words. She wondered what her father would say to Mr B. He was so brilliant with people. He was so brilliant at being interested without being patronising, being fully engaged without getting too involved.

'Was it all OK in the end?' she ventured, as she led him past the offending security camera and through the back door into the kitchen.

'It was fine. The perpetrators were brought to justice. And, of course, the fabulous Bluebell Cliff lived to fight another day. Did you know that it's not just an ordinary hotel? It's a place where people can go to live out their dream.'

'I did know that, yes.' Clara King had mentioned it when they'd met. She was relieved they were back on safe ground. 'It's a brilliant concept', although she couldn't think of any particular dream she would want to play out at an hotel. 'What sort of dreams do people have?'

'Pretty whacky ones usually.'

They must be whacky, if Mr B thought that. She hoped he was going to elaborate, but he didn't.

'Can I offer you a drink? I have coffee. Or herbal tea?' He looked like a man who might drink herbal teas.

'Are they fair trade?'

'Yes, I think so. Teapigs.' There was a joke there somewhere.

'Guinness World Records.'

'Excuse me?' Sam looked at the packet in her hand. Teapigs were good, but she wasn't sure they were that good.

'It was someone's dream to break a Guinness World Record and they did it at the Bluebell.' He puffed out his chest proudly. 'That wasn't entirely down to me, I must confess. But I did create a new dish in their honour. The Runner's Roulade. A fantastic concoction of meringue, raspberries, fresh cream, the lightest of sponges – it's a little like a pavlova, but infinitely superior. If I do say so myself.'

'It sounds amazing.'

'You must come to the Bluebell and I will give you a sample.'

'Um. Thanks.'

'It will be my pleasure.' He tossed his head. He was slightly camp and clearly as mad as a box of frogs, but there was something endearing about him.

'I have to tell you that I prefer my pigs to people. Most people,' he amended. 'Pigs are as intelligent as dogs, you know. They are reliable, entertaining, loyal and affectionate. They don't let you down. They don't lie, manipulate, deceive or betray. No, that is not quite true. Portia can be a touch on the manipulative side when it comes to food. Portia is a foodie.'

Sam warmed to him even more. He lit up when he was talking about his Kunekunes. 'I know what you mean about animals being more straightforward. I've always been a great animal lover.'

'I can tell. You have it in your face.' Mr B tilted his head slightly and she felt as if he was scrutinising her properly for the first time. 'You put me in mind of Clara King. Kind but firm. Fair but generous. Yes, I see generosity there.' His eyes glittered with humour and intelligence. 'You must think me a little crazy. Most people do.'

She was about to disagree, out of politeness, but she couldn't quite bring herself to do it. Instead, she burst out laughing and he laughed with her.

For a few moments, they stood in the sunny kitchen, that was now full of the scents of coffee and cinnamon tea and the fresh basil pot that was growing on the windowsill, laughing uproariously. Mr B occasionally doubled over and slapped his knees. He looked like a giant stick insect who'd become a little touched by the midday sun – a thought which made Sam laugh even more.

It was Mr B who stopped first. 'Where were we? Ah yes – now, as I think I said, there is no need for you to stay at my house. I understand you have other priorities.'

'Where exactly are your Kunekunes kept?' She was suddenly worried that they must be in his garden. That couldn't be legal surely.

'They are in a field in Kent Way. Two roads from where I live. I would usually visit them five times a day. That is probably excessive, but I worry.'

Sam nodded, wondering how he fitted that around being a full-time chef.

'My girlfriend helps. Meg adores Portia and Percy, but she will be away too. With me.' His eyes brightened. 'We don't have many holidays. Meg is a workaholic.'

'I see.' Sam blinked. The mention of a girlfriend had forced her to readjust her image of him slightly. 'And – um – how many times would you like me to go and check on them?'

'Four times daily would be ideal. It is only for three days, perhaps four. Mid-September, as I said.'

'That sounds fine.'

'Excellent news.' He rubbed his hands together. 'You will, of course, need to visit and be introduced properly. Shall we go now? We can discuss terms on the way.'

7

'So let me get this straight,' Abby said idly when she and Sam were sitting in the lounge later that Saturday night. 'You are actually going to be responsible for two Kunekune pigs whose owner, as far as I can see, is totally batshit crazy. Isn't that a little risky?'

'It's only for a long weekend,' Sam said, tucking a strand of hair that had come loose from its clip back behind her ear. 'And it's not until the middle of September. How hard can it be?'

'That's what you said about the goat, girlfriend. And look how that panned out.'

'I know.' Sam let out a breath. Snowy was back in the field again and Sam had decided not to give her the option to escape again so she was now safely tethered. Much to Sam's relief, she'd seemed unperturbed by the leather strap around her neck. The chain that was anchored firmly to a post allowed her access to water and shelter, but there wasn't enough wriggle room for her to get too near the fence. So she couldn't accidentally hang herself.

Sam was feeling unusually laid-back, possibly because they'd had a glass of wine with the spag bol Abby had made for their tea. She smiled. It had been fun meeting Portia and Percy and the set-up had all been surprisingly normal. They lived in a sectioned-off paddock that was part of a much bigger field and they had a fairly ordinary-looking ark made of wood, which they 'retired to' – Mr B's words – at night.

'Are they like hens?' she had asked him. 'Do they naturally go inside at night?'

'These two do.' He'd leaned over to scratch Portia's belly – she'd been lying on her side and she'd obligingly rolled over, flicking her ears in ecstasy.

The Kunekunes had been cuter, and tamer, than Sam had been expecting. They were the size of small pigs, both brown with darker spots, and they were obviously well used to people, which she supposed wasn't surprising if Mr B and his girlfriend visited them five times a day.

He'd also showed her a camera he had rigged up over their enclosure. She'd been tempted to ask him how he got around the security implications with the Chinese but had resisted. She did not want to set him off on another long rant.

Sam poured herself a second glass of wine. Everything was beginning to look mellow and lovely. 'Nothing's set in stone. I can always change my mind.'

'Yes, I suppose that's true. You won't though, will you? You're far too nice.'

'And it's not as though I'm overflowing with customers, is it? Despite your best efforts with my website. Thank you for that by the way.'

'My pleasure.' Abby yawned and in his cot upstairs Jack yawned too and shifted in his sleep. Baby monitors were pretty sophisticated these days, Sam had thought when they had fixed it up, wondering if they were also monitored by the Chinese in the world according to Mr B, but deciding not to mention this to Abby. Jack's had a sound-activated light and it worked really well. It was connected to an app on Abby's phone, which meant they could sit downstairs and she could keep a close eye on him too.

Abby had asked her health visitor whether she could have the occasional glass of wine while she was breastfeeding and she'd been told that was fine. So this evening, for the first time, she was having a glass of red. She sipped it thoughtfully. 'You could really do with giving up your day job and investing some more money in Purbeck Pooches.

'I know, but those two things are incompatible.' Sam blinked. 'In an ideal world, I'd take a lot more boarders – maybe have some kind of outside kennelling. It would be great if I had the flexibility to have dogs outside.'

Occasionally lately, she had to turn one of her regular clients down because she'd been full. She could only do dog boarding at weekends. Canine boarders lived in the house and were restricted by baby gates to the kitchen and utility room, but there wasn't room to have more than two or three at a time. Turning people down wasn't good for business.

'You're right though. I can't do very much more without investing a lot more time and money. And that's difficult while I'm still working at Fielding's.'

'Any chance of you going part-time or maybe working from home?'

'Rex doesn't want us working from home at the moment. Heather asked once before. Part-time would be good. Financially, I could probably get by.' This had been true ever since Abby had been paying her a proper rent. When she'd first moved in, Sam had insisted that she didn't want any – that if you couldn't help out a mate, then it was a pretty poor show – but for the last three months, Abby had insisted on paying her. Abby's website design job was well paid. She was currently on maternity leave, but her company had already agreed she could go back on a work-from-home basis.

'I don't think me going part-time would work for Fielding's. They really need two full-time typists to keep up.'

'That's a shame. So you're stuck with things the way they are then.'

'For the time being,' Sam said, feeling irked because she wasn't sure how that was going to change. 'Do you fancy anything to nibble? We never did have that Brie we were going to have for afters, did we?'

She wandered out to the kitchen, her mind on autopilot as she opened the fridge, got the Brie, then, on impulse, grabbed a bar of chocolate from the side compartment. When she and Abby were small, they'd often had sleepovers at each other's homes, which involved some kind of impromptu feast like this. She added a packet of cream crackers and some plates and a knife and took the whole lot back into the lounge on a tray.

Abby's eyes lit up as she put it on the coffee table. 'That reminds me of the midnight feasts we used to have.'

'I was thinking the same thing.'

Abby helped herself to a slice of Brie and some crackers. 'I'm never going to lose my baby belly at this rate.'

'You can't diet while you're breastfeeding.'

'Don't encourage me, girlfriend.'

For a moment, there was a contented silence.

Then Abby leaned forward, 'Do you remember that game we used to play? *What if?*'

'I do,' Sam said. '*What if* we were princesses and lived in a castle in a magic forest?'

'*What if* we could fly like the birds?' Abby spread her arms wide and made flying motions. '*What if* we could have ice cream for breakfast every day?'

'I think mine was jam doughnuts. I had a real thing about jam doughnuts when I was younger. *What if* I could have a pony?' Sam added. 'That was one of my favourites.'

'I wanted a unicorn,' Abby said wistfully. 'With wings. I had a thing about flying, didn't I? And I wanted a prince who would ride off on it with me into the sunset. That went well.' A trace of sadness had crept into her voice.

Sam glanced at her. She hadn't mentioned Paul lately. She couldn't believe he still hadn't turned up to see his son, but she'd decided not to mention him unless Abby did and she hadn't. Was now the moment?

'Have you spoken to him, honey? What did you put on Jack's birth certificate in the end?'

'I left the father's name off.' Abby's face flushed. She'd certainly kept that quiet. 'Don't look so outraged. I can always add it on later.'

'I'm not judging you, honey. I know he's unreliable.'

Abby's eyes went distant. 'The last time we spoke, I gave him an ultimatum. I told him he had to choose between being a sensible adult, i.e. get a job so he could at least contribute to the rent, and being a rock star. He chose... Well, you know what he chose.'

'But, honey, wasn't that before Jack was born? Have you spoken to him since?'

'No. And I don't want to. Can we please talk about something else?' Abby swallowed and made a visible effort to compose herself.

'Of course we can.' Sam sipped her wine, but before she could say anything else, Abby went on in her brightest voice.

'*What if* we could live together when we grew up. That one came true, didn't it? And it's totally as good as I thought it would be.'

'It totally is for me too.'

'What would be on your list now?' Abby asked.

That was easy. '*What if* I could give up work and make Purbeck Pooches my career? *What if* it became really successful? *What if*

Beach Cottage belonged to me? *What if* I could have a baby…? She clapped her hand over her mouth. 'That was the wine talking,' she amended quickly.

'No, it wasn't!' Abby's eyes were speculative. 'You're broody, aren't you? I knew it. It's Jack – he's cracked your I-Prefer-Puppies-To-Babies thing, hasn't he? Come on. Admit it.'

Sam put her hands up in self-defence. It was pointless lying to her best friend. It always had been. 'Busted. Yes. All right, he has. He's adorable.'

'I know.' Abby preened. 'He takes after me.'

'No, he doesn't. He's not a drama queen – or king, come to that. He's laid-back and easy-going. Not that you're not adorable. Of course.' She went to pour herself another glass of wine and discovered the bottle was empty.

'Sorry. I had an extra glass,' Abby said. 'Why don't we open another one as it's the weekend? I'd better not have another, but you can. It's ages since you properly let your hair down.'

'That's very true,' Sam agreed, reaching back to pull out the butterfly clips from her hair and letting it fall around her shoulders. 'Let's do it.'

'So what are you going to do about this baby thing?' Abby said when she came back with an open bottle of red, the only other one they had in the house. 'Do you have a "daddy" in mind?'

'No, that's the trouble,' Sam said, feeling her heart sink faster than a hot air balloon with a puncture. 'The last thing I want is a man. Which means I'm rather stuck, doesn't it?'

'Not necessarily.' Abby poured out a glass of wine and handed it to her. '*What if* you didn't need a man?'

There was a pause and Sam was aware suddenly of all the little sounds in the room that had been hitherto unheard. The ticking of the old-fashioned clock on the wall, Jack's quiet breathing on the other end of the baby monitor and, every so often, a little huff as he shifted in his sleep. She must be almost as attuned to the baby's movements as his mother, she thought with a little tug of longing.

'But I do need a man.'

'No you don't. What you need is a sperm donor.'

'A sperm donor. Abby, that's insane. I don't want some stranger's sperm on a turkey baster. And I sure as hell can't afford IVF.'

'I don't mean that. You're missing the point. I mean, you could have a quick fling. You don't need to marry him or even have a long-term relationship with him if you don't want to – you just need to spend a night or two with him. I know lots of women who got pregnant the first time they ditched the condoms.'

'I don't. Besides, it's hardly fair.'

'*What if* you were going on a mission to find the ideal dad?' Abby went on as if she hadn't heard. 'We could make a list. What would be on it? Hang on a sec.'

She disappeared and came back with a pen and the A4 pad that Abby kept by the landline on the hall table for bookings. She sat beside Sam on the sofa.

'Humour me for a minute.' She wrote 'Mission Perfect Dad' at the top of the page and underlined it. Then, in the left-hand margin, she wrote the number 1, which she circled. 'Top of the list has to be good looks. We'll put tall, shall we? What colour hair would you like?'

Sam frowned as she considered this. She supposed she might as well play along. 'I quite like dark, but I don't really care. As long as he's got some.'

'Tall, with hair and handsome,' Abby wrote and fell about laughing.

It was so infectious that Sam joined in. 'He'd have to be intelligent,' she said, getting into the swing of this. After all, it was only a fun game, what harm could it do to fantasise? 'I don't want a dimbo daddy.'

'Number 2. Intelligent,' Abby said and wrote it down.

'Kind,' Sam said. 'And honest. And he'd have to like animals.'

'Number 3, kind. Number 4, honest. Number 5, animal lover. See how easy it is.'

'Skilled between the sheets,' Sam added. 'Otherwise I wouldn't fancy spending the night with him.' Just for a second, her treacherous heart flicked back to an image of Gary Collins. He'd been skilful between the sheets. Understatement! But he hadn't had any of the other qualities. Not when it really came down to it.

Abby wrote, Number 6, good in the sack and chewed the end of the pen. 'You probably don't want him too old either, do you? So we probably need an age range. What do you think? Somewhere between thirty and fifty?'

'Forty-five tops.'

'Cool beans. That makes sense. I mean, I know men can have babies until they're ninety-five or something, but young fit sperm is probably best.'

'Yep.'

'I was thinking that he probably ought to be well-heeled,' Abby said. 'But I suppose that doesn't matter if he's only going to be a sperm donor. That's a pity actually because something just struck me.'

'What sort of something?'

'I was thinking that if you got together with your landlord, you could kill two birds with one stone. You could have Beach Cottage as well as a baby. He's mega rich, isn't he?'

'Yes, but Ben's more of a friend. We went out a few times before and it didn't work out.'

'It's got to be worth another try?' Abby glanced back at the list. 'He's definitely kind or he wouldn't let you rent this place so cheap. And he's intelligent or he wouldn't have made so much money. And he must like animals or he wouldn't let you fill up his house with them. What colour hair has he got?'

'Um, light brown...' The prospect of going out with Ben again definitely didn't appeal, she decided, after contemplating it briefly.

'Well, that's OK. You said you didn't mind what colour hair they had.' She went back to the list. 'We need to start another column.'

'What for? What are you writing?' she asked as Abby began furiously scrawling.

'Prospective candidates,' Abby said and underlined the words as she spoke. Underneath this, she wrote the words 'sperm donors' and then put that bit in brackets. 'We'll put Ben at the top. What's his surname?'

'Campbell, but—'

'He's just a prospective,' Abby said, writing down Ben Campbell. 'For comparison purposes.'

Sam gave up arguing. It was pointless when Abby was on a mission. She broke off a square of chocolate and let it melt in her mouth.

'Who else is there we know that fits the bill?' Abby said. 'How about my brother?'

'Your BROTHER?' Sam spluttered and very nearly choked.

'Totally. He's the right age, he's tall, he's kind, he's smart, he's good looking – if you like that sort of thing.' She smirked and Sam realised she must be drunker than she was letting on. Abby had never been a big drinker and she hadn't had any alcohol for months.

'I couldn't exactly abandon him after the event though, could I? He might notice that I'd suddenly got pregnant and given birth.'

'Mmmm, true. Bit close to home. OK – let's go further afield. Your boss – Suit Man. What's his proper name?'

'Rex. And no. Definitely not.' She shook her head vigorously.

'Why not? I bet he ticks a few of these boxes. He must be kind because he hasn't thrown you out yet, despite extreme provocation lately, and didn't you say he had a thing about honesty? What's wrong with him?'

'He's called Rex for a start. I can't tell my child that his daddy's name is Rex.'

'I'd have thought being named after a dog would be a bonus.'

'Well it's not. Why are you writing him down?' Sam leaned over Abby's shoulder and saw that she had written: 'Rex – subject to name change.' She tried to grab the pen.

'No, no, no.' Abby wagged a finger. 'This is only a longlist. We're going to do a shortlist later. What about the other engineers at work? Are any of them good daddy material?'

'They're all married.'

'OK, not them. What about the mysterious Mr B? A gourmet chef could be handy round here. And you sounded as though you were getting on with him well. What were you laughing about anyway?'

'I can't remember,' Sam said truthfully. 'But no, not him. He's bonkers. I definitely don't need a bonkers sperm donor for my child. Anyway, he's got a girlfriend.'

'Fair point.' Abby narrowed her eyes. 'You're warming to the idea of a sperm donor though, aren't you?'

'Yeah, but it's probably because I'm under the affluence of incohol.' Hmm, that wasn't quite right. Never mind. 'Tomorrow I'll have sobered up and decided it's a terrible idea.'

'How about online dating?' Abby said, her blue eyes sparkling with mirth. 'Let's do your profile before you sober up.'

'All right,' Sam said, feeling a flicker of excitement in her stomach. Not because she was taking any of this seriously, obviously, because she wasn't.

'What shall we put?' Abby said, tearing off the sheet of paper she'd written and starting a new page of the notebook. 'Let's write it down first. Something snappy. How about, "Gorgeous, long-haired, animal-loving brunette seeks fit hottie for fun and games.'

'Fun and games sounds pervy.'

'OK, I won't put fun and games. I'll put "uncomplicated fun times".'

Uncomplicated was the last thing it would be if she was going to end up pregnant. But this was the last coherent thought Sam could remember having.

8

The first thought Sam had the following morning was that she must have drunk too much. She couldn't remember the last time she'd had a hangover like this. Correction, she couldn't remember the last time she'd had a hangover at all. As she carefully got out of bed, with a pounding head and a mouth that felt drier than a sun-scorched sand dune, she remembered why she never drank red wine. Or at least why she never drank more than two glasses of the stuff.

What had they been thinking? What had *she* been thinking? She was pretty sure Abby hadn't got drunk. She crept downstairs so as not to disturb her and found her in the kitchen eating toast with Jack on her knee.

'Morning,' Sam said, pouring herself a pint of water from the sink and downing half of it in a couple of gulps. 'You're up early.' She started opening cupboards. There were some painkillers somewhere – hopefully the kind you dissolved in water. They worked best.

'No I'm not. It's nearly ten.'

'It can't be!' Sam stared blearily at the kitchen clock above the cooker. It was actually ten to ten. How had that happened? 'Why didn't you wake me? I've got animals to see to.'

'Only Houdini and she's fine. She's still in the field. I checked.' Abby eyed her carefully. 'Bad head?'

'I think I might be dying.'

'You're not. It's just a hangover. Chill.' She sounded distinctly smug.

Oh my God, when had they exchanged roles? She was usually the responsible one telling Abby to 'calm down' or 'chill out.' She didn't sound that smug when she said it, did she?

'What on earth did I drink?'

'Quite a bit of red wine,' Abby said, gesturing towards the two empty bottles on the worktop.

'Why didn't you stop me?'

'Why would I want to do that? We were having a nice evening.' Her lips twitched. 'Do you remember what we were doing?'

'It's a bit of a blur.' Sam found the painkillers, though not the dissolvable kind, swallowed two and decided that instant coffee would be fine. She couldn't be bothered with real. Toast might be good though. It would mop up the alcohol. Especially if it were spread thickly with honey. She had a feeling sugar was good too.

A memory hit her as she carried the plate over to the table. 'Did I create an online dating profile?'

'You didn't just create it, you put it online.' Abby looked gleeful.

'Oh please tell me I didn't.' Sam would have shaken her head if it hadn't hurt so much.

'You've had some responses too,' Abby said, raising her eyebrows and making a clicking sound with her mouth. 'Go Sam.'

'How do you know that?'

'You left your phone down here. It's been pinging away all morning.' She shoved it across the table. 'I haven't looked at them, obviously, as that would be an invasion of your privacy. But I couldn't help noticing them because they ping up on the front screen.'

Sam swore under her breath and then apologised to Jack, who blew a bubble at her. 'I'm going to have to delete it...'

'But why? Someone interesting might have replied. It's surely worth a look.' She reached for her own phone and clicked on the familiar icon of the horoscope app she was so hooked on. 'Your three-word horoscope today is "*Take a risk,*" and mine is "*Encourage a friend*".'

'That's convenient.' Sam's head was banging. The painkillers hadn't kicked in yet. 'I don't know if I want to do online dating.' She couldn't delete it right this minute. She felt too ill and, in her experience, it was much harder to delete things online than it was to set them up in the first place. For a start, she must have set up a password and she had absolutely no idea what it was.

Abby wisely didn't say anything else. She busied herself with Jack and when she next spoke, her voice was more contrite.

'I'm sorry about the hangover, sweetie. Maybe I should have stopped you, but it was fun. And you don't let your hair down very often.'

Judging by the way she felt now, that was a very good thing, Sam thought.

* * *

It was gone lunchtime and Sam had consumed several coffees and a plate of toast and honey before she had a proper look at her phone. Despite what she'd said to Abby, she was curious about the man/men who had contacted her. Had there really been more than one? What type of man did you meet online? She hadn't tried online dating before. She had never fancied it, although she didn't have anything against it either. Elannah had met Robbie on an online dating site and that had worked out brilliantly.

Sam went up to her bedroom to have a private look. Not because she didn't want Abby to know who had contacted her, she would tell her eventually, but she wanted to know first. She did not want Abby leaning over her shoulder and giggling and pointing and saying, 'Message him, he's hot.' She definitely wasn't going to message anyone.

At least she didn't think she was. She wasn't in the market for a man. At least she wasn't in the market for a serious relationship. No way was she going to risk being humiliated and heartbroken again. But maybe it wouldn't hurt to have some fun.

Abby was right that that she didn't let her hair down very often. For ages, Fielding's had filled her weekdays and Purbeck Pooches had filled her evenings and weekends. She'd been walking a poodle from Swanage at lunchtime for the last week too. And although she loved building up the business, she didn't have a lot of work/life balance.

She lay on her bed, opened up the dating app and scrolled through the messages. At least she hadn't enrolled herself on one of the big 'cattle market' ones. The site looked fairly niche and was called Countryside Lovers. A picture of a cow intertwined with a big red heart featured heavily on the branding. Oh my! It was just a different kind of cattle market!

She hoped she hadn't paid them any money.

Abby had been right about the messages. She already had several. The first three were from the site moderators, thanking her for joining and giving an outline of how the site worked. There was a list of dos and don'ts. This was headed up:

The Countryside Code. Don't be a Countryside Klutz.

- *Consider the needs of other people.*
- *Respect the Romeos.*
- *Protect the princesses.*
- *Leave no lurid messages.*
- *Keep carnal urges on a leash.*
- *Be responsible for your own safety. Don't meet members in dark deserted woods.*

Sam blinked. Romeos, princesses, carnal urges? This surely wasn't for real. They had to be taking the mickey. Maybe she was still a bit hungover.

She looked at the messages in her inbox. The first had been sent by a man whose username was *Hot Farmer Boy*. Judging by his photo, he was anything but. He had a shaven head, an earring and an amorous grin. In one of his pictures, he was standing beside a field of sheep with a shepherd's crook with a handle that was distinctly phallic. In fact, it was fashioned in the shape of a... Sam did a double take. Surely that wasn't an actual...? Yes it was.

She scrolled swiftly on to the next message sender. *Animal Loving Lee.* He claimed to be thirty-nine, but he looked nearer sixty. He had thinning grey hair and was wearing blue cotton shorts and a green vest, from which spindly arms and legs protruded.

Then there was *Sultry Simon4* who was scowling in every photo.

Sam wasn't sure whether to laugh or cry. She was about to abandon the site and go downstairs for another coffee when there was a soft knock on the door.

'Sam, are you in there? Are you OK?'

'Yes. Come in.' She glanced up from her position stretched out on the bed, as Abby popped her head around the door.

'I thought you might have had a relapse,' Abby said, looking irritatingly sparkly eyed and fresh-faced.

'A hangover relapse? Is there such a thing? No, I haven't.'

'Do you fancy another coffee? Or are you all caffeined out?' Abby came fully into the room. 'Have you been on that dating site?'

'No.'

'Yes you have. What do you think?'

'I think I must have been paralytic to have signed up to it in the first place.'

'You thought it was hilarious last night.' Abby put her head on one side. 'Now, how did it go? *Don't be a Countryside Klutz. Respect the Romeos. Protect the princesses.*' Abby snorted with mirth and sat on the edge of the bed. 'I haven't laughed so much in years.'

'Well, I'm glad you think it's funny. But then you're not the one who's being pursued by Animal Loving Lee and Sultry Simon4.'

'No. Are you serious? What are they like? Can I see?'

'I might let you.' Sam whisked her mobile out of Abby's reach. 'But first you need to answer two security questions. Number one. Did I pay any money for this? Did you notice me getting my debit card out at any point during the evening?'

'Nope and nope.'

'OK. Number two. Did I set up a new email address? Please tell me I didn't use my Purbeck Pooches one.'

'Technically, that's four questions, but yes and no. I wouldn't have let you use your regular email address. We made up a new one. You thought it would be quite fun to call yourself Animal-MadMaxine.'

Sam did have a vague memory of that. 'But my name's not Maxine. Never again am I going to get so drunk that I can't remember what I've done.'

'Yes, you will,' Abby said confidently. 'And no one puts their real name. Anyway, you should be grateful I didn't let you use your original suggestion. Cowpat Clarissa.'

'No way did I suggest that.'

'Yes, you did. You thought it was hilarious. Fortunately, I was there to rein you in, so to speak.' She burst out laughing. 'At least you're totally anonymous. You can fill them in properly later.' She held out her hand for Sam's mobile. 'Now, can I see? Oh please?' Abby fluttered her eyelashes and put on her most beseeching expression. 'Pleeeze.'

'Yes. OK. Let's go downstairs. Where's Jack?'

'He's catching some zeds in his Moses basket.'

* * *

By Sunday evening, Sam was feeling her usual self again. Snowy was back in Mrs Alsop's safekeeping. Mrs A had reluctantly agreed that a tether wasn't a bad idea as Snowy could be problematic in places she didn't know. Sam had resisted the urge to ask her why she'd felt it was a good idea to keep that vital information to herself, but at least they knew for next time. She was beginning to think her field wasn't quite such a useful asset for Purbeck Pooches as she'd once hoped.

She could also now see the funny side of the whole dating thing. Looking through the messages she'd been sent had kept her and Abby entertained for most of the evening. In amongst the no-hopers who had contacted her, Abby had pointed out that there was the occasional profile that looked OK.

'There's a guy called Ned here who looks nice,' she said when she and Sam were settled in their usual spots on the sofa.

'I'm not dating someone who's named after a donkey.'

'Don't be so prejudiced. He sounds nice. Honestly he does. Anyway, Ned is short for Edward. Matt used to have a friend called Ned, who was really an Edward. Shall I read out his details?'

'If you have to.' Sam was flicking through a Sunday supplement while Abby had commandeered her phone.

'Widowed father of one, works for the National Trust. Loves the beach and walking.' Abby gave a little squeal.

'What?' Sam said, putting down her magazine.

'It says one of his ambitions is to run a boarding kennels. He has a seven-year-old daughter called Milly, so he obviously likes kids.' She raised her eyebrows. 'Now that you've decided you like babies nearly as much as puppies you're perfectly matched. And he's hot.'

'Why don't you date him then?' This might be amusing but she had no real intention of dating Ned or anyone else.

'He's not my type. At least have a look.'

Sam knew she wouldn't get any peace until she did and it was also a good chance to repossess her phone, just in case Abby got any ideas about messaging people on her behalf. She wouldn't have put it past her.

Actually, though, Ned was hot. He had a nice face. Kind and a little rugged, with blue-grey eyes that looked straight into the camera. He put her in mind of Ryan Gosling, which was a definite bonus. Someone else she knew looked like Ryan Gosling. She racked her brains but couldn't think who it was. Never mind.

'So are you going to reply to him then?' Abby's voice interrupted her thoughts.

A minute ago, Sam would definitely have rejected the idea, but now... 'I'll think about it.'

Her phone buzzed in her hand and the words 'Mum Home' scrolled across her screen. Feeling a surge of pleasure at the prospect of a good chat, because they didn't often happen in holiday season, she answered it.

'Mum, hi. How's things? How are you?'

'We're very good, darling, thank you, mad busy as usual. How are you girls finding having a new baby in the house? Are you getting any sleep?'

'Actually, Jack's as good as gold. You'll have to come and meet him.'

'I'd love to and we will. As soon as it calms down a bit. We've been fully booked for the last month solid. It's the sunshine. It brings everyone to the coast.'

'That's good news.'

'I imagine you're pretty busy with Purbeck Pooches too. In fact, we want to talk to you about that.'

'You want to talk to me about Purbeck Pooches?' Sam said, intrigued.

'Yes. I won't tell you on the phone. It'll give you a reason to come and see us.' There was humour in her mother's voice. 'How do you fancy a spot of dinner on Tuesday after work? Or after you've seen to the animals, whichever is easier. You don't have to stay long'

'Perfect,' Sam said. 'Tuesday it is. We can have a good catch up. Can I bring anything?'

'Just yourself, darling.'

Sam hung up feeling curious. She loved going to see her parents but it was odd that they'd specifically mentioned wanting to talk about Purbeck Pooches. She was intrigued.

9

On Tuesday, Sam finished work on time, picked up some flowers and some of her mother's favourite macaroons and headed for her parents' B&B.

She contemplated getting a dessert too, but her mother would have made a far better one than she could buy. Her fabulous cooking was one of the reasons, along with her parents' genuine liking of people, that they were so busy.

On Tripadvisor, they were listed as one of the top ten places to stay in Swanage and rated as excellent. They also had a five-star rating from the AA.

These accolades reflected the fact that her parents really cared about their business. They lived on the premises and did everything bar the chambermaiding themselves.

Belinda's B&B was close to Swanage seafront and it was the most welcoming little house you could imagine. Set back from the road and standing slightly apart from its neighbours, its Victorian-style frontage was painted light blue like the sea and in summer it was adorned with window boxes and hanging baskets overflowing with colour. It had eight letting rooms and a residents' lounge cum bar. Her parents had owned it for thirty years and a decade or so ago they'd extended into the loft space to create the two extra letting rooms. It also had a delightful garden at the back that included a suntrap of a patio and five parking spaces on the front. Parking was in short supply in the town.

Belinda's B&B was licenced to sell alcohol and her father manned the tiny bar most evenings while her mother chatted with guests and made the occasional bar snack. It was a profitable business, but it was also full on. Sam knew it was very hard work, and not just in the summer. It was a long season, starting at Easter and finishing at the end of October when they closed for barely six weeks before reopening for Christmas and New Year. In the winter weeks, both her parents turned their hand to being decorators, sprucing up the rooms, repainting and adding improvements like better en suites and beautiful old chairs, which her mother bought on eBay and upcycled so that they looked like something out of *Homes & Gardens*. She was a skilled upholsterer and seamstress. She also made patchwork quilts for beds, cushions for the lounge and decorative seaside bits and pieces out of driftwood and shells.

Sam was proud of her parents. She had inherited their work ethic and she admired her father's good business brain, but she did occasionally wish she saw more of them.

Knowing their parking spaces would be in use tonight, she found one two streets away and strolled round to the house. The familiar smells of fumes from summer traffic and the scents of flowers in people's back gardens greeted her and the ever-present wails of seagulls and chatter of people drifting from the beer garden of a nearby pub assaulted her ears. These were the smells and sounds of home, but she knew she never wanted to live in a town again. The countryside had stolen her heart. She may only be a fifteen-minute drive away, but the buzz of a tourist town was a world away from the peace of a quiet road adjoining fields by the coast.

After they'd become independent, most of her school friends had been anxious to move into bigger more exciting towns than Swanage. She and Abby were the only ones who hadn't gone far and sometimes she'd thought that Abby had only stayed because of Paul. Abby might be enjoying the countryside now, but Sam was sure that her best friend would one morning come downstairs and announce breezily that she'd decided to move back to town. Hopefully she would stay a few months more though. Beach Cottage would be a lot lonelier without her and Jack.

Sam transferred her flowers and the carrier bag containing the macaroons into one hand so she could let herself in through the front door of the B&B, which was on the latch, as it usually was in summer. She walked up the Karndean oak-lookalike floored hall, which smelled of suntan lotion and wax furniture polish.

The lounge cum bar, which was through a door to her right, was empty of customers she saw as she reached the open door, but her father was polishing glasses. She cleared her throat and he turned.

'Hello, princess.' His face was instantly wreathed in smiles. 'I didn't hear you sneaking up on me. How's tricks?' He stood back a few paces to look at her properly. 'You've grown.'

'No, I haven't. Unless you count outwards.'

It was an old private joke to which they both knew their lines. Only their next words would be unscripted.

'Second thoughts, I think you've lost weight. And you're getting yourself a tan. It's good to see you, love.'

'It's good to see you too, Dad.' He looked the same as he always did. Smiley, a little tired around the eyes. Not surprisingly given it was high season.

He abandoned the tea towel with which he'd been polishing the glasses and enveloped her in a hug that lifted her off her feet and she breathed in the faint odour of seaside landlord – a mix of old beer and Old Spice.

'Where's Mum?'

'Cooking our tea, I hope.'

'Is that why you're in here? Skiving?'

'Got it in one.' They both laughed, as he drew her towards one of the circular tables and pulled out a chair. They sat down opposite each other. Daddy-daughter time. It was precious.

Both her parents had been at home all through her childhood. Her friends had been envious of this, but she'd never been able to properly explain that just because they were at home, it didn't mean they were available. Growing up in a business wasn't the same as growing up in a family home. There were other people around 24/7 and their needs often took priority. At least that's how it had seemed to Sam.

Her memories were of unfinished games of Scrabble and Monopoly and bedtime stories being interrupted by phone calls or guests wanting snacks or asking about local attractions. It couldn't always have been like that, but in her memories it was.

On cue, the bar door opened and a silver-haired man came in. 'Is the bar open yet, Alan? Any chance of a wee dram?'

'I can get you a drink, sir.' He sprung up to comply. 'This is my daughter, Samantha. Sam this is John. He hails from Dundee.'

The silver-haired man nodded politely at her. 'Sorry, I didnae mean to interrupt.'

They always said that, but they never went away.

Sam acknowledged him and said, 'Good to meet you, John, and you're not interrupting. I'm just on my way to see my mum.'

As she left the bar, she heard the rhythm of their chatter behind her – Dundee accent against Dorset. Fragments of banter followed her out into the hall.

Her mother was sitting on a stool at the kitchen island, her dark head dipped over a magazine while she kept an eye on a couple of pots that bubbled on the big old commercial cooker to her left. Her hair was shorter than Sam's, a shoulder-length bob, but like Sam she had it pulled back into clips to keep it out of her face. There were touches of silver at her hairline, but she looked younger than her sixty-four years. Being slim helped on that score, running a B&B meant that she spent hours on her feet.

Sam took a deep breath – the kitchen was full of the scents of aniseed and cinnamon – and cleared her throat.

Her mother started. 'Love, I didn't know you were here.' She jumped up, glancing with pleasure at the flowers. 'Are those for me? You shouldn't have. I told you not to bring anything.'

'When did I ever do what I was told? There are macaroons too.' Sam hugged her. 'Dinner smells delicious. What is it?'

'Thai curry. I'm experimenting. How's gorgeous Jack? Have you got any more pictures?'

'I have, as it happens.' She held out her phone. 'Abby sends her love.'

'We've got her a little something.' Her mother retrieved a package from the worktop, which turned out to be the most gorgeous knitted cream bootees. 'I made them before we knew whether she was having a boy or a girl. Are they OK?'

'They're stunning. She'll be thrilled.' Sam tucked them in her bag, feeling a little pang. Her parents would make wonderful grandparents.

'Is your father busy? Food's almost ready.'

* * *

They ate it at the kitchen island, perched on stools: informal, with forks and paper serviettes and bowls of fragrant Thai curry and jasmine rice and a lot of laughter. They were only interrupted twice by the visitor bell, which her father answered uncomplainingly.

There was no mention of Purbeck Pooches or what her mother had said they wanted to talk to her about and she didn't ask. She sensed they were leaving it until the end of the meal.

There *was* mention – as usual – of whether or not she had met anyone nice. Or whether dating was still off the cards.

On impulse, she told them about the online dating site she had joined. 'I had a nice message from a man called Ned,' she said. 'So I messaged him back.'

'And...?' her mother probed. 'What did he say?'

'Nothing yet, so I wouldn't get too excited. I might never hear anything again.' To her surprise she felt a twang of disappointment. She decided not to tell them about the others, including Wetsuit Willie or Alpha Al. Her mother would have laughed but her father would have come over all protective.

'Have you sent him a photo, princess? That'll get him racing to the phone.'

'Thanks, Dad, and yes – he's definitely seen my photo.'

'I'm not sure I hold with these dating sites,' her mother said. 'Aren't they a bit cattle market-y? It's a pity you don't meet anyone at work. Aren't there any nice engineers there?'

'They're all nice. And they're also all married. Apart from my boss.' She had a vague sense of déjà vu. Had she had this conversation with someone else recently? It must have been Abby. Half regretting that she'd mentioned it, she changed the subject, 'Thank you for a lovely meal, Mum. Wasn't there something you wanted to talk to me about?'

'Yes, darling.' Her parents exchanged glances and Sam sensed a thread of tension suddenly in the room.

'I'll make us a coffee, shall I?' Her dad's voice was ultra hearty. 'Then we can tell you our news.'

Sam helped with the clearing away and the coffee was made but neither of her parents said anything else until they were sitting down drinking it.

Her mother cleared her throat. 'Now then, I expect you're wanting to know why we've asked you over to talk about Purbeck Pooches?'

'I am.' Sam rested her elbows on the kitchen island and her chin on her hands.

'It's a bit of a long story. So bear with us. I'll start at the beginning. Your father and I have decided to retire.'

'Blimey.' That was something she hadn't been expecting, although she wasn't sure why. Dad was already past retiring age and Mum was sixty-five in September, but she'd never imagined them retiring. She'd imagined them working at the B&B forever.

'This is a young person's game,' he went on. 'We're both finding it much more hard work than we used to – as I'm sure you can appreciate.'

'I can,' Sam said, noticing that her mother looked tired too, despite the fact she was wearing make-up: a touch of her favourite pink twenty-four-hour lipstick and a trace of mascara. Understated could have been her middle name.

'We've talked about it a lot lately,' her mum said, 'and we've made the decision that this will be our last season.'

'We haven't gone public yet.' Her father drumrolled his fingers on the work surface. 'So none of our regular guests know, but I did put out some discreet feelers and a couple of weeks ago I talked to a friend of mine who runs a commercial estate agent and he actually has someone in mind who's very interested in buying the business. As a going concern, I mean.'

'Well, that's brilliant,' Sam said. Now she'd got over the initial surprise of their news she was pleased. They deserved a rest and a tiny selfish part of her mind acknowledged that this could be good for her too – she'd get to see a lot more of them. 'Isn't it? I mean if you're definitely sure this is what you want to do. I'd have thought it might take a few years to find a buyer.'

'That's what we thought too.' Her mum's face sobered a little. 'And yes it is good news. Great news. He's actually now made us an offer, so it could all happen very fast. I think we're a little bit shell-shocked. We expected to have loads of time to adjust.'

'Yes. I see.' Sam looked at both their faces and saw various emotions. There was excitement on her father's and something closer to fear in her mother's expression. 'Maybe the speed of things just means that it's meant to be,' she offered. 'A sign from the universe that you're doing the right thing.' Her mother wasn't really into signs from the universe. She amended it quickly. 'You know, a thumbs up from fate.'

'A thumbs up from fate,' her mother repeated slowly. 'Yes. I suppose.' She still looked doubtful.

'When's it all likely to happen?' Sam asked.

'We haven't signed anything yet. But he'd like us to be out by the third week of September.'

'This year? But that's only just over two months away! Is that even possible?'

'It's possible, yes. But it doesn't give us much time to find something else.

'You could always come and stay with me.' Cogs whirred in Sam's brain. This must be where Purbeck Pooches came in. 'There's plenty of room – even with Abby and Jack. I'm sure Ben, my landlord, wouldn't mind, but I could ask him.'

'Sweetheart, that's lovely of you.' Mum reached across and touched her arm. 'And maybe we could do that – as a very temporary measure – but we can find somewhere to rent. That won't be a problem. Most of the furniture would need to go in storage. A lot of it will go with the B&B of course. It's only really our living accommodation bits and pieces and a lot of that is fitted.'

'Yes, I suppose it is.'

'We could even leave the whole lot and start over,' her father said. 'A totally fresh start. Think how freeing that would be. Having a completely blank page.'

To Sam's surprise, her mother looked quite keen on this idea too. 'So where do you plan to spend your retirement?' she asked, sensing the tension rising in the steamy kitchen. She couldn't see her parents in a retirement flat. They'd want a garden.

'Probably in a bungalow,' her mum said, but it was her dad who delivered the killer blow.

'We're torn between Cornwall and Cyprus at the moment.'

'Cornwall or Cyprus?' Sam felt a tremor of shock. She couldn't quite get her head around that, even though she'd just repeated the words out loud. 'I didn't know you wanted to retire abroad...' Although now she thought about it, she did remember them talking once a few years back about retiring to the sun. But then everyone dreamed about that when they were stuck in the depths of endless English winter. She hadn't thought they'd actually meant it. 'Gosh,' was the only word she could think of to say that wasn't rude and it didn't come anywhere near to summing up how stunned she felt.

'I know we live a lot closer to each other now, princess, but it's not as though we live in each other's pockets is it. We probably wouldn't see much less of you if we did live in Cyprus. You could come out for holidays and we'd have quality time.'

'Great.' Sam was struggling now to keep the disappointment out of her voice. 'So it's definitely Cyprus then is it, Dad?'

'Nothing's definite.' Her mother's voice was soft. 'We really are still just thinking things through. We know that we could get a lot more for our money in Cyprus. The nicer bits of Cornwall are quite pricey. More expensive than we thought and...' She hesitated. 'Well, one of the things we'd like to do is to give you some money to invest in Purbeck Pooches. Dad and I – well, we know that's where your heart lies and we know that you can't really expand the business without some sort of investment...' She broke off as Sam stood up abruptly, the legs of her stool scraping violently on the kitchen tiles.

So that was where Purbeck Pooches came in – they were offering her a bribe, something to soften the blow of abandoning her.

'We would come back for Christmases and birthdays,' her mother said.

'I see.' She knew she was probably being unreasonable and childish, but she couldn't listen to any more. She couldn't bear to. 'I've got to go,' she said, turning on her heel. 'Talk another time. Yeah.' She was through the kitchen door and into the hall before they could answer. She thought she heard her father's voice call her name in a mixture of anguish and impatience. But nothing on earth would have induced her to go back.

10

Everything felt different as Sam hurried back through the sunny evening towards her car. Cyprus. Bloody Cyprus. Why on earth would they want to go there anyway? Wasn't it close to Syria? She seemed to remember that from her long-ago geography lessons. But she had never been good at geography.

She reminded herself it wasn't definitely Cyprus. It might be Cornwall. But what if it wasn't? It shouldn't make any difference where they retired – as they had pointed out already, they had never lived in each other's pockets.

The fact that they said they would be back for Christmases and birthdays had only served to twist the knife a little harder. Sam couldn't remember the last time she had spent a Christmas with her parents that was actually at Christmastime. The B&B was open at Christmas, so between Christmas Eve and the day itself, her mum cooked her heart out for the guests, her dad served drinks and toasted the season with the guests and, on Boxing Day, everyone headed off in a minibus to the pantomime.

They celebrated with Sam a few days later, so more often than not they would celebrate Christmas in the new year. Sam had always enjoyed these late Christmases, she thought now, or had she really just been making the most of them because there was no other choice?

On autopilot, she realised that she had gone past her car and had ended up on the sand-strewn pavement at Swanage seafront. It was getting towards sunset and the sky was streaked pink and purple. The sun hung suspended like a great fireball of gold above the sea.

For a moment, she stood in the faint breeze and looked towards the pier. The tide must have recently gone out, a stretch of wet sand led down to the sea and a solitary couple walked hand in hand, their feet making deep prints that swiftly filled up with water. She felt a wash of almost unbearable loneliness.

She had always assumed her parents would retire somewhere close by and that for the first time in her life they would do things that normal families did, like meet for a cream tea in the midst of summer in one of the chintzy tea rooms in Swanage and have Christmas at Christmastime. She'd had happy dreams of them coming to Beach Cottage and sitting by the log burner, eating mince pies and sipping mulled wine beneath a tree that glittered with tinsel and sparkled with multicoloured lights.

This could all still happen of course. She had no idea why she felt so bereft.

Suddenly worried one of her parents might have come after her, she glanced over her shoulder. But there were just tourists strolling about, eating ice creams and hot dogs and fish and chips out of wrappers. Further into town, all the shops would still be open, selling buckets and spades and inflatables and newspapers and overpriced instant coffee.

Sam hooked out her mobile and turned it off. She didn't want to talk to anyone right now. As she fumbled with it, she realised she was shivering slightly, although it wasn't cold. There was enough heat in the day to make the t-shirt and cotton jeggings and the light jacket she wore more than adequate. She must be in shock.

She knew she would have to apologise to her parents for leaving so abruptly, but it wasn't going to be today. She couldn't go back right now. She needed to process things, think things through and get it all in perspective. She just wanted to go home.

* * *

A few minutes later, she was in her car and driving back through the heavy summer dusk towards Beach Cottage. For the first time she could remember, she didn't feel her heart lifting at the sight of her home. She was too wound up, she realised as she went into the lounge to find Abby sprawled out on the sofa.

'Hiya, Sam.' Then, Abby, who'd been watching TV, with the baby monitor on the arm of the sofa, looked at her face more carefully. 'What on earth's happened? Hey. Are your parents all right? Sweetie, you don't look well.'

'They're fine,' Sam said, standing in the doorway, 'I think...' she rubbed at her forehead distractedly, '...that I may possibly be overreacting.'

Abby patted the sofa beside her. 'Come and tell me about it.'

Sam went across and sat beside her and took a deep breath. 'They invited me over to tell me they're retiring and emigrating to Cyprus.'

'Bloody hell.' Abby switched off the TV and put the remote control on the coffee table. 'That's a shock and a half. Did you not have a clue they were thinking of doing that?'

'No.' Sam felt tears pricking behind her eyes. 'I don't know why I'm so upset.' She had a sudden vivid image of both her parents talking to Ben Hillman on *A Place in the Sun*.

'Well, I do,' Abby replied. 'Matt and I were really pissed when our folks said they were emigrating. I didn't speak to them for a week. Matt got his head around it quicker, but that's because Matt's had an emotional-response bypass – he never reacts to anything. He takes laid-back to a whole new level.'

'Yes, I know he does.' Sam smiled despite herself. She had never known a brother and sister so different. 'Thanks. You always make me feel better. But what I meant was I don't know why I'm so upset because they haven't actually said they're emigrating yet. They haven't said Cyprus definitely either. To be fair, they mentioned Cornwall too.'

'Same difference,' Abby said unfazed. 'In fact, it'll probably be quicker to get to Cyprus than Cornwall. The roads are so crap. It's probably in your best interest to encourage them to go to Cyprus. Paphos is good, apparently. Great place for a holiday.'

'Have you ever been to Paphos?' Sam asked, surprised.

'No, but I saw it on a holiday programme. It's where Aphrodite was born.'

'I thought Aphrodite was a Greek goddess. Do they even get born?'

'No, I guess they don't. They just appear mythically out of the sea waving a sceptre. Actually, I might be thinking of Neptune. I wasn't paying much attention when we were doing Greek mythology. I need to watch *Jason and the Argonauts* again.'

On the baby monitor, Jack began to grizzle and they both looked at the screen.

'I might just go and check on him. Then I'll be down and we can talk some more. Maybe over a glass of wine.'

'No wine. But yes, let's talk.'

* * *

It was amazing how talking could put everything into perspective. Sam had never realised Abby had been so upset when her parents had gone to Spain. But that was probably because Abby had made light of it. In fact, at the time, she had made a big thing about never having to pay for a holiday again. But Sam only remembered her going there a couple of times and they'd been gone for eight years.

'The truth is I'm not very keen on flying,' Abby said when Sam asked her about this, 'and actually, I'm not a massive fan of Alicante. It's not all that different from Benidorm.'

'I see.' It was like glimpsing a side of Abby that she hadn't really known before. 'But your parents obviously like it there.'

'It's a home from home for them. There are so many expats there that it's like the UK, with the added bonus of permanent sun. That's another thing I'm not a fan of – permanent sun. I break out in freckles and I get sunstroke really easily. I'm too fair. I'm glad Jack hasn't inherited that.'

There was a little pause. Abby yawned. It was gone eleven.

'I guess it doesn't really matter what I think about Alicante though,' she added. 'It's not me who's living there. And I am pleased they're happy.'

'You don't wish they were around more so they could help out with Jack?'

'I thought I might, but no.' Abby gave Sam one of her beautiful smiles. 'Maybe it would be different if I didn't live with you. I feel as though he's got two mothers. What more does he need?'

Her eyes dared Sam to say, 'A father,' but Sam couldn't bring herself to mention Paul. Friends – especially best friends – didn't nag or make judgements or give unwanted advice – they just fought your corner and made sure they were around when they were needed. And Abby had certainly stepped up to the plate tonight.

By the time they did both go their separate ways up to bed, Sam had started to feel the beginnings of acceptance around the whole retirement and moving away thing. She was surprised she hadn't had a phone call from her parents. Then, when she looked at her phone, she realised with a jolt that this was because she had never turned it back on.

When she did, she saw there were two missed calls from her mother, the last one an hour and a half ago. It was too late to phone back now. Her parents had to get up at the crack of dawn to cook breakfast for their guests. She would phone and apologise tomorrow.

She was just about to go to sleep when her phone pinged with another message. It was from Countryside Lovers. Or, more specifically, it was from Ned. That too had been sent an hour earlier.

It was good to get your message. It sounds like we have a lot in common. I'm not very good at this online stuff. Would you like to talk on the phone?

Abby flicked back into his profile and read it again and then she looked at his picture once more, at those kind direct eyes. He sounded a bit serious and intense and she didn't want to lead him on. On the other hand, talking to him on the phone might be an entertaining distraction.

* * *

'How are you doing, girlfriend? Did you sleep OK?' Abby glanced up from her position at the kitchen table the following morning. She was cradling Jack on her knee, his head crooked into her arm, and reading the news on her phone. She looked like an old hand at motherhood now.

Sam had been surprised she was up. They'd had such a late

night. 'I'm OK, honey. And yes, I slept fine in the end, thanks. Did you?'

'He was a bit restless. Weren't you, my lovely? I thought we'd got this sleeping through the night thing cracked, but I may have just been lulled into a false sense of security. I think he's found his voice. He didn't wake you, did he?'

'No he didn't. Good morning, Jack.'

The baby gurgled and stretched out his arms out to her. Abby said he recognised her. Could babies of barely a month old recognise anyone? It happened too often to be a coincidence and, in truth, Sam liked the idea. She put her finger into his and he held on tightly.

She felt the familiar tug at her heart. When did you let go of your children? Did they have to get to a certain age? Sixteen, twenty-six, thirty-six? Oh my goodness, she really had got stirred up last night.

'Do you feel better about your folks?' Abby asked.

'Yes, I think I do, actually.' Sam helped herself to a bowl of cereal. 'I'm really pleased they're retiring. They've worked flat out for years. They deserve to have a lovely retirement and they should have that wherever they fancy. I think I was just being selfish. Making it all about me.'

'Not selfish, sweetie. Human.'

Sam glanced at her. When had Abby become the wise and responsible adult? That was usually her job. 'Thanks,' she said. 'Maybe you're right. But I'll feel better when I've phoned my mum and apologised.' She paused. 'I had a message from Ned last night. He wants to chat on the phone.'

'He's a quick worker.'

'Yes, that's what I thought.'

'Will you phone him?'

'I guess.'

'If nothing else, it would be a bloody good distraction. Sorry, Jack. Don't listen. I've got to stop swearing in front of him.' She shot her son a guilt-ridden glance.

'I expect he's too young to pick it up.'

'I know, but it's tone of voice, isn't it? Bad Mummy.'

'Human Mummy. And yes. You're right about the distraction. I could do with something fun to think about. It could be fun talking to Ned.'

Abby eyed her speculatively. 'I didn't think you were after his conversational skills. I thought it was more about his suitability as a – ahem – daddy. Mission Perfect Dad. Remember?'

'Oh God. I was hoping I'd imagined that. Or dreamed it or something. It's been coming back to me in bits. Didn't we write some kind of list? What happened to that?'

'I found it down the side of the sofa. I put it in the top drawer of the phone table in case you wanted to refer back to it.'

'Thanks.' Sam shook her head. That whole drunken evening seemed daft now. She couldn't imagine ever wanting to be reminded of it. 'Right then, I'd better get to work. I don't want to be late. I'm walking Seamus and Goldie at lunchtime. Catch you later, guys.'

'Don't forget it's this weekend my folks are coming to see Jack,' Abby called. 'They're staying with Matt, so we'll probably be over there quite a bit. Just in case you wanted the house to yourself for any reason, I mean. I was just saying,' she added in response to Sam's horrified expression.

They seemed to have reverted to their normal roles, Sam thought with amusement. Abby – the impulsive, irrepressible, slightly reckless drama queen and her, the – responsible-ish – adult. That was a relief.

* * *

At lunchtime as Sam sauntered along the footpath by Barbara Oldfield's house with Seamus and Goldie trotting ahead, she phoned her mother.

It was a huge relief when her apology was accepted with her mother's usual lovely grace.

'I'm sorry too, love, that we didn't find a way to tell you more sensitively,' she said as Sam held the phone close to her ear while a brisk sea breeze buffeted her face, swinging her ponytail about. 'Your dad and I aren't surprised you were shocked. We've been a bit shocked ourselves about the speed of everything.'

'I bet,' Sam said, watching Seamus mooch along the path just ahead of her. He was stopping to sniff at every patch of grass and occasionally cocking his leg on a particularly interesting bit. Goldie, who was half his size, but was definitely in charge out of the two dogs, would occasionally nudge him to one side so she could get to a patch of grass first. 'But I want you and Dad to know I'm happy with whatever you choose. Cyprus or Cornwall – wherever you'll be happiest. I had a good chat about it to Abby last night.'

'Ah yes. I'd forgotten her parents did the same thing. Didn't they go to Spain?'

'Alicante. They're flying back this weekend to meet their grandson.'

'That's nice.' There was sunshine in her voice. 'One thing I will tell you, love, is that if you were to present me with an unexpected grandson, I would definitely not leave it a month before I came to meet him.'

Sam felt a warmth spread around her heart. 'I was surprised they left it so long too, but Abby said it was partly her choice not to let them come until she felt settled. She wanted to get Jack into a routine.'

'I suppose that's fair enough.'

'By the way, you do know I'm not planning on having a baby,

don't you?' She certainly wouldn't be telling her parents about Mission Perfect Dad.

'I know that's what you've always said, love, yes.' Was she imagining the wistfulness in her mother's words or was it real?

Sam wanted to add, 'although you never know what will happen in the future,' but she didn't want to say something she might later have to retract. She thought back to Mission Perfect Dad. It was an insane and ridiculous idea. But she could see how she and Abby had ended up dreaming it up.

The longing to have a baby was there again, dancing on the horizon like the sparkle of sunshine on the sea.

The desire to have a long-term relationship with a man was not.

'Good luck with Ned, darling.' Her mother brought her crashing back to earth with a bump. 'You will let us know how it goes...?'

Sam was touched she had remembered that snippet. 'Of course.'

As she disconnected, she realised neither of them had mentioned the B&B money again – she didn't even know what her parents had in mind. Some misplaced pride hadn't let her ask.

11

Things always went quiet at Fielding's when the schools had broken up for summer. Only the most determined of house buyers carried on looking at properties when their kids were at home. It was also a prime time for holidays.

This July was no exception. So no one was surprised when Lightning strolled in on Thursday morning with a large pink cake box, fragrant with the scent of fresh cream doughnuts.

'Mmm,' Sam said, sniffing the air and feeling her mouth water.

Heather glanced across. 'We must be quiet – if even Lightning's not in a hurry,' she observed as he sauntered past their workstation and put the box onto Elannah's desk.

Elannah broke off from the conversation she was having with Rex and glanced at the senior structural engineer. 'Is that a reward or a bribe?'

'It's a reward, of course. I'll get us some plates.'

'I'll get them,' Rex said. 'It's a good time to have a break. I want to talk to you all about something anyway.' He headed for the kitchen, which was tucked alongside his office at the back of the open-plan area.

'What's happening?' Heather hissed to Elannah as soon as he was out of earshot. 'What does he want to talk to us about?'

'Yeah, is it good or bad?' Magpie piped up. He'd just slid over, attracted by the cake box.

'You'll have to wait and see,' Elannah said. 'But it's a good thing, don't worry.'

From his position behind Sam, Mike mumbled something that no one could quite catch.

Rex came back bearing plates and forks. 'Just in case anyone wants to be civilised.'

No one, apart from Elannah and Rex, wanted to be civilised, it seemed. The cakes were transferred from box to plates to mouths in about thirty seconds flat. The men made short work of them. The women nibbled theirs more slowly. Rex was the only one who didn't touch his. He left his fork alongside it and steepled his hands.

'I want you to know that I very much appreciate how hard you've all been working lately,' he began. 'And I think a reward is in order.'

Sam pricked up her ears. Was he going to give them a bonus? That could be good. An extra day's leave would be even better.

There was an air of hushed expectation as everyone waited.

Rex paused a fraction of a second longer, presumably for effect. His face had gone a little pink. 'Therefore, I have decided that we are going to have a work's fun day. As you know, this is Swanage Regatta Week, so we will meet for an early lunch at Berni's Bistro on the front at around midday. Then I'm taking you all to Hart's funfair.'

Elannah clapped her hands together and beamed. She was clearly thrilled at the prospect, but she looked as though she was the only one.

'When?' Heather asked flatly.

'Tomorrow,' Rex said.

'I have a survey booked for tomorrow lunchtime,' Lightning said quickly.

'Elannah has rescheduled all of our appointments for next week. Under my instructions. However, if anyone particularly doesn't like the funfair for a good reason...' He frowned as though he was struggling to think of one. 'Then I am more than happy for you to come in tomorrow and work as normal.'

'I think the fair would be OK,' Mumbling Mike said, or at least that's what it sounded like. 'The missus and I took the kids there last week. There are some good new rides.'

Sam couldn't imagine Mumbling Mike on a ride. With or without his kids. He was only in his forties, but he was on the chubby side and he was definitely a sports watcher, not a sports doer.

'I heard that,' Lightning said. 'We were planning to take the grandchildren there.'

'I'm not a fan of heights,' Heather said. 'They set off my vertigo. And the ones that spin make me feel sick.'

'Everything makes you feel sick,' Magpie said and shut up hastily when he caught Rex's pointed look, although Sam thought he had a point. Funfairs and Hypochondriac Heather were clearly a recipe for disaster, but she wasn't going to say this.

'How about you, Sam?' Rex's gaze focused on her. 'Are you a fan of the fair?'

'Why not?' she said because he looked like a drowning man desperate for someone to throw him a rope. She was surprised actually that he'd chosen to take them to the funfair. She couldn't imagine Rex on the dodgems or even tucking into a hot dog. 'Are you – er – planning to join us?' she asked him.

'Of course I will be joining you.' He nodded around solemnly. 'Team building is at the basis of all good working relationships.' He picked up a bowl and Sam realised it was the one that was usually on his desk. 'Can I offer anyone a Murray Mint?'

* * *

Abby was highly amused when Sam relayed the morning's events to her when she got in from work that evening.

'Your boss has never sounded like a funfair sort of guy,' she murmured. 'Isn't he quite up himself and a bit pompous?'

Had she really said that? Sam felt guilty. 'He's not all bad. He has his good points. And it turned out it wasn't his idea. It was Elannah's. She's a great fan of funfairs apparently. She persuaded him they were the perfect way for us all to let our hair down.'

'Well, rather you than me. I'm quite glad I work with a bunch of geeks I hardly ever see. Even when I'm not actually on maternity leave.'

'How long have you got left of that by the way?'

'Months – I've got a really good package. I'll probably start work again in November. I mostly work from home anyway and Jack is so good, I think it will work out. If it doesn't, I'll get some consultancy work. Anyway, enough of me. Have you phoned Ned yet?'

'I'm phoning him at seven thirty. In private,' she added, as Abby's eyes brightened with glee. 'In my room.'

'We need to talk about safety,' Abby said promptly. 'There are certain things you need to know about online dating...'

* * *

Just before seven thirty, Sam went upstairs. She had shut her bedroom door pointedly when she'd seen Abby go past on the landing. 'I will report back later. I promise. But you are NOT listening. I've taken note of all that safety stuff you were talking about.'

This wasn't quite true. She'd switched off after point 3, which had been never go straight home in case your date is a stalker and follows you. Always drive in a circuitous route and go via a petrol station so you can check if they're behind you.

Abby pouted before widening her eyes and tossing her head. 'I've got better things to do. As it happens.'

'No, you haven't,' Sam called after her.

A few moments later, she lay on the bed and dialled Ned's number. Her stomach crunched with a mix of anticipation and fear as she waited for him to answer. She felt like a teenager.

Abby had said that most people lied about something on their profile and then Sam had spent an anxious ten minutes reading blogs about it and discovered 81 per cent of people lied. What if nice Ned turned out to be nasty Ned?

He picked up the phone. 'Hello. You have reached Ned Collins.' She thought fleetingly he was a recorded message, but she could hear him breathing. He had a strong Dorset accent. You didn't hear the local accent that often in Swanage.

'Hi, it's Maxine. From Country Lovers.'

'He-llo, Max...ine.' There was warmth now, entwined with the accent. 'Thanks for ringing. Should I call you back?'

'No, it's fine.' On Abby's advice, she had withheld her number, as well as not yet telling him her real name. 'Just in case he turns out to be a maniac or a stalker,' Abby had said, widening her eyes dramatically.

'Not reassuring, honey,' Sam had replied.

There was an awkward pause. Oh God, the longer it went on, the worse it would be, but her mind had gone blank. Abby had also said she should write down some questions on a piece of paper. She hadn't done this. Abby's experience of online dating was based entirely on a vlog she had seen on YouTube. But now Sam was beginning to wish she had taken more notice.

There was the smallest of noises from the landing. It sounded like the squeak of the rocking chair. Could Abby actually be out there listening?

Before she could be bothered to get up and check, Ned broke the silence. 'Have you been doing this long then, Maxine? Online dating, I mean?'

'No. How about you?'

'A couple of years. But I've not seen anyone I've wanted to hook up with yet. Are you single?'

'Yes,' she said, surprised he was asking. She'd assumed that everyone who went on dating sites was single.

'Not everyone is,' he went on in explanation. 'Some people are polyamorous.'

'Which means?'

'Essentially it means they have many lovers. They don't settle down.'

'I see.' She felt out of her depth. 'I'm not one of those people.' She wanted to add, 'I'm not the settling down type either', but she decided to keep that to herself for now. 'Are you polyamorous, Ned?'

'Oh no. Don't get me wrong, I'm definitely up for having some fun, but I'm a one-woman man. I'd expected to be with my wife for the duration, but – as you can see by my profile – she died three years ago. But I do have my lovely Milly.'

There was a sudden vulnerability in his voice and she felt herself warming to him.

'Have you ever been married?' he asked.

'No.'

'Not met the right man?'

'No.' She wouldn't tell him about Gary Collins and he must have picked up on her hesitation because he steered the conversation on to more neutral subjects like work.

He told her about his job with the National Trust, which turned out to be a part-time voluntary position in their coffee shop. His full-time job was for an online tyre company. He worked as an audience development executive.

'What is that exactly?'

'Essentially it's a PR position. We sell tyres via our website and ads on big online communities like Facebook. My job is to respond to negative things people say about our tyres. So I deal with bad reviewers and other internet pests. You've heard of internet trolls.'

'Um, yes.'

'Well, my job is to respond to negative comments that might be left online. It can be intensive because they can leave comments at any time of the day or night.'

'Really?'

'Oh yes. We're an international company, which means that essentially I'm working across all timelines 24/7.'

Now he'd started talking, there was no stopping him. Was it her imagination or did he say the word 'essentially' ever such a lot?

'What do you do, Maxine?'

She was going to have to tell him her real name soon. Answering to someone else's was disconcerting.

On her profile it said that she worked in an office. That had been Abby's idea – 'Keep it bland, keep it anonymous. Don't lie but don't elaborate until you're sure you trust them.'

'I'm an audio typist. Essentially.' Blimey, it must be catching. 'I work for a group of engineers. That was anonymous enough. To put him off the scent, she told him her real passion was animals and she'd set up an animal boarding business in the Purbecks. 'On a very small scale. I only really take recommendations from people I know.'

There was more noise from the landing. It was impossible to sneak about out there without it being obvious. There were too many creaky floorboards. Abby was definitely listening in. She really must be bored. Maybe it wasn't that surprising. Other than for walks with Jack in his buggy and once into town to register the birth, she'd hardly ventured out since he'd been born. That wasn't like Abby. She loved being out and about.

Sam dragged her attention back to Ned. He was easy to talk to, although she couldn't say there was any real chemistry. Mind you, it had been such a long time since she'd felt any chemistry, her body had probably forgotten the feeling. Or maybe you had to meet a person in the flesh for that.

She thought about Mission Perfect Dad and shuddered. How could she ever have imagined she'd just be able to meet some random bloke and sleep with him in order to have a baby? It was a total non-starter.

'So what do you think, Maxine?' She realised he must have asked her a question, but she had no idea what. A moment before they'd been talking about taking pets on holiday.

'I think it's a great idea,' she said enthusiastically.

'Really? That's brilliant. As I said, Milly's on a sleepover tomorrow, so it's great timing.'

Oh crap, the conversation must have moved on without her noticing. She had a horrible feeling she'd just agreed to something she wouldn't want to do, once she'd found out what it was.

Before she could retract it, Ned went on, 'I love the fair – it brings back many a happy childhood memory. Let's go for about six then and we can wander around the stalls. Maybe even go on the dodgems?'

'Tomorrow?' she asked cautiously. Had she just agreed to meet Ned at the fair? Funnily enough, though, that could work out well, as she would be there anyway.

'Yes, it's great for me. Are you having second thoughts?'

'Er no...' What the hell. Abby was always saying she should let her hair down. Meeting Ned at the fair couldn't hurt. It was a public enough place.

'Do you look like your photograph, Maxine?'

'Yes. Of course I do.'

Before she could ask him the same question, he said, 'Great. Mine was taken three years ago, but you should be able to recognise me. I'll see you by the entrance at six.'

When Sam went out onto the landing, she found Abby in the rocking chair by the window, nursing Jack.

She looked up with her most innocent expression. 'What? We've just been enjoying a touch of evening sunshine, before bedtime, haven't we, Jack?'

Considering it was almost dusk, this wasn't very convincing. 'So what did you overhear?'

'Hardly anything,' Abby said airily. 'You could have talked a bit louder.'

'Did you hear I've just arranged to meet him tomorrow?'

'No way. So you liked him? Hey, that's brilliant news. Where's he taking you? Do you want me to come and keep an eye on you? We'll be at Matt's anyway. I'm sure my folks would be delighted to babysit Jack for an hour.'

'We're meeting at Hart's Funfair, so I'll be quite safe. But thanks for the offer.'

'But… Isn't that where you're going on your works outing?'

'Yep. We're meeting early evening. I thought I'd kill two birds with one stone.' Sam couldn't keep a straight face. 'Actually, that's not true. My mind was drifting off a bit and I kind of agreed to it without realising.'

'You agreed to go out with a complete stranger without realising.' Abby stared at her in amazement. 'Why didn't you just fess up and hang up on him.'

'I didn't want to hang up on him. I couldn't tell him I'd agreed by mistake. He was really pleased I'd said yes.'

'I thought I was supposed to be the scatty, irresponsible one. And you told him about Purbeck Pooches, didn't you? So he now knows where you live.'

'I didn't tell him the name.'

'You said you had a pet boarding service in the Purbecks. It's not going to be hard to work it out.'

'I thought you said you weren't listening.'

'I couldn't help overhearing that bit. Your voice gets louder when you're talking about something you're passionate about.'

'Does it?'

'Yes it does. So tell me all about him. I could only hear one side of the conversation. Obviously.'

'He sounded nice. Warm and genuine. And I'm looking forward to meeting him tomorrow.'

It was only much later when she was getting ready for bed, having laid out her favourite jeggings and ultra-feminine floral blouse for the morning, that it struck her that the second part of this statement wasn't actually true.

12

Sam woke on Friday morning with the niggling feeling that something bad was happening today. What was it? Oh yes, she was off for a 'fun' day out with her work colleagues. Deep joy. Contrary to what she'd told Rex yesterday, she was not a great fan of funfairs.

Then she remembered she'd also agreed to meet Ned there in the evening. She sat up in bed. Good grief, the fair twice in one day, what had she been thinking?

There was an email on her phone from Mr B, the eccentric chef from the Bluebell Cliff. What could he possibly want now? Maybe he'd changed his mind about her looking after his Kunekunes. Sam realised she'd be half relieved if he had. But she'd also be disappointed.

Purbeck Pooches wasn't very busy, considering it was holiday season. She'd taken her eye off the ball. A lot of her work came via word of mouth and repeat bookings, as she'd told Ned. But there was also the Purbeck Pooches website. Abby had both set up the website and updated it for her. There was a Facebook page too that Sam updated when she had time. There had been no updates on either lately and it was amazing how quickly business dropped off when she didn't advertise.

There had been a time, not very long ago, when she'd thought that life was panning out exactly as she had planned. Purbeck Pooches was going well. Fielding's was boring but bearable. Her parents were happily working just up the road.

Maybe life had been a little mundane, but it had all been perfectly under her control. Just the way she liked it. Lately she'd felt as if someone had pulled the rug out from under her and given it a good hard shake and when the pieces had landed again, they'd all been in a different place.

She pushed these thoughts away as she drove into Swanage, which was buzzing, the regatta was great for the town. She parked in Hart's car park, knowing it would be impossible to find a space anywhere else. Hart's Funfair was a permanent fixture – it took up three grassy fields on the outskirts of town and was open all day during the season.

As she walked across the rutted field, the sun-baked ground hard beneath her thin-soled trainers, Sam could smell the scent of burgers and hot dogs drifting on the breeze, mixing with the diesel fumes of the generators that powered the rides.

Through the slatted fence that surrounded the site, Sam glimpsed the teacup ride, its giant gaudily painted teacups, currently all empty of people, circling to a backdrop of tinny music. Alongside that was the Caterpillar Rollercoaster, its bright green front carriage in the shape of a grinning caterpillar with green stalks protruding from its head. Further in, she could see the dome of a red and yellow helter-skelter and beyond that a very tall ride called Scary Skyscraper that towered over everything else. That must be one of the new rides Mumbling Mike had mentioned.

It was impossible to feel downhearted when she could hear the boom of music from a marching band thrumming somewhere in the distance and children's laughter and their delighted shrieking closer by.

Out in the bay, dozens of brightly coloured boats bobbed on the sparkling blue water and there was a paraglider, his scarlet sail silhouetted high up against the perfect blue of the sky.

A few minutes later, Sam was back in town, once more, at Berni's Bistro, which Rex must have booked or they'd never have got a table. She was early, but she wasn't the first. Rex and Elannah were standing on the pavement outside.

'Morning, Sam,' Rex called cheerily.

She just about stopped herself doing a double take. It was the first time she'd ever seen him out of a suit. Elannah must have had a word with him. He was still wearing a white shirt, but it was open at the neck. No tie today – that was a miracle. He wore cool biscuit-coloured casual trousers and over the whole lot was a long casual dark jacket. The effect was a laid-back style.

Blimey. She dragged her eyes back up to his face. He was smiling, as if he had somehow been released from the prison of serious boss clothes and serious boss stance both at the same time. Even his sideburns didn't look pompous today. In fact, dressed like this, he looked completely different... He was the other person, she realised with a little stab of surprise, who'd reminded her of Ryan Gosling. How extraordinary. Ryan Gosling was hot, particularly in *La La Land*. She had never, EVER thought of her boss as hot.

'Hi, Sam,' said Elannah, breaking the moment. 'Isn't this exciting? I've been really looking forward to it. Have you?'

'Yes,' Sam lied swiftly. 'Much better than working.' Oops, that probably hadn't been very tactful, even if Rex was in team-building mode.

Fortunately, Mumbling Mike, Lightning and Hypochondriac

Heather chose that moment to rock up, which was a good distraction.

Magpie wasn't far behind them. He was talking on his mobile, which he pocketed as he reached them. 'Sorry, boss. It was a work call.'

'Today is not about work. It is about fun and, er, team building. But lunch first. Yes?' He was back to his usual rather strait-laced manner, the Ryan Gosling resemblance gone, Sam thought. Phew! That was a relief.

* * *

Lunch passed swiftly in a whirl of their usual banter. Then afterwards they threaded their way through the crowds, pausing briefly to look at a parade of vintage cars that were part of a procession involving the carnival queen, a sweet-faced blonde, before arriving at the golden-arched entrance of the fair.

Rex paid the bored-looking teenager for their tickets and they trooped through the turnstile. Sam felt her phone vibrate in the pocket of her jeggings and saw another message from Mr B. What with the excitement of speaking to Ned last night, she'd forgotten all about him. She took a moment to phone him back, apologised profusely, and discovered he wanted to change the booking from September to October.

'Work, I'm afraid. Unavoidable.'

'It's no problem. I will look forward to taking care of Percy and Portia in October.'

* * *

After the first half-hour, Sam realised that, against all odds, and completely contrary to what she'd expected, she was actually enjoying herself. To everyone's huge relief, Rex hadn't insisted that they go around the fair joined at the hip, but it had seemed natural to group together and this was supposed to be a team bonding day. Elannah had persuaded everyone, even Heather, to go on the waltzers. The girls were in one gaudily painted carriage while the guys took another.

Music blared out as the cars spun and whirled madly. Sam didn't remember them going that fast the last time she'd come to a fair, but that had probably been a couple of decades ago. Times had changed.

All the spinning and whirling had clearly affected Heather too. She'd been weaving about when they got off and had said she felt sick.

'It wasn't going that fast,' Mumbling Mike had pointed out. 'My ten-year-old daughter managed it fine.'

'She's just after a free pass to skive off home,' Magpie had taunted.

'I am not!' Heather had flicked back her blonde plaits in annoyance. 'I intend to be here for the duration.'

After that, she'd insisted that she cheer on the others from the sidelines, which she had done with great gusto to everyone's amusement. And also to the entertainment of the fairground boys, one of whom had watched with an astounded expression as the well-dressed blonde had clapped madly and given a piercing wolf-whistle with two fingers from the ground as her friends climbed into their carriages.

'Does she have special needs?' he had asked.

'Definitely,' Mike said.

'No, but she doesn't get out much.' Sam glared at Mike.

In a quiet moment between rides, Heather had confided to Sam that her parents were overprotective and hadn't approved of fairs. 'We never actually went to a funfair like this,' she said wistfully. 'All the other children from school went, but I wasn't allowed.'

Sam had looked at her sad expression and for the first time since she'd known Heather, she had felt empathy. Everyone was a product of their upbringing. She imagined Rex's parents must have had strict Victorian values. His father certainly had, judging by the decor in Rex's office, which, rumour had it, he had never changed. She presumed his mother was still alive, although she'd never heard him mention her. She imagined his parents had had him late in life and instilled in him traditional values; 'Waste not want not' – hence the battleship-grey filing cabinets. 'Our word is our bond' – he was certainly a fan of that one.

'I bet our boss has never been to a funfair either,' she told Heather, raising her voice over the sound of the ghost train's tinny music.

It was only afterwards that she'd realised Rex was walking behind them. Not that he'd given any indication of having heard.

Later, as they paused to watch a man win a prize for his son at hoopla, Sam found herself standing next to Rex.

'How's it going, Sam? You having fun?'

'I am actually. Considering fairs aren't really my thing.'

'They aren't really mine either. You were right earlier; I've never been to a funfair before. Today, as you probably know, was Elannah's idea. But then maybe we should pursue activities that aren't really our thing more often.' His blue grey eyes glinted in the afternoon sun.

'Maybe we should,' she said thoughtfully.

He turned to talk to Mike, who was on his other side. She heard him suggest it might be fun if they all had a go on the rifle range.

'Think of it as a works competition,' he said to Heather, who looked horrified. 'If you don't wish to participate, then maybe you could come along and keep score.'

There wasn't really a way Heather could disagree with this, Sam mused, thinking that maybe Rex had been right about the team-building exercise. The men were all up for the idea and so was Elannah. Sam had already decided that she'd go along. Why not? Not that she thought she had any chance of beating the others, but it would be pretty cool if she could win a teddy for Jack.

To Sam's surprise, and, she imagined, to everyone else's too, she turned out to be a crack shot at the rifle range, getting two bullseyes in a row.

'Go Sam.' Elannah and Heather cheered her on excitedly.

'You've done this before,' Magpie said in reluctant admiration.

'I really haven't.' She flushed beneath their compliments. 'I've never even picked up a gun.'

'Must be beginner's luck then,' said Lightning, who was also a crack shot and hot favourite to win.

Mike missed more times than he hit, but both Rex and Elannah were also good at this. Elannah admitted she'd had a fair bit of practice with her other half.

No one was more amazed than Sam when she got a third consecutive bullseye and zoomed into first place with an almost perfect score. Even the stallholder looked impressed as he handed her a large blue teddy bear with a sparkly gold sash around its body pronouncing, 'I'm a winner.'

'You should take up target shooting, ma'am. You're a natural. You could shoot pheasant – you'd feed your entire family.'

Sam pulled a face and Rex said, 'I suspect you'd be more inclined to rescue pheasants than shoot them, wouldn't you, Sam?'

'Definitely.' She was surprised he'd remembered the conversation they'd had in his office about her passion for all things feathered and furred.

'So who fancies going on a grown-up ride?' Magpie asked them. 'Who's up for Scary Skyscraper?'

'I'm still letting my dinner go down,' Elannah said.

'Me too,' Mike agreed.

'Heights are not for me,' Heather said. 'They set off my vertigo.'

Magpie strutted in a circle, making chicken noises and flapping his arms against his denim jacket. 'Wusses, the lot of you! We're supposed to be grown-ups. Grown-ups who are team bonding.' He looked at Rex. 'How about you, boss? Are you man or mouse?'

'I'm game,' Rex said, sounding coolly confident.

Sam was about to say that heights weren't for her either – they came a pretty close second to spiders in the fear stakes – when she saw Rex's eyes on her. Buoyed up with the euphoria of winning the rifle competition and also because of what he'd said earlier, she nodded. 'I'm game too. If I can find someone to teddy sit.'

Elannah put her hand up. 'I'll give him a cuddle. What are you going to call him?'

'I'll leave that to Jack and Abby.' She handed over the three-foot-high teddy with relief. She'd have to put him in the car before she met Ned.

A few minutes later, they reached the ride, which was in progress, and Sam shielded her eyes against the sun as she craned her neck to look. The seats of the ride were bolted onto the outside of a moveable metal framework that was presently crawling at a snail's pace up the vertical structure, higher and higher towards the top. She could see people's legs dangling. Oh my God.

Scary Skyscraper looked a lot higher close up. Being scared of heights was closely linked to being scared of falling and this, it seemed, was what the Skyscraper was all about. Yep, the seats and their occupants had just reached the top, where they hung suspended for a few seconds and then the framework dropped like a stone. Screams echoed across the fairground.

Sam met Rex's gaze.

'Are you sure about this?' His voice was mild, but there was definitely a sparkle of challenge in his eyes.

'Absolutely.'

It was only for a few minutes. It was obviously safe or they wouldn't be able to operate. She could close her eyes. And you were allowed to scream. That was the whole point of scary rides, wasn't it? Like scary films. They were designed to frighten you without actually being dangerous.

Sam squared her shoulders determinedly and followed Rex and Magpie to the turnstile. It was too late to back out now; they'd already paid. But her legs felt decidedly wobbly as she watched a dark-haired teenager with a fuchsia-pink bum-bag strung around her tiny waist release the last lot of occupants from their harnesses; a few of them looked decidedly pale. Was that bum-bag a bad omen? Sam chided herself for being ridiculous.

Then they were being strapped in: her, Rex and Magpie and a group of youngsters who couldn't have been more than about twenty. Sam didn't dare look at the rest of her colleagues, who were leaning on the barriers grinning. Instead she stared up past the red and yellow metalwork at the azure blue sky. She couldn't believe she was doing this. It would be a good story to tell Abby anyway. Presuming she survived to tell the tale.

Her seat jolted, the metal structure cranking as the whole thing began its upward trajectory. Oh my God, they were on the move. Up, up and up they went. It was the kind of ride that went up slowly and came down fast. Her stomach crunched with anticipation. She could smell sweat and she could feel the cool breeze on her neck. There was definitely a temperature change up here near the clouds.

Though, of course, they were nowhere near the clouds. She was turning into a drama queen like Abby.

Even when they got to the top, she didn't look down. She focused on the surrounding countryside and the strip of beach and the pier which looked even tinier than usual from up here. Her legs were dangling in terrifyingly empty air. She couldn't breathe. She was now confident that this had been the worst idea of her life.

As the ride hung suspended, Sam closed her eyes. She thought she might be about to have a panic attack. Oh God, oh God, oh God. She'd known she would hate this. Why hadn't she trusted her instincts?

And then the world dropped away. Her stomach lurched uncontrollably. A woman's screams were close by and yet somehow detached. It was her. She was screaming. She was vaguely aware of closing her mouth because her throat was hoarse. Adrenaline swept through her veins in a mad, supercharged dance.

The whole thing couldn't have lasted more than a couple of seconds, but it was without doubt the scariest two seconds of her life. And then, they were on the ground once more and she was trying not to sob.

But she couldn't get out. The ride was going up again. Why hadn't she realised it did it more than once? Why hadn't she paid more attention? Rex was in the seat next to her and suddenly she was aware that he had noticed her discomfort.

'You OK?' He mouthed the words and she closed her eyes and nodded.

She kept them closed for the rest of the ride, which went up and down twice more before they were finally back on the ground and the girl with the fuchsia bum-bag was releasing them. Sam jumped out and then found to her shock that her legs wouldn't support her. They seemed to be made of jelly. As she stumbled, she felt someone's arm around her, holding her up. Without it she'd have been on the ground. She was vaguely aware that it was Rex.

She could smell him, a mixture of mints and man and some vaguely exotic citrus scent, maybe this morning's faded aftershave. It was funny how much you noticed in moments of shock. But her boss, rescuing her from collapse – could it get any more embarrassing than that?

It seemed it could. She heard his voice close to her ear, 'It's all right. I've got you. Lean on me. We'll find a seat.'

She had no choice but to lean on him. Her legs still weren't working.

A few seconds later, she was compos mentis enough to realise that he'd led her to a picnic bench near a fast food van. She sank gratefully onto the hard wood and he sat opposite her. To her huge relief, the others had left them to it. More witnesses would have been dreadful. As it was, she was struggling not to burst into tears.

'I'm really sorry,' she managed eventually. 'I'm not sure what happened there... I...'

'It's fine.'

She risked a glance at him. His eyes were kind and calm and non-judgemental.

'To tell you the truth...' he went on, 'that was the most terrifying thing I've ever done. At least voluntarily. I can't think what possessed me.'

'Me neither. I don't know why I did it. I know perfectly well I'm scared of heights.' Now she wanted to laugh. She must be close to hysteria. She realised her hands were clammy with sweat. She wiped them on her dark grey jeggings.

'Maybe there's a limit to pursuing activities that aren't our thing,' Rex offered. 'Perhaps sometimes we should listen to our instincts.'

She nodded.

'Wait there,' he said, getting up.

She did what he said. Not that she had any plans to move. She wasn't convinced yet that her legs were under her control.

She saw him join the queue for the food van and when he came back, he was carrying two giant sticks of pink candyfloss.

'I wasn't allowed this stuff when I was a kid, but I've always wanted an excuse to try it. Sugar is good for shock,' he explained, handing one over.

She tore off a handful of the fluffy warm sweetness and put it in her mouth. He was right. Against all the odds, she was beginning to feel better. And something else unexpected had happened. Her opinion of Rex Fielding had gone up by several notches.

13

Now it was just before five thirty. Everyone else had gone home and Sam was sitting in her Chevy in the car park, having just come back to drop off Big Ted, who was now in the passenger seat beside her with a belt around his plump blue middle. His 'I'm A Winner' sparkly gold sash had slipped down and Sam felt as though her mood had slipped too. Things had gone a little flat after what had happened on the Scary Skyscraper.

Magpie and Lightning had had a row. Lightning had accused Magpie of taking some measuring device from his desk and Magpie vehemently denied it.

Elannah had said she'd had a cool day, but now had funfair fatigue.

Heather had said she felt queasy and was possibly sickening for something but had added swiftly when she'd seen her colleague's faces that she was sure it was just tiredness and she'd be fine when she got home.

Rex had been subdued. Sam felt guilty that she may have ruined the day, but she'd already apologised for the Skyscraper incident so she didn't do it again.

Now she had a moral dilemma. Like Elannah, she had funfair fatigue and she was desperate to go home. The very last thing she felt like doing was spending her evening at Hart's. In fact, if she never saw a funfair again, it would be too soon. She had tried texting Ned earlier to cancel their date, but her phone had come back with a message saying the text was undeliverable. Two further attempts had resulted in exactly the same thing happening and when she'd tried to phone him, she'd got an automated message saying it had not been possible to connect her call. That probably meant he was in a no-signal area.

Maybe she should just go home anyway. She had tried her best to contact him and cancel. Was that good enough?

Sam's conscience told her it was not. He'd seemed like a nice enough guy and she'd have hated it if someone she was meeting had let her down at the last minute.

She struggled with herself and finally she decided that she'd meet him and then she would tell him she didn't feel well and ask if they could reschedule. That was a compromise she could live with and it wouldn't be far from the truth anyway. She had a thumping headache, probably the after effects of the adrenaline dump of the Skyscraper.

As she climbed out of her car to go back towards the funfair, a blue Skoda drew in through the gate of the field. That's what Ned had said he'd be driving. Skodas were good cars these days, he'd taken pains to point out. Their engines were made by Volkswagen. Not that Sam was bothered what car he drove. She didn't know much about cars anyway.

She waited and, sure enough, it circled the field and then drew up in the parking space next to hers. He must have spotted her, although he didn't wave.

She waited for him to get out, which gave her plenty of time to study him. He was older than his photograph suggested. Heavier too, she thought, as he climbed out slightly laboriously. Hang on a minute, he wasn't as tall either. Nowhere near the six foot his profile had claimed he was. Height didn't alter. That couldn't be Ned. Oops, she must be gawping at a complete stranger.

She was just turning away, embarrassed, when a voice called her alter ego's name. 'Maxine? Is that you?'

She turned back again, startled. He sounded exactly like the man she had spoken to. He took a step closer. So he may have Ned's voice, but this was not the man whose profile photograph she and Abby had studied. He had a similar beard but his was scruffier and he had different coloured eyes. His were brown, not blue.

The penny finally dropped. He had used someone else's photo. What a flaming cheek. All that deliberating she'd been doing about letting him down and he had lied to her from the start. Her mind flicked back to the blog she'd read that said 81 per cent of people lied about their profile.

It felt like the final straw. 'You're a fake,' she said, looking him up and down.

'I'm not. I swear...'

'You used someone else's photo.'

'But I can explain that. I didn't have any current ones and...'

She wouldn't have hung around to listen even if he she had been in a good mood and hadn't had a headache. She turned her back on him and stalked over to her car. Thankfully, he didn't follow her, but as she drove away with Big Ted on the passenger seat beside her, she saw Ned in her rear view mirror standing in the middle of the car park sticking up two fingers. She'd clearly had a narrow escape.

* * *

Sam's mum was even more disappointed than Sam was when she telephoned to tell her. 'Definitely his loss, my darling.'

Abby was outraged.

It was now Sunday afternoon. Abby had got back from visiting her parents at Matt's about an hour ago and now she and Sam were pushing Jack's buggy along Studland Beach towards the dunes. Fortunately, the tide was out and it was a lightweight buggy, so it wasn't too heavy-going.

'I'm not bothered that it didn't work out,' Sam said. 'To be honest, he'd have had trouble impressing me if he'd been James Bond.'

'I didn't know you were a fan of Daniel Craig,' Abby puffed as she manoeuvred the buggy around some clumps of seaweed.

'I'm not really. But you know what I mean. It was a mistake to arrange to meet him at the fair when I'd been there all day. I probably didn't give it a proper chance.'

'Hang on a sec. The guy was a total phony – you surely aren't blaming yourself for that.' Abby's look of indignation made Sam backtrack hastily.

'No, of course I'm not. What I'm saying is that it wouldn't have mattered if Ned had been Mr Wonderful, I rushed into it. I didn't find out enough about him. I shouldn't have arranged to meet him at the fair when I knew it was a bad idea. I should have trusted my instincts,' she finished, thinking that Rex had said something similar.

'We should all do that more, I guess.'

'How did it go with your parents anyway?' Sam asked, keen to change the subject. 'What did they think of their grandson?'

'They loved him. Of course.' Abby paused and bent over the buggy. 'Didn't they, Jackanory?' She tickled the baby's tummy and he gazed at her. 'That's what Dad called him. After some old kiddie programme he used to watch. Mum wanted us to fly back out with them and stay in Alicante for a while. So she could look after us both and be a proper granny.'

'Would you like to do that?' Sam kept her voice neutral, even though the thought of Abby and Jack disappearing to Spain sent a cold shiver through her.

'No way.' Abby widened her eyes dramatically. 'Do I look like the kind of Clingy Carol who needs her mother butting in and telling her how to change a nappy?' She snorted with indignation. 'It was bad enough being around them for the weekend. Mum forever fussing about the way I was breastfeeding. Dad and Matt getting all awkward and embarrassed every time I got my boobs out. I have *so* got the hang of that by the way. I reckon I could do a YouTube video on breastfeeding. We could call it Breast is Best. Only, I think that's been done.'

They both giggled.

'I have no intention of going to Spain,' Abby went on. 'The older I get, the more the sun seems to affect me. And Jack's too young for plane rides. If my mother wants to see more of her grandson, she'll have to come back here for a bit longer. I'm not the one who emigrated.'

Sam sensed a thread of hurt beneath her words and then Abby added more gently, 'You see, I do get it, how you feel about your parents disappearing. I know we're supposed to cut the umbilical cord and all that, but sometimes I think we do things arse about face in England: families splitting up and going off to all four corners of the planet, rather than living in the same town and being there for each other like they are in Europe. It's different for blokes. They're not so close with their families, are they? Matt said to send his love by the way.'

'That's nice. Give him mine back.'

'He's got a new girlfriend,' Abby added. 'I don't think it will last long. She came over for a bit, but she spent most of the time on her phone. Not that Matt seemed to notice. He reckons she looks like a young Kylie.'

'Does she?'

'Maybe a bit. She's blonde and she's tiny and she was wearing these minute gold hot pants. I don't know if she sounds like her – she barely said a word.'

'That is pretty unsociable.' Sam paused. 'By the way, I think we're near the naturist beach,' Sam said, glancing back up the beach at the sand dunes, covered with spiky grass. 'Did you notice the sign?'

The air smelled of salt and marsh grass and it was very still. The faintest heat haze still hung in the air.

'No.' Abby shielded her eyes. 'I can't see any naked men.'

'They're usually ancient. Why is it that people who have beautiful bodies to show off rarely do it and people who definitely shouldn't be taking their clothes off in public are quite happy to flash it about?'

'Sod's law, I guess.' Abby gave up scanning the beach. Here the sand was a soft powdery white and the sea sparkled and glittered in the late afternoon sunshine. 'I thought there would be more people about. Shall we go a little bit further? The buggy's easy enough to take to bits. We could sit on the dunes for a bit and chill.'

Sam agreed and they found a spot in the dip of a sand dune and Abby got Jack settled on her lap. 'He loves his teddy by the way.'

'I'm really pleased.'

'...Don't let Ned put you off.'

'...I'm glad you're not going to Spain.'

They spoke at the same time and Sam gestured for her friend to go first.

'Promise me you'll give online dating another go. They won't all be muppets and liars.'

'Just 81 per cent of them,' Sam said, leaning back on her elbows and smoothing down a patch of extra spiky grass. 'That's how many people lie about their profile for online dating apparently.' It was odd but she'd barely given the Ned thing another thought. It kept getting eclipsed by the humiliation of her boss rescuing her from collapsing in a heap.

'They won't all use someone else's photo though. That's taking the mickey. I can see why they might use older pictures when maybe they were thinner or whatever. I mean, most people do a bit of that.'

'And he said he worked for the National Trust. When actually he just volunteered. I wonder if he was really widowed and had a daughter called Milly or whether he just made that up to reel in women who are a sucker for a sob story.'

'My, you're even more cynical than me. When did that happen?' Abby kissed Jack's head. 'I am going to teach you never to lie to women, to always have integrity and never to make stuff up on your online dating profile. Yes I am...'

Jack belched and they both laughed.

'Good start,' Sam said. She rolled over onto her side and rested her head on her elbow. 'So would you ever consider online dating?'

'Maybe one day. At the moment, Jack is the only man I need in my life. Aren't you? Did you know that they start to focus at this age? So he can recognise us? The two most important women in his life.'

'Shouldn't that be you and your mum?' Sam said, feeling her heart swell with warmth, nevertheless. There was a little pause and she added softly, 'Still no word from Paul?'

'No. My parents asked me about him too.'

'I'm sorry, honey. I don't want to pry.'

'You're not. You're my best friend. It's natural to ask. And I know that, much as I'd like to, I can't just forget Paul exists. Jack is going to want to know who his father is at some point. I know that too. I guess I've been in denial really ever since he was born. I've been in this little bubble where no one exists except Jack and you and me. It's been really nice. But I know it can't last forever… I know real life is going to come crashing in.' She frowned and stopped talking abruptly and Sam was sure she was going to say something else but had then thought better of it.

She waited patiently, but in the end all Abby said was, 'You were going to say something – earlier on. What was that?'

'Only that I'm glad you're not going to Spain. I think I might get a complex if everyone I know leaves the country.'

'Have your parents decided yet where they're off to?'

'No, I don't think so. Although the sale of the B&B is going through.'

Movement distracted them and when Sam glanced up, she saw a man walking past not more than a few feet away. They were partially hidden in the dip of a dune so she wasn't sure if he knew they were there. He certainly didn't act like he had. He must have been in his forties and he was very tanned and very trim, which was particularly apparent because his entire body was on show. From his muscled calves to his bronze six-pack and… Sam tried to drag her eyes away and failed… absolutely everything in between.

Abby was staring too. 'Woweeee,' she mouthed in a hushed breathless whisper that hadn't been quite hushed enough, it would seem, as the man turned.

'Good evening, ladies.' He didn't sound surprised to see them. 'Lovely weather for it.

For what? Strutting about in the altogether or sitting on a sand dune taking in the rays? Sam didn't like to ask.

It was Abby who recovered her composure first. 'Top of the morning to you, sir.'

'It's evening,' Sam hissed as the man nodded and walked on by.

'Yes, I know. It's a turn of phrase. My dad's always saying it and it just slipped out.'

'It certainly did.'

'It was a whopper, wasn't it? Fancy seeing one of them swinging about when you're just minding your own business sitting on a sand dune. I had to cover Jack's eyes. I didn't want him getting a complex.'

Sam stifled a laugh. 'I doubt he can focus that well, can he? And we are in the middle of a nudist beach. I guess it's our own fault.'

'Yeah, he probably didn't know we were here.'

'I think he did. Didn't you notice he was holding in his stomach? He let his breath out when he'd gone past.'

'Newsflash. I wasn't looking at his stomach. Don't tell me you were looking at his stomach. Samantha Jones, no wonder you aren't interested in online dating. Have you taken a celibacy vow or something?' She shook her head. 'I mean, I've got a reason not to be interested in dating. I've just had a baby, but you, girlfriend, are a hot-blooded woman in the prime of her life who should be up for a bit of hot rumpy-pumpy. Especially if you want a baby. Do you still want one? Or was that the drink talking?' She eyed Sam curiously and Sam felt herself blushing.

'I don't know, honey. Can we change the subject?'

'Of course we can. I'm sorry. Shall we head back for some tea? Or do you want to hang around and see if you can see anything you like the look of. At least, down here, you can check out all their equipment up front! Talking of which, have you ever seen that Channel 4 programme, *Naked Temptation*? It's unbelievable what they put on mainstream TV these days.'

'It's called *Naked Attraction* and I can't think of anything worse than choosing a partner on the basis of his or her bits!' She scrambled to her feet while Abby busied herself gathering up baby paraphernalia. 'Are you planning on getting Jack christened by the way? Or having a naming ceremony?'

'Probably not. It's not as if I'm a practising member of my church.'

'You haven't been out much at all lately,' Sam probed, as they made their way back. 'Even to the shops. Is that because it's more difficult, having Jack in tow? You do know I can look after him anytime?'

'It's not that. He's an angelic baby and I like online shopping...'

For a moment Sam thought Abby was going to say something else. But she didn't. And they walked towards home in companionable silence.

14

In the first week of August, Sam got chatting with another guy on Countryside Lovers, called Danny Bowkett. She'd barely looked at the dating site since Ned, but every so often a notification caught her attention. There was a thing called 'New Attractions' that flagged up anyone who'd recently joined. Danny Bowkett was one of these and his photo popped up on Sam's phone. He wasn't traditionally handsome. He had a slightly crooked nose and sandy brown hair and a gap in his front teeth, but he had a twinkle in his eyes that was appealing.

His profile said he was a builder who dreamed of emigrating to a hot country. He loved dogs and had a border terrier called Stan who accompanied him to work.

On impulse, Sam had sent him a message and he'd answered the next day. Ever since then they'd chatted back and forth and after a few days of this they arranged to meet for a coffee. She felt much more confident about Danny. Her instincts told her he was genuine, but then she'd talked to him far more than she'd talked to Ned. She'd even told him her name was Sam, not Maxine.

'You will be careful, won't you?' Abby warned. 'What if he's a weirdo like the last one?'

'We're meeting at the Bluebell Cliff Hotel. I don't have to stay if I don't like the look of him.'

'But isn't that place up on the cliffs in the middle of nowhere. What if he abducts you in the car park?'

'It's a hotel car park. It'll be jam-packed with walkers on a Saturday lunchtime. Besides, it means I can kill two birds with one stone. I want to thank Clara King for putting dog-sitting clients in my direction, not to mention Mr B's Kunekunes.'

'Is that the bonkers pig man? Has he been in touch again?'

'He's been in touch four times since he came to see me,' Sam said, relieved to have distracted her. 'I think that's a record. Although, to be fair, he had to change the booking because of unforeseen circumstances. I'm now looking after Portia and Percy for the third weekend of October. You'd think if you were that paranoid there wouldn't be any unforeseen circumstances, wouldn't you?'

'Hmmm,' Abby nodded, she'd clearly lost interest in Mr B. 'So, going back to your date, would you like me to phone you halfway through lunch to give you a get-out clause?'

'No, it's OK. We've arranged just a quick drink. I'll only stay for lunch if he seems nice. Otherwise I'll make my excuses.'

'Wow. That's brave. Would you really do that?'

'Yes. You were the one who said life's too short to spend it with a no-hoper. Remember?'

'Did I really say that? OK. I'll stop nagging. Have fun, girlfriend. I hope he's not a no-hoper.'

* * *

By the time Saturday lunchtime arrived, Sam wasn't feeling quite as brave as she'd made out to Abby. The memory of what had happened last time she'd tried a blind date replayed in her mind. Her stomach knotted as she walked across the Bluebell Cliff car park, breathing in the familiar mix of salt and sea on the breeze that flickered across the cliff top and listening to the haunting cries of the gulls.

The Bluebell Cliff was in a stunning location. The building itself was distinctive. It was a long, low, white Art Deco building – the car park lay on its northern side and it had the most perfect position a hotel could have. It was perched on the headland that overlooked Old Harry Rocks.

Sam had seen it from the back because she'd walked along the South West Coast Path just outside its grounds, but she'd never actually been here for a meal, even though it was open to the public. It was funny how you rarely went to places right on your doorstep.

It had been her date-to-be, Danny, who'd suggested it. 'I've always wanted to try it. It's got a great reputation.'

A quick glance around the car park revealed no lone males sitting in cars. Not that she knew what he drove. They hadn't touched on cars. Was he here already? It was five to twelve. They'd arranged to meet at midday.

Belatedly, she wondered if it had been a mistake to come here. She'd always fancied it too, but she didn't want to taint the experience by meeting someone here she may not like. She reminded herself it was the place where dreams came true. At least that's what it said on all the literature.

They'd agreed to sit outside if it was a nice day and it couldn't have been more beautiful. The sun shone down from a cloudless sky. That was a good omen.

She was directed through to the hotel's outside terrace by a girl wearing a uniform with a bluebell logo on the pocket of her white blouse. There were a dozen or so metal tables, each with a vase of flowers, dotted around a paved terrace. Lush lawns stretched down to the fence that separated the Bluebell's grounds from the coast path beyond.

Sam spotted Danny Bowkett almost immediately. He was chatting to a waitress near the back entrance of the hotel. He had his back to her, which gave her the chance to study him for a moment unobserved. He was wearing smart jeans and a checked shirt. From the rear, he looked exactly like his photo. If anything, he looked slightly slimmer and his sandy hair was shorter than it had been in his picture.

As she approached, the waitress spotted her and called out a welcome and Danny turned too.

He was definitely more attractive in real life. He was clean-shaven and the checked shirt was open at the neck and his eyes were bright and smiley.

'Sam, I assume?'

She nodded and the waitress moved discreetly away.

'You look just like your photo.' Was that relief in his voice?

'So do you.'

'Not always like that, is it? What are you drinking? Shall we find a table? Apparently we can sit anywhere we like. They don't do reservations at lunchtimes.'

By the time they'd sat down, the awkwardness of the first few moments was gone. Her first impressions were of a man who was at ease with himself. Someone who smiled often but wasn't a fake. He reminded her of her dad. A little self-deprecating, but big on bonhomie. He would have made a great front-of-house man.

'So what made you try online dating then, Sam? Have you been at it for long?'

She told him the truth. Or nearly the truth. She was definitely never telling anyone about Mission Perfect Dad. 'I had too many glasses of wine with my housemate one Saturday evening. I was mortified when I woke up the next day and realised what we'd done.'

'But not mortified enough to delete your profile? Mind you, by then I expect you had a horde of guys beating their way to your door. That's what usually happens to the pretty ones. So I'm told.' His open smile was reassuring.

'It wasn't quite like that, but thank you for the compliment. How about you?'

'I can't blame mine on wine. Or cider...' He indicated his half pint with a rueful look. 'I just wanted some female company. You don't meet many ladies in my line of work, so it seemed a good idea. My brother met his girlfriend online – not that he's a builder, he's an accountant – so I knew it worked. I figured the worst thing that could happen was that I'd make some new friends.' He broke off. 'Sorry. I'm babbling. I've got a habit of doing that...'

'You're not,' Sam said, warming to him even more. 'I guess it's quite an artificial situation, isn't it? Meeting a complete stranger for a drink.'

'Yeah. Although not that different from blind dates. That's what our parents' generation would have done.'

'But they'd have had the advantage of their mates filling them in on the bits to look out for. The good bits and the bad bits, I mean.'

'What are your bad bits?' he asked, tipping his head slightly to one side. He had a habit of doing that when he asked a question. 'I don't mean what are your faults, Sam. I'm not asking that.' He coloured slightly. 'I mean in your life. What bits would you change if you could?'

'Oh, definitely my job,' she said without stopping to think. 'I'm a typist for a company of structural engineers, which is OK as it goes – it pays the bills. But it's not my dream job. My dream job is to be self-employed, in charge of my own time and responsible for my own destiny. Free to pursue my passion.' Had she just said passion? Where had all that come from? She felt slightly embarrassed, but Danny was nodding. His eyes, which were hazel brown, were interested.

'What is your passion?'

'Animals.' She fiddled with a beer mat. Then she told him about Purbeck Pooches. 'When I started it up, just over two years ago, I was so full of what would happen in the future. I would gradually build up my weekend boarding clients, then one day I'd get to a point where I could give up my day job and do it full time.'

'And that hasn't happened yet?'

'No.' She sipped her half pint of orange juice and lemonade. 'I remember reading this piece of advice once from some famous entrepreneur, that if you want to work for yourself, you should build up your company in your spare time and then, when it's earning the same amount of money as your day job, you should halve your income by giving up your day job.' She stopped speaking. 'Now who's the one babbling? Sorry. You must be a good listener.'

'So I'm told,' he said without a trace of arrogance. 'Would you like to eat? Are you hungry?'

The smells of food drifting from other tables and the plates carried around by waitresses were enticing. Sam's stomach rumbled and she realised she was enjoying his company. She didn't want to make her excuses and leave.

'Yes. Good idea.'

They chose a ploughman's. Ham for him and Brie for her. Sam had spotted them going by, destined for other tables, with great chunks of warm bread and a pat of butter in a white pot and what the menu had said was homemade Dorset apple chutney.

As they waited for their lunch, they carried on talking. 'The trouble with the advice from that famous entrepreneur,' Danny said, 'is that it probably only works if your self-employed job is very well paid. Otherwise you would run out of hours. Not to mention energy.'

'That's exactly what I've found. I've got to the point where I'm stuck. I can't take on any more boarders without doing fewer hours at Fielding's. Boarding dogs and the occasional horse or goat is never going to make me a millionaire.'

'Will it make you happy though?'

'I think so.' She looked at him. 'I'm sorry. This is all about me, me, me. Tell me something about you.'

'All right. I used to be a self-employed builder. That was my dream too. And I made a lot of money. But I also wrecked the tendons in my arms. Building is physically very hard.' He held out his forearms and she saw the tattoo of an anchor on his tanned skin. 'You can't see anything different, but I still get quite a bit of pain. I couldn't do the heavy lifting these days. I thought it was the worst day of my life when I had to stop being self-employed, but actually it wasn't.' He paused to sip his drink. 'Am I being boring?'

'No, not at all.' But she liked that he'd asked. 'I'm interested. My parents are self-employed.'

'Then, as you already know, you need several different skill sets. You need to be an accountant, publicist, salesperson, advertising manager – and all of that on top of whatever business it is that you start up. And you need to work all the hours that there are. The freedom is an illusion.'

'Yes,' she said, thinking of her parents and how they worked flat out and did longer hours than anyone she'd ever met. Once again, she felt guilty for begrudging them retirement. 'So what do you do now?'

'I work for Bovis Homes. I'm a salaried site manager, so I tell other people what to do. I oversee the brickies, the ground workers, the electricians – in fact everyone who comes onto site. I troubleshoot. Then, at the end of the day, I go home, but unlike when I was my own boss, I don't take it all with me. I shrug off my hard hat and hi-vis jacket and leave the problems of the day behind. If that makes sense?'

'It makes total sense.'

Just at that moment, a shadow fell over their table and Sam looked up to see a woman in a gorgeous pale lilac suit with a badge that said Manager pinned to her blouse.

'Welcome to the Bluebell Cliff,' said Clara King. 'Please accept my apologies for intruding and also for the delay in your food. We've been extremely busy.' They recognised each other at the same time. 'Oh hello Sam, I didn't realise it was you.'

'Clara. We didn't even notice there was a delay,' Sam said, realising with a shock that half an hour had flicked by.

'It's our policy to offer you a drink on the house if there's a thirty-minute delay.' The manager's eyes sparkled. 'Also I'd love to talk to you on a business matter, if you have time before you go?' Her eyes flicked towards a dog, the colour of a fox, sitting patiently on the terrace outside the eating area.

Sam nodded with understanding. They had talked about the possibility of Foxy coming for a trial boarding night so she could get to know Sam when they'd met last time.

'I'll come and see you on my way out.'

'Thanks.'

Sam noticed two messages from Abby, when she sneaked a surreptitious look at her phone as Clara left. The first said:

What's he like?

And the second sent five minutes later said:

Do you need rescuing?

When Danny excused himself to pay a visit to the gents', Sam sent a quick message back – So far, so good with a thumbs up emoji.

By the time he came back, their food had arrived and as they ate, the chat moved on to other things. He told her about his dream of living in a hot country.

'I've always loved the sun. How about you?'

'Um.' She didn't tell him she didn't holiday abroad very much. She'd gone to Alicante once with Abby and it had upset her to see so many stray dogs and cats, haunting the tourists like skinny shadows. It had been difficult to resist bringing one back to England. Abby had told her she'd do more good by giving a donation to the local rehoming centre. So she'd done that in the end. But it had darkened the holiday mood. 'There are people who like animals and there are people who are batshit crazy animal lovers like you,' Abby had said with a look of exasperated affection. Sam came back to the present with a start. 'Where's Stan today?' she asked, remembering that Danny had a dog. 'He's not in the car, is he?'

'No, of course not. I figured it would be too hot. He's with my brother's family. Andy's got kids and they love having Stan round to play. When I go on holiday, he usually goes into kennels in Wareham. But, hey, maybe I could bring him to Purbeck Pooches in future.'

'I'd like to meet him.'

'Did you say you'd got a field?' he asked suddenly.

'Yes. I don't own it, but it goes with the house I rent. It's next door.'

'Could the owner be persuaded to sell it? Or is it prime building land?'

'I think it's agricultural, but it's definitely green belt. Why?'

'Because there's another way you could make use of your field. Have you heard of dog fields?'

She shook her head. 'I don't think so.'

'I take Stan to one sometimes. They're aimed at people whose dogs can't be let off the lead. Stan was a rescue and he can be anti-social with other dogs.' He steepled his hands on the table and rested his chin on them. 'Basically, a dog field is a fenced area where dogs can run free but can't actually escape. You have total use of the field. You hire them out by the half-hour. The one I go to has an online booking system, so it's not too time-intensive for the owner, although I believe the woman who owns it does actually live on site.'

Sam felt a flicker of excitement. 'Wow. What a great concept. It must give you huge peace of mind, knowing your dog is totally safe.'

'Yeah it does.' He grinned at her. 'They're very popular, dog fields. I'm a mine of useless information.'

'A mine of very useful information, I'd say.'

'I'm quite good at coming up with money-making ideas. Maximising financial potential, my brother calls it. I sometimes think I should have gone into the accountancy profession like him.'

'But you'd have found it boring?'

He clicked his tongue. 'You're on my wavelength.'

He was so nice and so easy to be with, yet something was niggling her. Something she couldn't quite put her finger on.

Before they left, Danny had gone inside to pay the bill – she had insisted on giving him her half – and she'd popped in to see Clara King to make arrangements for Foxy's trial boarding night.

'Was this your first visit to the Bluebell?' Clara asked her as they booked a date.

'It was, yes.'

'Did you have a good time?'

'Lovely, thanks.' On impulse, she added, 'This was actually our first date. We met online.'

'How fantastic. Was he nice?'

'He was certainly good company.'

When she got back to the terrace, she saw Danny was waiting. He ticked all the boxes. He was tall, not bad-looking. He was intelligent, kind, easy to talk to and he was definitely an animal lover.

So what was it that was niggling her? It was the same thing that had bothered her when she'd first talked to Ned. But she'd been trying to ignore it because Danny was so much nicer.

There was no chemistry, she realised with a tiny shock of disappointment. None whatsoever. She couldn't imagine herself kissing him or feeling sparks flicker between them. Had they even touched? Yes, probably when they'd passed the drinks and once as he'd pulled out her chair. That had been a nice chivalrous thing to do.

It had been lovely, but it had felt as though she was talking to Lightning or Mumbling Mike – or even her father. Her head might see Danny Bowkett as potential boyfriend material. But her heart most certainly didn't. It was like one of those TV programs, *First Dates* or *Dinner Date*, when everything seems to go so well, but at the end of the night no one arranges a second date.

15

'You are seeing him again though, aren't you?' was Abby's take on it when Sam finally got home at nearly four o'clock.

'Um, I don't know. Maybe.' Sam frowned. 'We've left it open.'

'What do you mean maybe?' Abby followed her into the kitchen. 'He sounds perfect. Kind, generous, tall, not bad-looking. What didn't you like about him?'

'Nothing. I liked him a lot. But I'm not sure he's boyfriend material. I just didn't fancy him.' She sighed and stared out of the window that overlooked the back garden. The grass needed cutting. Another job to put on her list. 'Do you think it's possible for the chemistry to kick in later or does it have to be at the beginning?'

'Do you need chemistry for father material?' Abby looked at her face. 'I was joking, girlfriend,' she added swiftly. 'I think anything's possible. I guess chemistry could be a slow burner. How did you leave it with him?'

'He said he would call. We didn't actually arrange anything else. Maybe he won't call.'

'I bet he will. Did he seem keen?'

'Yes,' Sam said, remembering the moment, back in the car park, when they'd stood rather awkwardly at the parting point.

'So, would you like to do this again over dinner?' Danny had asked her.

A cool breeze had lifted her hair and she'd hesitated and she'd seen in his eyes that he knew how she felt.

There had been the slightest of drops in his shoulders and he'd given a half nod and put his hands in his pockets. 'Or we could just be friends?'

'I'd like us to be friends,' she'd said. 'And see how that pans out.'

To give him credit, he'd nodded and said, 'That's cool, Sam. I've really enjoyed your company. And it's always good to make a new friend.'

'I've really enjoyed yours too.' After that it was awkward. There was nothing else to say. As she had driven home, she'd felt a despondency settle like dark clouds on her shoulders. She'd been oh so tempted to pull over into a layby and phone him and say, 'I think I've made a mistake. I would really like to see you again. Let's do dinner.' But deep down she knew she hadn't made a mistake. Was it fair to lead him on if there was no chemistry?

'Are you OK? You look really sad.' Abby's voice jerked her back to the present and Sam realised she had wandered over to the fridge, deep in thought.

'I feel a bit sad. What if I never find anyone I click with? What if I'm destined to end up a batshit-crazy cat lady surrounded by animals and isolated from the human race, alone on a smallholding in Somerset.'

'Where the hell did that come from?'

'Don't look so shocked. You're the one who's always accusing me of preferring animals to humans.'

'You do know I'm joking though, right? Well, I'm kind of joking. I can't see you as a crazy cat lady. Maybe a crazy dog lady.' She winked. 'Sorry, I couldn't resist that. Anyway, why Somerset? What's wrong with Dorset?'

'I can't afford a terraced house in Dorset, let alone a smallholding.' Sam picked up a tea towel and threw it at her friend and Abby ducked so it landed in the washing-up bowl instead, which was half full of cold dishwater.

Abby stuck her tongue out and Sam went across and hooked out the sopping-wet tea towel. But at least their banter had chased off the melancholy.

'How's Jack? Is he asleep?' Sam asked.

'Dead to the world.' Abby held up her arms. 'So these arms are baby free and hug ready, should you need a girlfriend hug?'

'I do,' Sam said, hugging her friend, who smelled of babies with a faint undertone of apple shampoo, and thinking again that she was glad Abby and Jack were here. Beach Cottage would have been a much lonelier place without them.

* * *

For the rest of that weekend, Sam buried herself in activity. She mowed the grass, did a whole pile of domestic stuff and washed the dog bedding in the utility room ready for her next doggie boarders.

Her mind kept flicking back to Danny Bowkett. OK, so things may not have panned out in the way she'd hoped, but she had liked him and he had said some thought-provoking things about her work. The dog field idea was brilliant. She had done some research online and discovered he was right. There was a rising trend across the country for securely fenced fields that were hired out in one-hour slots, or in some cases half-hour slots.

The prices varied and so did the facilities that were offered. Some fields had play areas for dogs. These ranged from baskets of dog toys and some old spare tyres piled in a heap, to a venue in

Cornwall, which Sam nicknamed 'The Ultimate Dog Field', that had a full 'all-weather fixed agility course'. There was everything you could imagine in between. Another field she looked at had a search and find area and what the owner called 'sniff zones', which were, apparently, especially grown areas of dog friendly herbs and flowers. The mind boggled. Sam bookmarked that page so she could have a proper look later.

The facilities for the dog owners varied just as much. Most had wooden picnic benches and some had covered areas for humans to stand in, which made sense if it was raining. People still needed to take their dogs out in the rain.

She flicked through to the bookings page on a few and found that they were surprisingly popular. The closest one to Beach Cottage was in Blandford, thirty-odd miles away. That must be the one Danny used. He lived in Swanage, so it was slightly nearer for him, but not much. When she clicked through its online booking page, she saw they had bookings up to Christmas. They even had two slots booked on Christmas Day. Blimey. She could feel her heartbeat quickening. Might this be a feasible option for her?

Purbeck Pooches had not been the success that Sam had hoped for when she'd first dreamed up the idea. She'd envisaged that her pet care service, which had started with such lowly beginnings – walking Seamus and Goldie and looking after them for the odd weekend while Barbara Oldfield was away – would build up into a viable business.

This had probably been naïve. Weekend dog boarding was all very well, but she would always be limited by space and it was incredibly time-intensive. She knew from experience that dog walking was more profitable. She had thought that building kennels would be good, but a dog field would be better. A dog field could run with far less supervision.

Could Ben be persuaded to sell her the field? How much were

fields even worth? Maybe she wouldn't need to actually buy it. After all, she already used it for equine guests and the odd grumpy goat. Maybe Ben wouldn't object if she turned it into a dog field. The questions tumbled over themselves.

Fencing it so it was safe enough for dogs to run free in might be expensive though. The four-foot panel fencing that it currently had wouldn't be enough. Snowy had managed to get out of it without any problem, and a determined dog could probably do the same.

The thoughts churned in her head, going nowhere. In the end, she decided to talk it through with her father, who had a very good instinct for business. She wanted to ask how the sale was progressing anyway, so on Sunday evening she gave her parents a call.

'You must be psychic,' her mother said when she picked up the phone. 'I was literally just about to call you.'

'For anything particular?' Sam asked, sensing it was. There was a thread of excitement in her mother's voice.

'We exchanged contracts on the B&B yesterday.'

'Oh my goodness, that was quick. When's completion?'

'On 21 September. So there isn't a great deal of time to get everything packed up. But, on the bright side, the new owner does want a lot of the furniture left in situ – so there's not a huge amount to pack up.'

'That's really good news. Do you need some help?' Sam had a sudden vivid image of her parents trying to squash a lifetime of memories into a few small packing cases.

'We won't need any help, thanks, darling. We've got that in hand. But I did want to talk to you about what we've decided.'

Sam felt her heart sink a little, despite all her efforts to stop it. So they were going to Cyprus then. She bit the inside of her lip. She must not put a downer on things. She must be happy for them. She was so focused on putting a brave face on that she didn't properly hear her mother's next words. Something about a short let.

'Um, sorry, Mum. Bad signal. What was that?'

'We've decided to get a short let somewhere local while we look at houses. That will take all the pressure off and it will also put us in a stronger position to buy.'

'Good idea. Have you decided what part of Cyprus yet?'

'We haven't decided on Cyprus at all. All things considered, I think we're now edging towards Cornwall, or maybe even North Dorset. It's a lot cheaper to buy in the north of the county than round here. Especially if we pick somewhere a bit rural.'

Sam let out a breath that until that moment she hadn't been aware she'd been holding. Relief was washing through her like balm. She thought she'd accepted the fact that her parents were retiring abroad. She said carefully, 'But I thought you and Dad wanted to retire to the seaside?'

'It was an option. But that's more your dad's thing than mine. It's very expensive to retire to the seaside and we're not sure it's worth it.' She lowered her voice slightly. 'To be honest with you, darling, I've seen enough of the sea, lovely as it is, to last me a lifetime. I'm fancying a pretty little semi-rural town with facilities – doctors, chemists, bus routes, that kind of thing – for when we're in our dotage. And a community that we can be a part of – get involved in. Your dad would love that too. You know what a socialite he is.'

'Oh, Mum, that's brilliant news. I'd love you and Dad to be close. It would be wonderful – not that I mind if you're not. I can travel. That would be fun too.' No it wouldn't. She was such a liar. At least she was lying for the right reasons.

'Also, darling, do you remember we mentioned before that we wanted to give you some money?'

'Yes, but I don't need you to give me any money. I'm fine and you'll need every penny for your new place.'

'We've factored it in, Sam. It was something we'd always planned to do when we sold the B&B. We both know how keen you are on working for yourself and the truth is that we wouldn't have been able to set up in business ourselves if we hadn't had some help from your grandparents.'

Sam did know that. She had heard the story many times. Gran and Grandad had sold up their chain of family grocers when they'd retired to the Orkneys, where they had lived in a remote bothy on an island accessible only by boat.

She had fond memories of going there as a child. Of how exciting it was, being allowed to stay up late on summer days when it stayed light until well after ten. Gran and Grandad had both died within months of each other in the last five years, but up until then they had loved their retirement, both of them being active in their community to the end.

'We're not giving you a fortune. It'll be about £22,000. Think of it as an investment in your business. Or you may even want to put it down as a deposit on a house. It's up to you, darling. The main thing is we don't want any arguments. We've decided to give you the money. It's not up for discussion. If you want to just put it in the bank. That's fine too. There's inheritance tax implications, but only if we die within the next seven years, which we're not planning to...'

She paused for breath and Sam felt her head spinning a little. This was not a conversation she'd expected. 'Wow,' she said at last. 'Thank you. That's really amazingly generous. I don't know what to say. Are you sure?' She'd never envisaged they meant that kind of money – it may not be much to them, but it was massive to her, especially at the moment.

'Totally.' Her mother's voice grew brusque. 'Anyway, I've just remembered you phoned me, didn't you? Was it just for a chat?'

'Yes and no – um.' Her head was still spinning at her parents' generosity. 'I wanted to run something by you as it happens, just to see what you thought. A business proposition, funnily enough…' She broke off. It sounded like someone was banging on the front door. That was odd. It was nearly nine, and she didn't think they were expecting anyone. She certainly wasn't. She had been talking on her mobile in the lounge. Now she poked her head out of the door and saw Abby coming downstairs. 'Do you mind getting that, honey? I'm just on the phone.'

Abby gave her the thumbs up and Sam shut the lounge door again.

'Sorry, Mum. Where were we?'

'You were talking about a business proposition?'

'Yes.' Was she imagining it or could she hear raised voices coming from the direction of the hall? No, she wasn't imagining it. She definitely could. 'Hang on a minute, Mum. Sorry. Can I call you back? I think Abby might need my help.'

She disconnected and went into the hall. Abby had her back to her, but she was talking to someone on the doorstep. A man whose voice was familiar. Oh my goodness. It sounded like Paul, Abby's ex. What on earth was he doing here?

Sam took a step closer. 'Is everything OK, Abby?'

She turned. Clearly it wasn't. Her face was ashen.

Behind her, Sam caught a flash of dark hair and the familiar profile of Abby's ex. It was Paul standing on the doorstep. No flowers, no chocolates, this clearly wasn't a social call then.

He swore quietly and Sam saw his face properly for the first time in the reflected light of the hall. His eyes were dark and angry. He looked absolutely furious.

16

'He's just leaving,' Abby said.

'I'm going nowhere.' Now Sam could see that he had his foot wedged in the door so that Abby couldn't shut it. She wondered fleetingly if he was drunk. He didn't sound it.

She stepped forward, intending to tell him to sling his hook, although she'd probably have worded it in stronger terms than that. Abby was in tears and every protective instinct Sam had was bristling. But then Paul said something, directly to Sam, that stopped her in her tracks.

'Until three hours ago, I didn't even know I was a bloody father. Do you think that's fair? I know you're her friend, Sam, but can you really look me in the eyes and tell me that's OK?'

Sam halted beside Abby. Somehow she didn't even need to look at Abby's face to know that Paul was telling the truth. Everything suddenly made sense: his lack of communication, his apparent lack of interest in his son, not to mention Abby's total point-blank refusal to talk about any of it. Sam had thought that was odd, but she'd also thought Abby would talk about it in her own time.

Sam's heart was thudding hard. Confrontations were never

good, but an out-of-the-blue Sunday night one on your doorstep was right on up there with the worst. Aware of Jack in bed and Abby's pain she felt her placatory instincts kick in. 'I'm sure we can get this all sorted out. Let's calm down.'

There was a small silence, filled only with the sound of their breathing. Paul's was heavy with anger, Abby's was ragged and her own felt faltering. She put an arm around Abby's narrow shoulders and Abby sagged very slightly against her.

'It might be best if we took this into the lounge,' she said gently, aware that unless Paul removed his foot from just inside the door, they couldn't shut him out anyway. Brute force wasn't going to work. He was a big guy. Not that she expected him to get physical or violent, but he was clearly a man on a mission. 'I'll make some coffee,' she added as Abby nodded, defeated. 'Are you OK with that?'

'I'll have to be, I guess.' Abby sniffed and stood back from the door so that Paul could get in.

'Thank you.' He came into the hall, bringing the smell of night air in with him on his wax jacket and jeans. His hair was the same dark unruly mop that Sam remembered.

Paul was the epitome of rock musician cum bad boy. Abby had been smitten with him on and off for as long as Sam could remember, right back to when they'd first left school. Paul had grown up in Swanage like they had, but their relationship had always been more storm-blasted beach than calm seas.

Sam sighed as she watched the pair of them head towards the lounge door, which she had left ajar. She went to make coffee. She should probably have said more, set some kind of boundary about how long he should stay. She didn't want to be unsupportive, but she was acutely aware that this this wasn't her battle either.

She didn't blame Paul for being angry. Anyone would be angry in his shoes. On the other hand, Abby must have had her reasons for not telling him about Jack. There would be a lot more to it than met the eye. There always was with Abby. Sam knew this wasn't going to be sorted out in five minutes.

In the kitchen, her phone pinged while she was making the coffee. It was her mother asking if she was OK.

Sam phoned her back and told her in swift, hushed tones about Paul's reappearance. 'I'll phone you tomorrow and, Mum, thanks so much again about the money. I'm blown away.'

She took the tray of coffee mugs into the lounge. There were no raised voices as she pushed open the door. Progress then. She discovered they were sitting at opposite ends of the couch. Paul's arms were folded and he hadn't taken off his coat. His long jeans-clad legs were bent stiffly in front of him. He looked as though he was poised for flight.

Abby's hands were clasped in her lap.

'I can't believe you thought I wouldn't want to know,' Paul was saying quietly.

They both glanced up and Sam put the tray on the table. 'I'll leave you to it, guys. I'll be in the kitchen if you want me.'

* * *

About half an hour later, Sam heard the front door bang, and a couple of moments after that Abby came into the kitchen. She looked tear-stained but resolute.

Sam got up from the kitchen table where she'd just opened a pack of chocolate biscuits, having felt in dire need of a sugar fix. 'Are you OK, honey? I'm sorry about letting him in. But I didn't think we'd get rid of him if we didn't.'

'No, I'm sorry. I shouldn't have put you in that position. I knew he'd find out sooner or later. I guess I wasn't expecting him to just turn up. He bumped into Matt, would you believe, in the Co-op in

Swanage. It didn't help that my brother gave him a right mouthful about abandoning me. Oh shit. What a mess.' Her eyes were full of tears.

'Did Matt tell him you were here?'

'No, he worked that bit out for himself. Process of elimination. Where else would I be?' She wiped her face with a tissue and sighed. 'I didn't even know he was back in the area.'

'Where did you think he was?'

'Glastonbury. That's where he went last time we split up. To join some fecking band who were right on the brink of fame but needed a lead guitarist. They were about to sign with a big label.' She yawned. 'Like I said before, same old, bloody same old. They didn't. Needless to say!'

'Is that where he's been ever since?'

'No. He came back a while ago apparently, when things didn't work out. Honestly, Sam, when will he ever learn?' There was hurt in her voice. 'Mind you, I guess it's only luck that he hasn't bumped into Matt – or anyone else who knows about Jack – before.'

Sam nodded. So that explained Abby's reluctance to go out very much. She must have been worried she'd bump into Paul sooner or later.

'The last time we split up, I gave Paul an ultimatum. Do you remember?'

'Yes. Settle down and get a steady job or ship out, wasn't it?'

'I think it was ruder than that, but yeah, basically that was it. I didn't know that I was pregnant then. I didn't find out until a few weeks after he'd gone.'

Sam knew there was a gap, but she'd always assumed Abby had told Paul as soon as she'd found out. In fact, she was pretty sure Abby had said she'd done this and he hadn't been interested, but she let this go.

'He just walked away without a backward glance.' Abby reached for a chocolate biscuit and broke it into quarters. She put one quarter in her mouth. She always ate them like that. 'He gave me all the usual bollocks about how this time it would be different. I've heard it so many times, Sam. Something inside me just snapped.'

Sam could understand this perfectly. She'd heard it quite a few times too. OK, so it had been second-hand from Abby, but she had found it wearing, so God knows what it had been like for her friend having a boyfriend who would always put his music dreams before anything else in his life. 'I do get it,' she said gently.

'I know you do. I was fed up with being the breadwinner, the responsible one, and Paul being totally selfish.' Abby ate the second of the biscuit quarters. 'And I know that sounds mad to you, because you've always been hyper responsible and I just bound along like a baby kangaroo who hasn't learned to jump in a straight line, but out of Paul and me, I am definitely the responsible one.'

'I know you are, although that's quite a good metaphor.'

Abby acknowledged this with a raise of her eyebrows. 'When I realised I was pregnant, I didn't feel as though anything had changed. I know that probably sounds crazy now, but at the time it seemed totally logical. Paul would come back for a bit until the next big opportunity came along and then he'd be gone again. But this time he'd be deserting us both. I didn't want that to happen. I couldn't bear that to happen.'

'The only thing I don't understand is why you didn't tell me all this before, honey.'

'Because I thought you'd try and talk me into telling him. But you wouldn't have done, would you?'

Sam shook her head.

'It's easy with hindsight. I should have trusted you.' Abby ate the rest of the biscuit. 'Matt's sent me three texts tonight to warn me that he bumped into Paul today. Too little too late.' There was an echo of bitterness in her voice. 'Although I suppose I can't blame Matt. He'd assumed Paul knew. There was nearly a punch-up.'

'How did you leave it with Paul?'

'He wants to see Jack, which I said he could. It wouldn't be fair on Jack to stop him seeing his father. Not long term. The time frame's up to me. Talking of time frames…' she glanced at her watch. 'It's nearly midnight. Sorry again, Sam. You've got to get up for work and you look worn out. We should go to bed.'

At the top of the stairs, they paused and, just before they went off to their respective bedrooms, Sam said, 'You didn't let Paul see him tonight, then?'

'Only through the baby monitor. I didn't want to disturb Jack. Paul's got the rest of his life to catch up with his son.'

'For what it's worth, I think you're doing the right thing.' Sam held out her arms. 'Girlfriend hug.'

'Sweet dreams,' Abby murmured as they drew apart and Sam echoed the sentiment, even though she had a feeling that sleep wouldn't come easy tonight.

She was right. It took ages to drop off and then when she did, it felt as though seconds passed before her alarm blared into action.

* * *

'How was your weekend?' Elannah said, as Sam slid, bleary-eyed, behind her workstation. She'd managed to get in on time with seconds to spare, although there was no sign of Hypochondriac Heather. Great. That was all she needed – covering Heather's work today as well as her own. She could manage on no sleep as long as she didn't have to concentrate too much.

'I had a great weekend, thanks. Er busy. Where's Heather?'

'In the loo, chucking up.' Elannah's eyes gleamed with curiosity. 'Do you think she's pregnant?'

'Heather? No way.' Sam wasn't sure why the idea should be so surprising. Heather was married and she wasn't that much different in age to her. Sam realised that she had no idea what Heather's views on children were. Unlike Elannah, she kept her cards close to her chest as far as her personal life went. She had pictures of villas and tropical islands, white beaches and palm trees, pinned onto the corkboard at her workstation.

There was one particularly big photo in the middle and that was of a white villa in the Bahamas. It was set on a hillside and in the distance you could see the turquoise sea. For ages Sam had assumed, like everyone else in the office, that it was some dreamed-of holiday destination and then one day Heather had told them it was actually a picture she had downloaded from Rightmove.co.uk

'It's the kind of place I'm going to live in one day,' she'd said, her face completely serious. 'I'm practising visualisation. If you can see it, you can dream about it and then one day you can have it. It works,' she had snapped when Magpie had burst out laughing. 'You should try it.'

Sam had pictures of dogs, cats and horses over her workstation, along with the odd Charlie Mackesy illustration. Perhaps she should pin a few pictures of dog fields up there. Maybe that would help her to acquire one.

'I can't imagine Heather having kids,' Lightning said, coming across to give Sam a USB stick and jolting her back into the present. He must have been eavesdropping. 'When would she ever be well enough to look after them? She's more likely just building up to another sickie...'

'Shhh,' Elannah broke across him and Sam saw that Heather was just coming back across the office.

She must have sensed they'd been talking about her because she glared around at their faces.

'We were just wondering if you were OK?' Sam said, embarrassed. It was horrible knowing you were the subject of unknown gossip.

'I'm fine. Just something I ate.' Heather wiped her face and sat at her desk. She did look a little pale. But at least she wasn't going home. For now.

* * *

The day ticked along. At lunchtime, Sam switched on her mobile and called her mother. 'Sorry about last night. Is it OK if I pop round after work tonight or tomorrow for a catch up?'

'Either's fine, darling.'

Then she sent Ben, her landlord, an email, asking him if he'd ever considered selling his field. She got an email back almost immediately and her heart banged with anticipation, but it wasn't from Ben. It was a notification to tell her she'd got a message from a man on Countryside Lovers who was wondering if she'd like to 'get to know him better'?

She deleted it. After the lunch with Danny Bowkett – good grief had that only been Saturday? – Sam had gone off the whole dating idea. It may be better, she decided, to focus on work, or more specifically, Purbeck Pooches.

She wasn't as enamoured with the concept of visualisation as Heather was, but she did know one thing for certain. If you wanted to do something, then focusing on it, was quite a good first step.

When she switched her phone on again at the end of the day, she had a flurry of messages. There was one from Abby saying she had gone out to talk things through with Paul and that Sam shouldn't worry if she wasn't back early. That lifted Sam's spirits. It would be great if they could work things out and come to some kind of amicable agreement. There was one from Danny Bowkett, thanking her for the lunch and saying he meant it about them being friends. And there was one from her mother saying tomorrow would be better than tonight.

She texted a good luck message to Abby, told Danny she felt the same and an 'OK, thanks' to her mum.

There was nothing from Ben about the field. Sam wasn't surprised. Ben often took ages to answer his emails. She would phone him in a couple of days if she hadn't had a reply. It would be good to know what her options were.

She was just signing out of her PC – she had somehow managed to be the last one to finish work again – when Rex came out of his office. She hadn't seen him all day. She hadn't seen much of him at all since their works fun day. He'd been immersed in some new data protection regulations that had just been brought in and which had involved him having to update some databases. Elannah was doing some of the work, but apparently there were certain bits he had to do himself.

He seemed as surprised to see her as she was to see him.

'Sam…' He paused by her desk. 'Is everything OK?'

'Yes. I was just finishing something.'

'Thank you. That's very conscientious.' He rested his briefcase on the adjoining desk and put his hands on it. 'I'm going to The Anchor on my way home for a drink. Would you like to join me?'

She looked at him. She couldn't have been more astounded if he'd asked her to accompany him on a trip to the moon.

'Don't worry if you have other plans.' Surely he wasn't blushing. It must be a trick of the light.

'I don't.' The words came out of her mouth unbidden. 'That would be nice. Yes. Why not?'

Her body agreed. There was a little flutter of pleasure in her stomach as she picked up her bag. It must be the thought of a nice relaxing glass of wine.

17

It made sense for them to go in convoy and as Sam followed Rex's top-of-the-range metallic silver Saab along the narrow country road, she wondered if he'd just asked her on impulse, or whether he'd actually wanted to talk to her about something work-related.

Neither option seemed that likely – Rex didn't seem to do much on impulse and if he'd wanted to talk to her about work, then surely she'd have been summoned to his inner sanctum, where she presumed he felt at home, with his mints and the smell of dust and old books.

Sam stopped trying to second-guess his motives. She would find out soon enough. Ten minutes later, they arrived at The Anchor. Because of its position on the main road, it got a lot of passing trade, but it also attracted the locals because the food was good. The season was short in the Isle of Purbeck and the competition was fierce, which meant the food was excellent almost everywhere you went because bars and restaurants had to attract the locals as well as tourists.

Sam parked beside Rex in the large car park and they walked across towards the pub, alongside which was an outside seating area, a patio garden that was chock-a-block with colourful hanging baskets and tubs of bright flowers.

Rex paused just before they reached the doors. 'Would you prefer inside or out?'

'Inside, please.' The patio was for romance and lovers, an intimate little Garden of Eden. Inside, there was a bar and a large eating area with tables galore, where people gathered for after-work drinks or pre-dinner ones with their friends. It still felt odd, though, to be out with her boss.

Sam watched Rex come back to the table she had picked with two tall glasses. She'd asked for a lime and soda and it looked like he'd got something similar. Ice clinked in both glasses as he put them down and sat opposite.

'I've been meaning to catch up with you, Sam. And there never seems to be time at work. I wanted to ask you how things are going with Purbeck Pooches?'

Oh my goodness, so that was what this was about. He wanted to talk to her about moonlighting. Sam was surprised he'd remembered the name of her company. It must have been playing on his mind. Did he think she wasn't doing her job properly?

Before she could answer, he smiled at her. 'Don't look so worried. It's just idle curiosity. I'm aware that you having your own business doesn't impact on you working for me.'

'I don't think it does.' She was wary nonetheless. What was this? A fishing expedition to see if she was planning on leaving any time soon?

'I've done a fair bit of moonlighting myself,' he went on before she could decide what else to say.

'Really? How come? I thought you'd always worked for yourself?' She should probably have edited that. It sounded a bit rude, but he didn't seem fazed.

'Well, yes, Fielding's was my father's company, as I suspect you know. I grew up knowing that I was expected to go into the family business. Follow in his footsteps, if you like. I'm an only child and my father was keen that I work for him. With him,' he amended with a slight frown. 'I wasn't so enthusiastic.'

'What did you want to do?' Sam was intrigued despite herself. Rex didn't seem the type to go against family tradition. He hadn't gone against it, obviously, but she'd always assumed, as she was sure everyone else who worked for him did, that he'd been happy to take on the mantle of the family business when his father had died.

'By trade, I'm a carpenter,' Rex said and he sounded hesitant, as if he wasn't used to saying the words aloud, as though they felt slightly awkward on his tongue. 'I make furniture. When I was young, I had a dream that one day I'd set up a high-end furniture business where I'd make things to order.'

'Gosh. What kind of things?' Sam leaned forward, totally fascinated, and Rex looked startled.

'Tables, er, chairs... I still make the odd thing as a hobby. Just to amuse myself, you know. It would be easier to show you.' He hooked his phone out of his pocket and she saw him touch the photos icon. For a moment, he scrolled through a screen of pictures. There seemed to be dozens. She wondered what kind of pictures they were – they were unlikely to be the silly WhatsApp pictures that cluttered up her phone. Then he passed the phone to her and Sam found herself looking at a coffee table. It had a small half moon-shaped base, joined by one curved leg to the bigger circular table itself, but instead of being made entirely of smoothly polished wood, on one side its edges looked more like natural bark. The effect was rustic and stunning.

'Oh wow. That's beautiful. Totally gorgeous.' She knew she was gushing but it was true.

'It's what you call a live edge,' he said, in the same serious tone of voice he always used. 'It's horse chestnut. It echoes what the tree once was, I don't like things to be too forced and manufactured, too uniform.'

'No,' she breathed. 'Are there more?'

He nodded and shifted his mismatched chair round closer to hers so he could show her other pictures.

For the next few minutes, she scrolled through shots of tables. None of them were the same. Some, like the coffee table, had what he'd called a live edge. Others were more traditional, with rounded edges or polished corners, but none of them, as he'd said, looked like the IKEA mass-produced perfection. In each one, echoes of the tree it had once been were still visible. Each had a nod back to its heritage, as if some part of it was still alive. And every single one of them was undoubtedly beautiful.

Sam was speechless. In her wildest dreams, she would never have thought that Rex would have a skill like this.

She glanced up at him. He looked nervous. Suddenly they were no longer employee and boss, but two people sharing a passion.

'They're fantastic,' she said. 'This is what you should be spending your life doing. Not just in your spare time, I don't mean that. But all of your time. You're so talented. How did you learn this stuff?'

He dipped his head in that self-deprecating way he had, but she could tell he was really pleased by her enthusiasm.

A waitress was hovering by their table. 'Would sir and madam be wanting to eat tonight?' Her words broke the spell.

Rex looked at her. 'Are you hungry? I don't want to keep you from anything?'

'You're not,' Sam said, realising it was true. Abby wasn't at home expecting her. There were no animals needing her attention. Also, she realised in the next heartbeat, and with a little flicker of surprise, she didn't actually want to be anywhere else right now. She wanted to be here. The smell of food filtered into her awareness. 'Actually I am hungry. Shall we have a sandwich?' She looked back into his eyes. They were more grey than blue in this light.

'A sandwich it is.'

They ordered swiftly, neither of them was particularly interested in food, and when the waitress had gone again, they got back to wood. Sam felt as though she'd pushed open the door to Rex's world a crack, but now it was open he had let her in.

'When I was younger, I had a workshop in our garden at home. It was a shed really... but it was my sanctuary. It was where I learned to make things.'

'On your own?' Sam had a sudden vivid image of a serious little boy. A much smaller version of Rex holed up in a shed playing with wood. This was so reminiscent of her own childhood that it momentarily stole her breath. Only she had escaped to the company of animals, to Felix and to Spot. And animals had become her passion. Maybe all passions began in childhood and were born out of loneliness.

'No, not on my own. My grandfather was a master craftsman. I learned huge amounts from him. He liked to work with oak. He was more of a traditionalist than I am, but I prefer ash. Ash,' he said, 'is a bit like oak on steroids. If that makes any sense. It's more like oak than oak is and it's much easier to work with.'

It didn't really make sense, but it didn't matter, because his eyes were on fire. She had never seen Rex like this – he was light years from the stiff and serious persona that had earned him the name RoboBoss.

'You're right though,' he continued. 'When I'm working with wood, I feel as though I'm doing what I was put on this earth to do. I've never looked at it like that before.'

'I think it might be like that with all passions: music, writing, art...' She spread her hands to indicate that it didn't matter what subject it was as long as you were passionate. 'I can't do any of those things. As you know, I'm just passionate about animals, but I completely understand the feelings.' Bloody hell was she really having a conversation about feelings with Suit Man? RoboBoss? Where had that come from? It was definitely time to change the subject. 'What do you do with the things you make?'

'I've got some at home in my garage. Actually, I can't get in my garage for all the furniture.' He shook his head ruefully. 'I've given away the odd piece to people who've admired it. Friends, the occasional girlfriend.'

That was another thing she'd never heard him mention before. Girlfriends. Of course, he must have girlfriends. She didn't think he was gay, but she realised she had never heard him discuss going on a date. But then he wouldn't, would he? Rex wasn't the sort of boss who shared out his private life in snippets of gossip to entertain the troops. He was aloof – she'd always thought of it as uptight, but he hadn't been uptight tonight. The man sitting in front of her was as far from uptight as it was possible to be. He was relaxed and confident and at peace with himself.

Weirdly, the mention of girlfriends had twanged something in her stomach. *Reality check, Sam. He's your boss. Not a friend with whom you can be indiscreet.* She mentally reined herself in. And almost as if he'd picked up on it, he changed the subject.

'You say I should spend my life focusing on my passion,' Rex said, 'but that isn't what you're doing, is it? I had the impression when we talked before that Purbeck Pooches is your passion, but you work for me.' He steepled his hands in RoboBoss fashion and studied her. 'So how does that compute?'

They were back where they'd started, Sam realised. Moonlighting.

Fortunately, their food arrived at that moment so she didn't have to answer him straight away. Their sandwiches came with chips that smelled glorious and reminded her she was hungry, and little bowls of salad. There was the dishing out of knives and forks and serviettes and the polite passing of condiments, which gave her time to gather her thoughts. She couldn't think of a tactful way of telling him that Purbeck Pooches might be her passion, but it was working for him that paid the bills. Anyway, surely he must know this. So in the end she just came straight out with it.

'Purbeck Pooches isn't established enough for me to give up my day job. Maybe one day I'll have to choose, but I thought at the beginning I would just do both for a while and see what happened. I didn't really think of it as moonlighting. I don't want to stop working for you.' To her surprise she realised this was true and it was no longer just financial.

'I'm glad to hear it. You're very good at your job.' He opened a sachet of tomato sauce and squirted it carefully onto a corner of his plate. 'They don't call it moonlighting any more. I think the modern term is portfolio working, isn't it, Sam?'

She nodded. 'My parents say that portfolio working is just another word for not putting all your eggs in one basket.'

'Your parents sound wise.'

For a while they ate in silence, but it was a comfortable silence. Sam felt as though they were in a bubble of peace that only they inhabited within the background hum of chatter in the pub. It was Rex who broke it by bringing the conversation back to Purbeck Pooches.

'Going back to your situation,' he said carefully, 'I suppose the best way to do portfolio working is to have a job that brings in money without having to put in too many hours.'

She nodded. Danny Bowkett had said much the same thing. The dog field swirled in her mind.

'One of the things I wanted to talk to you about is hours.'

'Oh?' She looked at him.

He cleared his throat. 'I trust that you will keep this confidential for now, but Heather is going to be off on maternity leave in the not too distant future.'

She didn't tell him that the office grapevine was already ahead of him. 'I see. Wow. And yes of course I will.'

'Obviously I will need to employ someone to cover her maternity leave, but I thought it would be good to talk to you first. It's an opportunity to change how we do things in the office. We could, for example, have job sharing, or we could have a couple of part-time employees, or more than a couple. Or we could keep things as they are, whatever suits...'

'Are you saying that I could go part-time or I could job share?'

'That is exactly what I'm saying. You could also stay full-time, if that's your preferred option, but I wanted to give you the choice, Sam. I thought that maybe, in your current situation, you might like some more flexibility.' He had gone all formal again, but then maybe that wasn't surprising. They were back on office talk.

She realised with a little start that he was waiting for her to answer.

'I need to think about it, if that's OK? I'll need to work out my finances and stuff. But thank you. Yes, I think job sharing could be really good. I would love to be able to build up Purbeck Pooches. When do you need a decision?' Aware that she was babbling, she shut up.

'There is absolutely no rush.' He wiped a smear of tomato sauce from his mouth with a serviette. He had really nice-shaped lips. Ryan Gosling-shaped lips. It wasn't just the eyes.

Sam blinked. Good grief, what was she thinking? He was Rex Fielding. He was not Ryan Gosling. He may look like him a bit, but he was not him. He was her boss. RoboBoss. He was not even vaguely fanciable. There was some part of her that disagreed with that last thought.

Flustered, she reached for her glass of lime and soda and

realised it was empty, there was just ice clinking in the bottom of the glass.

'Would you like another one?

'Um, thanks.

She had time to gather her thoughts as he went up to the bar. She glanced after him and was struck with the force of déjà vu. A different man, a different location and a totally different feeling. Had it only been Saturday that she had looked at Danny Bowkett and had thought dispassionately that he was a nice-looking guy but she was totally uninterested?

Yes it had.

She glanced at Rex's rear view. He was wearing a suit, as always. Today's was light grey, but he had taken off his jacket earlier when they had been talking about wood. His trousers were close-fitting enough for her to be able to see the muscular curve of a thigh, the outline of his bum.

She became aware that she was staring at her boss's bum, but it was difficult to drag her gaze away. There were gremlins playing with her head. Or maybe she really was finally losing the plot. Perhaps she was working too hard and was overtired. She should definitely take up his offer to reduce her hours.

By the time he got back from the bar, she had recovered control over her feelings. They were all firmly stuffed back in a locked box and she had the key safely back in her pocket.

It must have been shock, she decided, that had made him seem so attractive. The shock of discovering that Rex Fielding was human after all. That RoboBoss had a passion. Not to mention the fact that he had also just offered her a way out of the dilemma she'd had for some time. She could go part-time and focus on Purbeck Pooches. If Ben agreed, she could set up a dog field. With the support of her parents' gift, she could give Purbeck Pooches a fighting chance of becoming a success.

Thanks to Rex's thoughtfulness she had even more options. No wonder she was re-evaluating him in her mind. She was re-evaluating everything. Over the past twenty-four hours, everything had changed. Actually over the past twenty-four minutes, everything had changed.

Rex placed her glass in front of her and picked up his own. 'We should have a toast,' he said.

'To what?'

'Possibilities and passions?'

'I'm up for those.' She clinked her glass against his.

'Possibilities and passions,' they said in unison. Their fingers touched. She felt the jolt of something that was much more powerful than static electricity. She met his eyes and looked hurriedly away. Heck, had he felt it too?

18

Sam had been surprised to find Abby had got back to Beach Cottage before her until she'd realised it was gone nine p.m. She and Rex must have sat in The Anchor chatting for three hours solid. Where had the time gone?

She and Abby were now in the kitchen, which smelled deliciously of creamy hot chocolate and cinnamon, sipping from mugs which had dark chocolate sprinkles on the froth. The perfect nightcap, Abby had decided recently, for a breastfeeding mother.

'So how did it go with Paul?'

Abby looked flushed and buoyant, which was a good sign. She was in her *Friends* jimjams now, but she'd obviously got dressed up to see Paul because she hadn't yet taken off her make-up. She still had her rose dust lippie on. She hadn't worn that for a while.

'It went very well. All things considered.' Abby pursed her lips. 'I didn't cave in, though, Sam. I told him exactly what the score was. Having a kid changes things.' She cupped her hands around her mug of hot chocolate and, for a second, she looked so vulnerable that Sam wanted to hug her. 'I'm not gullible enough to think that Paul's had a personality transplant,' she said more softly, 'but I do think he wants to make a go of being a dad. He was lovely with Jack. He was holding him as though he was some precious fragile vase and there were tears in his eyes.'

'That is such great news.' Sam studied her across the kitchen table. 'Does he want you to be part of the package, too?'

'Yes, he wants us to get back together.' Abby dipped her gaze. 'I haven't agreed to that. I've told him that we'll have to take things slowly. We'll have to see how it goes. I'm not about to rush back into anything. I'm being a grown-up.' Her lips quirked as she met Sam's eyes again. 'Well, I'm trying my best to be a grown-up.'

'I have trouble with that too.'

'I don't think you do. I think you have trouble being irresponsible. Where have you been anyway?'

'Out with my boss. I think I've fallen for him.' Gosh, had she said that out loud? She hadn't meant to, even though she had felt the sizzle of that touch still tingling in her fingers all the way home.

'You've fallen for Suit Man? No way.' Abby leaned forward and rested the back of her hand on Sam's forehead. 'Have you got a temperature?

'I think I must have.

'Hmmm, it doesn't feel like it. What were you doing going out with your boss anyway? I thought he was allergic to socialising. Apart from "Designated Works Outings for Team Bonding".' She spoke in her plummiest voice and mimed the inverted commas around the words. She'd only met Rex a couple of times, yet she had him down pat.

'He is. He was. I didn't say it made sense, did I?' She was still trying to get her head around it too. 'He wanted to talk about restructuring the office. Hypochondriac Heather is pregnant. He mentioned job shares. It means I could go part-time. I could focus on Purbeck Pooches.'

'Well, that's brilliant news. I'll help you with the website and marketing. That'll be fun. You've wanted this for months. No wonder you've fallen for him.'

'I know.' Sam felt light-headed. Abby wasn't taking this seriously. 'But I don't think that's the reason.'

'Sleep on it. That's my advice. It worked with Paul.'

No wonder she wasn't taking anything seriously. She must be all over the place.

Sam forced herself back into a world where her housemate and best friend was dealing with serious things like her child's future with his father. 'It really is great news about Paul.'

'Baby steps.' Abby rested her chin in her hands and considered something. 'So what happened with Suit Man? Did he make a pass at you?'

'No.'

'Did you make a pass at him?'

'No.' Sam's thoughts flicked back to the memory of the moment when she'd noticed Rex's lips. The moment of electricity when their fingers had touched.

'Was anything said? By him or by you?' Abby pressed.

'Nope.'

'So it was all in your head?'

'I guess it probably was.'

She didn't really think this was true. There had been something in his eyes when he'd made that toast. And she had felt that jolt. She guessed she would find out the next day whether she was or wasn't imagining it. Things would be different when they were both in the cold grey daylight of the office.

She would go and see him and tell him that, yes, she would like to cut her hours. He'd said it wouldn't be straight away. Heather could only be a few weeks pregnant. There would be time for her to build up Purbeck Pooches. Do more advertising. Think about what she could and couldn't do in terms of boarding. In truth, she knew she just wanted an excuse to see him again.

* * *

But the next day when she got into work, Rex wasn't in. 'He's taken some time off to go and see his mother,' Elannah told her. 'Apparently she had a fall and she's broken her hip.'

'Oh my goodness. Is she OK? When did that happen?' Sam leaped out of her chair and went across to Elannah's workstation.

'Late yesterday, I think. He said he had a call about ten and he went over to take her to hospital.'

So he must have got home from seeing her to get that awful news. Sam shook her head in distress.

'How old is she?' Heather piped up from her desk. She hadn't mentioned being pregnant yet and everyone was pretending they hadn't noticed her frequent trips to the cloakroom. 'Broken hips are very dodgy once you get to a certain age. It's the beginning of the downhill slope.'

'I don't know how old she is,' Elannah said. 'He doesn't confide in me about his personal life. I didn't even know she was still alive.'

Sam felt a little pang at the memory of how much Rex had confided in her the previous evening. She wondered if Elannah knew about their after-work drink. Or if Elannah had ever been out with him herself. She had certainly never mentioned it. Sam decided not to mention last night either, unless Elannah did.

Maybe Rex hadn't told his PA about the possible restructuring of the office. Actually, he probably hadn't. He would have needed to make sure there was going to be a restructuring first and that had been partially dependent on her. His PA couldn't job share as easily. Audio typing was easy to divvy up. PA work would involve more complicated handovers.

Sam was disappointed that he wasn't in though, a little too disappointed for it just to be about discussing job shares. She turned her thoughts resolutely back to work.

* * *

Rex didn't come back in for the rest of the week. Sam's loose arrangement to see her parents on Tuesday got put back to Friday. 'We'll have slightly more time then,' her mum had said. 'Especially if you come early.'

She went straight from work. It felt odd, she thought, as she walked through the summer evening up to the tree-lined road, to know that she wouldn't be making the familiar journey very many more times.

The completion date on their sale, 21 September, was five weeks away. Belinda's B&B would belong to someone else. Sam wondered if the new owners would still keep the name.

'I think they will for now,' her mother told her. 'It's part of the branding. Part of the good reputation that the business has. They might rebrand eventually, but then they'd have to start again on everything – Tripadvisor reviews, Yelp, the lot.

'Yes, I guess they would.'

Sam glanced around them. Her father was in the bar serving, but she and her mother were sitting in the small sitting room at the back of the kitchen, which was the private accommodation part of the B&B. There were packing boxes piled up everywhere and there were gaps on the shelves and oblongs of space on the walls where framed pictures had been. Her mother had said they'd agreed to leave virtually everything behind. They would take only what was most personal to them.

'Will you miss this place?' Sam asked her now.

'Yes and no.' There was an air of suppressed excitement about her mother. 'It's hard to imagine not being in a place where you've spent the last thirty years of your life. I won't miss the workload, I can tell you that for nothing. It's definitely got tougher these last couple of years.'

Sam looked at her face. There were creases of tiredness around her eyes and today's make-up had faded until there was barely a trace, but she did look animated.

'The thought of getting up and not knowing what I'm going to be doing for the next twenty-four hours is hugely exciting. I can't believe that's going to be us in a few weeks' time.'

'Me neither. You and Dad won't know yourselves. And I'm sorry again about being so selfish before.'

'You weren't being selfish, darling. It was a shock. Change is always a shock.'

'Have you found somewhere to rent yet?'

'No, but we've got two places to see this weekend. There are some details over there.' She gestured and Sam jumped up to get the printed A4 sheets. She found herself looking at two pretty bungalows.

'They're both really local,' she said in delight. 'I never thought you'd end up in Swanage.'

'Neither did we, but it's a question of what's available. They're both short-term lets, three months, with an option to extend on a month-by-month basis. That'll give us some breathing space while we look properly for somewhere to buy.'

'Have you had any more thoughts on that?'

'We're keeping our options open. But neither of us want to be too far from you, darling. We have decided that. We've been talking a lot about how it was when your gran and grandad upped sticks and went to the Orkneys. We wished them well, but we missed them too.' Her eyes clouded. 'Now then, enough of us. How about you? How is the online dating going? Have you met anyone nicer than that Ned chap? Why do people use fake photos? He must have known he'd be rumbled the second you clapped eyes on him.'

'You would think so, wouldn't you? But he seemed to think that it was perfectly acceptable to use someone else's photo if you didn't have a recent one of your own. Not only that but he was deluded enough to think that he actually looked like the guy. He didn't. Believe me.' She hadn't given Ned another thought until now, she realised.

Her mother stifled a giggle and Sam met her gaze. Moments later, they were both laughing out loud.

When they'd recovered enough to speak, her mother leaned across and patted Sam's arm. 'I guess things were easier when I was young. People couldn't hide behind a computer. I was really lucky meeting your dad the way I did.'

Sam nodded. The story of how her parents had met was legendary. They had both been at a Shakespearean-themed fancy dress party where neither of them had known anyone except the host. Her father had gone as Romeo and her mother had gone as Puck and they had got chatting over the buffet table.

'Please can you rescue me from Juliet,' he had whispered halfway through their conversation, indicating a woman in a white dress who was bearing down on them. 'I mean, she's a nice enough girl, but she won't leave me alone.'

'Maybe it's your destiny to end up with a woman called Juliet.'

'God, I hope not.'

'But you did come dressed as Romeo. What were you expect—'

He had chosen that moment to grab her in his arms and kiss her full on the mouth.

'In normal circumstances, he'd have got a slap for his trouble,' her mother usually said at this point in the story. 'But I was so surprised. And he was such a good kisser.' It was also at this point that her voice would soften and her parents would look at each other tenderly.

It was her father who normally supplied the punchline. 'It wasn't until I asked her to get engaged that she told me her middle name was Juliet. So destiny did have a hand after all!'

Sam was jolted out of the memory by her mother's voice. 'Will you risk meeting someone again?'

'I already have. I went out with a really nice guy last Saturday, although I don't think that's going anywhere.' She definitely owed Danny a drink, though, for the field idea. 'There was no chemistry.'

'There has to be chemistry,' her mother agreed.

Sam decided to keep quiet about Rex. She still wasn't sure what had happened between them. Maybe nothing.

She realised her mother had just asked her a question. 'Sorry. What did you say?'

'I was wondering whether you had decided what you were going to do with your business bonus yet.'

She dragged her thoughts away from Rex. 'Actually, I want to talk to you and Dad about that. I do have an idea. This might sound crazy, but I'm thinking of buying a field. Is Dad going to be in the bar all evening, do you think?'

'No he isn't,' said a voice from the door. 'Hello, princess. I've excused myself from landlord duties for a bit. They can ring the bell if they want more drinks. What's this about a field?'

For the next ten minutes, Sam told them about her plans to set up a dog field and then she showed them the ones she had found online on her phone. 'I think it would be a really good investment. People will always have dogs. Lots of people have more than one these days and they don't want them racing around as a pack in public spaces. There's too much litigation.'

Neither of her parents spoke immediately, but the atmosphere had changed in the room and she could tell that they weren't quite as enamoured about her plans as she was. It was her father who broke the pause.

'It sounds as though you've thought it through and I agree that a field could be viable, but fields are expensive. What is it – about an acre?'

'About that.'

He was frowning she realised, perturbed.

'What?' she asked.

'You'd need to get in some pretty secure fencing, Sam. That won't be cheap for an acre. But it would be essential to make it dog-proof.'

'Yes, I know that.' Sam thought about the ease with which Snowy had made her escape and she felt her heart ratchet down anther few notches. Maybe she had let her heart rule her head. If the expression on her father's face was anything to go by, he didn't think it was a good idea.

'Does your landlord definitely want to sell it?' her mother asked tentatively.

'He's phoning me this weekend to have a chat about it.' Ben had finally texted her back. 'But he hasn't actually said yes or no yet.'

Her dad was nodding slowly. 'I'm not against the idea in principle, princess, but it would probably take up most of your money. It won't be cheap and what will you do if you decide to move house? Or if Ben decides to sell Beach Cottage? It would be hard to oversee a field if you weren't on the premises.'

'What sort of agreement do you have with Ben regarding the house?' her mum asked. 'Isn't that fairly informal?'

'Yes.'

She saw her parents exchange glances. Everything they were saying made sense and, unlike her, they were looking at her business idea without the benefit of rose-tinted glasses, but that didn't change the fact that she felt as though her dream was being dismantled before her eyes.

'You don't think it's a good idea, do you?' she said, trying to keep the disappointment out of her voice.

'As I said, I think it's a good idea in principle, princess, but I'm wondering if there's a better approach.' His voice was gentle.

Sam looked around her at the little room where she had spent so much of her life: the faded burgundy, but incredibly comfy two-seater where her father was sitting, the big picture of Durdle Door that took up half of one wall. The smaller one, painted by a friend, that usually sat on the sideboard was missing. Presumably that had already been packed away. The novelty clock with the seascape background that she had bought them one Christmas was still in situ over the fake stone fireplace. She guessed that was going with them, but not until the last minute as it was the only way of telling the time out the back and neither of her parents wore a watch.

It felt as though the room was full of endings, whereas just a few minutes earlier, there had been a breathy sense of hope.

Sam looked at the patterned brown carpet. Half a dozen platitudes came to mind: It was a good dream while it lasted; As one door closes another opens. But she felt too choked to say anything.

'Maybe she could think about leasing the field, Alan?' her mother said suddenly. 'Would that work? What if you were to ask Ben for a more formal arrangement? You could arrange a long-term lease. That wouldn't be so expensive or so permanent.'

'And it would give me a chance to see how it went,' Sam said, feeling a little of her despondency lifting. 'What do you think, Dad?'

'I think that's a much better plan. That way, whatever money you spent on making the field secure would be a good investment. If you could get him to agree to a five-year lease, and maybe have something a bit more formal in place on the house as well, I think you'd be in business. There's no sense in throwing money into something that could be put at risk by someone else.'

Suddenly they were all smiling again and Sam felt a huge wash of relief. It was that relief that decided her. She had told Rex he should follow his passion and she knew she wanted to do the same, yet it was so easy to say things like that. Having rock-solid plans that actually had a chance of working was the hard bit.

'Ben might not agree. But I'm definitely going to ask him about the leasing before I take this any further.' She let out a breath. 'There's something else I need to tell you too. I've just been offered the chance to go part-time at Fielding's. I've always wanted to do that – and with your really kind offer of that money – well, it means I can focus on building Purbeck Pooches into a proper business, rather than just doing weekend boarding and the ad-hoc pet sitting I do at the moment.'

'That's excellent news,' her father said and her mother clapped her hands together. 'That's a definite – what did you call it the other day – a thumbs up from fate?'

'I did,' Sam said, pleased she'd remembered.

Also, no one had rung the bell to summon her dad back to the bar. So they'd actually managed to have a completely uninterrupted conversation for once. That was a thumbs up from fate if ever she had seen one.

19

At the weekend, Sam spoke to Ben and discovered he would be happy to lease her the field on a five-year renewable basis.

'I'm not so keen on selling just the field, Sam,' he had said in his unhurried voice. 'Which is why I've been a bit tardy about getting back to you. But I'm more than happy to give you a formal lease and for you to hire it out as a dog field. Sounds like a bloody good idea. I'm also happy to do something similar on the house front. It makes sense, so why not? I do get that you'd want to feel secure there.'

Sam was so pleased about this that she messaged Danny Bowkett to update him and to say thank you for suggesting the idea.

He messaged her back the next day saying that if she needed anyone to quote for the fencing he knew people who would do 'mates' rates'.

I meant what I said about being friends

He had added at the foot of his message:

So don't worry, there are no strings attached. If you like, I can also offer Stan's services as a scout to check your field. He's a born escape artist. All border terriers are. If your field has a weak spot, Stan will find it.

When Sam showed Abby Danny's message, she widened her eyes and said, 'Wow. He's keen on you and he also sounds like a really nice guy. Are you sure you don't fancy him? Is it worth having another date with him just to check?'

'Sadly not. But while we're on the subject of dates, how's it going with Paul?'

'We are definitely not dating.' Abby crossed her arms in denial. 'But it is going well. He's plying me with chocolates, though that's not helping my diet. And he bought Jack a "Daddy's Little Rocker" t-shirt. He is definitely not wearing that. I can't quite get my head around it. Paul's always been so anti the idea of kids. I've known him cross the road to avoid a buggy.'

'No you haven't,' Sam said, amused.

'Well, OK, I may be exaggerating slightly, but I've never known him show the slightest bit of interest in babies.'

'Yes, well it's very different when they're your own. Not to mention the fact that Jack is the most gorgeous of babies. Aren't you, angel?' Sam leaned over the Moses basket that was between them and Jack reached out chubby fingers towards her in that way he had that made her heart melt. She kissed him on the forehead, breathing in his gorgeous baby smell, and when she straightened, she felt Abby's eyes on her.

'How's the online dating going? You can't have a baby by divine conception, you know.'

'Stop it.' Sam bit her lip. Why had Rex's face swum straight into her head?

Tuning into her thoughts with unerring accuracy, Abby said, 'So have there been any developments with Suit Man? Has he seduced you over the photocopier?'

'No. He hasn't been in to work since our after-work drink?'

'Flaming heck, did you frighten him off? Hey, he doesn't know you have a potty-mouthed housemate, does he? Did he ever say anything about me telling him to eff off that day on the way to hospital?' She glanced at Jack.

'No he didn't. I'm beginning to think it couldn't have been him you spoke to. Or I'm sure he'd have said something by now.'

'Hmmm. Good. By the way, your three-word horoscope today was "*Go for it*" should you be interested. I'm not sure if that's a reference to new men or new businesses. Maybe it's both.'

Sam sighed heavily. 'Rex hasn't been into work because he's gone to look after his mum. She broke her hip.'

'Oh.' Abby frowned. 'Sorry. That's not a laughing matter. I hope she's OK.'

'So do I, and can we please change the subject? I've decided I don't have time to do any more dating anyway. If I'm going to focus on starting up a new business, I can't get distracted with men.'

Abby drew a line across her lips with her finger and thumb. 'My lips are sealed. No more nagging. If you want to find a man, you will. If you want to have a divine conception, who am I to stop you?'

Sam laughed despite herself. 'I do love you.'

'I know. I am very lovable.'

Sam rolled her eyes.

* * *

Rex was back at work the following Monday. As soon as Sam got the chance, she caught him on his own at his desk. 'How is your mother doing? I was sorry to hear she'd had an accident.'

He looked tired. He was wearing his usual suit and tie (dark olive) and outwardly he was his usual well-pressed self. But his face looked ruffled somehow. There were shadows beneath his eyes and those Ryan Gosling lips had a hint of a downturn.

'She's fine, Sam. Thanks for asking. She's back at home. She can't do much, but I'm going in once a day and so is her neighbour, Sheila. I think she was more shocked than anything. She's never broken a bone in her life. But breaking her hip has highlighted the fact that she has osteoporosis.'

'Ah. That's not good. Can they do anything about it?'

'There's medication, diet, not to mention being more careful. She fell off a ladder. She was halfway through painting the hall. Heaven only knows why she didn't get someone in. She's seventy-two. But she's got this thing about independence. I keep telling her, there's independence and there's incredibly reckless, but she doesn't take the slightest bit of notice of me. She never has... She was exactly the same with my father. Too damn proud and stubborn.' He broke off, looking slightly dazed. 'Sorry. Too much information. You didn't come in my office to talk about my mother. How can I help? Have a seat.'

Sam sat in the visitor chair. 'I hope she'll be OK. Does she live far away?' It didn't feel right to ask him about changing her hours now. He was clearly under enough pressure without having to restructure the office.

'She lives in Tolpuddle, near Dorchester. It was made famous by the Tolpuddle Martyrs. Dad used to joke that she got him to move there so she could join them.'

Sam knew the story. Six men were caught forming one of the first trade unions back in the 1800s and were sentenced to be transported to Australia. She was wondering what to say to this when Rex blinked.

'Sorry, Sam. I haven't had much sleep.' He visibly drew himself in and straightened his shoulders. 'Did you want to talk about your hours?'

'If it's not a good time, I can come back.'

'It's fine. Truly.' He pushed the bowl of Murray Mints across the desk.

She took one of the wrapped sweets. She was actually beginning to like them. 'I was only going to say that yes please, I'd like to reduce my hours to maybe twenty. I don't mind if I job share or go part-time. Whatever and whenever suits. Also...' she hesitated. 'If the situation has changed and you'd rather I just stayed full-time for a bit longer, that's OK too.'

'That's good of you.' She caught a fleeting softening in his eyes. 'But it's fine. Nothing's changed. I actually want to get this underway as soon as possible. I think it will give us a lot more flexibility. We'll be having a team meeting about it this week.'

* * *

As it turned out, things moved faster than Sam could have hoped. She had now told everyone at work about Purbeck Pooches and they'd all been very supportive. Heather had clapped. Elannah had given her a 3D bookmark with a cute picture of donkeys on it. Mumbling Mike had said he'd always known she was wasted at Fielding's, or at least that's what she thought he'd said, and Lightning had brought in cakes to celebrate. Even Magpie, who was prone to teasing, had pronounced that she'd be very good at dealing with awkward people – after all, she'd had plenty of practice with Heather.

August bank holiday flew by. Sam looked after a King Charles spaniel puppy called Dash, who had apparently been named after one Queen Victoria had owned. Dash chewed the left foot off the gender-neutral teddy bear Matt had given Jack.

'Don't worry about it,' Abby said. 'Jack much prefers Teddy Eddy who you won at the fair. Just don't tell my brother.'

Jack met a new set of grandparents – Paul's parents – who cooed over him and made Sam feel quite envious.

Foxy came for her trial night and the three-legged dog with the burnished red gold fox coat and beautiful temperament even won Abby over and she let her sneak up onto the sofa for a cuddle.

By the middle of September, Rex had advertised for the position of part-time audio typist and had sifted through dozens of CVs.

One of the candidates he liked was a woman in her sixties called Janet Brown, whose hobbies were watching murder mysteries and spending time with her grandchildren.

'She seems a very solid type,' Rex said, showing Sam her CV. 'Reliable and down-to-earth, although she hasn't been qualified long.' He pointed to the relevant section. 'She spent most of her working life being a chambermaid, but a couple of years ago she decided to go back to college and retrain. That shows initiative, don't you think? She did a secretarial course in her spare time and qualified with flying colours. She's just become a grandmother for the third time and she wants to help out with her new grandchild, hence only wanting to work part-time. What do you think?'

'She used to work at the Bluebell Cliff Hotel,' Sam said in surprise. 'That place has a great reputation. She's put Clara King down as her reference. I know Clara. I could maybe have a discreet word to ask if she's as good as she seems.'

'That would be great. I'll arrange for her to have an interview. I'm seeing a few people next week. You can meet the shortlist before I decide. You'll be the one who'll be job sharing with them. So that's only right.'

When Sam rang her, Clara King gave Janet a glowing reference and confirmed Rex's theory that she was both reliable and had initiative. 'I wouldn't have thought she would let you down. I don't think she ever let us down once. I was sorry to see her go. But getting a job in an office was her dream. It's funny actually how many of the staff who work at Bluebell Cliff end up deciding they're going to live their dream. I think the hotel must bring them luck. I think there's a little bit of magic at the Bluebell.'

'Me too,' Sam said, because while things may not have worked out with Danny on a romantic level, the Bluebell was where the idea of her dog field had been born. 'I'm looking forward to having Foxy whenever you need a pet sitter.'

'Foxy says she's looking forward to it too.' Clara chuckled.

'Thank you again for recommending Mr B,' Sam added.

'I hope that works out. Our chef can be very demanding. You should pop by for a cream tea some time. He does an amazing Dorset apple cake and his scones are to die for.'

Sam said that she would. It would be a lovely place to take Abby and Jack. Or maybe even her parents when they were no longer tied to the B&B. Sam had begun to let herself get excited about the future.

Danny Bowkett had been as good as his word too. He'd recommended a bloke he knew in the building trade to come over and quote for the fencing. The fencer, whose real name was Simon Dennings but who was known to everyone as Ginger thanks to his unruly shock of flaming red hair, turned out to be very friendly and his quote was so good that Sam only asked one other fencer, who couldn't compete.

As soon as Sam had signed the lease paperwork with her landlord, Ginger started work. As well as the red hair, he also turned out to have an impressive six-pack that was very apparent because he was inclined to work with his top off.

'You can get quite a good view from the first-floor landing, but it's better from the garden,' Abby told Sam with a wicked grin, when Sam caught her with her head out of the window one morning.

It was two thirds of the way through September but still blazing hot, and a Saturday so they were both at home. It was stifling in the upstairs part of the cottage, even at just after nine thirty. Goodness knows what it would be like outside.

'You shouldn't be ogling him. He'll be embarrassed,' Sam said. 'Anyway, it's sexist to stare at men's chests.'

'I am not being sexist, I am admiring a thing of beauty. It's more like art,' Abby flicked back her blonde bob, which she'd had restyled, Sam noticed with interest. She'd been wearing make-up regularly too since Paul had come back on the scene. 'Anyway, he likes being ogled.'

'He told you that, did he?'

'More or less. Besides, if you're not interested why are you standing so close to the window?'

'I am not,' Sam said, stepping back hastily. 'I'm not interested in men's chests. Or men.'

'You liar. Anyway, the window is all yours. I've got a whole pile of washing that needs hanging out.' Abby skipped away across the landing. 'And Jack needs some sunshine. Did I tell you Paul is coming over in a bit? He's taking us to Monkey World. How cool is that?' She paused at the top of the stairs. 'What are you doing? Why haven't you got any dogs cluttering up the place?'

'Because it's today that my parents are moving house. I'm going over to give them a hand. They haven't got that much to move. Most of it will be staying in the B&B, but I wanted to help.'

Abby clapped her hands. 'A historic day for them. Or is it "an historic" day? I never know. They both sound wrong.'

'It's a milestone,' Sam said. 'I do know that.'

Abby ran downstairs and Sam followed more slowly. Abby was still insisting that she and Paul were sharing parenthood, they were being partner parents, nothing more, but she had been very bubbly lately, so Sam didn't totally believe this. But Abby was right about one thing. Today was a – an? – historic day. Her parents were moving to a bungalow in Swanage and they had also chosen a long list of potential properties to buy, all of them in Dorset. When they had whittled it down to a shortlist, which they were really looking forward to doing, Sam was going along to help them choose their new home. That would be very exciting.

* * *

It was bittersweet saying goodbye to her childhood home, Sam thought as she lugged boxes out into the small removal van.

'We're having a celebration meal tomorrow night,' her mother said when they were finally done and had just hugged her in the hallway, which still looked like home but no longer felt like it. 'Probably fish and chips. Come over, darling. We can talk about your dog field and we can all toast our new beginnings.'

When Sam got back from her parents' early evening, Ginger was still working. She went across the field to see if he wanted a cold drink. He was making great progress with the fence on the side that was furthest from the house. He was beavering away, putting up stock fencing above the panels that were already there, which had worked out to be quite economical. He didn't have his top off any more, she saw, as she got closer. He was wearing a very skimpy vest tee, though, which made it difficult not to ogle, although she wouldn't tell Abby this.

Just before she reached him, he turned round and looked so startled it was almost comical.

'Sorry, I didn't mean to make you jump. Don't worry, I'm not checking up on you. I just came to see if you fancied a drink?'

'I'm good, thanks.' He indicated a glass on the grass, which had a couple of slices of lemon beginning to dry out in the bottom of it. 'Your housemate got me one. She's very – um – helpful.'

'Not too helpful though?' Sam asked, her radar on full alert. He looked a bit embarrassed.

'Nope – not at all.' He didn't meet her eyes though. That was odd.

Sam left him to it and went back into the house. As she passed the rotary washing line in the garden, she noticed that Abby had filled it up as she'd said. But it wasn't just the usual mix of nappies and staid white M&S pants – oh no. There was a whole different class of undies on their line today: wisps of lace panties, and 'barely there' bras, a black lace camisole and a fantastically feminine red silk teddy with a matching red suspender belt, which jiggled in the faint sea breeze. It was much more Victoria's Secret than No VPL. Where had that lot come from?

Sam marched into the house to find out.

'Hey, girlfriend, chill. I've just been sorting out my drawers...' Abby smirked. 'Things needed a wash. That's not a crime.'

Sam shook her head in affectionate exasperation. 'How was Monkey World?'

'Great. Jack loved it.'

'Paul OK?' she asked meaningfully.

'Fine.'

'Do not scare off my fencer before he's finished the fence, Abby Martin. I'll never get another one as good as him.'

'I won't.' Abby's eyes sparkled with feigned innocence. 'Anyway, *he* started it, not me. Getting his kit off and flaunting his six-pack. I haven't been flashing it about doing topless sunbathing in the garden. Despite the fact I've got every excuse to get my boobs out.' A beat. 'I've still got a bit too much of a mummy tummy to get the rest of my kit off,' she added ruefully. 'Although I have started doing stomach crunches – there's this brilliant YouTube video. Anyway...' She saw Sam's look and changed tack. 'Today, girlfriend, I have simply been doing my laundry. And in the process I may have been giving Six-Pack Si a little reminder that a couple of gorgeous women live here.'

'Hmmm,' Sam said. 'Well, stop it. I don't need a man right now, no matter how good a six-pack he has!'

20

Sam asked Danny Bowkett to bring Stan the border terrier to test the security of her fence once it was finished, as he'd offered. She had felt slightly awkward about doing this. She'd been half-worried he may have changed his mind about them being 'just friends', but he'd shown no sign of it. He'd been his usual chirpy self as he introduced Stan, a shaggy-haired terrier with sandy-coloured fur very similar to his owner's hair.

Stan had wagged his tail politely. Then, as soon as he'd been let off the lead, he'd done exactly what Danny had said he would. He'd run straight to the perimeter fence and proceeded to do a complete circuit. Sniff, stop, run. Sniff, stop, run. Sniff, stop, run.

'If there's a weakness, he'll find it,' Danny said as they watched him go from post to post, occasionally putting his paws up onto the fence as if to test it. 'He was like this in my garden when I first took him on. I think it's one of the reasons his previous owner gave him up. They lived on a main road.'

Sam had given Danny one of her premier memberships (these had been her dad's idea), which entitled him to twenty slots a year free in her field to be used as and when he chose.

'You're not going to make a fortune if you give too many of those away,' he scolded.

'I will, because most people will pay for them and they're expensive. They also include priority booking. I've actually sold five already, thanks to Abby's all-singing, all-dancing online booking system, and we're not even open.'

'Good on you.' He looked impressed.

'How's the dating going?' she asked and he tapped his nose.

'I haven't met Miss Right, but I do have a full diary. I reckon you can never have too many friends. How about yourself?'

'I've been concentrating on Purbeck Pooches, but I agree with you about friends.'

'It's not just about romance.' He bent to stroke Stan's head and the dog leaned into his touch with a small grunt and a snuffle.

'Absolutely,' Sam said, thinking again how nice he was and making a mental note to ask Abby if she had any single friends, looking for love.

* * *

Ginger's fencing had passed the Stan test with flying colours and the dog field was certified as 'Stan-proof' on the website where Stan's photo now had star position. Sam had also managed to get a great video of two greyhounds playing in the field. They belonged to a woman she'd met on Studland Beach very early one Saturday when she'd been walking a Rhodesian ridgeback from the village.

The greyhounds, named Coal and Pewter, after the colour of their sleek coats, were both muzzled and Sam had fallen into conversation with their owner, Maureen Grey. 'They're ex racers,' she'd said, 'and they both have high prey drives. I only let them off when the beach is empty. I can't trust them around small dogs, though, so they have to wear muzzles. It's a real shame.'

Sam had told her about the dog field. 'You'd be more than welcome to some free sessions if you don't mind me taking some footage to put on my website.'

Maureen Grey and her greyhounds became her most viewed video and Sam wasn't a bit surprised. When the dogs had realised they were free to roam, they began to race around like lunatics and the joy on their faces was palpable. Maureen herself had stood watching, her cheeks flushed pink with pleasure.

'Oh my word, look at them.' She had turned towards Sam with tears in her eyes. 'If I'd known a place like this existed, I'd have come to it long ago.'

Sam had hugged her. This was what it was all about – the feeling that she wasn't just making her own dream come true but other people's as well.

Seamus and Goldie had been good models too when Barbara Oldfield had brought them over for a photo shoot.

Seamus had been particularly enamoured with the sniff zone, which was close to the gate and was comprised of a three-metre square paved-off section of the field, in which there was a selection of dog-friendly plants, including, thyme, chamomile, wheatgrass and valerian which Sam had put in raised tubs and pots at various levels so they would appeal to dogs of all sizes.

Seamus had ambled obligingly around the tubs and pots, stopping occasionally to lower his great grey head for a sniff or to cock his leg. Sam hadn't taken any photos of him doing that. When a wolfhound cocked his leg, they could flood the average back garden.

There were also some old tyres she'd asked people to donate and a woodpile. Dogs seemed to love woodpiles. In addition to the fence, Six-Pack Si (annoyingly Abby's nickname had stuck) had built a wooden bus-stop-type shelter for humans and Sam had ordered a wooden picnic bench from eBay. She'd bought a crate and filled it with toys for dogs. She would need a poop bin too.

Although Sam had jumped through all the legal and health and safety hoops the council had put in front of her, which included insurances and licences, there was still a checklist of other things to do and so the end of September and the first few days of October were frenetic because she was still working full-time at Fielding's. Rex had employed Janet in the end – Sam had liked her – and she would be starting soon. But he'd put off employing anyone else until Heather was nearer her maternity leave.

* * *

'I think we should launch the Purbeck Pooches dog field officially before you open for business,' Abby said as they were eating breakfast one morning. She had Jack on her knee and he was gurgling happily. He couldn't say actual words yet – after all, he was only three and a half months old – but he had just started making a variety of sounds that started with Ah or Ga or Goo, which he shouted with gusto.

'I am having an official launch. Kind of…' Sam buttered another slice of toast and spread it thickly with Nutella. She preferred cold toast and Abby liked it hot, so they were the perfect breakfast companions. 'I've got that advertising feature going in the *Purbeck Gazette*, remember? It's timed to coincide with National Love Your Dog Week, which is the third week of October apparently.'

'Yes, but I thought you weren't open for actual bookings until the first of November. Anyway, I don't mean an online launch. I mean for real. We should have a big launch party and break a bottle of champagne on the five-bar gate and maybe even get someone to open it.'

'The gate!' Sam quipped.

Abby glared at her. 'No. The field. We could find a celebrity to name it… The Purbeck Pooches Paddock – or whatever you're going to call it.' She waved a hand. 'The celebrity can break the champagne – or maybe prosecco if champagne's too expensive.'

'Or we could just drink the prosecco,' Sam said, warming to the idea. I like the idea of a launch, but I don't actually know any celebrities. Anyway, wouldn't we have needed to book them a year ago?'

'We could ask someone really local. How about Perrie Edwards from Little Mix? She lives in Dorset, I think. I'll Google it.'

'Goo Goo,' said Jack.

'Yes, darling, Mr GooGoo. See, I told you he was gifted.' Abby looked smug. 'He's going to be a computer genius like his mother. And not an overgrown teenager with rock-star dreams like his father.' Despite the dig, there was a softening in her face when she talked about Paul.

'I think you're probably right,' said Sam. She was still as besotted with Jack as ever and equally on the lookout for every tiny milestone. She blew him a kiss.

Jack blew bubbles back at her.

Abby wiped a dribble from his mouth. 'We could ask a not-so-famous celebrity. How about that woman who plays the piano in The Anchor on live music nights – the one with the little dog with the pink and yellow ribbons? She's pretty flamboyant.'

'She's also not a woman.'

'So…? She'd be excellent fun. And she does have a dog.'

'No.'

Abby pouted. 'Your trouble is you're not adventurous enough. We need to make a splash. Take photographs of people enjoying the new dog field. We could post them on the Facebook page.'

'We've got loads on there already.'

Unperturbed, Abby went on, 'We could have a Halloween launch. That would be fun.'

Sam checked the diary. 'That's a Saturday. But won't people be going to parties already?. And it's probably too short notice to have it the weekend before. Anyway, that's when I'm looking after Mr B's Kunekunes.'

She was slightly regretting that she'd ever agreed to do this as he was on the phone so often. He usually began with the words, 'I'm not sure if I told you about...' followed by things that ranged from, 'Portia likes her belly rubbed but hates it if you touch her ears' to 'Percy must only have the pig food in the orange bag.'

She didn't want the distraction of a party while she also had the responsibility of checking the Kunekunes four times a day. What on earth would she do if something happened to one of them while Mr B was on his four-day break? It didn't bear thinking about.

'I like the idea of a launch though. I'll make a list of people to invite.' Sam grabbed a notepad. 'I can ask everyone who's helped me set it up. Mum and Dad, Danny Bowkett, Six-Pack Si, all my clients.'

'Don't forget everyone at Fielding's. When's Janet thingamy starting? It would give her a chance to socialise with her new workmates.'

'Good idea. She's starting the week after next.'

'I'll invite some people too. I could ask Matt. He split up with the girlfriend who looked like Kylie.'

'Oh did he?' Sam glanced at her. 'Is that what this is all about? Setting me up with your brother?

'Of course it isn't.' Abby widened her eyes as if this was the most outrageous suggestion she'd ever heard. 'I gave up on that years ago.' She shook her head. 'I'll help you make a buffet. Nothing too elaborate. It won't cost the earth.' She clapped her hands. 'It'll be awesome!'

'It would be fun.'

'Go girl,' Abby squealed.

'Ah goo,' added Jack.

* * *

Paul, Abby's 'non partner' as Sam had started to call him, had recently got himself a job in Out Of Town Music, which sold musical instruments and all sorts of other musical paraphernalia on the same industrial estate as Fielding's. Abby had told Sam excitedly that this was his first EVER full-time job so maybe he really was finally settling down. She had taken to visiting him there and having lunch.

It was on one of these lunchtime visits that she popped into Fielding's to see Sam.

'Paul's had a brilliant idea about your launch party,' she said, puffing slightly because she'd just lugged the buggy up the stairs. She was instantly the centre of attention as both Elannah and Heather left their desks to coo over Jack. 'And I couldn't wait until teatime to tell you.'

'What idea?' Sam said, feeling slightly jealous as Elannah made silly faces at Jack from behind her geek-girl glasses and he responded by giggling.

Heather, not to be outdone, was making puppet motions with her hands and bobbing her head from side to side. She was starting to get quite a baby bump herself.

'Paul suggested you get a local businessman to open the Purbeck Pooches field. Like your boss, Rex.'

'I'm not sure he would—'

'Oh I think he would.' Elannah interrupted cheerfully. 'He'd be honoured. Wouldn't you, Rex?' She raised her voice on the last sentence and Sam realised that, to her embarrassment, Rex had chosen that moment to come out of his hidey-hole office, presumably to see what a buggy was doing in the middle of his workplace. He looked tired and a bit pale. He was still paying regular visits to his mother, Elannah had told them.

'What would I be honoured to do?' he asked, glancing into the buggy. 'Aren't you a fine fellow?' This was addressed to Jack.

Sam glanced at him curiously. He'd never struck her as a man who'd fuss over kids and a warmth stole through her, which she suppressed firmly. It certainly didn't make any difference to her whether he liked kids or not.

'Officially open Sam's new dog field,' Elannah told him. 'There's food and champagne in it for you. And we'll all be going – it'll practically be a works outing.'

'I'd be delighted,' Rex said, before Sam had the chance to object. 'When is it?'

She told him. 'I'm sure you have better things to do on a Saturday night...'

'Like go to a Halloween party dressed as a vampire,' quipped Magpie with a wicked grin.

Rex blinked and rubbed his eyes. 'I know I've been burning the candle at both ends, but I don't look that bad, do I?'

'It was a joke, boss.'

'I know.' Rex's lips twitched.

Magpie grinned, then absentmindedly picked up one of Sam's pens and put it in his top pocket.

'Hey!' She glared at him. 'No wonder I can never find one.'

'What would I be required to do?' Rex asked Sam. 'Would it just be cutting a ribbon? Should I prepare a speech?'

She hadn't expected him to agree so wholeheartedly or to be so interested. She felt her cheeks heat up with pleasure. 'It would be great if you could say a few words. Nothing too onerous.' She could feel his eyes on her. She could also feel that slight edge of awareness she had started to feel every time he was around. Not that he had been around much lately. He'd been out of the office a lot, preoccupied with his ill mother who still needed a fair bit of help. 'Are you sure you don't mind?' she added. 'I know you have a lot to do.'

'I don't mind at all. I don't get out much.' His lips twitched again.

'Then thanks. We can touch base about the arrangements some time before then.' Oh God, had that been too forward? Would he think she was flirting? She could sense Abby grinning from ear to ear beside her, but she dared not look at her face.

* * *

'I could throttle you,' Sam told Abby when she got home later that day. 'Putting Rex on the spot like that.' Although actually there was a part of her that really wanted an excuse to spend more time with him.

Abby, who was changing Jack's nappy on the lounge floor, and was therefore not in a position to flounce off, shot her an unrepentant look. 'He didn't sound like he minded very much to me. He sounded well up for it. Besides...' She paused while she fastened the nappy into place. 'You can ply him with alcohol once you've got him over here and see if you can seduce him.'

'I don't want to seduce him,' she blurted, even though her body had other ideas.

'That's not what you said when you went out for that drink. You said you'd fallen for him. And you haven't been on any dates since then either.'

'That's because I've been rushed off my feet getting the dog field up and running. You know I have.'

'About time you seduced someone then. There you are, gorgeous boy.' She leaned over to give Jack a kiss. 'All lovely and sweet-smelling again.' She turned her attention back to Sam. 'OK then, if it's not Rex who tickles your fancy, how about Six-Pack Si? He's pretty hot, you have to admit.'

'I thought it was you who had your eye on Six-Pack Si. I still haven't forgotten the Victoria's Secret Washday Incident.'

'Oh that.' Abby didn't look at her. 'He didn't think they belonged to me. I told him they were yours.'

'Bloody hell, Abby, no wonder he would never meet my eyes when I looked at him. I thought it was strange. I can't invite him to my party now. He might be standing there wondering what I'm wearing underneath my outfit. What if he's told Danny Bowkett?'

'So what if he has?'

'How's it going with Paul?' Sam asked to divert her. 'You haven't mentioned him lately. Is he still just as besotted with Jack?'

'Yes. Yes he is.'

Sam sensed hesitation in Abby's voice. 'And are you two still just being partner parents – or have things progressed?'

'We may have had a snog the other day.' She sounded slightly guilty.

'What? Why didn't you tell me?'

'Because…' Abby sighed and gently turned Jack over onto his tummy on his play mat on the carpet. He was beginning to try and lift himself up a bit when he was on his tummy and she wanted to encourage him. She glanced back up at Sam 'Because I'm not sure if it's going anywhere. Or even if I want it to go anywhere. We'd both had a glass of wine. I let my guard down a bit. He'd made me a nice tea – well, he'd cooked pizza and cut it into slices. Which is as much cooking as he ever does. We were at his.'

'Sounds nice. What's his flat like?'

'Pretty poky. It's basically a studio, although he has got a separate kitchen. But at least he's not sharing. He's doing overtime so he can save up and get something better. There's an assistant manager job coming up. He's going to apply.'

'Wow. That's a major leap for Paul, isn't it? Is he doing that because he wants you two to move in with him?'

'He says not. But I'm not sure I believe him. I know I've said it before, but he really does seem to have changed. It's this little one, isn't it…?' She glanced at Jack with so much love in her eyes that Sam was moved just looking at her. 'Being a parent changed everything for me. And I think it has for Paul too.'

'Bottom line. Do you still love him?'

Abby gave the slightest of nods. 'I guess I still do, girlfriend.'

'So maybe you should give him another chance?'

'Maybe I will.'

21

Eleven days before the Purbeck Pooch field launch party, something happened that threatened to disrupt all of Sam's carefully laid plans.

It began with a phone call from Mr B. Sam was at work at the time, although she had actually finished for the day. She was slightly late because she had the next day, which was Friday, and also the Monday booked as leave so she could look after Mr B's pigs and she also had Max, an ageing black Labrador, coming to board for the weekend.

It was just gone five thirty. She was packing up to go home when she saw Mr B's now familiar number flash up on the screen. She wavered about answering it and then decided that she may as well because it was probably some last-minute detail he'd neglected to tell her, although she couldn't imagine what. She felt as though she knew the ins and outs of every detail of Portia and Percy's history, not to mention a fair bit about the history of Kunekunes in general.

She picked up the phone.

'Sam, how are you?' He had his most charming voice on, which made Sam instantly wary. 'I'm so glad I caught you.'

'I'm good thank you. I'm looking forward to babysitting Portia and Percy tomorrow.'

'Ah yes. About that. I'm afraid there's been a change of plan.'

Sam closed her eyes. This clearly wasn't going to be a quick call and, yes, technically she had finished work, but she still didn't want to be talking to one of her clients when she was at her desk in Fielding's office, particularly as Rex was also still at his desk. 'I'm going to have to call you back, Mr B.'

'It won't take a minute,' he insisted.

Unless she actually hung up on him, there was no getting out of it. 'OK. I'm listening.'

'I need to reschedule.'

'What? Why? It's a bit late notice. I thought you were going away tomorrow?'

'I know. I'm so sorry. It's not work. This one's totally out of my hands. There's been a bereavement.'

'A bereavement – oh. I'm really sorry to hear that.'

'Yep. It's been a difficult week. ' He sucked in a deep breath. 'My girlfriend's pet python died.'

'Her pet python...!' Sam could feel her patience slipping away. Not that she didn't appreciate that people could have bonds with all sorts of creatures and she could imagine that if you had an ill pet you wouldn't want to go off for a short break, but a dead pet was different. Wouldn't you want to get away? Wouldn't a change of scene away from the sadness actually help?

She was trying to think of a tactful way to say this when Mr B continued, 'I know it's short notice, but we've decided, Meg and I, that the best thing to do is to go next Friday instead. Meg will be feeling a bit better then and she'll be able to enjoy it more. I know you'll understand – being such an animal lover yourself.'

'I totally understand. But next weekend is difficult. I'm launching my new dog field.'

There was a sound like a strangled yelp on the other end of the phone. 'But I've just rescheduled the hotel. It's the only time they can do it. I won't be able to get anyone else at such short notice.' There was a thread of panic in his voice and Sam wavered. 'I don't trust anyone else. What if I pay you double?' Mr B's voice had risen an octave. 'Treble? I'm more than happy.'

Blimey that was tempting.

'And we could cut down the number of actual visits. Maybe two of the visits can be virtual. There's an app that goes with the security camera over their pen. It's called Watch Me From Afar. I could set it all up on your phone. It would take seconds.'

She caught a movement out of the corner of her eye and realised she needed to get out of the office. 'Sorry, Mr B, I really do need to go. I'm in the middle of something. I'll call you back first thing in the morning. I'm sure we can sort something out.'

He was still babbling when she hung up, but Rex had just come out of his office and he'd paused by her desk. He obviously wanted to ask her something.

'Sorry. That was a personal call.' She looked up at him. There were shadows beneath his eyes, although he wasn't as pale as he'd been recently. 'It was about some Kunekunes I'm supposed to be looking after for the next four days.'

'Didn't you do that once before?' He looked interested.

'I haven't actually done it yet – the owner had to reschedule and he's just phoned me to reschedule again.' As she spoke, her mobile began to buzz in her hands like an angry wasp. She didn't answer it. 'I told him I'd ring him back. He doesn't listen to a word I say. I don't think he's the listening type.' She was aware that her voice was rising and that Rex was looking at her curiously.

'I don't think I've ever seen you rattled.'

'I'm sorry.' She remembered where she was. 'You didn't need to hear that. How are you? How is your mum doing?'

'She's doing fine. Thanks for asking.'

There was a pause.

'Was there something I could help you with?' Sam asked, turning off her phone before it could ring again.

'I was only going to ask you about next Saturday. Find out what you would like me to say as regards the launch?' She noticed he had his jacket over one arm and his briefcase in his hand. He was clearly about to leave. 'I thought we could maybe discuss it over a drink – if you're not in a hurry? Or we could do it another time?'

'Now is absolutely fine. I could do with a drink. In fact, I could probably do with several.'

* * *

They went to The Anchor again and Sam had the strangest sense of déjà vu as they parked alongside each other and walked across to the main doors. How long ago had it been since their first visit? More than two months, yet she could remember every detail of the evening. It had been when he had told her about wood being his passion and she had told him about her dream of making Purbeck Pooches a full-time business. A lot had changed since then. She had now taken her first steps towards making her dream a reality. Rex was a big part of the reason. She remembered the moment their hands had touched and how she'd felt, although she'd since decided she must have been overreacting.

Tonight the fire was lit and the scent of wood smoke hit them as they went in. They were given the same table, which only added to the sense of déjà vu, but this time they didn't order sandwiches – they decided on a main meal.

Paella was chalked up on the specials blackboard. It could only be made freshly to order and came subject to a forty-five-minute lead time. They both spotted it at the same time.

'Paella is one of my favourite things,' Rex announced, sounding pleased.

'Mine too,' she said, surprised. It was uncanny how much in common she had with him once you had scratched the surface. What was the old saying? 'Don't judge a book by its cover'. This certainly applied to Rex.

He clearly wasn't in a hurry tonight, Sam thought, as they ordered food and drinks from a cheerful waitress. And neither was she. In fact, as they slipped into easy conversation she realised there was nowhere in the world she would rather have been.

How odd.

She told him about the dilemma with Mr B. He hadn't called her again, but when she turned on her phone just before they'd come into the pub in case anything urgent cropped up, she had discovered a lengthy text outlining the details of the app he had mentioned and how it could all work and how it would barely take up any of her time at all to supervise Portia and Percy from afar. It would have been handy if he'd mentioned this before.

'Maybe you should do it,' Rex said. 'It does sound as though it wouldn't be too much trouble – or am I being naïve?'

'I don't know. But I will honour the booking if I possibly can. Despite the fact he's the trickiest person I think I've ever met.'

'You didn't meet my ex-wife,' Rex said, stopping her in her tracks.

'I didn't know you'd been married.'

'No. I don't tell many people. It wasn't my finest hour.' He met her eyes. 'I don't really know why I told you.' He looked puzzled for a moment.

'But now you've started you may as well finish,' Sam prompted. 'I'll keep it to myself. What I mean is – it... um, won't be the subject of office gossip.'

'I know,' he said. 'I know that about you, Sam. You have integrity.'

'As do you,' she said, feeling ridiculously pleased.

He paused for a moment, looking oddly vulnerable before taking a deep breath. 'Her name was Katrina. She was the daughter of my father's best friend. We were the same age and we hung around together as kids a lot and it was always assumed that we would end up together.'

'And you did.'

'We did.' His eyes clouded. It clearly hadn't been a good memory. 'It's a long story. But the short version is that Katrina's father died in a boating accident when she was nineteen. She turned to me for support, which I was happy to give. Don't get me wrong, I liked her very much as a friend. For a long while that was all it was and then one night we were at a party. We both had a bit too much to drink. One thing led to another and we ended up spending the night together.'

Sam held her breath. It was so odd hearing him speak like this. She'd always thought of Rex as being uptight and aloof, buttoned up, but the more she got to know him, the more she realised what a misjudgement she had made.

'I guess we all made mistakes like that when we're young,' she said gently. His face was sad and she felt enormously privileged to be taken into his trust.

'Yes. And I think maybe it wouldn't have been a mistake if it had ended there, but it didn't. A few weeks later, she told me she was pregnant. That wasn't the mistake either.' A beat. 'I wanted a family in those days. We had spoken about it often. So we decided to get married. All the arrangements were made very quickly. Within six weeks. Then, on the night before our wedding, Katrina told me that she had lied about being pregnant. There had never been a baby.

But she was in love with me. She begged me not to call it off. She begged me to stay with her.'

'Oh my God.' Sam realised that she was leaning forward to hear his quiet voice above the buzz of chatter that surrounded them. The pub was filling up with after-work drinkers and the occasional tourist on a late-season break. The scent of freshly cooked food, as waitresses carried plates to tables, was threading through the wood smoke.

'I agreed that I would stay with her.' Rex blew out a breath and gave the slightest shake of his head. 'That was the mistake. I should have listened to my instincts and run for the hills. I was only twenty-one. But I didn't. We got married the next day. Both of us smiling for our families – for the cameras – but I know that neither of us were happy with the decision we'd made. Katrina was guilt-stricken and I was still in shock, I think. Over the next few months, she managed to reconcile herself with her lie because she had told me before I'd actually married her.' He paused to sip his drink. They had both ordered lime and soda again. 'But I never did. It rankled and grew in me like a bitter thing. I was stupid to let that happen.'

Sam met his direct gaze across the table. His eyes were shadowed and vulnerable.

'The most bizarre bit about it, Sam, is that we never consummated our marriage. In the end, we got divorced as soon as we possibly could. There was a lot of backlash about that from our families. Most of it aimed at me. But I was stupid to let it go on that long.'

'Stupid is the last thing you are,' she said, feeling fiercely protective. 'It's not stupid to trust what people tell us. It's human. And when we find out, we are hurt and angry. Of course we are.' She had a vivid recollection of Gary Collins. 'I had a serious relationship a couple of years ago. He lied too – but in his case it was about me being his only girlfriend.'

She told Rex about that awful day when she had got a text from a stranger asking her if she knew what her boyfriend was doing that night. And whom he was seeing.

'I went to his house and I parked outside and I saw them through the window together, I saw him kiss her. I didn't have the courage to confront them there and then. I went home and sat with it. I tried to find an excuse for him when there were none.'

'He didn't deserve your trust.' Rex sounded aggrieved on her behalf.

'Katrina didn't deserve yours.'

'I know, but it took me a long time to realise it.'

'You were young. You had an excuse. My disastrous relationship was only a couple of years ago.'

'Have you been out with anyone since? Are you seeing someone now?' He dropped his gaze, suddenly flustered. 'Sorry. That's none of my business... Forgive me. You don't have to answer that.'

Just then, their paella arrived. 'Sorry to keep you waiting,' the waitress said as she put it in front of them. 'But I'm told it's worth waiting for.'

The steam rising from the paella was certainly fragrant and delicious.

When she had gone again, Sam picked up her fork. 'I haven't seen anyone since,' she said. 'And no, I'm not seeing anyone now. Are you?'

Rex shook his head.

Sam's heart gave a little leap, which she tried to ignore. For a while they ate in silence. Not that Sam wanted to eat now. She had thought she was starving, but suddenly she wasn't hungry. She wanted them to carry on talking. She wanted to know more about him. She felt as though she had gone to sleep in a familiar world, but then woken up again in one that was new and different. Wonderfully new and different, where all the colours were brighter and the feelings more intense and the scents of the food more present. It was the most curious and delicious of feelings.

After they'd eaten, they carried on talking, noticing fleetingly when their plates were cleared from the table and they were given a plastic-backed dessert menu. They talked about Rex's mother and her slow, but good recovery. They talked about Sam's forthcoming launch day and the part he would play in it. They lapsed briefly into formality for that, but Sam was aware that they were touching each other frequently. Touching each other's hands, fingers, often to demonstrate a point, as naturally as though they had been good friends for years.

Eventually Rex picked up the menu and said, 'Would you like a dessert?' When she agreed, he looked around them to summon a waiter and so did Sam.

The pub looked fairly empty. There was a clock over the bar and she narrowed her eyes as she focused on it. 'I think we may have missed our chance. It's coming up to ten!' Blimey, how had four hours whizzed by?

'It can't be.' There was disbelief in his voice.

They stared at each other.

Rex cleared his throat and frowned. 'Do you think we could do this again? Over dinner? Would that be… er, inappropriate?' He blinked a few times and rubbed his forehead. 'I've always wondered about – um – mixing business and pleasure…'

'I think it would be terribly inappropriate,' Sam said, trying and failing to keep the smile out of her voice.

He was nodding, but she knew he was listening to her smile and not her words.

'Where shall we go next time?' she asked. 'I could cook you dinner? Are you free tomorrow night?' The question was out of her mouth before she'd edited it. But suddenly she didn't want to edit it.

'Yes I am. I'd like that very much.' He unhooked his jacket from the back of his chair. 'I'll just get the bill. Don't go anywhere.'

It was cute how he suddenly seemed to have more confidence now she had offered him dinner. He was such a strange mixture of uncertainty and confidence, vulnerability and authority. She didn't think she had ever seen so many conflicting emotions wrapped up in one person, and quite frequently displayed all at the same time.

Outside in the car park, they stood in the gap between their respective cars. It was a bright beautiful night and a million stars were visible out here where there was virtually no light pollution. Sam tilted her head back to look. The full moon soared high above them. A great fat orange ball of a moon that seemed almost surreal in its brightness.

'Wow,' Sam said. 'Isn't that stunning.'

'That's a hunter's moon,' Rex said. 'So called because it's rumoured that Native Americans traditionally went hunting by moonlight in October so they could gather in food for the coming winter.'

'Wow. I didn't know that.'

'My father was a keen observer of the night sky. He taught me a little about stars.'

'How romantic.'

'It was.'

She breathed in the fresh scent of the coastal air and pulled her light jacket a little tighter around her shoulders.

'I really enjoyed tonight, Sam.' Rex hesitated. His eyes were dark in the light of the moon. 'If you change your mind about cooking me dinner, it's OK, I'll understand. Let me know tomorrow.'

'I'm not in tomorrow. I took the day off – remember? I was

supposed to be looking after a pair of Kunekunes. But I won't change my mind.'

His eyes softened and he caught her hands in his. 'Good.'

Every part of her was aware of his touch as she met his steady gaze. A beat. Then, as he bent to kiss her, she tilted her face up to his and their lips touched and once again the ground shifted beneath her feet. She had thought that the kiss would be a peck, but it wasn't. It was a full-on, tender and very beautiful kiss beneath a tangerine moon. Sam never wanted it to end: the soft warmth of him, the strength, the passion that she could feel deep within him, matched by the passion in her. It was a kiss that put every other kiss she had ever had firmly in the shade. It was a kiss that told her with an utter certainty that this was a beginning. Nothing was ever going to be quite the same again. That feeling she'd experienced earlier about waking up in a new and different world had returned, but now it was multiplied by the power of ten.

When they did finally draw apart, she knew that it had changed him too.

'I'll see you tomorrow,' he said, touching her face with his cupped hand in a gesture that was infinitely tender.

'I'll look forward to it,' she said.

That was the bloody understatement of the year.

22

Abby was almost as excited as Sam was when Sam finally got home at nearly eleven and explained why she was so late.

'Oh my God. That's so brilliant. I want to know everything. What was his kiss like? I need a blow-by-blow account. Did you do tongues? How dark was the car park? Did he touch anywhere that he shouldn't?'

'I'm not telling you stuff like that. It's classified information.' She could feel herself smiling at the memory of driving home beneath that amazing tangerine moon with the memory of their first mind-blowing kiss against the perfect backdrop of the stars.

Abby pouted. 'Oh OK, but what about the kiss? Was there a hint a tongue?'

'There may have been the merest hint of tongue. The car park was lit by moonlight – have you seen that stunning moon - and frankly...' She stretched her hands up above her head in a delicious cat-like stretch. 'Frankly... I am amazed I managed to resist dragging him into the bushes and ripping all his clothes off.'

'How fantastic.'

'It's been a long time since I wanted to do that. Oh no! Maybe that's why it was so good. Because it's been so long since I kissed anyone. What if that was the reason it was so good?'

'It wasn't. Remember Danny Bowkett. Not to mention that other dork you met Ned the Nobhead and "It's Not Even My Photograph" Numpty. How much chemistry was there then, huh? Zilch, nada, none. You told me that yourself. Chemistry either exists. Or it doesn't!' Abby rested her elbows on the kitchen table, which was where they were sitting. Sam had caught her just about to make a hot chocolate nightcap. They'd progressed from sprinkles and were now on miniature marshmallows as a topping. 'By tomorrow night you could be in bed with him.'

'I could not. He's not that type of guy. And I'm not that type of girl.' Sam felt an ache of longing. Her body definitely disagreed with that statement.

'I think I might go and stay with Matt tomorrow. Just in case you change your mind,' Abby said with a glint in her eyes. 'He keeps saying he wants to see more of his nephew.'

'There's no need.' Deep down Sam hoped there might be.

'We can argue about it in the morning.'

* * *

When Sam woke up the next day, Rex, and the memory of their lovely evening, not to mention that amazing kiss, was the first thought that she had. Her second thought featured Mr B, but that was because there was another missed call from him.

She got dressed and rang him back. He answered within one ring and he sounded hugely relieved to hear from her.

'Samantha. I have been both a timewaster and a rapscallion and I must apologise.'

That was a first. He had never apologised before. She wondered what a rapscallion was, but before she had time to ask, he swept on.

'Is there the slightest possibility that you would still be able to...?'

'Yes,' she cut in before he had the chance to get going again. 'We can arrange something, maybe along the lines of using that app you mentioned – it's fine...'

'Oh, that's wonderful. I can't tell you how much of a relief that is to hear. I will pay you double what we agreed.'

'That won't be necessary. What we agreed is fine. Although I will charge you for my time if we are going to be meeting again to set up the app. Maybe we could do that later today.'

'Absolutely. That's fine. Wonderful.' He had the grace to sound a little shamefaced.

'How is Meg coping?' Sam asked, because she was feeling in such a conciliatory mood. No one – not even Mr B – could upset her today.

'Meg is – er – recovering. She has got over the shock. Thank you for asking. Monty belonged to a very dear friend of hers. He had been alive on the earth for forty-two years. Longer than any of us. I wonder if there is any significance in the fact that he died when he was forty-two. Isn't that a magical number of some kind? The answer to life, the universe and everything. Or maybe that's only in a book.'

Sam had stopped listening. She was still smiling at the idea of anyone having a python called Monty. *Monty Python and the Holy Grail* was one of her dad's favourite films. She wasn't sure about magical numbers, but she certainly felt as if there was magic in the air today.

* * *

Part of Sam wished she was going into work and part of her was relieved she wasn't. It would have been difficult to sit at her desk while Rex was sitting at his and to be surrounded by all of her workmates. And to know that everything was the same, but also that everything was totally different.

She had just finished eating breakfast with Abby and Jack when Rex phoned.

'Good morning, Sam.'

'Good morning, Mr Fielding.' A beat. Maybe she shouldn't have said that. He might not realise she was being ironic and now Abby was craning her neck to listen.

'I thought we may have progressed to first-name terms,' he said without a flicker of irony. 'After that spectacular kiss.'

Oh my God, so he had felt it as strongly as she had. She hugged the warmth of his words around her like a duvet on a frosty starlit night and walked out into the hall so she could get some privacy.

'I am really looking forward to tonight,' she said, imagining him in his office, surrounded by the smell of dust and old books and with the door firmly closed.

'So am I. What time would you like me to arrive? Can I bring anything?'

'Just yourself,' she said. 'And please come at seven. If that suits?'

* * *

Sam spent the rest of the morning tidying the house.

'I don't know why you're bothering,' Abby said. 'He already knows you're not tidy.'

'I am tidy.'

Abby put her hands on her hips and formed her lips into an O shape. 'How can you say that? Your desk at work is a complete mess.'

'It's an organised mess. Oh my God, what am I going to cook him? I haven't thought this through. I don't even do cooking.'

'Buy a posh ready meal.'

'More importantly, what am I going to wear?' She wandered into the lounge, spraying air freshener. 'Does it smell of dogs in here?'

Abby sniffed the air. 'Dogs and babies,' she said happily. 'But if he doesn't like dogs and babies, you might be in trouble. Let's go and sort out your outfit, girlfriend.'

* * *

After lunch, Sam went to see Mr B, which didn't take as long as she thought. He was at his most charming. She knew he was relieved that she was still going to pig-sit Portia and Percy – even if some of it would be via the app. He showed her how to set up the Watch Me From Afar app on her phone and it worked perfectly. She could see both the ark itself and most of the surrounding paddock.

'Unfortunately, this app can only be used on one phone at a time,' he said. 'So when I switch over the control to you next Friday, you will be the only person who is able to see it. I will email you the link and give you the security code to activate it.' He frowned. He was clearly struggling with the concept of handing over control of his precious pigs to her. 'The main thing is to make sure that they go in at night and come out in the morning. I don't like the idea of them staying out all night. Someone might pinch them. Kunekunes are quite valuable.'

Someone could just as easily pinch them during the day, Sam thought but didn't say, although, in truth, she suspected they would not be that easy to pinch, given they were more safely guarded than the Crown Jewels. There was a very heavy-duty lock on the five-bar gate of their paddock. A thief would have needed a big pair of bolt cutters, night or day. They'd also have needed transport. She couldn't imagine anyone wanting two largish pigs romping around in the back of their hatchback, however valuable they were. They'd need a trailer or horsebox. So it wouldn't be any old opportunist thief. Mind you, an opportunist thief probably wouldn't be after pigs in the first place.

'Thank you again.' Mr B clasped her hands firmly and looked into her eyes. 'I will recommend you to everyone I know.'

'I haven't done anything yet,' she reminded him.

'Until next week then.' He let go of her hands and Sam left him standing by the five-bar gate.

As she drove away, she wondered what she was letting herself in for. Not just with Mr B, but with every future whacky animal owner she had yet to meet. Did she really want to give up her boringly safe, well-paid audio typist job for a life of economic insecurity and clients like Mr B?

'Oh yes, I do', she answered her own question.

Her parents would laugh when she told them that. They were having a whale of a time looking at houses. They'd seen a few, mostly in Dorset, and a couple in Wiltshire. They'd been emailing details back and forth, but they hadn't yet drawn up a shortlist.

Mum had smiled when she'd heard about Mr B and the Kunekunes and Dad had asked if she'd considered changing her name to Purbeck Pets. If there hadn't already been a Purbeck Pets in existence she might have been tempted. Goats, pigs, whatever would she be looking after next?

* * *

Sam picked up the food shopping on her way back from Mr B's. When she got home just after four thirty, she found Abby packing a bag of Jack's things. There were already several bags piled up by the back door. Taking Jack anywhere required a mountain of accompanying baby paraphernalia.

'I said you didn't have to go out.'

'Yes, girlfriend, I know you did. But I'm hardly going to hang around to cramp your style while you're busy with the seduction of the decade, am I?'

'I'm not planning a seduction,' she protested, although the thought was very appealing.

'Well, let's hope he is then.' Abby picked up Jack. 'Did you still want him to change his name? Frank's a good name. Hanky-panky with Franky.'

'Stop it,' she said, trying not to laugh.

'You can help me carry this lot out to the car if you like.'

'Are you really going to Matt's?' Sam asked as they carried the bags out. She wouldn't have put it past Abby to be sneaking off to Paul's. Not that she needed to lie about it.

'Yes I really am. And we're staying over. Matt's quite excited – well, he's as excited as my brother ever gets. He's ordered Chinese for later and we're all going to watch reruns of *SpongeBob SquarePants*.'

'Isn't that a bit old for him?'

'Matt – yes probably, but he'll grow into it.' Abby giggled. 'Oh, you mean this little one. I know, but he may as well get used to some Martin family traditions. A gentle introduction before we go on to *The Simpsons*.' She strapped Jack into his car seat. 'Wave goodbye to Sam, gorgeous boy.'

Sam felt an ache in her throat, which she knew was ridiculous. They were only going for the night. The coolness of the coast breathed across the fields as the beginnings of dusk swirled around them. The countryside was beginning to turn red and gold. Autumn was a time for endings. She suppressed a little shiver of premonition.

'Cheer up. You're supposed to be excited,' Abby quipped, giving her a long look. 'You're not regretting asking him, are you?'

'Absolutely not.'

'Well, you might want to tell your face that.' Abby rummaged through her bag. 'Just checking I've got my phone,' she said, locating it and nodding. 'I'll leave it switched on. Just in case you need me. Have fun, darling. I shan't be back too early tomorrow. In case you need a lie-in.' She couldn't keep the grin off her face.

'I will not need a lie-in. Max is getting dropped off at 10 a.m.'

'Blimey, girlfriend. Rex one night and Max the next morning?'

'Max is my Labrador boarder,' Sam said primly.

She watched them drive away, trying to ignore the pang of sadness, and went back indoors. Rex wasn't arriving for another two hours, but her stomach was racked with nerves. At least she had plenty to do.

She wasn't taking any chances on the cooking. She'd followed Abby's advice and bought a Cook lasagne and she would make up a side salad to go with it. Their starter was Kalamata olives because she knew he liked them and some gorgeous bread (from the bakers where Lightning got the awesome cakes), with virgin olive oil in little ceramic bowls for dipping.

Sam felt like a virgin herself. A very nervous one. That was nuts. She'd been listening to Abby too much. Probably nothing at all would happen tonight. It was – effectively – their very first date. No, it wasn't. This had been building for a while and that kiss – that mind-blowingly wonderful kiss – had cemented the fact they would, sooner or later, end up being a great deal more than friends.

Rex wouldn't want to be a friend with benefits and neither did she want that of him. She wanted much more than that, she thought as she put on the outfit she had planned – a beautiful teal silky blouse that Abby said made her dark hair and olive skin look stunning and a grey skirt that hugged her hips and was informal enough to be casual but still smart and maybe the tiniest bit sexy. She wasn't used to feeling sexy.

* * *

Rex arrived at two minutes past seven. From the hall window, Sam watched him park outside, take his satnav out of its holder, and then reach across to the passenger seat to pick something up. Flowers, she saw, and a wrapped bottle of wine. So he'd ignored her instructions to bring just himself then, although it was a nice gentlemanly thing to do and she was secretly pleased.

She went to let him in with her heart doing a tippy-tap dance of excitement and anticipation.

'Good evening, Sam.' His eyes were lit with warmth, which softened the formal words. He kissed her cheek and her senses swam.

He was wearing those biscuit-coloured trousers he'd worn when they'd gone on their works outing to the fair and a pale blue shirt that brought out the colour of his beautiful eyes and in the narrow confines of the hall he smelled delicious. He had on some subtle but expensive scent that underlaid the headier scent of the flowers.

'These are for you.'

'They're beautiful. Thank you. Didn't I tell you not to bring anything?'

'Do *you* always do what you're told?' he countered and then she was leading him down the flagstone hall, past the lounge door and into the beamed farmhouse kitchen. 'This is a fabulous location. And an absolutely beautiful house. One day I shall exchange my practical house full of mod cons for a quirky thatched cottage like this.'

He lived in a house full of mod cons? He was full of contradictions. She'd expected him to live somewhere more reminiscent of his office. A house full of antiques and ornate heavy furniture. With a sudden stab of insight, she remembered the office with its battleship-grey filing cabinets hadn't been his. It had belonged to his father and he had clearly kept everything the same. Family loyalty. Of course he would have done that.

'I wish Beach Cottage was mine,' she said, leading him straight into the kitchen and liberating the flowers from their paper and cellophane wrapping to put into a vase. 'But I do feel very lucky to live here.'

They fell easily into conversation and it was just as it had been every other time they had talked since that day at the funfair. She had thought there might be awkward moments, but there were none. Even when he asked where Abby was.

'I thought she lived with you?' His eyebrows rose in a question.

'She does, but she's staying with her brother.'

'Ah. Good.' A beat. 'So she's not avoiding me. She does realise that I've forgiven her for what she said to me on your phone the day she was in labour.'

'So it *was* you she told to—' Sam gasped.

'Eff off. Yes, but I think that was perfectly excusable in the circumstances.'

'I'm so glad you didn't mention that before. She may not have been so keen to march into your office and suggest you officially open my field if she'd known it was you.'

'I'm very glad that she did ask me. It'll be an honour.' He gave her a look that made her fizz with pleasure.

It was just as it had been before, Sam thought. They were so interested in each other that neither of them had huge appetites, although he did compliment her on the lasagne and she did confess she hadn't made it.

'I was going to pretend I had to impress you,' she said, as she cleared away the plates. The washing-up could wait. 'I even hid the packaging in the outside bin. How's that for subterfuge?'

'But you decided integrity was more important,' he said in a tone so mild she couldn't tell whether he was being ironic or serious. 'I would expect nothing less of you, Sam.'

They retired to the lounge and were now sitting on the sofa about six inches apart. She hadn't yet offered him coffee. Coffee seemed a prerequisite to the end of the evening and she didn't want him to go. Neither of them had drunk more than a glass of the wine he'd brought either. As the time had flicked by, the chemistry had been building between them. She didn't even have to be that close to him to feel it like a powerful force field of electricity.

'Thank you for another absolutely lovely evening,' he said at around ten and she nodded.

'Thank you too. I... I don't want you to go.' Hell, was that too forward? He kept talking about integrity. Did that mean that you kissed on date two and possibly cuddled on date three, before waiting until date five or six until you ripped each other's clothes off?

Sam knew she couldn't kiss him again without wanting to do a whole lot more. She was incapable of leaning even one centimetre into that force field and still having the restraint to hold back. How on earth had she ever thought there might not be any chemistry?

'I won't go just yet then,' he said, reaching out his hand and touching her face with his fingertips, which caused a million-volt charge of electricity to shoot through her body. Then he leaned closer and she saw in his eyes that it was exactly the same for him. They were kissing again and Sam knew without a shadow of a doubt that they had leapfrogged straight from date three to date six – smashed through every barrier – if there ever had been any barriers.

There were none now. There was nothing but him. The last thought she had before she gave up any pretence of this just being a goodnight kiss was, thank goodness Abby had gone out for the night. Thank goodness Abby had known her better than she knew herself.

23

In the morning when she woke up in her bed, it was to find Rex already awake, although it must be still early because there was only a dull light visible around the edges of the pale blinds at her window.

He was propped on one elbow, smiling at her. She could see quite a bit of bare chest and a smattering of dark hair and it all came flooding back. The way they had raced up the stairs. The way she had tripped on the bottom one in her haste and he had held her to steady her and her body had remembered his strength, his touch from the fair. Hart's was where it had all begun – the first inkling she'd had that he was going to be so much more important to her than simply being her employer. Even though she had been in denial off and on ever since.

Poor Ned wouldn't have stood a chance even if he had matched his photograph. Neither would Danny Bowkett. A part of her heart had already been reserved for someone else.

When it came to it, they hadn't ripped each other's clothes off, either in the lounge or upstairs. In her bedroom in the quiet basil and lime candle-scented darkness – that had been Abby's idea, just in case – they had undressed each other, item by item, and they had watched each other's faces as they did so and Sam didn't think that she had ever found anything so exciting, or so arousing, in her entire life. Although she swiftly had to revise this after what had followed.

'Good morning, Miss Jones,' he said, fetching her back into the present.

'We must definitely have moved on to first-name terms now, Rex. That's an unusual name, isn't it? I don't think I've ever met another one.' It was lovely to know that she could talk openly and honestly with him about anything now.

'I was named after my father. He was a Rex too.'

There was a pause and in the pale light of morning she studied his face. There were touches of grey in his sideburns, but no evidence of it on his head and he had the kind of defining cheekbones that would ensure he was attractive even in old age. His nose was straight, his lips gently curved and his blue-grey eyes darker in the shadows.

'Why are you staring at me?' he asked and she was reminded again of that vulnerability that was never far away from the surface.

'I didn't mean to. Sorry.'

'No need to apologise.' His eyes warmed and then shadowed again. 'No regrets?' he asked.

'None at all. You?'

'Absolutely none.' He touched her collarbone, his fingers tentative. 'It's still early. I didn't wake you, did I?'

'You didn't. Would you like some coffee?'

'I can think of something else I would like more.'

* * *

In the end, he didn't go home until ten minutes before Jess Bradshaw was due to drop off Max. Sam didn't want him to go home then, but he said that there were things he needed to do and there were things she needed to do too, unfortunately.

'Shall we meet up later?' he said as they stood together by his car because she still couldn't quite bear to let him go. 'I could take you out for dinner. Or I could cook for you? I'm actually a half-decent cook.'

'I think I may have met the perfect man,' she said, still unwilling to leave the warm circle of his arms.

'Where is he?' He looked over his shoulder. 'I'll kill him.'

They both laughed, standing there bathed in the morning sunshine with the scent of a soft breeze curling in from the sea and rustling the trees, and then he finally, finally left.

Sam went back inside to start the reality of her day, which seemed to have become imbued with a new sunshine. A sunshine that had nothing to do with the real sun that was climbing into a perfect blue autumn sky – how had she ever thought that autumn meant endings? – and everything to do with the warmth that buzzed in every cell of her body.

* * *

'It went well then,' Abby said, when she breezed in about lunchtime.

'How do you know that?' Sam asked, raising her eyebrows in her best imitation of innocence.

'Because you are alight, girlfriend. Every little bit of you is shiny and sparkly. And...' She leaned forward for a closer look. 'You've got a love bite on your neck.'

'I have not. Where?' Sam made a dash for the mirror in the hall.

Abby followed her more slowly. 'No, you haven't. I was kidding.

I think it's just a red mark. But the fact that you thought you might have says it all. So I take it you had a good night. Not that you're going to tell me the details of that. It's classified information. Yada, yada, yada.'

Sam's smile was bursting out of her. 'I had a bloody awesome night and morning.'

'That is superb news. So there was a shedload of passion beneath that stiff upper lip, was there? That's good to hear. What star sign is he?'

'Scorpio, I think. And yes, there certainly was.' Sam swallowed the emotion that had suddenly leapt into her throat. 'This is going to sound really OTT and sappy, but I think that he might be The One, Abby. I think that I may have found the person I'm meant to spend my life with and I wasn't even looking.'

'Oh MY, you do have it bad.' Abby went back into the kitchen, summoned by a yell from Jack. 'I'm really pleased. And do you know how he feels? Did he give you the impression that he felt like that? I guess it's too soon to know.' She picked Jack up and cuddled him against her chest. 'How will it work with you still working for him? I know it's only part-time now, but do you think that will make it awkward? Or will you keep it secret? It's hard to keep things like that secret, isn't it?'

'I don't know.' Sam bent to kiss Jack's head. 'Good morning, gorgeous. We haven't really had the chance to talk about any of that yet.'

'No, I don't suppose you have. It's not the first thing that springs to mind, is it in the postcoital glow – what shall we tell the office?'

Sam nodded in agreement. 'We'll work it out. I'm going to take Max for a saunter around the dog field. Lots to think about.'

'But all good by the sound of it.' Abby gave her the thumbs up sign. 'By the way, Jack and I are going to see Paul later – just in case you were wanting a repeat performance.'

'This is your home,' Sam paused at the back door, 'you don't have to go out every time Rex comes over.' She decided she should probably keep quiet about the eff off thing. Abby would definitely avoid Rex if she knew about that.

* * *

It was one of the happiest weekends that Sam could remember. She spent most of it with Rex.

When he'd discovered she was looking after Max the Labrador for the weekend, he had suggested she bring him with her to his house.

'Unless you would rather I came to you again?' he'd added. 'I could cook at mine and bring the food over. That wouldn't be a problem.'

He was climbing higher and higher in her estimation.

'It's fine, I'll bring him to yours,' she said, partly because she didn't want to put him to the trouble of lugging food about, but mostly because she wanted to see where he lived and also because she wanted to see how he would be around dogs. It wasn't a deal breaker if he was totally indifferent, but it might be a major red flag.

His house was on the outskirts of Brancombe, a suburb of Swanage, not much more than a twenty-minute drive from Sam. The address was 22 The Avenue – the poshest part of Brancombe. She found it easily with the aid of her satnav and parked outside a low red brick wall with the number 22 in black lettering on one of the pillared gateposts. Then she helped an enthusiastic Max to jump down from the back of the car and had a proper look at where Rex lived.

In some ways, it was exactly what she'd expected. She knew Rex was a fan of old houses and this one was classic Victorian. It was a large two-storey red-brick building with four lots of sash bay windows and a gable at one end with a finial poking skywards. Sam walked through a small gate up a path to the front door and rang a bell, which she could hear jangling loudly somewhere inside but distant.

Rex had also told her to bring only herself and Max, but she had ignored him – two could play at that game - and brought some posh after dinner mints that she'd had in the cupboard waiting for an occasion, and a nice bottle of red she had bought especially.

His eyes lit up with pleasure as he let her in, dropped a light kiss on her cheek and bent to give Max a tentative stroke. That was a good start. She could smell something delicious drifting down the hall.

'Come in, come in. Long time no see.' There was that twinkle in his eyes again. How had she managed to work for with him so long and not notice how often his eyes sparkled?

He was wearing blue corduroy slippers and he had his formal white shirtsleeves rolled up to the elbows – a curious combination, that made him look vulnerable, but she was learning that most things about Rex were a curious combination.

His house was no different. The inside was a total contrast to the outside. The inside, as he'd said, was full of mod cons and had what an estate agent would have described as a good flow. There were also some old-fashioned touches that blended beautifully with the old/new theme.

A modern breakfast island sat in the centre of a stunning chrome kitchen, which also housed an Aga, set back against the pale vanilla wall, that looked as though it had been there forever.

'I think it probably has,' he said when she mentioned it. 'It dates back to 1964. The original was coal fired, but it was converted to gas before I bought the place.'

The whole house also had great architecture. High Victorian ceilings, beautiful old-fashioned dado rails, and a William Morris stained-glass window in the porch. The mixture of old and new reminded Sam of how much of a mixture Rex himself was – a paradox of confident and insecure, formal and warm, mathematical and creative, engineer and carpenter.

'I've never had much to do with dogs,' he confessed as the conversation got round to Max. 'I've put a bowl of water for him on the floor and a blanket. Is that OK?' He gestured to a Pyrex dish that was in a space alongside the Aga and a dark blue sleeping bag that looked new. 'I thought he may like the warmth,' he added blinking.

For someone who wasn't used to dogs, his instincts were spot on. She loved that he was so thoughtful. 'That's brilliant. Thank you. I've brought his bed. You don't have to sacrifice your sleeping bag.'

Rex waved a hand. 'Max is welcome to it. I doubt very much I'll ever go camping again.' He gave a little shudder. 'Once was enough.'

Also dotted around his house were pieces that he'd obviously made. In the kitchen, there was a spice rack and a fruit bowl on a stand. In the lounge, there was a coffee table. In his bathroom, she spotted a light wood cabinet made with his unmistakable flair and containing miniatures of Molten Brown shower gel and a bottle of indigestion remedy, Sam saw when she sneaked a look.

Once more, they talked about anything and everything. Sam felt as though they were catching up on every part of their lives before they'd met.

After they had eaten dinner, an exquisite fish pie Rex had made for her, followed by a rhubarb crumble – the rhubarb had come from his mother's garden – he told her why he had given up his carpentry dreams and decided to work for his father.

'They were very let down when things didn't work out between Katrina and myself and I... I... felt as though I wanted to redress that somehow and the only way I could think of to do it was to stop resisting their wishes that I go into the family business.'

'But it wasn't your fault that things didn't work out with Katrina,' Sam said, shocked. 'She lied to you.'

'They didn't know that. As far as most people outside of our marriage knew, Katrina had lost the baby. She begged me not to tell people the truth,' he said. 'And so I went along with it, as long as she didn't make any objection to the divorce.'

Sam gasped. 'But didn't that mean everyone thought that she'd lost the baby and then you'd divorced her? So you were painted as the bad guy?'

'Pretty much.' He looked downhearted.

'That's awful. Didn't you mind?'

'I've got broad shoulders. I knew anyone who was close to me would know I wasn't "the bad guy", as you put it.' He mimed the inverted commas around the words. 'I have an uncle I'm close to. Uncle Len. He knew the truth. So did my best man, Peter Bennett. He's local. He has a butcher's shop in Brancombe – Bennett's Butchers. I'll introduce you to him one day.'

The words, 'one day', warmed her. So it wasn't just her who thought they had a future. He was looking ahead to the day he would introduce her to his friends and family.

'To cut a long story short,' Rex continued, 'I felt I had some making up to do to my parents. My father was thrilled when I told him I'd decided to retrain as a structural engineer. I told him I didn't intend to stop working with wood, but that I planned to make it more of a hobby than a career. That was what my parents had wanted me to do in the first place, not because they didn't want me to be happy, but because being an engineer has far better prospects, particularly if you go into an established company. And the rest, as they always say, is history.'

'Yes,' Sam said, thinking again that it all made so much sense now she knew the full story, although that didn't mean her heart didn't go out to Rex for giving up on his dreams. She was no longer surprised he hadn't changed anything in his father's office. Her mind flicked back to the picture of Rex Fielding Senior on the wall. A sombre unsmiling man dressed in a suit and dark tie similar to the ones Rex always wore. Had Rex unconsciously also modelled himself on that man? Could he have taken on his father's persona when he'd given up on his own dreams in order to join the business?

A small whine interrupted her thoughts and she glanced at Max, who was at her feet in Rex's kitchen.

'Oh my gosh, I should take him out. Is it OK if we go in your garden? I have poop bags.'

'Be my guest. I'll make us some coffee.'

* * *

After the coffee, Sam had regretfully taken Max and herself back home to Beach Cottage. She didn't think it was fair on the old dog to have to sleep in a strange kitchen that he wasn't used to. Also, as Rex had said, when he'd walked them both out to her car, they had plenty of time to do all of the things they wanted to do.

'I'm so glad I found you,' he said. 'I know real life will get in the way from time to time, but I'm not planning on going anywhere. We have all the time in the world for it to be just the two of us, don't we?'

Sam nodded. She couldn't have agreed more.

24

They had agreed that for the time being they would keep their relationship a secret from the rest of the staff in the office.

'What I would really like to do is shout it from the rooftops,' Rex had said when they'd discussed it. 'But maybe not just yet. I think it might alter the dynamics when we tell people. For you, as well as for me.' He'd touched her cheek.

Sam knew he was right. The rest of the team were bound to treat her differently when they knew she was sleeping with the boss. She had seen it happen before in other places she'd worked. It was almost like having a spy in the ranks. People were more careful what they said, no longer sure that casual throwaway lines wouldn't be misconstrued and fed back to the boss as pillow talk.

It did feel slightly odd going into Fielding's the following week. But Sam knew it would have felt slightly odd anyway because it was her first week of being part-time. Janet had finished her induction and training. They'd had a desk reshuffle in order to make this work.

Heather still needed a desk, although she'd already had quite a bit of time off with various pregnancy-related ailments. Sam wasn't surprised Rex had wanted to cover himself. He and the other three engineers easily generated enough work for two full-time typists and Heather took time off at the drop of a hat in normal circumstances, let alone when she was pregnant, which, 'wasn't a breeze actually,' she told anyone who would listen. 'And if you haven't had a baby, you're not really in a position to comment.'

As this applied to absolutely everyone in the office, no one dared to say very much. Rex had decided that training three new people simultaneously would put them under too much pressure so the plan was that once Janet was up to speed, Rex would ask the two women who would cover Heather's official maternity leave to come in for an induction. Rex didn't think the training would take too long as it was mainly a case of 'learning the lingo'.

'Don't forget translating Mumbling Mike's surveys,' Heather had added darkly. She certainly wasn't going to be the one who would play down the skill level of her role.

Sam had done Janet's induction. Luckily, Janet had a 'nothing's too much trouble' approach. She was keen to get to grips with her new job as quickly as she could.

She did also talk a lot.

'I'm so glad I reinvented myself,' she told Sam as they were sipping coffee in a break. 'Sitting down all day's a breeze compared to being a chambermaid. It's the stairs that were the killer. Up and bleeding down them all day long. That's very hard on the knees when you get to my age. What did you say you were going part-time to do? It wasn't the holiday trade, was it?'

'Yes, but for animals. I've got an animal boarding service and a dog field for hire. I won't be looking after any people.'

'No, but you'll still have to deal with their owners, won't you,' Janet said darkly. 'They're likely to be as nutty as fruitcakes, some of them. I could tell you some stories about fruitcakes. We had this couple stay at the Bluebell once who were convinced there was a murderer up on the flat roof above their bedroom, dragging a body around in a sack.'

'Why?' Sam stared at her in astonishment.

'They'd been watching a late-night thriller was most of the reason, as far as I could tell. They actually got the night porter to go up there and check.'

'What did he find?'

'Well, he didn't find no murderers with body bags,' Janet said gleefully. 'Overactive imagination, if you ask me. I love crime dramas myself, but you've got to have the stomach for them. I think my ideal job would be working as one of them courtroom typists. That would really be something.'

'Well, if you can translate a structural engineer's babblings you can translate anything.'

'The chef was as mad as a hatter too,' Janet added, draining her mug and slanting a glance at Sam. 'He refused to tell anyone his real name in case someone stole his identity. We all had to call him Mr B.'

'I know. I've met him. I'm looking after his Kunekunes this weekend.'

'You're kidding – right?' Janet stared at her in amazement. 'You're not kidding. Rather you than me. He's besotted with those flaming pigs. And I've heard they're quite sickly. I hope you've got good public liability insurance.'

Sam frowned. Mr B hadn't said anything about them being sickly.

* * *

It was strange leaving Fielding's at lunchtime that first week, but Sam hardly noticed she was doing fewer hours because she was too busy. She was still putting the finishing touches to the dog field.

She'd managed to buy a couple of old wooden tea chests from charity shops and these contained a selection of dog toys: tennis balls, KONGs, throwing rings, tug-of-war ropes and squeaky toys.

The tea chests were in the bus stop-style shelter in the dog field, which now sported a wooden sign over the top with the words, 'Purbeck Pooches VIP Owners' Enclosure'. Matt had arranged for this sign to be done without telling her and given it to her as a surprise. Sam was touched he'd taken the trouble.

She had also picked up some more dog-walking business. Two of her regular clients, who'd known she was about to have more time, had immediately upped their bookings and one of them had recommended her friend, who also made a regular afternoon booking.

One of the things Sam had done with her parents' money, apart from the fence, had been to trade in her Chevrolet for a nearly new van, which she'd had sign-written with the name Purbeck Pooches and then, in smaller letters, 'We walk dogs while you work' and 'Dog field for hire'.

It had been Abby's idea to put the word 'we'. Sam had been more reluctant. 'They might think I have a whole team working for me,' she'd said.

'Well you might have, soon. Think big,' Abby had countered. 'Anyway, it sounds better.'

The van had also been fitted out with specialist crates for dogs, which was so much easier than transporting them in her car and meant Sam could also pick up dogs from different households and know they'd be safely separated.

Sam had also been stressing a fair bit about the swiftly approaching launch party. She was worried about the weather. The BBC weather app gave a 40 per cent chance of rain. She had visions of twenty-five people and half a dozen dogs getting drenched and then traipsing around the house covered in mud.

'Don't be so pessimistic,' Abby told her. 'Anyway, they can stand in the VIP Owners' Enclosure.'

'I know. I just want it to be perfect.'

Sam, Abby, Paul and Matt were included in the twenty-five guests. Abby had persuaded Paul and Matt to dress up as wine waiters and serve prosecco. And of course, Rex would be there. Sam felt as though Rex was threaded through her life like a bright strand of gold. They didn't speak much more than usual at work, both of them too aware of their surroundings, but they had stolen some time together in the evenings. On Wednesday, he'd shyly presented her with a beautiful carved wooden sign with hooks for hanging up dog leads and the words Purbeck Pooches carved out. She'd been blown away.

In between clandestine meetings, they had chatted on the phone for hour-plus sessions. Sam was amazed they didn't run out of things to say, but they didn't. They were still in the discovery phase and the more she discovered about him, the more she liked him and the more she knew that he was the perfect man for her.

She was also in almost daily contact with her parents too, chatting about house updates. Her mum was thrilled to bits about Rex. 'We can't wait to meet him at the launch. Don't worry, darling. We won't expect an official introduction. We'll be super discreet.'

* * *

'Let's hope he doesn't have any dark secrets tucked up his sleeve,' Abby said when she came into the kitchen on Thursday afternoon and found Sam sitting staring into space with a big grin on her face, having just put the phone down after talking to Rex.

'Like what?'

'I dunno. A secret wife somewhere. Or a love child.' She had brought in Jack's bouncy chair, which he had just started to use, and he giggled as she strapped him in. 'A love child could be good. It would save all the hassle of giving birth. Wouldn't it, Jackanory? I'm going to adopt if I want any more.' She turned her attention back to Sam. 'Have you discussed children yet with Mr Wonderful? Does he want a family?'

Sam felt a twang of unease. The closest they had got to discussing children was what Rex had told her about Katrina's deception before he'd known it was deception and he had said that he'd been pleased. He'd also said, 'I wanted children back then.' It was the words 'back then' that had bothered her. Did that mean he didn't want children now? She hadn't asked him because it would have felt wrong. They were such a new couple. She could hardly drop that on him.

'It's a bit soon for that kind of discussion,' she told Abby.

'OK, just asking.' Abby narrowed her eyes. 'Don't leave it too long though. It'd be a pain if he'd had a vasectomy.'

'He hasn't,' Sam snapped, because they had discussed that when the 'precautions' word had come up. 'Sorry,' she added more softly. 'I think I'm a bit stressed. To be honest, I'll be relieved when this weekend's over.'

'Yeah, I bet. I know you've never been a massive fan of parties. But it'll be fun. A chance to celebrate new beginnings.'

'I know it will. Sorry. The last person I want to take it out on is you.'

They moved on to lighter things, like what they were going to wear, and Sam felt the tension she'd been feeling flitter away.

One thing she had stopped worrying about was Mr B's Kunekunes. Right up until the last minute, she had thought he might not go away. But on Friday morning, he and Meg set off on their minibreak to Edinburgh as planned. They had flown from Southampton airport to their luxury break at a four-star hotel which had water frontage and a top chef and Mr B had said he was looking forward to four days of being an awkward customer and sending his meals back if they weren't cooked to his exact specifications. Sam wasn't sure whether he'd been joking or not.

She had checked on the Kunekunes twice since then, once on the Watch Me From Afar app and once in person. All had been well. They'd looked as perky as a pair of pigs can look and had posed for a photo. One of the things Mr B had stipulated was that she send him a breakfast photo of Portia and Percy each morning.

She was beginning to wish she had not got caught up in his paranoia or listened to Janet about them being sickly, although Mr B had dismissed this when Sam had mentioned it.

What Sam had told Abby still held true though. She would be relieved when this weekend was over.

* * *

Saturday kicked off with a hazy sky and an autumn mist that hung over the pasture meadows like an army of wandering ghosts.

'That'll clear by eleven,' Abby said confidently and she was right.

A lemon-coloured sun popped through the haze and it turned into a spectacular blue-skied day. There was a slight chill in the air, but the fields looked like a patchwork of perfect English countryside – a montage of greens and yellows and rustic browns. Harvesting was done and the farmland had been ploughed for their next crops or laid to fallow.

In the distance, the sea was a sheet of navy gabardine. Not a breath of a breeze shivered the bronze and golden leaves on the surrounding trees and the ivy that clambered over the back wall of Beach Cottage was transformed into a waterfall of fiery red every time the sun splashed carelessly across it.

'It's going to be awesome,' Abby told Sam as they put the final touches to the food. There hadn't been too much to do because they weren't having anything extravagant. Sam had bought in canapés and nibbles like crisps and nuts and olives and dips with carrots and celery for those who were watching their weight. There were several bottles of prosecco and several more of sparkling elderflower, orange juice, apple juice, cranberry juice and tea and coffee for those who didn't drink or were driving.

Sam had put out a selection of stainless steel and ceramic bowls of water for the canine guests and she had also supplied a bucket and a roll of poop bags for the field.

More than a handful of dogs were coming to the party. They included Seamus and Goldie and Max and three border terriers who belonged to a new client and were known affectionately as the snapdragons by their owner, who had also promised to keep them on leads. Maureen Grey was coming, but Coal and Pewter would be staying at home. Clara King was bringing Foxy. Apparently Foxy got on with everyone, canine or human. She had once been a street dog so being convivial had presumably been key to her survival.

Sam had done her morning visit to Portia and Percy in person. They'd grunted at her affectionately and had posed obligingly for their breakfast photo. Sam had sent it off to Mr B and had got a thumbs up emoji in return. There was a part of her that was surprised he hadn't asked for today's newspaper to be lined up in the shot, but maybe that was going a bit far even for Mr B.

At lunchtime, the Watch Me From Afar app showed the Kunekunes to be still grazing contentedly. She had decided to check that they were safely tucked up for the night on the app once more, just before Rex did the official opening – which was happening at 4 p.m.

She and Abby were ready a good hour early. Sam was wearing jeggings and a metallic gold fitted t-shirt with her long hair up, twirled in a bright clip with a few escaping strands, and the minimum of make-up. Jeggings and trainers were part of her identity. That was who she was. And who she was was what today was all about. It was the first day of her properly beginning to live her dream. She had made a slight concession on footwear and had swapped her usual trainers for some very stylish mustard-coloured Converse High Tops, which had been eye-wateringly expensive but served the dual purpose of being both cool and comfy.

Abby had gone for a gorgeously upmarket multicoloured bohemian dress with lace edges that showed off her curves and hid the bits she wanted to stay hidden – despite the fact Sam had repeatedly assured her there was nothing that needed to be hidden – and a little jacket because it would be chilly by four. Jack was wearing a very cute pale blue waistcoat that she said she would put on at the last minute in case he was sick down it.

Before anyone else arrived, Sam and Abby pushed Jack's buggy across the lawn and stood by the five-bar gate that led through to the field. It looked amazing. The Purbeck Pooches VIP Owners' Enclosure was immediately on the left as you opened the gate. The Purbeck Pooches Sniff Zone, which now also sported a wooden sign, made by Rex, was in the right-hand corner. Between the two, the short grass ran in a smooth sweep down to the rear fence. There was plenty of room for even a wolfhound like Seamus to get up a bit of speed and have a run, if ever the mood took him. Seamus wasn't a dog who liked to overexert himself, Sam had noticed.

'You should be really proud of yourself,' Abby said, touching her arm as they stood in the golden October light.

'It's just a field,' Sam said, swallowing the ache in her throat.

'No it's not. It's the start of a dream.' Abby's eyes were sparkling. 'And it's goodbye to Fielding's. I'll give it six months before you can give up the other half of your job. That's assuming things don't hot up with the boss. I can't see Suit Man wanting his girlfriend working for him.'

'Stop calling him that. Although, actually, he did say he planned to wear his best suit today! Anyway, honey, things can't get any hotter. I can tell you that much for free.'

'Oooh, that is exciting. I knew you'd cave in and confess all sooner or later. So how is he in the sack? Does he take his tie off? How about his socks? What does he take off first? I can't be doing with men who keep their socks on.'

'He takes his tie off. And that is all you're getting. A lady doesn't kiss and tell,' she smirked.

'Cool beans. By the way, I thought you might like to know that your three-word horoscope for today is, "*No going back*".'

'Sounds OK. What's yours?' Not that Sam put anywhere near as much faith in those horoscopes as her best friend did.

'"*Tonight's the night*".' Abby giggled.

So did Jack. 'Dag,' he said.

'Did you hear that, Abby? He just said dog. He really is the perfect little man.'

'Are you sure it wasn't Dad?' Abby glanced at her son with affection. 'Apparently they usually say Dad before Mum. Typical. We do all the work and Dad gets all the credit.'

'Dag og, dag dag dog,' repeated Jack, waving his hands vigorously, delighted as usual at being the centre of both women's attention.

* * *

Sam's parents were the first to arrive. They came at quarter past three. It was great to see them looking so relaxed and happy, Sam thought as she poured her mum a glass of sparkling elderflower and her dad a tot of Irish whiskey, his favourite drink, from her secret stash in the drinks cabinet in the lounge.

Paul arrived next and Sam was thrilled to see that he'd done as he'd promised and dressed as a waiter. He scrubbed up well, his darkly gypsy looks were fabulous in black trousers and a crisp white shirt.

Sam noticed the way he and Abby looked at each other. She'd have put money on the fact that if they weren't already a lot more than 'partner parents', they would be very soon. Perhaps Abby's "*Tonight's the night*" horoscope was more accurate than she'd thought.

Matt wasn't far behind Paul. He looked good in a suit too. His fair-haired, slightly windswept beach-surfer looks were also perfectly complemented by a waiter's outfit. 'Hey, Sam babe. How's it going? My spies tell me you're already booked up till Christmas.'

He kissed her cheek and she looked at him with affection. 'Not quite. Your sister has been amazing, though. Superwoman as far as websites go. As well as being supermum.'

'It keeps her out of mischief,' Matt said, shooting a swift glance at Paul, which made Sam wonder if he had come to the same conclusion she had – it wouldn't be long before Abby was back with the father of her son.

After that, everyone seemed to arrive at once. All the staff from Fielding's and their partners turned up close together, as did the geeks from Abby's company, two of whom had also brought their dogs.

Clara King, Danny, and Six-Pack Si were hot on their heels. Soon there were people and dogs milling freely around the house and garden. Rex had agreed with Sam that it would be a good idea, more exciting and official, if he didn't arrive until just before 4 p.m. which also gave Sam the chance to get everyone out of the dog field for him to cut the ribbon. They'd arranged to have a late supper when everyone had gone and he would stay for the night. They hadn't done that since that first unforgettable Saturday. Sam couldn't believe it had only been a week ago. She was really looking forward to the moment they could sit down, just the two of them, to relax.

While she was on a trip to the bathroom – she'd either been drinking too much sparkling elderflower or she was nervous – she sneaked another look at the Watch Me From Afar app. Neither of the Kunekunes were in the paddock as far as she could see, which meant that they'd taken themselves off to bed. They had done that last night too.

Mr B had said that as long as she could see they were in the ark, she could forgo the evening visit if she was too busy with the launch. She was about to switch the app onto the indoor camera when she heard the slam of a car door. It sounded as though her guest of honour had just arrived. With a flutter of pleased anticipation, she ran downstairs to let him into the party.

25

'How's it going, Sam? You look... beautiful.' Rex stood on the doorstep at the front of Beach Cottage, and his eyes were tender. She still hadn't got used to him looking at her like that.

'You look pretty hot yourself.' He had, as promised, put on his best suit, the one he'd told her he'd had tailor made when he'd been going to a posh wedding.

'My cousin's wedding, not mine,' he had added, 'which wasn't long ago, so it should still fit me perfectly. And at least you'll be able to tell the difference from what I usually wear at work.'

That was true. Rex Fielding was a man who wore suits and looked good in them. But this suit was something special. It was beautifully cut in a gorgeous charcoal grey that totally set off his eyes. Sam had never been a fashionista, but she could see it was in a class of its own.

'I wish I could whisk you upstairs,' she said. 'I need to remind myself of what you look like underneath that fabulous suit.'

'Don't tempt me,' he said, stepping into the hallway, close enough for her to smell his cologne and feel the fizz of that force field that sparked up every time she got within a foot of him.

A voice from behind them broke the moment. ‘Sam, have you got a piece of paper anywhere? I need to write down a phone number.’ It was Matt, looking flustered. ‘My phone’s out of battery. Bloody typical. They always do it at the worst possible time.’ He broke off when he saw Rex. ‘Oh sorry. I didn’t realise…’

‘Hall table,’ Sam said, gesturing as she ushered Rex past him towards the lounge. ‘Right then, let me get you a drink. Do you need wine for Dutch courage?’

‘I think I’m OK,’ Rex said, glancing at his watch. ‘It’s just about time, isn’t it?’

‘Yes it is. But, in the interests of making an entrance – or maybe that should be exit as we’re going outside – I think you should stay hidden in here while I rally the troops.’

‘No problem. I’ll stay in the hall. I’m actually pretty nervous. I don’t think I’ve ever done an official opening before.’ He touched her arm in a little gesture of solidarity. ‘Sorry. How are *you* feeling?’

“Butterfly tummy. I know that’s totally mad. Ten more minutes and we can all relax and have a drink. I’ll be back to get you in about thirty seconds.’

Matt had gone back outside. It looked as though he had already rallied the troops too, bless him. She could see that everyone had crossed the garden and they were gathering around the five-bar gate that led into the field. Earlier on, she had tied a bright sunshine-yellow tape across the entrance that would show up beautifully when the gate was actually open. Matt had instructions to push the gate open a fraction. Then Rex could cut the tape and push the gate the rest of the way open. Meanwhile, Paul would change from being a waiter into his second role of being official photographer and snap shots of the whole thing, which would, of course, go on the website and Facebook page.

‘We could live stream it all if you like?’ Abby had suggested, but

Sam had said they were probably better off showing videos of dogs playing in the field than a live stream of a gate!

Now, she caught Abby's gaze across the heads of her guests and they exchanged a nod. Everyone was in position.

It was time to fetch Rex.

He was still standing in the hall where she had left him. Was it a trick of the light or did he look paler than he had a few moments ago? He looked very tense too. Gosh, he obviously hadn't been joking when he'd told her he was nervous.

Sam held out her hand. 'Everyone's waiting for our guest of honour.'

'Then the guest of honour had better not disappoint them.' His voice was so formal and grave that Sam was momentarily startled, but then, after what seemed a lifetime of hesitation, he took her hand and she was reassured as she led him out into the Beach Cottage garden. They crossed the sweet-smelling lawn and walked towards the small crowd of people and dogs crowding around the five-bar gate.

She'd had no idea what he had planned to say, but he had clearly put a lot of thought into it.

'I first met Sam,' he began, 'when she came to work for me at my own family business. I can't say that I'm not a little disappointed that she has decided to begin her own business, because it means I am losing her. Although I am not losing her completely.' He paused and in the pause Sam read an ocean of meaning. He was not going to lose her at all. She would be sharing his life. She knew it, as surely as sunrise. Not, of course, that he could say anything like that in his speech, but she hugged the warmth of this truth close to her heart.

Rex went on to speak about her love for animals and the dream she had of starting a business she was passionate about. He mentioned her supportive parents and Sam saw them both glow pink and smiley with pride. He said that he was touched and honoured to be the person she had asked to officially open it. Then he leaned forward. 'It now gives me great pleasure to announce the Purbeck Pooches Paddock officially open.'

Everyone was smiling. There was a smattering of applause and one or two shouts of 'Hear, hear,' and 'Go for it, princess.' The latter was from her dad, who was beaming from ear to ear.

Rex cut the ribbon and pushed the gate open wide and people and dogs poured into the paddock.

Sam was being showered with congratulations. When she next had the chance to look up, she couldn't see Rex. Maybe he had gone for the drinks refill she had promised him. She hoped so.

After a few more minutes, she extricated herself from a conversation with a very earnest woman who was a partner of one of Abby's geek colleagues apparently and had a rescue whippet she was sure would love a run in the dog field. Then she went into the house to track him down.

There were a few people in the kitchen helping themselves to drinks refills, but Rex wasn't amongst them.

Matt was though. He was mid-conversation with her parents.

'Have you seen our guest of honour?' she called over.

He shook his head, but he came across. 'No. He was here though. Have you tried the bathroom?'

'No. But I guess if he's in there, he won't be long.'

'It is what it is!' Matt was nodding thoughtfully. He patted his shirt pocket. 'I'll give you these back before I forget.' He handed her a wad of yellow Post-it notes. 'They were in the hall table drawer. I couldn't find a notepad – there were a few bits of paper, but they mostly had writing on. I'm not sure if I put them back.'

'Don't worry, I'll do it.' She took the Post-its and went out into the hall.

The pieces of paper Matt had mentioned were still on the hall table as he'd said. They were face up. Sam reached for them absently and glanced at the writing. The one on top was headed up with the words, Mission Perfect Dad.

She felt as though a finger of ice had just trailed down her spine.

Oh God. She had forgotten all about this. But now, aided by a written prompt, the memory rushed back into her mind with horrifying clarity. It was the night she and Abby had waded through two bottles of wine – actually she had done most of the wading – and made a list of the attributes that a perfect father/sperm donor must have.

Abby clearly hadn't been anywhere near as inebriated as she had because her writing was beautifully neat.

Mission Perfect Dad

1. Tall with hair and handsome.
2. Intelligent.
3. Kind.
4. Honest.
5. Animal Lover.
6. Good in the sack.
7. 45 years (tops).
8. Well heeled.

Alongside the first list, there was a second and even more damning column, should a casual observer be reading it.

Prospective Candidates (sperm donors)

1. Ben Campbell.
2. Matt Martin.
3. Rex Fielding (subject to name change!!!)
4. Mr B.

The piece of paper clipped to the back of it said simply, *Gorgeous, long-haired, animal-loving brunette seeks fit hottie for uncomplicated fun times.*

Had Rex seen this? Matt clearly hadn't or she knew he would have mentioned it. But then Matt had been looking for something else and he'd been in a hurry. He would have been too distracted to be reading random bits of paper.

Rex had been standing here in this hallway with nothing to distract him but the impending speech that he'd been trying not to think about. The icy shock morphed into a wave of heat as Sam felt her cheeks flood with embarrassment.

The lists would have been right under his nose. He surely couldn't have avoided seeing them. It certainly explained his absence. It also explained his pallor and the tension she'd spotted when she had come to fetch him. She hadn't imagined it, after all, and it hadn't been due to nerves.

With a tiny gasp of distress, she crumpled up the pieces of paper and stuffed them into her back pocket. She had a vague memory of Abby telling her she'd put them in the hall table drawer. Why hadn't she got rid of them long ago?

Clinging to a tiny last vestige of hope that Rex hadn't seen them and he'd just nipped to the bathroom, she took the stairs two at a time. There was no one in the bathroom. The door was slightly ajar.

She looked out of the landing window just in case he was still outside and she'd somehow missed him. It was almost dark now, but the outside lights were on and most of the garden and much of the dog field was illuminated clearly.

Most people were in the garden in small groups chatting. Clara King was talking to Janet Brown, and Danny Bowkett was deep in conversation with Barbara Oldfield. Sam registered they were standing very close together – they were clearly getting on well. But there was no sign of Rex's familiar outline.

Then she did what she should have done before, she raced back downstairs and went out of the front door to see if his car was still there. He'd been one of the last to arrive so he would have parked at the back of the line in the country road. She ran along it to the end. There was no sign of the distinctive silver Saab.

Oh God, what must he have thought when he had seen that list? That he was part of some kind of elaborate sperm donor programme? What on earth must he be feeling now? All of the joy and hope and expectation and excitement that had filled her less than an hour before had gone. It had been replaced by a chilly darkness.

Sam ran back into the house to get her phone. When she pressed his number, which was already in her favourites list, it went straight to a tinny voice that said, 'The person you are calling is unavailable'. She couldn't even leave him a message.

Rex had left her with no easy way of reaching him quickly. And she didn't blame him one little bit.

* * *

Sam wasn't sure how she got through the next hour, but she did. Every instinct she had urged her to go after him: to drive round to his house and hammer on the door until he let her in. But a cool and rational voice in her head was insistent that this was not a very good idea and was unlikely to work. He clearly didn't want to speak to her or he'd have left his phone on. He might not even have gone home.

Heading off on a wild goose chase around the countryside was counterproductive. Not to mention the fact that it would look very odd if both the host and the guest of honour left the launch party. Also, not having anticipated driving, she'd already had two glasses of prosecco.

She forced her face into a mask of composure and went back to mingle with her guests. Abby and Paul and Jack were sitting on the bench by the summerhouse. Abby had her head on Paul's shoulder and Jack was in the buggy between them. The perfect little family.

Sam wanted to tell Abby what had happened, but she couldn't bring herself to interrupt what she suspected was going to turn into the reunion of the decade. She wanted to tell her mum too. Mum wasn't stupid – she knew something was up – but Sam couldn't risk letting the mask drop for fear she would fall apart.

Instead, she made small talk, handed out business cards, accepted people's congratulations and stroked all of the canine guests. The dogs were the easiest part. Sam had worried that a fight might break out, having so many dogs in such close proximity to each other. She hadn't, even in her worst nightmares, predicted that Rex would leave the launch of her dream business without even saying goodbye.

26

'Not that I blame him,' she told Abby, for the umpteenth time 'How could I have been so stupid?'

It was now 9.35 p.m. on Saturday. Even the most determined of stragglers had gone. She'd managed to convince her parents she was fine – that Rex had shot away because he hadn't been feeling too good – that was true. Now she and Abby were clearing up the wreckage of the party. They had already washed and dried endless glasses and the plates used for the nibbles were in the dishwasher, which was rumbling through its cycle.

'The question is – what are you going to do about it, girlfriend? Stand here hoping it didn't happen or head round to his house and hammer his door down?'

'Do you really think I should do that?' Sam put down the tea towel. 'I'm scared he won't let me in.'

'He'll have to talk to you sooner or later. You still work for him, remember?'

'No he won't. He barely talked to me for the first two and a half years I worked there. He's not really the talking kind.'

But that wasn't true, was it? He had opened up to her that very first time they'd gone out. When they had talked about wood and about their passions and their dreams. He had let her in, let her see the vulnerability of him. He had told her all about Katrina.

'Yes, OK, but that was before. He'll surely want to hear what was behind that list. I know you haven't been seeing each other long, but you had something special. You weren't the only one who thought that – not from what you've said.'

'I think he may be too hurt,' Sam said with a deep sigh. 'He was married very briefly to a woman who tricked him into it by telling him she was pregnant after a one-night stand. That list was the worst possible thing he could have seen.' She pressed her fingers to her forehead, which had been throbbing for a while.

'Oh shit,' Abby said.

For a moment, there was silence in the steamy kitchen while the implications of what had happened tonight rattled around in Sam's head. At worst, Rex would banish her from his life. At best, he would never trust her again.

She gave up trying to ignore the headache and found some paracetamol to take.

Abby came across to where she stood and caught hold of her hands. 'What if we were both to explain what happened? I could talk to him. Tell him that I wrote that list when we had been drinking. Tell him that it was all just a silly joke.' Abby's eyes were more sombre than Sam had ever seen them. 'Surely he'd listen? Surely he'd give you a second chance?'

'Maybe.' Sam checked her phone again to see if there were any messages. There weren't. She tried his phone again. It was still switched off. 'I'll go round there and see him first thing in the morning. I'll do it on the way back from the Kunekunes. Oh my God, the Kunekunes. I meant to check they'd put themselves to bed. I got side-tracked. It'll be too dark to see now.' She switched the app on anyway. She was right. It was too dark to see if they were in the ark.

'They'll be fine,' Abby said. 'They're pigs. Get some sleep. Everything will look better in the morning, I promise.'

* * *

Sam was amazed that she slept, but she did. Her dreams were a disturbing mix of Mr B wagging a finger at her and saying with Rex's voice, 'Our word is our bond. Trust is the basis of all good relationships. Where are my Kunekunes?'

She woke up properly around 7.00 a.m. and for a moment she was still too caught up in the dream to remember. Then reality came crashing in. She flashed back to Rex's face as he'd stood in her hall. That slight pallor and the tension in him.

'Everyone's waiting for the guest of honour.'

'Then the guest of honour had better not disappoint them.'

She remembered how formal he had sounded and how she'd been fleetingly shocked. How she had reached for his hand and how there had been that long second of hesitation before he'd taken it.

He must have been wondering in that moment if he should go through with it. He must have wanted to just walk out. But he hadn't. He'd stood outside and he'd said all those lovely things about her – he'd sung her praises, launched her business as he'd promised he would.

'Our word is our bond.'

He'd showed himself to be the man of integrity she had come to know and respect and oh so much more than that, even though he must have thought that she'd been lying to him and using him from the start.

It was this that somehow hurt the most. Sam felt the tears that she hadn't cried last night blocking her throat as she jumped out of bed, showered and put on make-up with slightly trembling fingers. She had to put this right. She had to do it as soon as humanly possible.

While she was waiting for the kettle to boil – no breakfast but she couldn't leave the house without coffee – she opened the Watch Me From Afar app on her phone. The Kunekunes were up early. They weren't in the ark. She flicked to the outside camera and saw with a small shock that the field was empty too. That was impossible. Her fingers felt sweaty as she went back to the images inside the ark in case she'd missed them in her haste. Two brown pigs were easily camouflaged in the dim interior of an ark, even in daylight. She scrutinised every corner. They definitely weren't there.

Fuck. Unable to believe the evidence of her own eyes, she went back and forth between cameras. Maybe there was a fault with a camera. But surely if there was, she would simply see a blank screen.

The sound of footsteps coming downstairs heralded the arrival of Abby and then she was there in the doorway, still in her jimjams, her hair all tousled, rubbing sleep from her eyes.

'Hello, darling, I heard you come down and I figured you might be in need of a hug. Hey, what is it? Have you spoken to him? You look...' She tailed off as Sam showed her the phone.

'The Kunekunes have disappeared. I've got to go over there. They must have been stolen.' She reached for her coat from the hook by the door.

'Are you sure? Do you want me to come with you? It won't take a minute to get Jack ready.'

'We both know that's not true. No, it's fine. You won't be able to do anything I can't do. Shit. Shit. Shit. Mr B will be apoplectic if anything's happened to those pigs. Why didn't I go and check them last night?'

'That wouldn't have made any difference. It's hardly your fault if someone's stolen them in the night.'

'Yes, but the last time I checked at three thirty, I only checked the paddock, not the ark. I was about to do it and then I got side-tracked. What if they were stolen yesterday afternoon? I won't be able to tell the police when it happened. I wasn't doing my job properly, Abby, that's the bottom line.'

'Do not tell the police that.' Abby folded her arms. 'Getting sued is very bad for business.'

'I can't lie to the police.'

'You have to, Sam. Think about the consequence. Two Kunekunes versus your whole career. You have to lie.'

She shook her head. 'I'd better go and see what I can do before Mr B gets on to ask where his breakfast photo is.'

Five minutes later, Sam was in her newly sign-written van, hurtling through the blue-sky morning along the coast road on her way to the Kunekune paddock. Why hadn't she looked last night? Why hadn't she checked? It would have still been bad if the Kunekunes were stolen, but at least she would have honoured her part of the agreement.

Exactly like Rex had done last night, her conscience reminded her. She had let him down utterly, but he had still honoured his end of the agreement. That was integrity. That was what it meant. Doing the right thing no matter how bloody hard that might be.

She knew in that moment that, on day two of her business launch, her integrity was about to be called into question. If she lied to the police about the facts, she would have proved she didn't have any.

Her hands sweated on the steering wheel as the countryside

flashed past in a film reel of breathtaking autumn beauty. It all looked exactly the same as it looked yesterday, but today its beauty was bittersweet. In twenty-four hours, it seemed that her whole life had changed.

This time yesterday, she'd been full of expectation for the future: full of hope and possibilities. The golden thread of Rex and their fast-growing connection, the tenderness in him, the way she knew that she felt about him. Love. She hadn't dared give it a name, but that's what she knew that it was. And she had seen it reflected back at her in his eyes.

This time yesterday, she'd been keyed up with excitement about finally getting Purbeck Pooches properly off the ground, the culmination of a long-held dream. One that had been taking shape in her head since she'd been a little girl sitting in the back room at the B&B cuddling a ginger cat called Felix and a Jack Russell pup called Spot.

This time yesterday, autumn had been awash with hope and beginnings. Now it felt as though every door had slammed cruelly in face.

Abby's face flashed once more into her mind. *'You have to lie to the police.'*

But as Sam turned into the road that led to Mr B's Kunekune paddock, she knew that she was not going to do that. She might have lost everything else, but she didn't intend to lose her integrity too.

* * *

Her stomach crunched as she parked in her usual place in the layby by the five-bar gate.

That was odd. She'd expected to find it open, but it was still closed and the lock was still intact. She supposed that it wasn't totally impossible for the Kunekunes to be lifted out over it. Mr B had once told her that the word Kunekune was a direct translation of the Maori words, fat and round. But they weren't as heavy as standard pigs – according to Mr B, they were about 140 pounds apiece. If there had been more than one Kunekune rustler, it was doable.

Sam climbed over the gate and walked towards the ark, which was in the top right-hand corner, scanning the field as she went in case, by some miracle, Portia and Percy had miraculously reappeared. But there was no sign of them and the ark was empty too.

Feeling sick, Sam began a metre-by-metre search of the perimeter fence. She supposed it was possible they could have escaped. If they had, then there was a good chance of finding them again. She wished briefly that she'd had Stan, Danny's border terrier, to help. It would have been quicker. Not that it took that long anyway. The paddock wasn't that large. After ten minutes of looking for gaps and testing for loose panels, she had to concede it was unlikely that Portia and Percy had made a bid for freedom.

She couldn't put it off any longer. She had to phone Mr B and face his wrath. She walked slowly back towards the ark across the yellowing grass. Something was niggling her. Something was different. Then it struck her what it was, the black food bucket was missing. The thief must have used it to entice the Kunekunes away.

Back at the ark once more, she checked inside. No bucket. Then she walked around the back into the two-metre oblong of space behind the wooden structure, just in case they had somehow managed to get stuck behind it and she stopped dead in her tracks. They were both there, wedged into the small space. They weren't stuck though. They were tied up – both of them had collars on and they'd been chained up to a hook on the far side of the ark with what looked like long dog leads.

What the hell? Sam stared at them in disbelief and Portia, who was the one with the least number of splodges, shook her head up and down impatiently, rattling the chain as if to say, 'Well, you took your time, but now you're here, can you get us out of this?'

Sam's heart pounded in an explosion of relief and shock. It took seconds to unfasten the collars and encourage the pigs to back out of the small space, rear ends first, into the field once more, where they both began to nose around in the grass, apparently none the worse for their experience.

In amongst the relief buzzed half a dozen questions. Who the hell was responsible for this? And why would they do it? What on earth had been the point? Why would you tie up two Kunekunes so they had no access to food or water? Actually they did have access to water. Someone had filled the bucket with water and left it at the far end of the gap – with a bit of a shuffle round, they could both have reached it, theoretically anyway.

Sam looked around the field. Had someone planned to come back later and steal them? That didn't seem very likely. It wasn't as though they were hard to catch, as their abductor must already know. Portia would do anything for food and Percy would do anything for a belly rub.

Was it possible that she'd interrupted someone who was in the process of stealing them? That didn't seem very likely either. They would have had to be parked close by and she had seen no other vehicles in the vicinity. She ran back to the gate and scanned the road to check.

There weren't any nearby houses, apart from the one that this field belonged to, a few hundred metres away. There was an old Citroen parked outside that. It wasn't big enough to transport a large dog, let alone a couple of Kunekunes.

It was a complete mystery. It also left Sam with a new dilemma. Should she tell Mr B about this? She knew she must. It was that or camp out in the field until tomorrow when he got back from Edinburgh. There was no way she could risk someone coming back to finish what they had started.

27

Sam got out her phone and scrolled through it until she reached Mr B's number. As she stood in the sunshine with her hands on the cool top bar of the gate, breathing in the sharp countryside smells, she hesitated. Was it too early to phone? It was only just after 8.15 a.m. and she knew that he was an insomniac and didn't sleep. But he was on a break with his girlfriend.

She glanced back at the Kunekunes, who were now grazing peacefully. Maybe she should leave it a while before she called.

Fleetingly, she wondered what Rex was doing. Had he got any sleep last night or had he lain awake going over the events of the afternoon, thinking about what he must have seen as her betrayal?

Her heart clanged shut on the painful images. What would Rex do if he were standing here? She doubted he would be hesitating.

Taking a deep breath, she called Mr B. It rang several times before going to voicemail, which increased her anxiety no end.

Now what? She took the morning photograph of the pigs, checked their water and she was just checking that the pig nuts were topped up when Mr B phoned her back.

'I just had a missed call,' he said without preamble. 'Is everything OK?'

'Yes and no,' she said and told him what had happened.

At the end of it, there was a brief silence before he exploded into such a tirade that Sam had to hold the phone away from her ear.

She could still catch the odd word. 'Scumbags' featured quite a lot, before he finally ended on the phrase, 'flagitious bloody bastards'.

Sam decided that a good dollop of placatory politeness was called for, plus a bit of common sense and practicality. She wasn't sure that Mr B had either of these. He might be the brilliant chef that everyone said he was and she had no doubt that he had an IQ higher than Everest, but common sense didn't seem to feature very much. 'I'm extremely sorry that this has happened. They do seem to be perfectly fine. The intruder hasn't hurt them at all, which is a blessing. They were even left a bucket of water...' She broke off because he was off again.

Again she held the phone away from her ear, an idle part of her mind thinking that this would have made a superb comedy sketch. You couldn't make it up, except that being caught in the middle of it and knowing it might bring an end to her dream was far from funny.

She let him come to a halt. Her father had once told her that if people were in full rant mode it was much better to give them the time to finish than to interrupt. 'Interrupting a ranter,' he had said, 'is like putting your finger over the hole of the whistle on an old-fashioned kettle when it's just come up to the boil. You're gonna get hurt.'

'What would you like me to do?' she said when she was sure he wasn't going to start up again.

'Play back the camera footage,' Mr B said with a clipped authority. 'Whoever carried out this vile act will be on it. Yes?'

'Er, yes,' Sam said. 'I suppose they will. Is there an easy way to do that?'

'I will email instructions. I would do it myself, but, as you know, only one person can access the app. It's a great weakness – I should have gone for a different version. None of the versions were that great. I thought that some of its other functionality would compensate. I was wrong.'

Sam could hear a woman's soft voice in the background. His girlfriend must be wondering what on earth was going on. Or maybe she was used to his ranting. Yes, she probably was, poor thing.

'I will also send instructions on how to freeze-frame the image of person or persons unknown to send to me,' he went on. 'I will get to the bottom of this. Did I ever tell you that I once saved the Bluebell Cliff from a predacious saboteur? This will be no different.'

'The only thing is, I will have to leave Portia and Percy unattended while I go through the footage,' Sam said when he paused for breath. 'I'll need to go home. My phone won't have enough battery.' She didn't want to leave any mantraps in this plan, which she might subsequently fall into. She was already keeping her fingers crossed that whoever had done the tying up hadn't done it too early in the day, because then her lapse yesterday would be highlighted and goodness knows what Mr B would have to say about that.

'I will arrange for a guard,' he was saying, in the same matter of fact tone he might use to say he was arranging for a haircut. 'Until the footage can be examined and sent.'

'Um, I do have some other things to do today.'

'I understand totally. If the worst comes to the worst, I will cut short my break and return.'

'Please don't,' Sam said, her distress mounting. 'I will do it as soon as I can today. Do you know how long it will be before you can arrange the – er – guard?'

'It will be done within the hour,' he said in an imperious voice, so that Sam found herself wondering if he was planning to instruct one of his minions from the Bluebell Cliff. She imagined that he must have a few. Given Mr B's paranoia and connections she wouldn't have been all that surprised if he managed to magic up an actual security guard.

'I am sending the instructions now,' Mr B said and hung up.

Sam breathed a sigh of relief and decided she would stay at the field for another ten minutes or so. It didn't seem very likely that someone would come along and steal the Kunekunes in broad daylight. But something was obviously afoot.

She phoned Rex again while she was waiting and this time his phone was on. She braced herself waiting for him to answer, but it rang and rang and eventually went to voicemail.

'Rex, please can we talk? Please will you give me the chance to explain...?' She could hear the raw emotion in her own voice. 'Please...' she said again. 'None of this is what you think. I hope you're OK.'

She hung up. Of course he wasn't OK. That had been a stupid thing to say. At least she had made contact. She had apologised. No she hadn't. But that was something she wanted to do face to face.

As she got into the van, she was aware that her phone had pinged with a message. With a jolt of hope she reached for it, but it was just Mr B sending through the instructions on how to play back the camera footage.

She sent him a quick reply saying they'd been safely received and that she'd be in touch soon.

But first Rex. His home wasn't far from Mr B's paddock. Even so,

Sam felt as though she made the whole journey without taking a breath.

* * *

She drew up outside Rex's house, in the same place she had parked before. There was no sign of his Saab, but then she hadn't seen it last time either. He had said the one thing he didn't like about his neighbourhood was the lack of parking when everyone in the road was home.

With her heart thumping hard, she got out of the car. It was perfectly possible that he wouldn't want to see her again, but she did think that if he were in, he would open the door.

She felt a sense of déjà vu as she listened to the bell jangling in some distant part of the house, but there was none of the expectation and excitement she had felt the first time she'd come here.

Rex didn't answer. Nor was there so much as a flicker of a curtain to betray anyone's presence inside. There were no lights on either, as far as she could see.

Sam wondered in a mad surge of hope if he had gone to Beach Cottage, having had a few hours to think things through. Or maybe he'd responded to her message just now. If he did turn up, she knew Abby would have let her know. There were no messages from Abby. Sam felt her heart sink once more.

She tried phoning him again but got his voicemail as before. Eventually she was forced to give up and head for home. If Rex had decided not to speak to her, there was nothing she could do – at least until tomorrow morning when she would be turning up for work as usual. He'd have to speak to her then, unless of course he planned to barricade himself in his office.

* * *

Back at Beach Cottage, Sam found Abby had finished the clearing up they hadn't done the night before, which had involved emptying the dishwasher and bringing in more glasses and plates she'd found in the garden, which she was now washing up by hand, elbow deep in bubbles.

Jack was in his bouncy chair. When he saw Sam, he waved his hands and said, 'Gag ga ga.'

'Good morning to you too,' she said, going across and crouching down by him. 'Gorgeous boy.'

'Ga ba ba...'

'He'll be saying proper words soon.'

'I know,' Abby replied.

'Thank you for washing-up. You're an angel.'

'It's the least I can do. What happened? Did you have to speak to the police? What did you say?'

Sam told her what had happened and Abby's face grew more and more astounded. 'Unbelievable. Bloody unbelievable.'

'Guddy,' said Jack. 'Gud gud Guddy.'

'Oh crap, I really must stop swearing. He's picking it all up. He's so flaming bright.'

'Mr B knows some good alternative swear words. At least I think that's what they are. I must look up flagitious. That's how he described the person who chained up Portia and Percy.'

Abby dried her hands on a tea towel and tapped on her phone. 'It means wicked and nasty, apparently. Anyway...' She glanced back up. 'Moving on. Is there any news on Rex?'

'No. I've left him a voicemail. I've also just been round to his house, but I don't think he was there. I was hoping he might have come here.'

'He may still. He may be on his way now.'

'I don't think so. I would have passed him, wouldn't I? He's obviously avoiding me.'

'Well, he can't do that forever, can he? Worst-case scenario, you'll see him tomorrow.'

'I really hope so, honey.'

Abby held out her arms. 'Hug available. If you would like one.'

'I need all the hugs I can get,' Sam said, stepping into her best friend's embrace. 'What are you up to today?' she asked as they drew apart.

'Jack and I are seeing Paul for lunch at The Anchor.'

'That sounds nice. You two seem to be getting on well.'

'We are. Very well. He's wearing me down.' Abby gave a slight frown. 'Not enough so that I've leaped back into his bed – I just want to point that out – but it is going well and I think I might do soon. Sorry – that probably wasn't very diplomatic... in the – um – current circumstances.'

'Abby, stop it. I'm pleased for you. You know I am. I'd love it if you got back with Paul and the three of you lived happily ever after. You do know that, don't you?'

'Yeah, I guess I do. Thanks. That said... you are very welcome to join us for Sunday lunch. It's not going to be a romance extravaganza with Jack throwing his toys about and yelling.'

'Thanks, but I'll have to pass. I've got a pile of CCTV footage to go through. I'd better get started.'

28

Half an hour later, having read Mr B's instructions and answered two more emails from him advising her he'd got a temporary 'guard' in situ, Sam finally sat down to watch the footage.

Mr B was right. Somewhere on the recordings was the answer to who had caught and tied up the pigs. She was almost sure they would have done it in daylight because the last time she had checked it had been light and the paddock had been empty then. She'd assumed the pigs were in the ark.

The Watch Me From Afar app had a slow fast-forward button – at least it did on Sam's phone. As she scrolled through footage of endless grass, with the occasional shot of a Kunekune strolling past, her mind skipped back to Rex. Where would he have gone? She didn't think she could bear another twenty-four hours of silence. Would he go to his mother's house? Sam didn't have the impression they were very close. Although of course he had looked after her when she'd broken her hip.

She was still pondering this when she spotted something on the footage. A person had just crossed the grass and was heading in the direction of the ark. She freeze-framed the image. It was nearly dark and they had their back to the camera. They were dressed in dark clothing: black jeans, black hoodie with the hood up and they were carrying a bucket. The dog leads must be in there – and probably a few pig nuts too, although they wouldn't have been essential. Portia would follow anyone who had a bucket, empty or not – just on the off chance that they were going to feed her.

Sam zoomed in. He – it was most likely a he, although it was hard to tell from the unisex clothing – was tall and reasonably slim. She played back the image, but the software had chosen that moment to switch to the camera on the inside of the Ark and for a minute or so she found herself watching a screen of empty darkness.

Then the screen changed back to the field. This time, the abductor was coming the opposite way. It was definitely a man. That was clear by the way they walked: a slightly cocky saunter. He was in no particular hurry and as he got closer to the camera, Sam could see why. As well as having his hood up, he had a dark scarf covering most of his face. He was clearly aware of the camera. It would be impossible to identify him from this footage, that was for sure.

Sam carried on searching in case she came across any better shots. But she didn't. The footage was too dark. Eventually, she decided to screenshot the best images she could find and then, with a slight feeling of dread, she emailed them to Mr B.

She would have liked to turn her phone off so he couldn't call her and do any more ranting. But she didn't want to miss Rex so she left it on.

Precisely two minutes later, it rang and Mr B's name flashed up.

Sam answered it, bracing herself for an onslaught. 'I'm really sorry there weren't any better pictures. But—'

'Those pictures were fine,' he interrupted. 'I now know exactly who the perpetrator is and I believe I know why.'

'You do?' She waited. She was half expecting him to launch into a rant about the Chinese. Although why the Chinese would want to abduct someone's pet pigs, she had no idea.

'I am 100 per cent sure that my Kunekunes are not in danger,' Mr B continued. 'The person who did this is Phil Grimshaw.'

'Um, OK,' Sam said, none the wiser.

'Phil Grimshaw is the maître d' at the Bluebell Cliff Hotel,' he added as if this would explain everything.

She was still none the wiser. 'Do you need me to do anything?' She was probably going to regret asking that, but it seemed only fair to ask.

'I do not. The fopdoodle is merely engaged in what someone with an intellect like his would see as a practical joke.' He drew a deep breath and blew it out again and she was reminded of a snorting dragon. 'He will not think it's so funny when I am back in the country.'

'I see.' She gave a little shudder. What sort of person would think pretending to abduct a pig was funny?

'Thank you,' Mr B continued. 'For being so diligent and for alerting me so swiftly to what was afoot.'

'It's fine.' Sam had been feeling slightly less guilty about yesterday's slap-happy timing after she'd realised exactly when the Kunekunes had been tied up. Checking the app wouldn't have made any difference. The abductor had struck after her final check-up time.

'I will be leaving you a very lengthy five-star review on Tripadvisor.'

'Thank you.'

'I trust that you will go back this afternoon, as per our plan, to check up on Portia and Percy.'

'Yes I will. And I will let you know immediately if there is anything amiss.'

'There won't be.' He sounded very confident about this. 'Neither will it be necessary to go tomorrow morning. Meg and I have decided not to take our optional extra night. We are flying back this evening. So that I can resolve the situation with Phil Grimshaw.'

'Right,' Sam said, deciding she wouldn't have traded places with the unfortunate Phil Grimshaw, whoever he was, for absolutely anything.

* * *

On Monday morning as Sam got ready for work, she was no longer quite so sure she wouldn't have traded places with Phil Grimshaw.

There had still been no word from Rex. No text. No call. Nothing to indicate he had got any of her messages.

'It'll be OK,' Abby had said. 'One way or another at least you'll find out where you stand. He can't fire you. He can't do anything that would be seen as constructive dismissal either.'

'He wouldn't do anything like that anyway.' Sam was sure about this. Rex may not want to have anything to do with her on a personal level, but he wouldn't let his personal judgement affect his professional one.

Thank goodness no one in the office knew about their relationship. At least she didn't have to face people's sympathetic, knowing glances. She could carry on being one of the crowd. But could she really do that? She asked herself as she parked in Fielding's car park, where there was no sign of the silver Saab, and went into the building.

Climbing the stairs to the first floor felt a little like climbing to the gallows. No it didn't. She was being a drama queen.

She took a deep breath and went into the main office. She was slightly early – ten minutes or so – but she could see that Heather was already in. So was Elannah and Magpie was on a call.

The air smelled of coffee and doughnuts and there was a pink box on Elannah's desk. They didn't usually have cakes on a Monday. Maybe it was someone's birthday.

A quick glance towards Rex's office showed he hadn't somehow got here without his car. He definitely wasn't in yet.

'Hi everyone.' Her voice came out a little croaky. Blimey, she was nervous.

Everyone else was in weekend chat mode, a lot of which was directed at her because of the launch.

'Great party, Sam.'

'Here comes our entrepreneur.'

'Sorry I didn't stop to help with the clearing up.'

'You must be excited. Six months down the line and you'll be out of this place completely.' That was Lightning, who'd just rushed in, having done an early-morning survey already.

In the end, Sam could bear it no more. 'Is Rex not in today?' she asked Elannah.

His PA shook her head. 'No. He's taking a few days off. He messaged me earlier.'

Sam felt her heart nosedive towards her kitten heels. She had been dreading seeing him and facing his disappointment, but not seeing him was ten times worse. 'Did he say whether he was going away?'

'No.' Elannah was shuffling papers on her desk. 'Why? Did you want him for something specific? Can I help?'

'No, it's nothing important,' Sam said, forcing a casual tone into her voice.

God, this was far worse than if he'd barricaded himself in his office. At least then she'd have known he'd have to come out by the end of the day. Now there was an open-ended time limit. He clearly didn't want to see her. He might stay away for weeks.

Her forced brightness couldn't be very convincing because

when Janet arrived just before lunch and made them both coffee she saw straight through her. Janet patted her arm and said, 'You OK, love? I must say you're not looking much like a woman who's on the path to her dream job. You're not having second thoughts, are you?'

'No. No. Definitely not. I – um – I had a tricky weekend. It was also the weekend I was looking after Mr B's Kunekunes. Do you remember me telling you?'

'I do.' Janet sipped from her mug and looked suspicious. 'They didn't take ill, did they?'

'Oh no, nothing like that.' She told Janet what had happened, ending with the story of her spending yesterday morning going through the footage and sending Mr B a photo of the perpetrator. 'Apparently it was Phil Grimshaw who moved them,' she concluded, raising her eyebrows curiously.

Janet guffawed with laughter and clapped her hands. 'I'll be blowed. That's priceless. Brilliant. Top marks.'

Sam looked at her in astonishment. 'What?'

'Those two have had an ongoing feud for years. Feud may be too strong a word, but it's all about the wind-ups. They've been doing it for as long as I can remember. It started off with quite small things. Once Phil ordered ten tubs of anchovies from the wholesalers in Mr B's name. You should have seen Mr B's face when they turned up.' She laughed. 'He went ballistic. Although that one did actually backfire on Phil because Mr B ended up inventing some new anchovy dish that became really popular and Clara King gave him a bonus.

'Another time, Mr B put something in the wash on the commercial washing machines so that Phil's white shirts ended up a pale pink colour and so did a pile of napkins. That was entertaining too.' She put her head on one side. 'Although Clara was a bit pissed off about that.

'The last one I heard about on the grapevine was in January. Mr B helped himself to Phil's car keys apparently and moved his car about a mile up the road. He didn't let on until after Phil had reported it stolen to the police, which he then had to retract and he only just avoided being charged for wasting police time.'

'Oh my goodness.'

'I know.' Janet shook her head. 'Some men never grow up.'

'I wish Phil hadn't decided to retaliate when I was looking after the Kunekunes. I nearly had a heart attack when I thought they'd been stolen.'

'He probably didn't realise you were looking after them,' Janet said, after a few moments' consideration. 'Everyone at the Bluebell knew that Mr B had that app thingie on his phone. So he could check on his blessed pigs from wherever he was.'

'Watch Me From Afar.'

'Yes, that. Phil wouldn't have realised that Mr B had hired you as a pet sitter. He'd have assumed Mr B would be watching from his hotel room in Edinburgh. That's classic. Oh my goodness.' She burst out laughing again and then stopped herself. 'Sorry. It must have been insanely stressful for you being caught up in the middle. Is that why you look so tired?'

'Probably,' Sam said as Janet drained her coffee.

'Mr B was never going to be an easy customer, love. I hope you charged him double for the inconvenience.'

* * *

As far as stress levels went, Mr B was a minor blip compared to the stress that Rex's refusal to talk was causing her. Somehow she got through the morning without making too many mistakes on the surveys. After lunch, once she'd finished at Fielding's, she had a few email enquiries about boarding availability to answer and one woman phoned about dog walking. But Sam was on a different mission.

She left Rex another message, asking him to please call her. Then she paid another visit to his house, which still had an air of desertion about it, and finally she went back home.

'He seems to have vanished off the face of the earth,' she told Abby. 'I don't know where else to look.'

'Maybe he decided to hole up in a hotel for a couple of nights. Is he the type who'd want to think things through?'

'Yes. I think maybe he is. I'm not sure about a hotel, though.'

'A friend then?'

'I've never met any of his friends. That's the problem. He's such a private person. Hang on.' A memory was surfacing. 'He did mention his best man once. I can't remember his name, but I think he said he had a shop in Brancombe. A baker's. No... No, I think it was a butcher's. There can't be that many butchers in Brancombe.' She grabbed her phone and tapped into it swiftly. 'I've got it. Bennett's Butchers.' She glanced at her watch. 'If I go now, I could catch the shop before it closes. He might at least have an idea where Rex is.'

'He might not tell you,' Abby warned.

'I know. But it's got to be worth a try,' Sam reached for her coat again. 'Anything beats sitting here doing nothing.'

29

It was four thirty by the time Sam found a parking space in Brancombe and walked round to Bennett's Butchers, which was in the high street. The shopfront had a traditional red and white striped canopy over it, marking it out from some distance away. When she got closer, she saw that the proprietor's name, Peter Bennett, Master Butcher, was etched in black over the door.

A bell chimed as she opened the door and walked in to be hit by the distinctive smell of raw meat, which was displayed in a glass-fronted case beneath a stainless-steel counter.

The butcher himself appeared, dressed in a white coat with a black apron. All very traditional.

'Are you Peter Bennett?' she asked.

'No, love. I'm his manager. I'm John. Can I help?'

'I'm really anxious to talk to him. I don't suppose you could tell me where he is?'

'Is it business or personal?' He gave her a keen look.

'It's personal. It's really important.'

Something in her tone must have alerted him because he gave a swift nod and said, 'What's the name?'

'Sam Jones. He won't know me,' she added, but he had already gone through a beaded curtain into the back of the shop. She guessed it must lead to the flat above.

A couple of minutes went slowly past. During it, someone else came into the shop: a woman in a turquoise headscarf that put Sam in mind of the sea in Studland Bay on a bright summer's day.

The woman glanced at Sam. 'Does he know you're waiting?'

'Yes, he'll be back in a sec.'

The sound of two sets of footsteps heralded the butcher's return and then the bead curtains swished and rattled and John, the manager, reappeared, closely followed by Rex.

'Hello, Sam.'

His face was grave, but her heart still leapt. She hadn't been expecting to find him so soon, but it seemed her instincts had been spot on. He was dressed for work. At least, he was wearing his customary suit, although not the one he had worn to open her launch. That evening, barely forty-eight hours ago, seemed as though it had been a hundred years in the past. An evening from another lifetime.

Rex gestured to her at the same time as the manager opened a hatch so she could go through into the walkway beyond the counter. She went, following Rex through a doorway that led to some stairs. He went up the first flight and opened a white-painted door that led into a bright airy lounge with two long caramel leather couches that were positioned end to end, making an L shape. There was no one else in the room, but it smelled of coffee and something sweeter, air freshener maybe. It must be hard to stop the smell of the butchery below from drifting up the stairs.

'Have a seat,' Rex said.

Sam sat at one end of a couch, feeling a faint edge of surrealness.

He sat at the closest end of the other so that they were less than a couple of feet apart, but it might as well have been an abyss, she felt so far away from him.

Rex cleared his throat. 'If you're worried about your job, then don't. I'm sure we can still work together perfectly amicably.'

Oh my God, she hated that formal tone. As if they had never shared anything at all. As if she meant less to him than a desk or a management handbook on his bookcase at work.

'I'm not worried about my job. That's not why I'm here.'

'I see.' His hands were clasped together in his lap. The knuckles of his fingers were white. So he was a lot tenser than his composed appearance suggested.

'I'm here because I wanted to apologise... for that piece of paper that you saw in my hall. I—'

Unusually he cut across her. 'There's no need to apologise for the truth.'

'But it's not the truth.' She flicked back her hair, which had been tied up properly earlier but had been loosened by the rush through the seaside town to the shop so that long wisps of it were now around her face. 'It's not the bloody truth,' she repeated. 'That piece of paper was a joke. Mission Perfect Dad was a stupid thing that Abby and I did. It was the first night she'd had a drink since having Jack and I was much drunker than she was. I didn't even know that piece of paper still existed until I saw it on Saturday night. I have never once looked at it since. I swear.'

His eyes flickered.

Sam went on more haltingly. 'It was back in July. Not long after she'd had Jack. I'd really bonded with him. Which was quite a surprise to me. Everyone who knows me well will tell you that I've always much preferred puppies or kittens to babies.

'Abby and I have been best friends since we were kids. When we were little, we used to play this game. "*What if?*" For example, *what if* I could fly? *What if* I could have a pony? That was my favourite one. It was all imagination – my parents could never have afforded a pony.'

Rex's face was unreadable, but she knew he was listening.

'So on that night in July, Abby was joking about the fact that I should have my own Jack and I said that I may want a baby one day, but I also said...' She slowed down, remembering, and thinking that she should probably have edited her words. But it was too late now. 'I also said that I didn't want a boyfriend. That was true back then.' Oh crap, in for a penny in for a pound. 'So Abby said, what if I could have a baby without having a boyfriend? And she asked me what I might want in a man. And that was where the list came from. I would never have done it. I would never have tricked anyone into being a father. I'm not that selfish.' She stopped and stared at her hands.

Rex didn't say anything.

After a while, she risked another look at his face.

He was nodding.

She felt the need to explain further. 'That list was the result of a stupid drunken joke. Your name was on it because Abby added it. She added all of the names. I didn't actually have any input to that.'

'So you're not totally turned off by the name Rex then...?' he said in a voice that had thawed out considerably since the last time he'd spoken.

'That would be ridiculous.'

He gave a deep sigh and put his head in his hands. 'To be honest, Sam, I've been wondering ever since I walked out if I'd overreacted. That's why I haven't returned your calls and messages. I had to think things through. I know I'm easily triggered by what happened in the past.'

'That's not really surprising.'

'It was the lies Katrina told me that hurt the most.'

She swallowed. 'Yes, I do get that. It was like that with Gary. But that's what we do. We trust what people say. Until we are given a reason not to. I've been thinking about things a lot too. I know how that list must have looked. I don't think you overreacted one bit. I couldn't have done anything more hurtful if I'd set out deliberately to do it.'

'I guess we are all very much products of our past.'

During the time they'd been talking, he had moved a little closer to her. The atmosphere in the room had thawed. But she didn't dare let herself succumb to wanting him again in case he didn't feel the same.

'While we're on the subject of the truth,' she said finally, 'I need to tell you that I have loved every second of our time together. For what it's worth, you've restored my faith in the opposite sex. I know I've buggered it up, but I just needed to tell you that.' She hesitated. 'Is your friend Peter actually here?'

He shook his head. 'He's on holiday with his girlfriend. When I phoned him to ask if I could come and stay for a couple of days, he just told me to see John for the keys.'

'And you told John who I was…' she finished.

'I thought it was a pretty long shot that you'd actually turn up here, but I did mention your name to him. Yes.'

She stood up. 'I'd better get out of your hair.'

He stood up too. For a moment, they faced each other with a foot or so of force field between them. It was Rex who stepped into it.

'Don't go.' He held out his arms and it was as impossible to resist as it had ever been. She went to him and for a few seconds there was nothing else in her world except him. His familiar citrus cologne mixed with the testosterone scent of man. His strength – the strong muscled arms beneath the deceptive white shirtsleeves. His warmth – every atom of him was warm. And the chemistry that buzzed between them, making every atom of her feel alive.

She rested her head on his shoulder.

'Shall we draw a line under this and get back to where we were before?' he asked, when they drew apart.

'Yes. Yes please.' His words sent a delicious peace stealing through her heart.

* * *

They had gone back to Rex's house in the end. It would have felt wrong to have stayed in Peter Bennett's spare bedroom. Even though, as Rex had said, Peter Bennett was the kind of friend who definitely wouldn't have minded.

Sam had updated Abby, who had been thrilled that they'd managed to talk things through and sort them out. She had even held the phone to Jack's ear and Sam had chattered away to him and been delighted when he'd said, 'Gah gah goo,' excitedly down it.

She and Rex had also done a great deal more talking.

'So how do you feel now about starting a family?' Rex had asked her as they had cleared away the supper things at his house: plain omelettes with a blob of ketchup – as he said that even he couldn't create a gourmet meal with only one ingredient. Not that either of them was that bothered about eating, she knew. They were just relieved that they had worked things out. 'Could you live without a baby, Sam? Would it spell the end of our relationship if I didn't want one?'

'I honestly don't know,' she told him, biting her lip. 'The truth is that I would love a family, yes. But if that meant I couldn't have you, I'm not so sure. It's a big question and one I'd need some time to answer.' She put down the tea towel she'd been holding and met his eyes. 'I think that maybe I fell in love with Jack because I was looking for love. And the love between a mother and child is overwhelming. Jack is so full of love. I was there at his birth.' She broke off. 'Of course you know that, don't you?'

'It was the same day you had that urgent appointment at the dentist, wasn't it?' His eyes sparked with amusement.

'The very same.' She batted the question back at him. 'So do *you* want a family, Rex? How do you feel about it now?'

'Let's say I'm not averse to the idea. But I've always been quite traditional. I'd prefer to do things in the right order. You know, step one the dating, step two the falling in love, step three the deciding to spend our lives together...'

Her heart registered that he'd said 'our'. 'That sounds good. Which step are we on?'

'Somewhere between step one and step two,' he said after a moment's consideration. Then he gave her a direct look. 'Closer to step three, if I'm honest.'

'Me too,' she whispered.

They had gone to bed after that. There had been a great deal of passion. Sam didn't think she had ever met anyone as passionate as Rex, once he was out of that formal suit.

Just as Sam was dropping off to sleep, spooned around him, she remembered the Kunekunes. She sat bolt upright in bed, before realising she no longer needed to check up on them.

'What's wrong?' Rex murmured.

'Do you want to hear a funny story about two disappearing Kunekune pigs?'

30

Sam spent the first two weeks of November feeling as though her feet didn't touch the ground. This was partly because she was walking on air – love did that – and partly because a great deal was going on. She was still working mornings at Fielding's and her afternoons were spent dog walking and supervising the field.

It didn't need much supervising. There was a ten-minute handover period between bookings to allow the previous dog walker time to get out and most people were really good about not overstaying their time. She had discovered that the 7-7.30 slot was very popular, as was the 1.10-1.40. Presumably this was because people wanted to run their dogs before work and during the lunch break.

It was very satisfying watching dogs playing in her field and quite interesting watching the owners too – she usually did the latter discreetly from the house. Some made full use of the toy basket and were as active as their dogs were. Others spent the time engrossed in their smartphones while their dogs mooched about undisturbed.

Sam was beginning to get enquiries for a few more boarders, but she was very selective. The experience with Mr B had made her careful, although that had turned out very well in the end.

He had, as he'd promised, given Purbeck Pooches a five-star review on Tripadvisor in which he'd done what her parents would have called 'waxing lyrical' about her going above and beyond the call of duty. He'd also insisted on paying her a bonus because of the extra time she'd spent helping him catch the 'perpetrator'.

In addition, he had invited her and three guests for a VIP afternoon tea at the Bluebell Cliff, at his expense. This had to be booked on a Saturday afternoon because he was always there Saturdays. Rex and Sam had already arranged to go there for dinner on his birthday on 21st November, so Sam had invited her parents and Abby who was back at work full-time now and deserved a treat. Paul was working in the shop and Matt was babysitting. She and Abby had arranged to meet Sam's parents in the Bluebell car park at two thirty.

* * *

'What exactly is a VIP afternoon tea?' Abby asked curiously as she parked and unbuckled her seat belt.

'I've got no idea, but I suspect we're about to find out. Like I told you, he did say we shouldn't eat lunch and that we probably wouldn't need any dinner either.'

Sam could see her parents getting out of their black Volvo a few spaces away and once they'd exchanged hugs they paused for a moment and all of them looked up at the white-painted hotel. She'd only seen her parents once since the launch and that had been to view a bungalow they had fallen in love with, so she'd been really looking forward to this.

'What a stunning location,' her dad said.

No one could argue with that.

'I love the fact it's got its own lighthouse,' her mum said. 'I bet that's gorgeous inside.'

'Apparently it gets hired out a lot for weddings and special occasions. It's the place where people come to make their dreams come true.' Sam breathed in a lungful of the chilly November sea air and tilted her head back to watch a lone seagull soaring high up in the moody grey sky.

'I haven't been here since the refurb,' her mum said. 'But it has a great reputation.'

'I'm starving,' her father added. 'I took you at your word and I haven't eaten since breakfast.'

'To be fair, that was a full English, Alan,' her mother remarked good-naturedly. Her parents looked more relaxed than she'd ever seen them. Retirement obviously suited them.

'My tummy's rumbling too,' Abby said. 'So I hope this isn't the type of place that does all that two peas on a plate nonsense, with one of those physalis thingamabobs on the side and a fancy sauce.'

'It isn't,' Sam said, remembering her afternoon with Danny Bowkett. 'Anyway, afternoon teas definitely involve cake.'

They went through the hotel's main entrance, which smelled of vanilla and coffee and the scent of food that wafted through from the doorway of the restaurant.

They were greeted by a maître d' who had a sombre look about him. Black eyes, black hair and the kind of mouth that in repose looked slightly sulky. He would have made a great Heathcliff.

Then he spoke and the impression of sulkiness was gone. 'Good afternoon, welcome to the Bluebell Cliff. I'm Phil Grimshaw. May I ask if you have a booking with us today?' His voice had a deep baritone richness that would have sounded great on a stage.

So this was Phil Grimshaw, the fopdoodle, who had moved the Kunekunes. Sam and Abby had looked it up and fopdoodle, which meant a dim person, was now Abby's favourite word. Phil didn't look in the slightest bit dim, though. And Sam guessed he couldn't be if he worked here in this prestigious hotel. After Mr B's threats of revenge, she was quite relieved to see he was still in one piece.

'We do have a booking.' She gave him her name and he swept them through the restaurant – which managed to be both modern but intimate, thanks to the layout and lighting – to a window table, which was clearly one of the best in the house. It overlooked the terrace where she and Danny had sat. At the end of the terrace, a lush green sweep of lawn ran down towards a fence, beyond which was the clifftop that was part of the South West Coast Path.

'I will tell Mr B you're here,' Phil said as he seated them and handed each a leather menu.

'Wow,' Abby said. 'He's fit. And what a voice.'

'I'm sure I heard somewhere that he's an actor when he's not being a maître d',' Sam's mother said. 'He looks like he should be on the stage, doesn't he? I must say I'm looking forward to meeting this chef. What did you say his name was?'

'I've never known him as anything other than Mr B. I think he likes to be a man of mystery.' She wouldn't tell them about the conspiracy theory aspect of that. She had to admit she had warmed to Mr B quite a lot lately. When it came to it he was just another person, albeit a quirky one, who was passionate about their pets.

Her mother leaned across the table and Sam saw her eyes were bright with excitement. 'We've put in an offer for that gorgeous bungalow in Harman's Cross we all went to see. Did your dad tell you?'

'No, he didn't.' She glanced at him. 'I thought that bungalow was out of your price range?' Hope surged up in her. It had been perfect for her parents. The perfect distance from her too, it was barely a fifteen-minute drive from Beach Cottage.

'I wanted it to be a surprise, princess. And yes, it was out of our price range. But they dropped it the day before yesterday by 10k. They've just fallen in love with another one apparently and they're keen for a quick cash sale.' He tapped his nose. 'It's always worth stressing the point that you can manage a quick sale – if the price is right.'

'That's fantastic news. That's only up the road from me.'

'We haven't got it yet,' her mother cautioned. 'And we can't really go up much more.'

'We're waiting for a call from the agent.' Her dad held his mobile up. 'I've got it on silent. But if it buzzes, I might have to nip out and answer it.'

'Fingers crossed,' Abby said. 'Actually, I'm waiting for a call too.' She glanced at Sam. 'Paul's hoping to get that assistant manager promotion. He said he might find out whether he'll get a second interview this afternoon.'

'Well, we are in the place where dreams come true,' Sam said.

Mr B chose that moment to arrive. It was interesting seeing him in his own domain. If anything, he was slightly more imperious than usual, Sam observed, as he stood at their table in his chef whites.

'If you would allow me to take the liberty, I would like to recommend an extra-special menu that I will prepare just for you.'

'I thought we were having an afternoon tea,' Sam said, 'but I'm certainly game.'

'It is an afternoon tea plus,' the chef said. 'It is, in fact, a creation made for you by a master chef. Myself. We will begin with some savoury starters – a selection. Then we will progress to more traditional savouries. Then there will be a brief pause before we go on to mini desserts, a selection of little cakes and some petit fours.'

'That sounds awesome,' Abby said.

'Amazing,' Sam agreed. 'Thank you.'

Mr B didn't disappoint. For the next hour, they were treated to a selection of exquisitely made and presented savouries, all brought out on silver platters by Phil Grimshaw.

Sam couldn't have identified many of them, although Phil Grimshaw did tell them names as he brought each course, names such as 'Delicious Delights of the Sea', or 'Little Bits of Heaven'. He also told them whether they were seafood, meat or vegetarian. They ranged from spicy filo pasties to what looked like mini vol-au-vents to more regular canapés with anchovies, prawns and chicken, but they were all delicious.

'Oh my God,' her dad said at one point. 'That chef is a genius. No wonder they put up with him being as mad as a box of frogs.'

Sam had thought the maître d' was far enough away not to overhear this, but clearly he wasn't, as the next time he came to their table he leaned forward and said, 'Do not under any circumstances be tempted to tell Mr B he's a genius. He is insufferable enough already.' He said this with an absolutely deadpan expression. So it was impossible to tell how serious he was being. Then he looked straight at Sam and said, 'I am, at the moment, ahead of him in one respect. He has not yet been able to top what is, to date, the wind-up of the decade: the curious incident of the kidnapped Kunekunes.' His lips twitched.

'I am surprised,' Sam said, expecting Mr B would have already enacted his revenge.

'Oh I have no doubt he is still plotting,' Phil said with the slightest raise of one eyebrow. 'He might be able to create a gourmet feast when the mood takes him, but it takes him ages to plan and execute a half-decent caper! He's far too paranoid to take any risks.'

Luckily, Clara King chose that moment to appear. 'I just came on shift,' she told Sam, 'and a little bird informed me you were in for one of Mr B's specials. Are you having a lovely time?'

'We're having a fabulous time. This is a gorgeous place.'

'I'm glad you're here because we are now going away for Christmas, so I'd like to confirm Foxy's booking if that is still possible?'

'Consider it booked,' Sam said, aware that her dad, who was sitting on her left, had just picked up his phone and was now excusing himself from the table.

When he reappeared a few moments later, he had a serious expression. He shook his head slightly as he reached them.

'They turned down our offer,' her mother guessed and her shoulders slumped a little.

He frowned. Then his face broke into a huge grin. 'All that talk of wind-ups, I was going to tease you for a bit, but I can't do it. They only bloody accepted it.'

'Oh my goodness. Did they really? Oh that's fabulous.' In the next moment, they were all on their feet for a group hug.

And Clara, who was still at the table, was looking delighted. 'Another dream comes true at the Bluebell Cliff,' she said. 'Now it is customary that I offer you a celebratory drink on the house. Shall I bring it with the dessert course?'

Nothing could have dimmed the mood after that. The desserts, which turned out to be mini versions of old favourites like apple and blackberry crumble and bread and butter pudding, not to mention Mr B's famous Runner's Roulade, came served with tiny earthenware jugs of custard and cream.

They were also treated to Mr B's scones with clotted cream and what was apparently the most perfect Dorset apple cake in the county, if not the whole of England. 'That's his opinion, not mine,' Phil had told them with another twitch of a smile. Sam decided not to mention she thought Mr B might be right. The Dorset apple cake was melt-in-your-mouth divine.

Sam was aware that, although Abby had discreetly checked her phone a couple of times, there was no news from Paul about the promotion.

'Maybe it's just not meant to be for Paul yet,' Abby said as she and Sam walked back out into what had become evening while they were feasting. A cool sea breeze blew in flurries across the clifftop site. Dozens of stars were beginning to pinprick the velvet canopy of the night and a silver moon sailed high, casting moonlight over Studland Bay. This really was one of the most beautiful bits of England, Sam thought as she turned to Abby.

'Don't write it off just yet, honey. Bluebell Cliff still has time to make Paul's dream come true.'

Abby nodded and they squeezed hands.

'I don't think I'll ever need to eat again,' her mother said as they stood in the car park.

'It'll see me through until breakfast,' her father agreed, patting his stomach with a sigh of contentment.

'What a spectacular place. Thank you so much, darling. That was absolutely lovely.'

'Fingers crossed for the bungalow. Did they say how soon you could move in?'

'Our solicitor has promised that she'll fast-track it her end. As far as she's concerned, we can move in within three weeks. We'll definitely be in by Christmas.'

Wow, Sam thought, not only would they not be working for the first time in decades, but they'd be in their new home too. There were new beginnings all round.

* * *

Much later when Sam told Rex about the afternoon's events, he said, 'I'm very much looking forward to going there for my birthday meal.'

'Make sure you've got some wriggle room in your trousers,' Sam told him. 'Oh, and you might want to have a dream or two up your sleeve, seeing as we now have evidence that it's the place where dreams come true.'

31

SIX WEEKS LATER

It was Christmas Eve. Sam, Rex, Abby, Jack and Paul were all in the lounge of Beach Cottage. The room was warm and snug. It was filled with the delicious scent of wood smoke from the log burner in the old inglenook fireplace, over which stockings were also currently pinned, and the scents of spices and cinnamon from the mulled wine in a jug on the drinks cabinet.

The subtler scent of pine came from the six-foot-high living fir, with its roots in a pot so it could be planted outside after the festivities. It towered over a higgledy-piggledy pile of brightly wrapped presents. The tree was festooned with red and gold baubles and tinsel with a sparkly gold star on top.

There were also some homemade paper chains that, according to the packet, were supposed to be red and gold but had turned out more pink and garish yellow when Abby and Sam had put them together one evening to amuse Jack. They were lowering the sophisticated tone, but Abby had said babies and sophistication didn't really mix no matter how much of a yummy mummy you tried to be.

Christmas cards jostled for space on every available surface. A few had teeth marks around the edges. Jack was teething and this had involved a few uncharacteristic bouts of prolonged yelling. None of this dulled Sam's rose-tinted view of him one iota. She just cuddled him at every opportunity.

'I don't know about you guys, but I'm exhausted,' Abby said, picking up her glass and taking another sip before putting it back on the coffee table in front of her. She was sitting on the floor beside Jack, who was on the rug, dressed in an elf romper suit that Sam had given him as an early Christmas present and looking extraordinarily cute.

'That'll be all those potatoes you were peeling,' Sam said.

'You did a really good job,' Paul offered. He was behind Abby in the armchair, but he was leaning forwards, his arms on his knees and his eyes alight as he looked at his small family. He'd missed out on the assistant manager's job by a whisker to someone with more experience, but his boss had told him there would be other chances and he'd been offered some formal managerial training.

'Single-handedly, as well.' Abby dug an elbow backwards into his leg.

'Hey. I did a mountain of sprouts,' he protested, moving his leg swiftly. 'I don't even like sprouts.'

'Sprouts for ten people is hardly a mountain, Paul. At least we didn't have to worry about the main course. Thank you, Rex.'

'Yes, thank you, Rex,' Sam said, thinking that Paul and Abby had settled into life like an old married couple – they both seemed really happy. 'It's been brilliant knowing I haven't got to do Christmas dinner.'

'For us too,' Abby quipped.

Sam threw a cushion at her, which missed and landed just in front of Jack's head on the rug, which made him giggle. He'd been playing with a green teething ring, which was fast becoming his favourite toy.

'I love cooking,' Rex said and Sam turned towards him. They were side by side on the sofa, their knees barely touching yet she could feel the force. Time hadn't dimmed it one iota.

He looked back at her, his eyes light grey in the soft glow of the firelight and she knew he felt it too. She loved the way things were between then, that odd mixture of contentment and passion that she hadn't realized could be possible.

Rex had been introduced to her parents properly now and they had loved him. She'd met his mum, Carol, too, and found her to be both sweet and feisty. Tomorrow they would all have Christmas dinner together. Ten people and a baby would be crowding around the table, complete with an extension piece Rex had brought over, at Beach Cottage.

That meant the five of them in this room, plus Matt and his girlfriend, who looked much the same as the last one, Sam's parents and Rex's mum. It was going to be a proper fusion family Christmas and Sam couldn't wait. Her father had even volunteered to dress up as Santa Claus to dish out the presents after dinner. It was brilliant seeing him and her mum so happy, living in the gorgeous Harman's Cross bungalow up the road. She had seen them more in the last six weeks than she had in the last six years.

Christmas wasn't complete without a dog and Foxy would be there too. Well, she was already in situ. She was curled up on the sofa on Sam's left. Every so often she would open a watchful eye to see if there was anything interesting going on, which, in Foxy's world, meant food. Then she would slip back into the land of nod and snore and flick her paws – the three she had – and she would make little squeaking noises which Sam guessed meant that she was dreaming of chasing rabbits.

Everyone had dreams and one of the things Sam had realized over the past six months was that most dreams were better if they were shared. Like passions, they became brighter and bigger and shinier for doing so.

She leaned against Rex, aware that his eyes were on Jack, who had just rolled over onto his front and was banging on the rug with his tiny fists.

'Da... da... da... da... dad,' he shouted.

'Did you hear that?' Paul's voice was awestruck in the warmth of the Christmas scented room. 'He said Dad.'

'I think he actually did,' Abby said, glancing back at Paul and then towards their son again. 'Hey, Jack, say it again. Say, Dadeee. Dad, Dad, Dadeee.'

'Da... da... dad... Eeee,' Jack said obligingly and Sam saw that Paul's eyes had teared up. Bloody hell. He really was changing into a responsible adult. It was amazing what fatherhood could do.

She leaned her head against Rex's shoulder.

'One day,' he said in a voice so low it was barely a breath in her hair. 'One day that will be us.'

'One day soon,' Sam said.

EPILOGUE

Paul finally got the assistant manager job he'd been working for and Abby and Paul and Jack moved into their own little house in Brancombe. Sam had been sad to wave goodbye to Jack and Abby, but she couldn't have been happier for her best friend.

* * *

Sam's parents enjoyed settling into the rather aptly named Hope Cottage, which was actually a bungalow with roses around the door and a larger than average garden, where Belinda planned to grow vegetables and invent new dishes for them to feature in. She also signed up for an online course called The Creative Master Chef, invented and run by Mr B.

Alan joined the local Toastmasters club and was loving every minute of his new-found hobby.

* * *

Mr B continued plotting what he claimed would be the wheeze of the decade to pay back Phil Grimshaw for the curious incident of the Kunekune kidnapping.

* * *

Phil Grimshaw was confident that he would have left the Bluebell to take up an acting role with a travelling theatre before Mr B actually got his act together.

* * *

Danny Bowkett and Barbara Oldfield started dating after Sam's launch party and were now going steady. Fortunately, Stan, Seamus and Goldie also seemed to rub along quite well and the three dogs could often be seen racing like mad things around the Purbeck Pooches Paddock.

* * *

Sam was able to give up her mornings at Fielding's in order to run Purbeck Pooches full-time. The Dog Field was a great success and she soon had to employ two more dog walkers to keep up with the workload.

* * *

Rex asked Sam to marry him at a glittering Valentine's evening banquet at the Bluebell Cliff Hotel. She said yes and they were planning their wedding day there too, though the date for this was in question as not everything went according to plan.

Rex decided that some traditions were best broken. 'When you know something's right, why wait?' he said, one night as they lay in bed at Beach Cottage.

'Um, what did you have in mind?' she said sleepily because he appeared to be rummaging in the bedside drawer on his side of the bed.

'I think you should take these.' He produced a small bottle of pills and handed it to her.

Sam glanced at the label and saw that the pills were a folic acid supplement recommended for women who were trying to conceive.

'I thought you might like to take them instead of those other ones you have,' he had said, his eyes alight with love.

Three months later, they were expecting their first child.

'If it's a boy, I'm going to teach him all about being a master carpenter,' Rex said.

'And if it's a girl…?'

'I'll teach her all about being a master carpenter,' he said without a flicker.

FOOTNOTE

Mr and Mrs Fielding recently became the new owners of Beach Cottage and its field. Mr Fielding has plans to turn the wooden summerhouse into a proper workshop where bespoke wooden items will be created and advertised on eBay and Etsy.

Mrs Fielding has plans to build kennels in the dog field, once all the planning applications have been approved.

They both have plans to have another daughter or son very quickly to ensure that their first born, Abigail Belinda Carol Fielding, will not be an only child. She has already taken a liking to her older friend Jack, who they visit as often as they can.

Another thing Sam and Rex have discovered they have in common is that they both believe families and friendship can grow outwards in ever-expanding circles, especially when an individual, or indeed a couple of individuals, are motivated by something powerful – and nothing is more powerful than love.

ACKNOWLEDGMENTS

Thank you to: Gordon Rawsthorne, Ian Burton, Jan Wright, Pam Lant, Rosie Edser and Tony Millward for your advice, both about living and working in Dorset and for your support and enthusiasm. Thank you to the random cyclist I accosted on South Beach who filled me in on pertinent details about the area. Thank you to Judith Murdoch for believing in me, and Caroline Ridding for adding that extra colour to my work and everyone at Team Boldwood, with a special thanks to Jade Craddock. You are all amazing.

MORE FROM DELLA GALTON

We hope you enjoyed reading *Moonlight Over Studland Bay*. If you did, please leave a review.

If you'd like to gift a copy, this book is also available as an ebook, digital audio download and audiobook CD.

Sign up to Della Galton's mailing list for news, competitions and updates on future books:

http://bit.ly/DellaGaltonNewsletter

Sunshine Over Bluebell Cliff, another glorious escapist read from Della Galton, is available now.

ABOUT THE AUTHOR

Della Galton is the author of 15 books, including the Bluebell Cliff series. She writes short stories, teaches writing groups and is Agony Aunt for Writers Forum Magazine. She lives in Dorset.

Visit Della's website: www.dellagalton.co.uk

Follow Della on social media:

facebook.com/DailyDella

twitter.com/DellaGalton

instagram.com/Dellagalton

bookbub.com/authors/della-galton

ABOUT BOLDWOOD BOOKS

Boldwood Books is a fiction publishing company seeking out the best stories from around the world.

Find out more at www.boldwoodbooks.com

Sign up to the Book and Tonic newsletter for news, offers and competitions from Boldwood Books!

http://www.bit.ly/bookandtonic

We'd love to hear from you, follow us on social media:

facebook.com/BookandTonic

twitter.com/BoldwoodBooks

instagram.com/BookandTonic